Praise for

'Sheer joy.'
Katie Fforde

'Sparkling and festive!'
Milly Johnson

'Will make you laugh and cry.'
Miranda Dickinson

'Gloriously uplifting and unashamedly warm hearted!'
Faith Hogan

'Combines romance, humour and intrigue so well . . . The whole
thing was so captivating.'
Cressida McLaughlin

'A delicious festive treat.'
Jules Wake

'Between the gorgeous setting and the uplifting feel, this is a cosy
and charming festive read.'
My Weekly

'If you enjoy love stories and the Lake District, this is for you . . . As
delicious as hot chocolate sipped under the fairy lights.'
Woman & Home

'Serious escapism . . . like a big warm hug.'
Popsugar

'Romantic and life-affirming.'
Woman's Weekly

PHILLIPA ASHLEY is a *Sunday Times*, Amazon and Audible best-selling author of uplifting romantic fiction. After studying English at Oxford University, she worked as a copywriter and journalist before turning her hand to writing.

Her debut novel, *Decent Exposure*, won the Romantic Novelists' Association New Writers Award and was filmed as a Lifetime TV movie, *12 Men of Christmas*, starring Kristin Chenoweth and Josh Hopkins.

Since then, her novels have sold well over a million copies and been translated into numerous languages.

Phillipa lives in an English village with her husband, has a grown-up daughter and loves nothing better than walking the Lake District hills and swimming in Cornish coves.

🐦 @PhillipaAshley

Also by Phillipa Ashley

The Cornish Café Series
Summer at the Cornish Café
Christmas at the Cornish Café
Confetti at the Cornish Café

The Little Cornish Isles Series
Christmas on the Little Cornish Isles: The Driftwood Inn
Spring on the Little Cornish Isles: The Flower Farm
Summer on the Little Cornish Isles: The Starfish Studio

The Porthmellow Series
A Perfect Cornish Summer
A Perfect Cornish Christmas
A Perfect Cornish Escape

The Falford Series
An Endless Cornish Summer
A Special Cornish Christmas
A Golden Cornish Summer
A Secret Cornish Summer

A Surprise Christmas Wedding
The Christmas Holiday

Four Weddings and a Christmas

Phillipa Ashley

avon.

Published by AVON
A division of HarperCollins*Publishers*
1 London Bridge Street
London SE1 9GF

www.harpercollins.co.uk

HarperCollins*Publishers*
Macken House
39/40 Mayor Street Upper
Dublin 1
D01 C9W8
Ireland

A Paperback Original 2023

3

First published in Great Britain by HarperCollins*Publishers* 2023

A catalogue copy of this book is available from the British Library.

ISBN: 978-0-00-849438-4

This novel is entirely a work of fiction. The names, characters and incidents
portrayed in it are the work of the author's imagination. Any resemblance to
actual persons, living or dead, events or localities is entirely coincidental.

Typeset in Birka by Palimpsest Book Production Limited, Falkirk, Stirlingshire
Printed and bound in the UK using 100% renewable electricity at CPI Group (UK) Ltd

MIX
Paper | Supporting
responsible forestry
FSC™ C007454

This book is produced from independently certified FSC™ paper
to ensure responsible forest management.

For more information visit: www.harpercollins.co.uk/green

To the Friday Floras

Prologue

Bannerdale Church, the Lake District

'Freya, can you *please* stop fidgeting!'

Freya's hand froze at her mother's warning. They'd been hanging around in the church porch for *ages*. Her veil tickled her nose and her knickers had ridden up her bottom and were horribly uncomfortable. If she held her posy in one hand, surely she could reach down under her wedding dress, for a sneaky tweak.

She and her mum, Sandra, had been allowed to wait in the vestry while everyone took their seats and settled down. Her 'bridesmaids' – two classmates – were standing outside with her teacher, chattering excitedly. The buzz of anticipation from the church full of schoolkids, parents and villagers, sounded like a swarm of angry bees.

And they were all waiting for *her* to make an entrance.

Despite the warmth of the sticky July afternoon, Freya shivered.

'Are you OK, love?' Her mum smiled down at her from beneath the brim of her new feathered hat. 'It's normal to be nervous, dear. Travis might be feeling the same way.'

Freya knew he wouldn't. Travis Marshall might be angry or bored or plotting something wicked but he'd never be nervous. No one scared Travis – though many were scared of *him*.

'Though why the teachers picked him, goodness only knows,' her mother said with a heavy sigh. 'He's always causing trouble at school, his mother neglects him and as for his father, we *all* know what kind of a man he is.'

'I don't think he wanted to do this . . .' Freya murmured, dreading someone overhearing.

Her mum tutted. 'Then *why* ask him at all?'

Freya didn't bother putting Travis's case. Her mother had made up her mind about the Marshalls and nothing she could say would have any effect, but if only her mother could have heard the fuss Travis had put up about being groom at the mock school wedding.

During the weeks before, he'd driven their teacher mad.

He'd tugged the teacher's sleeve. 'Can't I take the photos, Miss?'

'No. You're the groom.'

'But I want to take the pictures. Can I borrow the camera?'

'No, it's very expensive. Leave it to Mr Patel. The groom is a very important person. You're very lucky.'

'I don't want to be important. I want to be the photographer.'

'It will do you good to take a central role that will teach you about responsibility and commitment. It's a privilege. Your mum will be pleased.'

'Maybe Mr Patel will let me look at his camera afterwards,'

he'd said with a sly grin that Freya secretly admired. 'If I'm good.'

'Look, I'll ask him,' the teacher had said, finally worn down. '*If* you're good.

The bargain had been struck. Travis would go along with the 'wedding crap' if he got to hold the camera.

'You should see the state of his trousers,' her mum muttered, adjusting Freya's flowery headband. 'The hem's come down. I'd have sewn it up it for him myself, but you don't like to interfere, do you?'

'No, Mum,' Freya murmured, cringing. Her mum meant well but she was obsessed with making sure Freya always looked perfectly turned out. She'd said she didn't want people thinking she couldn't manage, because she was on her own, but Freya just wished she'd let things go once in a while; let Freya get messy and make mistakes.

'I expect she's got enough on her plate, with her husband locked up, but to send her child to school in dirty clothes on such an important occasion.' Her mum shook her head in despair. 'Never mind, you look gorgeous, darling. I can't believe it's been ten years since I wore that veil myself. Your dad would have been so proud if he could have been here.'

Her dad, again. Her mum had talked about him more these past few weeks than Freya could ever remember. The school wedding seemed to have made her mother very emotional, and prone to sharing memories of her father that Freya hadn't heard before. Some of them had made her mum smile but others had made her cry a little bit too.

Freya felt helpless to understand and at a loss how to react. Her dad had died in a car accident when she wasn't even two and she had no memories of him whatsoever. All her knowledge of this perfect being had come from her mum, who'd always made him sound like the perfect man: strong and kind and loving.

Her mother gazed down at her, her eyes glistening. 'It makes me feel all teary, thinking of the future. One day, we'll be doing this for real . . .'

'B-but I might never get m-married,' Freya muttered.

Her mother laughed. 'Don't be silly. You're only eight. I'm sure you'll meet someone nice. When I was younger, I never thought I'd find anyone, then along came your dad and I fell head over heels. I bet he's up there somewhere looking down on you today.'

Freya shuddered, thinking of the carved angels peering down at her with their stone eyes from the church walls. When she was tiny, her mother had once told her that her dad had gone to be with the angels, and she'd found them creepy and ghostlike ever since.

Freya's head went a bit swimmy, and her stomach rumbled. She hadn't had any breakfast, too nervous to eat her Coco Pops – maybe that's why her tummy felt so peculiar. She didn't dare tell her mother how weird she was feeling; there was so much riding on this wedding. So many people looking forward to it, so much hard work and fuss by the grown-ups and all her classmates waiting for her in church.

Oh no, she might be sick . . .

'Are we ready, then?'

The vicar loomed in the doorway. He seemed so big in his long white and purple robes, his few remaining hairs plastered across his head while bushy ones protruded from his nostrils.

'Your bridesmaids are outside along with half the village. Shall we make a start?' his voice boomed.

4

Her mum grasped Freya's hand. 'We're ready, Vicar!' she said, her feathers dancing wildly. 'Now remember to smile, love. This is meant to be the happiest day of your life.'

'Excellent. Now, who's walking you up the aisle?'

'I am,' said her mother. 'We decided on a break with tradition.'

'That's fine. I had a bride accompanied by a Shetland pony once.'

'A *pony*?' Her mother smiled back but had a steely look in her eye that Freya knew all too well. 'Shall we make a start? I'm sure Freya's keen to get it over with.'

Her mum steered her out into the church and the two bridesmaids took their places behind her. Her teacher had chosen them; one of them – Roxanne Jameson – stuck out her tongue at her.

Freya's stomach did a somersault. If she got this wrong, she'd be teased and tormented for months.

The organ started, incredibly loud and scary like the vampire TV show Roxanne had persuaded her to watch which had left her with nightmares for weeks.

Her mother's arm tightened around hers. 'Smile . . .' she murmured.

Freya tried but her jaw was frozen with terror. So many people staring at her; the other kids who'd spent weeks making paper flowers for the church; the mums and dads grinning like idiots at her; and the stone angels staring down from the roof, their eyes boring into her.

The only one not looking at her was Travis. Facing the altar, he had his hands shoved so far down his pockets that one finger poked out of a hole in them.

She hesitated but her mum's hand tightened around hers.

5

'It'll be all right, love,' she murmured, and finally let go of her arm so she could stand next to Travis in front of the vicar, who was beaming down at them.

'Hold her hand, lad,' he said, 'though you'll have to take them out of your pocket first.'

'Yuk,' Travis muttered, yet a moment later his fingers closed around hers and squeezed them gently.

'Dearly beloved . . .'

Freya's stomach was swishing like a washing machine.

'. . . we are gathered here today . . .'

Her heart was thumping so hard, it would surely burst out of her chest and she was definitely going to be sick.

'. . . to celebrate the marriage . . .'

She couldn't do this, not in front of all these people gawping at her, with the angels and ghosts staring down, all expecting her to be perfect. In fact, maybe not ever.

'. . . of Travis and Freya . . .'

Freya tore her hand out of Travis's and ran down the aisle. She carried on running, out of the church and down the path, into the street, heading for the hills as if her life depended on it, with her mother's screams ringing in her ears.

Chapter One

Many years later
December 1st

Oh God, no, not again . . .

Freya sat bolt upright, jolted from her nightmare by
the ringing of her mobile. She was drenched in sweat even
though her bedroom window was rimed with frost. That
stupid, ridiculous dream . . . It had surfaced out of nowhere,
plunging her back to one of the most humiliating days of her
life.

Fumbling for her phone on the bedside table, she stabbed
the green button.

'Freya? Phew. Am I relieved you've answered! I've been
trying you for ten minutes! We've a major crisis on our
hands!'

Freya pressed the phone to her ear. '*Another* one?' she said
croakily, wishing she'd taken a glass of water to bed. Her best
friend Roxanne's hen night had gone on two hours and several

drinks past what she'd intended. She was meant to be having the day off while her business partner, Mimi, took the helm of their property management company.

'Yes. But this is *serious*.' There was an edge of panic in Mimi's voice that rang alarm bells.

She flicked on the bedside lamp and winced. 'How s-serious?'

'Pretty bad. I knew this freeze would spell trouble. There's been a burst pipe at Waterfall Cottage and the guests are sitting in the office in their pyjamas. I've made them hot drinks but lot of their stuff has been ruined and I need to find them alternative accommodation.'

'Poor things.' Freya grimaced at the image of guests trying to deal with a flood on an icy December morning. It was no more than Mimi could deal with, however. 'Have you phoned the owners and the cottage letting company to get them to find somewhere else?' she said, wondering why her partner was in quite such a state.

'Yes, and it's being sorted out, but I can't leave them until the new place is ready. We've also had a – um – canine-related incident in one of the posh flats by the lake. The cleaners arrived first thing to find the guests' three miniature dachshunds must have been on the vindaloo and left a trail of destruction in their wake. The carpets are ruined.'

At least they weren't Great Danes, thought Freya as her stomach turned over. 'Yuk. Where are the dogs' owners?'

'They scarpered before dawn apparently, leaving the evidence behind.'

'Some people are truly disgusting. Never mind. Joe will sort that. He works miracles. He could make a cow shed look like Buckingham Palace.'

'He's on my list to call, but there's more, Frey. We're two cleaners down.'

'*Two?*'

'Yeah. One's off sick and the other's wife has gone into labour. I'm so sorry to bother you on your day off, but this is a shitstorm. Literally.'

'It's OK. I'll come in now. You find somewhere for the guests to stay and I'll come and deal with Poomageddon. I'll cover the cleaners and do the changeovers myself.'

'Thank you so much, partner! Promise I'll make it up to you.'

'I'll make sure you do.' Freya swung her legs out of bed, wincing at the pulse in her temple. She hadn't had *that* much to drink, but she'd been tired after a busy week at work and too busy to have dinner before heading to the cocktail bar in Bowness. She'd have to dose up on paracetamol and put a peg on her nose before she inspected the House of Doggy Doom.

She and Mimi had started Cottage Angels five years previously as a cleaning and changeover service for the many holiday cottages around the Lake District village of Bannerdale, but it had now expanded to a full-blown property management service.

With experienced cleaners in short supply, and many more homes being turned into holiday lets, their services were in great demand. Most of the owners lived miles away – sometimes abroad – so Cottage Angels were often the guests' first port of call in emergencies.

It was demanding and relentless, but Freya adored being her own boss, and Mimi was a great business partner – if prone to the odd freak-out.

Freaking out . . . Freya shuddered as her nightmare came

back to her in lurid detail – except it hadn't been a nightmare when she was eight. Running out of the village church during her 'wedding' to Travis Marshall had made her the laughing stock of the school for *years*. Even now, some of the kids who'd been there – now 'grown-ups' – still referred to her as 'Bolton the Bolter'.

Squashing down the memories, Freya made a gallon of coffee and a pile of toast before making calls to the owners of the flooded cottage and to Joe the carpet cleaner.

'Thanks for the business,' he said, sarcastically.

'You're welcome,' she said cheerily. 'I'll meet you there at ten to see how bad it is then leave you to it.'

The previous night's celebrations seemed a long way off as she drove from her tiny cottage to the chic lakeside apartment where the dogs had had a field day. Sleet pattered the windscreen of her van and the high fells were hidden under a blanket of cloud. She knew they would be covered with snow after the recent freeze.

Joe was waiting for her at the lakeside apartment. While Freya tracked down the culprit guests to inform them they'd be paying a hefty cleaning fee, he set to work restoring the floorcovering to pristine condition.

Like many of the properties they managed, the apartment had already been decorated for Christmas by Krystle, a professional Christmas decorator whose work had impressed Freya so much that she'd added it as an optional service for their property owners.

Krystle and her team had been busy putting up owners' decorations, or using their own, over the past two weeks, so that come December 1st, the cottages and flats were already sparkling and festive.

Next on the agenda were two contrasting properties to be cleaned and prepared for arriving holidaymakers.

Freya stuck some Christmas tunes on the smart speaker while she made the two-bed 'boutique' flat sparkle enough to make the guests feel they were the first people ever to set foot in the property. She hadn't done a house prep for a while and was reminded how hard her freelance housekeeping team had to work. Every nook and cranny had to be pristine; the kitchen had to gleam, the bathrooms furnished with sweet-smelling toiletries and fluffy towels and the beds made to five-star standard.

No real home was ever presented to such a standard – but that's what guests expected.

She arranged the welcome tea tray with fresh coffee, local tea and Grasmere gingerbread, and added a welcome hamper with a chocolate advent calendar as a special festive touch. With one last check of the property, she dropped the keys in the door safe and headed to her final job.

Squirrel Cabin was situated up a long track on the outskirts of the village, virtually the last dwelling on the steep slopes that led up to the high fells. It was located in the grounds of a big house but had been empty for a few months while some basic work was done on its electrics and roof. It wasn't a trendy bolthole; the furnishings were quirky cast-offs from the main house – but Freya had always had a soft spot for it.

The large wooden squirrel beside the front door had been there as long as she could remember, although it was rather battered by the Lakeland elements these days. With snow dripping off the trees behind it, and sheep grazing the fells above, the cabin looked very picturesque. Being one bedroom, and having been unoccupied, she liked it even more because it would be a relatively quick job to make it look warm and welcoming for its next guests.

A small tree had already been set up in the corner of the lounge area, trimmed with woodland creatures and rustic decorations by Krystle.

Singing along to her Christmas mix tape, Freya vacuumed and dusted, made up the bed and attempted to turn the towels into waterlilies before giving up and leaving them neatly folded on the bed.

Next she replenished the tea and coffee, and put an advent calendar and welcome hamper on the counter before adding a basket of logs next to the wood burner.

There were only the flowers to arrange now. She found a vase from under the sink and unwrapped the crimson alstroemeria stems. She was almost done and could go home, enjoy a long soak in the tub and do some planning for the festive events taking place in the village over the next few weeks.

Cottage Angels had two big community events coming up: a stall at the Bannerdale festive fair and the annual carol concert, of which they were the major sponsor that year. When she'd first started the 'little cleaning firm' as her ex had once referred to it, she could never have dreamed of her business playing such a key role in the life of the village.

She'd come a long way from the terrified little girl running out of the church with the whole village laughing. Or had she?

The words dried in her throat, and she gripped the vase tighter, as other memories surfaced.

Now was *not* the moment to dwell on the darker times since.

As Mariah Carey reached the climax of the song, Freya stuck the vase under her mouth as a mic and let rip:

'All I want for Christmas is you-uuuuuuu!'

'Wow. I've heard of a warm welcome, but this is beyond the call of duty.'

Still clutching the vase, she turned around slowly, unwilling to connect the familiar voice with its owner.

The man framed in the doorway was tall and muscular with curly brown hair, a backpack slung over one shoulder and a tripod balanced on the other.

The vase slipped from her hands with a crash that made her heart almost leap out of her chest.

Blood pumped through her limbs and her stomach flipped as she tried to process the fact that the handsome guest glaring back at her was Travis Marshall: the man she'd tried and failed to marry – twice.

Chapter Two

Abandoning the tripod and bag, Travis darted forward. His boots crunched on the shards that had exploded all over the tiles. 'Are you OK?'

'I'm fine but you be careful of this glass,' she warned, her pulse still racing.

'I don't care about me. I didn't mean to startle you but I heard the singing and . . .' His eyes widened. 'What are you doing here, Freya?'

'I could ask you the same.' She glared at him 'What are *you* doing here?'

'Well, it appears that I've rented this place.' His thinly disguised sarcasm riled her instantly.

'You're three hours early. The instructions for guests *clearly* state there is to be no access until three p.m.'

'Ah, but the cabin owner said I could turn up earlier if I liked – in view of the circumstances.' His cocky grin maddened her further – because it hadn't changed one bit from their youth.

'What circumstances?' she said icily. 'What makes you

different to every other holiday guest? Don't you know we need time to prepare the place without guests under our feet, making a mess and causing trouble?'

His eyes flashed with annoyance. 'I didn't mean to cause trouble and – forgive me, but I'm not the one who's made a mess.'

Her jaw dropped.

'I accept that I might have caused it, however. I'll help you clear up the glass.'

'There's no need,' she said haughtily. 'That's my job – as you're on holiday.'

'*Holiday?*' A deep frown bisected his forehead. 'I'm not on holiday. I've taken the cabin on a long-term let.'

Freya tried to compute the meaning of his words and failed miserably. 'You mean, you're back in Bannerdale?' she exclaimed.

'It seems like it, doesn't it?' he said, adding with a mocking smile, 'though I can see I might not be welcome by everyone.'

'I didn't say that,' she shot back.

'You didn't have to.'

It had been several years since she'd even glimpsed him in person and fourteen years since they'd had an actual conversation. The last one of those had been bitter and hurtful.

Travis had never tried to contact her on his occasional visits to see his family in Bannerdale and she'd never wanted to speak to him anyway. This was exactly the reason why: because the moment they did have the misfortune to spend time in close proximity without anyone around, they were facing off like two warring kids again.

His eyes – deep brown flecked with amber – held hers without flinching. His chin and jaw were set in a determined

15

line, yet she would *not* be the first to look away. She wasn't sure she could, drawn to that annoying, handsome face like iron filings to a magnet. He was even better looking in the flesh than on his Instagram feed and she'd been checking that out for the past three years.

She let out a snort of derision – at him and at herself for even noticing his good looks.

'I didn't mean to be *rude*,' she said, 'but this is the first I've heard of anyone moving in here long-term. Actually, I wasn't meant to clean the cabin today, but we've a temporary staffing crisis so I had to come in on my day off. If I'd had time to check, I'd probably have seen your name on the booking list and realised you were on a long-term let.'

He raked a hand through his thick mahogany curls. 'Look,' he said in a slightly more conciliatory tone, 'it was a bit of a last-minute decision. I've taken over the lease on a gallery in the village and I needed somewhere to stay. There's not much to rent as you know, but Hamza heard about this place from a mate.'

'Hamza?'

'A friend from uni. Anyway, I only heard about it a few days ago and – well, here I am.' He shrugged and held out his hands as if to say: and what are you going to do about it?

The gleam of challenge in his eyes set off an annoying gymnastics routine in her stomach. No matter how many times she might have rehearsed this meeting, she wasn't prepared for his impact in the flesh. Whenever she'd fantasised about what she might say to him when they met again, she'd imagined making brief, polite conversation before moving on again.

The problem was that all these scenarios had taken place

16

in a public place, a pub, a shop, the street . . . not in the intimate space of a tiny cabin where moments before she'd been making a bed – *his* bed, she realised.

'Shall I help you clear up the broken glass?' he said, softening his tone. 'As it was me who caused you to drop the vase.'

'You didn't. I just didn't expect anyone to waltz in at that moment,' Freya shot back then regretted being so snarky. 'Thanks,' she muttered. 'I'll get the dustpan and brush and try and find an old newspaper.'

'I've got one in the car. I'll fetch it.'

Returning with a crumpled copy of the *London Evening Standard*, he crouched down next to her to pick up the slivers of glass from the floorboards.

His fingers brushed hers as they both went for the same piece of glass at the same time. Freya snatched back her hand and let him retrieve the shard. He dropped it into the newspaper.

She really wished he'd let her take charge of the clear-up so she wasn't forced to be so close to him. Briefly, her hand skimmed against his woollen sweater and she couldn't help catching a subtle hint of his aftershave, a warm, woody fragrance.

With relief, she straightened up and murmured, 'I'll get rid of these.'

Scuttling outside, she sucked in fresh air and emptied the shards into the bin. Travis was unloading another large bag of camera equipment into the cabin. The stuff looked very heavy, and his Insta had shown him in so many remote, mountainous places, it was no wonder he'd beefed up from the teenager she'd once known.

Tearing her focus away from his broad shoulders, she marched inside, meaning to turn off the music and leave. 'I'll be out of your hair soon. You'll want to unpack.'

'It'll wait. My camera equipment is the only thing I want safely in the house, not that I think Bannerdale is a hotbed of crime, though you never know.'

Did she detect a touch of acid in the comment? She'd no idea if his father was still in jail or had gone straight.

'The cabin looks good,' he said, directing a smile her way as if he regretted his cynicism, though she couldn't be sure with Travis. 'Thanks for making it so *welcoming*.' His gaze slid to the flowers in their new vase, lips twitching in amusement. 'You really shouldn't have bought roses.'

'I wouldn't if I'd known it was you.' She laughed. 'That was a joke by the way.'

He raised an eyebrow. 'I couldn't tell.'

She sighed. 'Look, they're not roses. They're alstroemerias and they're standard in *all* the properties we manage. You'll find tea, coffee and biscuits in the hamper – also standard – and milk in the fridge too.'

He nodded. 'It's been a long drive. I could do with a coffee.'

Freya wondered if that was a hint for her to leave which she was on the verge of doing anyway, when he added: 'You must be desperate for a drink too after cleaning this place?'

Her dry throat was testament to that, but she ignored it. 'I really should be getting back to work.'

He raised a quizzical eyebrow. 'I thought it was your day off.'

'It *was*.'

'Then you've more than earned a cup of coffee. I'll make it,' he added with a grin.

Cleaning was thirsty work and the thought of some of the dark roast in the welcome hamper was very tempting. 'I wouldn't mind . . . I had a late one last night.'

He quirked an eyebrow in interest. 'Hot date?'

'No! It was Roxanne's hen night.'

'Roxanne Jameson? She still lives round here?'

'Yes. Why wouldn't she?' Freya was piqued by the surprise in his voice.

'She was always boasting that she couldn't wait to get away from here when we were at school. She wanted to be an actress, didn't she?'

'Yes, but she's a paralegal now, at Beresfords.'

He made an 'o' of surprise. 'That place is still going too?' he said with a curl of the lip. 'I bet Jos works for his dad, doesn't he?'

'As a matter of fact, yes. He's a partner now.'

Travis snorted. 'Well, I could have predicted that one.'

'It's a good job,' Freya said haughtily, already rueing how easily she'd caved in and agreed to some coffee. What happened to her plan to make polite conversation and move on? 'I need to make a few calls while you make the drinks. Like I said, I can't hang around long.'

She carted the empty linen crate and slung it into the car. Travis could probably hear the boot slam from inside the cabin, but he'd touched a raw nerve with his comments about Roxanne and Jos Beresford. He made it sound strange that anyone would stick around in Bannerdale . . . just because *he'd* gone off to have an exciting lifestyle in exotic places.

She was on the verge of jumping in the car and driving off, but that would have seemed childish, and the last thing she wanted was to revert to their schooldays. Travis had caught her off-guard, and, she reminded herself, he was a guest, so she ought to at least be civil, and find out exactly *why* Travis had deigned to return to Bannerdale after so long.

Before she went back inside, she made a quick call to Mimi, who informed her that 'everything was in hand'. The flooded guests had been accommodated in another property and Mimi had helped retrieve some of their possessions.

Back inside, she found Travis had placed two steaming mugs on the coffee table and was opening the complimentary biscuits.

Finally, she felt she could breathe a little, apart from the fact she was sitting in Travis Marshall's new home, enjoying a cosy cuppa with him. He seemed to have rapidly made himself at home in the small space. She thought of the pine bed with its end boards and doubted it would be long enough for him, then regretted thinking of him in any kind of bed.

He lounged on the sofa, resting one jean-clad leg on the other, annoying Freya who perched on the edge of her chair, feeling as if she'd woken up in a parallel universe. Was it really him? Was it really her? Perhaps the answer was 'no', because they were very different people than the two lovesick teenagers who'd parted with so much anguish half a lifetime ago.

'I – um – saw you followed my Instagram account,' he said, taking a great interest in his coffee.

'Your photos are very good. I enjoy looking at them,' she replied, trying to sound appreciative but not too enthusiastic. He had so many followers on Insta, she'd been amazed he'd even noticed her or followed her back. 'Cottage Angels has a long way to go to match up,' she added, attempting a joke.

He smiled. 'Oh, I don't know. I like a bit of towel art.'

Was he teasing her? 'It's a business account to showcase our services,' she said, then regretted her haughty tone. 'It can't compete with a snow hare in the Cairngorms.'

He laughed. 'Cute animals and beautiful landscapes are what Insta was made for, but where would we be without a place to stay?'

She slurped her coffee. Maybe it had been a bad idea to stay.

'Sorry. I didn't mean to patronise you. I really admire how you've grown the business, building it up from nothing. I admire anyone who makes a go of things on their own.'

He turned his brown eyes on her, with the intense gaze that used to make her melt, but Freya refused to thaw. Romantic notions were for teenagers.

'I never liked having a boss,' she said firmly. 'It's why I left the holiday marketing agency to set up Cottage Angels. It was a big risk but if it all went wrong, it's down to me and that's fine.'

'Same here. Photography's a cutthroat business and you've no guarantee of success but at least you know you're alive.'

It was said with an intensity he couldn't hide under a veneer of cynicism. He'd given her a glimpse of the Travis she'd – long ago – fallen for. The one whose wild and crazy plans she'd allowed herself to be caught up in.

Even now, so many years later she felt that Travis ran at life full tilt. Under the bravado and laddish exterior, he had the soul of an artist: intense and romantic. No wonder he'd been so successful in a career that required creativity and obsession. She'd always been the sensible one, the practical one – perhaps, a small voice whispered, *too* sensible at times . . .

'Exactly. I like to make my own decisions; I don't have to answer to anyone else.'

Deep lines appeared between his brows. 'Shame that wasn't always the case, was it?'

'What's that supposed to mean?' she snapped. He must be referring to her mother, and her influence in Freya's decision to break off their engagement. Stung by the barb, Freya folded her arms defensively.

He shrugged. 'Nothing. Forget I said it.'

'No, Travis, I won't. If you're referring to what happened when we were at school? We were eighteen. There was no way that we should have even contemplated a serious relationship, let alone get married.'

'Of course. You're right. It was . . . crass . . . of me to bring it up. We're grown-ups now and in hindsight, you're right, it would have been a huge mistake.'

'Exactly,' Freya declared. 'A *massive* mistake. Look at us now: running our own businesses, doing what we love.' She thought back to the flat earlier, her hands encased in Marigolds, trying to help Joe clear up after the dogs, but wasn't mentioning that. 'That might not have happened if we'd ended up married at eighteen. You'd have had to get a proper job. I might have had three kids by now.'

'Three?' He raised an eyebrow.

'Or one or two,' she said, embarrassed at the idea – her own – that they'd have been at it like rabbits.

'In that case, I'd probably have had to get two *proper* jobs,' Travis said, an edge of sarcasm in his voice. 'I couldn't have swanned off round the world doing what I loved and making a name for myself.'

He folded his arms.

She bridled, resenting his tone. 'Well, clearly I'd have held you back so you should thank me for deciding not to run away with you to Gretna Green!'

'We never actually made it to Gretna Green. Your mum put a stop to all of it, didn't she?'

Freya thought back to the moment she'd told her mum that Travis had asked her to marry him and that they were engaged. She'd shown her mother the ring he'd bought her from a catalogue store.

Her mother had been on the verge of tears. 'A ring? You're both serious, then? Oh, Freya, you can't be! You're far too young to tie yourself down. You haven't even left school yet and nor has he. Please tell me that you're not going through with this?'

Before Freya could start to defend Travis, her mum had landed another blow: 'Darling, you may think that he's the only for one for you now, but trust me, you'll be making a massive mistake. His family life is far from ideal. You've no idea how he might turn out in the future. What if he drags you into a life of crime?'

'That's ridiculous, Mum!' Freya had cried.

'Well, having such a chaotic upbringing is going to have a bad effect on him, you can't deny that. It's a terrible way to start a life together and I worry you'll be trapped in a miserable situation, regretting marrying him and bitter about all the things you're missing out on. Come to think of it, is that really fair on Travis too? Tied to a partner who resents him?' her mother added, wiping her eyes with a tissue. 'I know your dad would say the same if he was here.'

Freya had almost walked out of the house and gone off with Travis in that moment, but she'd held back. She couldn't leave her mother alone, Freya was all she'd got and a tiny voice had nagged at her: what if her mum was right? What if she *was* taking a disastrous step in marrying Travis at such a young age. What if it was better for both of them to rein back?

In the intervening years she'd come to terms with her decision to break it off, but now he was back, she'd allowed a sliver of 'what-if' to enter her mind. That moment of doubt, however brief, made her feel queasy before she reminded herself that her hangover and lack of sleep were to blame for her light-headedness, rather than being confronted with one of the most painful moments of her life.

'Freya?'

His voice jolted her back to the present.

'We were different people then,' she said firmly. 'Just kids. Let's not rake up all those bad memories.'

'Bad memories?' he echoed. 'Of course. They were all bad ones.'

She knew what he wanted. He wanted her to soften her statement, say there had been good times too. The amazing, heart-stopping, spine-tingling rush that came with the intensity of first love.

She snatched up her coat and bag and held them to her defensively. 'Goodbye. I trust you'll find everything to your satisfaction.' She opened the cabin door. 'If you do need anything, our office number is in the welcome folder.'

'I know that. Freya! Please don't run away again.'

'"Run away"?' She snorted. 'You're surely not still pissed off that I bailed out of that stupid school wedding?'

'I'm not talking about the first one,' he said coldly. 'I'm talking about the second.'

Her stomach turned over. Surely, he couldn't still be hurt, after all these years? He must have moved on by now and got over her? She felt a sudden rush of anger, however unfair, that he'd thrust himself back into her life and dragging up emotions she'd buried long before.

'That's not fair,' she said, marching off to her car and climbing in.

Travis followed her to the car and shouted through the glass of the driver's window. 'Wait, Freya, I'm sorry.'

'Goodbye,' she muttered, pressing her foot down on the accelerator. With a tortured groan, the wheels spun in the slush.

Travis banged the window. Ignoring him, Freya's foot hovered above the gas pedal then stopped. If the van did lurch forward sharply, she might run over him and no matter how annoyed she was with him, she didn't want *that*.

She turned off the engine and pressed the window button. 'I don't need your help.'

He leaned down to her level. 'Good, because I only came out to finish what I was trying to say.'

She gripped the wheel. 'I don't want to hear it. Can I please leave now?'

'Sure. I'm not stopping you.' With that, he marched off to the cottage.

Praying the van would behave, she turned on the engine and gently let the clutch out while pressing the gas. If the worst came to the worst, she'd have to get out and chuck some grit under the wheels from the bag she kept in the boot. If the very worst came to the worst, she'd have to ask Travis for a push but she would rather clean up after the incontinent dachshunds every single day of her life than do that.

The van moved an inch. *Come on, baby, do this for me . . .*
The wheels turned, slipping a little, giving her hope.
A little bit more . . .
Yes.

The car slithered away from the cabin, with Freya praying it didn't do a Bambi on the steep track to the main road. She risked one fleeting glance in the rear-view mirror to see if Travis might be taking pictures, but the door was closed and there was no sign of him or his long-range lens.

Chapter Three

'Seb? Are you there?'
Travis called from the doorway of his brother's flat and winced at the smell of stale food, unwashed clothes and a couldn't-give-a-tossness.

Their older sister, Bree, had given him a key and he'd let himself in after several buzzes at the bell had resulted in silence. It was dark outside and the sleet had turned to rain by the time he'd climbed the stairs to the flat, situated in the attic space at the top of a building in the village centre.

The building had been a guesthouse when Travis was a kid but had long ago been converted into small flats catering to the local population of students and singles like Seb. However, in the current rental market, Travis was pleased his brother had a home at all.

He closed the door behind him and flicked on a light switch. Jeez. The illumination did nothing for the ambience. You could hardly see the furniture for discarded clothes and takeaway cartons. He hadn't expected anyone in Bannerdale to hang out the bunting, but so far, his homecoming hadn't resulted in the welcome he'd hoped for.

Why would it? He'd left the place as fast as he could and left very few people behind who'd miss him. There were probably more people who'd be happy to see the back of him, expecting him to turn out like his father.

Freya's mum had probably popped the champagne when he'd taken off after Freya had broken off their 'engagement'.

Ignoring the mess for the time being, he bellowed: 'Hey, Sebast-ian!'

Using his brother's full name always provoked a reaction.

However, instead of hearing swearing or groaning, Travis detected no human sound. Was Seb even *in*? Bree had said he should be up and getting ready for his shift at a nearby mini-market at this time of day.

Travis picked his way through the sitting room to the kitchen area where the 'breakfast bar' was piled with sticky mugs, crusty plates and empty lager cans. He winced as he saw the bin overflowing with cartons and stinking of rancid curry.

He turned back into the tiny hallway and heard snores from behind another door. Bracing himself, he opened it a crack and spotted a body-shaped heap under a duvet. By the whiff, this room also hadn't seen a vacuum or cleaning cloth in a long time.

Travis pushed the door open, allowing light from the hall to spill inside, but the sleeping figure stayed dead to the world.

Travis switched on the lamp and touched Seb gently on the arm. 'Hey, bro.'

Though he was twenty-seven, the sleeping Seb still looked

like a teenager, and snuffled like a toddler, blissfully dead to the world.

'Hey there, time to wake up,' he said and shook his arm more firmly.

'Urghhhh . . .' Seb rolled away, pulling the duvet tight around him.

With a sigh, Travis gave his sleeping brother a moment longer.

'Wakey! Wakey!' he shouted, yanking the duvet off.

'Jesus Christ!' Seb's eyes flew open, and he scrambled off the bed, blinking. 'What the fuck are you doing here?' he said hoarsely.

Travis grinned. 'Santa came early this year. It's four o'clock in the afternoon. Why aren't you at work?'

'I'm on the night shift . . . I don't start until six. Plenty of time.'

'Looks like you're going to need all of it to clean yourself and this hellhole up.'

'Hellhole? There's nothing wrong with this place.'

'It's a stinking pit, bro, and it looks like you need to use that washing machine I saw in the kitchen. Come on, get yourself out of bed and I'll make some tea.'

'*Tea?*' Seb's expression couldn't have been more disgusted if he'd been offered a cockroach cocktail.

Travis suppressed a smile. 'I hope you weren't expecting anything stronger?' he said with an eyebrow raise.

'Did I say that?' Seb growled. 'Tea will have to do.'

'Good. I also bought some bacon. While you have a shower, I'll make some sarnies – after I've detoxed that health hazard of a cooker.'

'Jesus, when did you turn into Mum?'

'Mum wouldn't have been interested in your domestic situation, as you well know. You can thank Bree for the visit. Now, get in the shower.'

A few minutes later, Travis heard water flowing. He found a couple of bin bags and started clearing all the crud off the floors and surfaces into them.

'Sh—' He stumbled over a pile of clothes and trainers, though it was the object underneath that had almost caused him to fall. He exhaled in relief as he picked up the guitar case from beneath the clothes. If he had landed or trodden on that, Seb would have killed him.

Although . . . his brother seemed to have little respect for what would once have been his most precious possession. God knows how long it had been since the instrument had been lying neglected on the floor.

Travis ran a finger through the dust on the case and his stomach ripped with unease. If Seb had stopped playing his music, he really must be at rock bottom.

The sound of running water ceased so Travis filled the kettle and switched it on. He found some half dried-up scouring cream and wiped out a couple of mugs. At the back of a cupboard, there was a frying pan, which mercifully looked as if it had never been used.

By the time Seb wandered in, wearing jeans with a towel around his neck, Travis was sizzling the bacon and eggs he'd brought with him.

Seb smacked his lips. 'God, that smells good.'

'Surprised you can smell anything at all. Your nostrils must have totally seized up.'

Seb sniffed. 'Whaddaya mean? There's nothing wrong with this place.'

'My point exactly.'

Travis slid the eggs and bacon onto the plate he'd managed to scrub into submission. He handed it to Seb who sat on the sofa with it balanced on his lap.

'Tea,' Travis said, placing a mug on the coffee table. 'I brought some milk. Yours was turning into a bioreactor in the fridge.'

'Thanks. You not eating?'

'I'm going to the pub for dinner later.'

'The pub?' Seb frowned. 'With who?'

'Hamza.'

'He's here too? Why are *you* even here? I'd no idea you were coming back.'

'Neither did I until a couple of weeks ago.'

'Don't say Bree dragged you back to nursemaid me?' Seb scoffed.

'Don't flatter yourself,' Travis countered, although it was a barefaced lie. 'I'm here looking after number one. The gallery became available so I took my chance. I can sell my own work from there and run photography tours. There's a big market for them right now.'

'You mean there are plenty of wrinkly wannabes with more money than sense?'

'Well, I wouldn't describe my customers like that,' Travis said. 'Firstly, they're not all "mature" and even if they are, it's fine because I'm quite happy to run workshops and tours for anyone if it means I can carry on taking my own pictures. I like teaching people; I've had a great time travelling and I don't mind some downtime for a while.'

'And conveniently, you can also hassle me while you're in town?' Seb pointed his fork at Travis before dropping it onto his empty plate with a clatter. 'I bet you fifty quid that Bree asked you to come back.'

Travis shifted uncomfortably because Seb was very close to the truth. 'Is there anything wrong with wanting to spend more time with my family?' he said wryly.

'Depends on how much you plan on interfering in their lives.'

Travis smiled. 'Depends on how much they need my interference. As you've finished dining, you can get off your arse and start clearing up this place. We've got a good hour before you have to start work at the shop.'

'I usually go on my bike.'

'No need. I'll drive you. Wouldn't want you getting lost on the way in one of the pubs.'

'You cheeky bastard,' said Seb, cheerfully enough but with murder behind his eyes.

As Travis had issued a dire warning to Seb about spending too much time in the pub, he thought it ironic – Seb would have said hypocritical – that he was headed there himself.

The Red Lion was one of many local hostelries and the stone exterior had changed little since he'd had last been in there – at a guess, three years previously on one of his rare and fleeting visits to Bannerdale.

The interior had, however, been given a makeover. Gone were the pine tables, stained by years of pints – replaced by grey upholstered benches, and pale wood furniture. Mood lighting and trendy bar stools had given the former snug the air of a cocktail bar.

He felt out of place until he spotted a familiar face – and figure – waiting for him in a booth in what had once been a favourite corner of the pub.

Travis had known Hamza Eassa since they were studying photography at art college in Manchester. His Sudanese family had been incredibly welcoming to Travis when he'd first turned up in the city and had even invited him into their home for a few months until he found somewhere to live.

While Hamza had gone on to be a renowned wildlife filmmaker, Travis had concentrated on still photography. When Hamza had heard about the gallery, he'd insisted on coming up to help Travis get it into shape, before heading off to a filmmaking assignment in Scotland.

'Sorry, I'm late,' Travis said, eyeing the pint on the table appreciatively. 'Thanks for the beer. You know me too well.'

Hamza was nursing a Peroni Zero. 'No problem. I've been people watching.' He grinned. 'Everything OK?'

'Not really.' Travis checked himself. Hamza really did know him well and must have sensed Travis was stressed. 'I had to drop Seb off at work. Well, I didn't *have* to, but I wanted to make sure he got there.'

Hamza nodded sagely. 'Still the big brother?'

'Big pain in the arse according to Seb and he has a point. Anyway, it's great to see you, mate. You found the cabin, OK? Sorry I wasn't there to meet you.'

'No problem. I've found my way round the Arctic and Amazon; I can handle the mean streets of Bannerdale.'

'And there are no polar bears to worry about here . . .' Travis laughed, feeling the tension of his spat with Seb slowly ebbing away. There was a feeling of calm and strength that seemed to surround his friend and seep into the people around him.

'I'm glad you found the time to come up and see me.'

'I'm between jobs. What else was I going to do but catch

up with you while we're both in the same country?' Hamza said.

'Well, you never know,' Travis said archly. 'There might have been someone a lot more interesting to spend time with than a cynical old mate.'

Hamza smiled, with an edge of ruefulness that was impossible to miss. 'Now, why would you think that?'

'You tell me?'

Hamza laughed. 'There is someone, actually.'

'Woo!' Travis whistled. 'Serious?'

'Kind of . . .' Hamza hesitated.

'Oh? This is news to me?'

'It was news to me. She's called Caz and she's a paediatric consultant and the daughter of a mate of my mum's. We've been family friends for a couple of years and lately, we've been seeing each other a lot more . . .'

'Am I sensing a "but"?'

'Why would there be a "but"?' Hamza said. 'She's extremely smart, kind, loves kids. She makes me laugh – and she's gorgeous and my parents adore her.'

'*But* . . .'

'Everyone thinks we're going to announce our engagement at any moment.'

'And are you?'

Hamza shrugged in a dismissive way that set Travis on the alert. 'We haven't got around to discussing it yet.'

'Have you actually asked her to marry you?' Travis said lightly.

'Mate, you don't know Caz. She would be the one doing the asking.'

Travis laughed. 'Are you sure about that?'

'I'm not sure about anything where women are concerned. I'm not sure about Caz either, but I think when we decide – it would be a joint thing.'

'OK. I'll back off and besides, I am the last person to be offering advice about relationships, let alone long-term ones.'

Hamza seemed relieved to shift the attention to Travis. 'So, there's no old flame who's lured you back to Bannerdale?' he said.

Travis snorted in derision. 'That's the last reason I'd ever come back. No . . . it's far less romantic.' Travis rubbed condensation off his glass before continuing. 'There's a bunch of reasons. Number one, being that Bree asked me to keep an eye on Seb. He's been feeling low, drinking again and she doesn't like the company he's been keeping.' He looked around at the pub, sad to see its rough edges smoothed by the bland, slick finish.

Hamza looked thoughtful. 'He's still young but I can understand why you're concerned too.'

'To be honest, it's his mood Bree's most worried about. You know, he used to play the gigs in this room. It was hardly the big time but he always looked happy with a guitar around his neck, playing and singing with a couple of mates.'

Poor Seb; was that why he'd abandoned his music? Was it because he felt he didn't fit in any longer, Travis wondered.

'Bree's concerned, nonetheless. Seb can't afford to lose another job or his flat. When I'd finished my latest job, I had some breathing space and you know I was already thinking of starting my own gallery, so here I am.'

'Sounds like fate, to me,' Hamza said.

Travis wasn't so fatalistic.

'Bree knows how to manage me. She held the stick of Seb over me and dangled the carrot of the gallery. I've enjoyed my adventures but there's only so many airstrips and shacks and tents in the wild I can take. I don't mind sleeping in a proper bed and having a place to call my own for a change.'

He could have added a third reason: that he'd developed an intense and annoying curiosity to see Freya. When she'd popped up as one of his followers on Instagram, he'd reciprocated and been following her feed far more closely than he'd let on, though not for the towel art.

The few videos she'd posted of herself and 'the team' had been viewed by him far more times than he cared to admit.

He raised his pint. 'So now I'm the proud new proprietor of Peak Perspectives.'

'Peak Perspectives?' Hamza echoed. 'I like the name. It has a ring to it.'

Travis took a nervous swig of his pint. 'Well, I needed a name. It's not brilliant but I thought it does what it says on the tin.' He smirked. 'The place was previously called Daffodils.'

Hamza snorted. 'I can't see you as a daffodil. Peak Perspectives is much more you.'

'I hope so though I'm not quite sure *what's* me. This is all new . . . I'm still feeling my way.'

Hamza slapped him on the back. 'Back yourself, mate. It'll be great and I'd love to lend a hand even in a small way.'

Travis sipped his pint and sighed appreciatively. 'I'm grateful for any help. I'm hoping to have it up and running for the Christmas Fair. The place will be rammed with people wanting to buy gifts and book tours.'

'I wish I could stick around until launch day but this BBC job is too good to turn down.'

'You mean you'd rather be filming eagles and sea otters than hanging around a rundown gallery?'

'It won't be rundown when you get to work on it and get the tours running. You're the one with a gift for teaching. I'm far better on my own with a bunch of wild creatures than people.'

'I wouldn't say I had a gift, but I do enjoy tutoring people,' Travis said, a little embarrassed by his friend's praise. 'It's a buzz to see them finding a whole new world with the camera and the look on their faces when we encounter the wildlife is priceless. It reminds me of how I felt when I was young and spotted my first pine marten or wildcat. I was so overexcited, I almost dropped the camera a few times.'

Suddenly his eye was caught by two women who were giving their order to the bar man.

Sensing Travis's interest, Hamza's eyes lit up in curiosity. 'You know them?' he said.

'Kind of. I was at school with them. The dark-haired one is Roxanne. Head girl. Never even knew I existed, probably.'

'And the other woman?'

Travis savoured his pint before replying. 'Oh yes. That's Freya.'

'Old flame?'

'Actually, we were almost married,' he said.

Hamza gasped. 'No way! You've never said anything about an ex.'

Travis grinned. 'When we were eight. It was one of those mock ceremonies they have at primary school.'

'Not at my school!' Hamza said with raised eyebrows.

'It sounds weird and it was, in hindsight. It was all part of some module on life rituals – but probably about so-called adults projecting their hopes and fantasies onto a bunch of eight-year-olds. I was forced to be the groom and Freya was the bride.' Travis watched Freya chatting to Roxanne.

Hamza was still agog. 'Tell me more. Are there photos of the big day?'

'I've no idea what happened to them,' Travis said, unwilling to let on that the bride ran away before they got to that point.

Fortunately, he was interrupted by a nudge from Hamza. 'She's coming over,' Hamza said, clearly relishing all the intrigue. 'Will she recognise you?'

'Well, as I had coffee with her earlier, I should think so.'

Hamza's eyes widened. 'This is getting juicier by the minute. Are you sure you want me in the cabin, cramping your style?'

Travis laughed. 'She runs a cottage management company. She was cleaning the place when I arrived. We had a drink for old times' sake and she left. End of.' He didn't elaborate on the tense row they'd had – and the strained way they'd parted.

Freya walked over, a Coke in her hand.

'Hello again,' she said, pausing briefly by his table while Roxanne nabbed a seat on the other side of the pub.

'Hi,' Travis said, marvelling at how lovely she looked and how confidently she strolled over to his table. She smiled politely at him as if their morning spat had never happened, making him feel like a gauche schoolboy again. Her eyes glinted, as if she was revelling in his discomfort.

'Er. This is my friend, Hamza,' he said, glancing away.

'Welcome to the bright lights of Bannerdale,' Freya said. 'Roxanne's waiting for me. I'll see you around – again?'

'We don't seem to be able to avoid it,' Travis replied.

'Enjoy your meal. Nice to meet *you*, Hamza.'

She was gone, trailing a cloud of perfume and obvious antipathy towards him. Travis felt as if he'd been pole-axed.

'Well, well . . .' Hamza said. 'You need oxygen, bro?'

Travis forced a grin to his face. Despite their row earlier, he couldn't bring himself to say anything against Freya. 'She always was quite a girl.'

'You seem to be unable to take your eyes off her now. I've a feeling she's more than interested in you too. Are you sure this school wedding is the only history between you?'

Caught off-guard, Travis buried his awkwardness under cynical laughter. 'We did go out together – briefly – when we were in the sixth form but that was a long time ago. We're completely different people now and I'm not here to rake up old memories. As far as I know she might have a partner.'

'I don't think so. Not the way she was drinking you up. She kept trying to hide her interest but she couldn't stop glancing at you.' Hamza smiled. 'All these years of observing wildlife have taught me to recognise the signs.'

Travis rolled his eyes. 'Mate, you're forgetting one thing: we're not otters or penguins.'

'Yet as well you know, we still have the same impulses,' Hamza said.

Travis rolled his eyes. 'I suspect Freya's only impulse towards me would involve tipping her Coke over my head. Now, let's talk about the photos for the gallery. I'm too close to my own work to judge what might appeal to the punters.'

He heard laughter from across the pub. Freya's laughter. Was it possible that as he lifted his pint, his hands weren't quite steady? Would his observant friend notice *that*?

In the space of hours, Freya had transported him back to the heady days of his youth, bursting with hormones and feelings he couldn't handle then – and wasn't sure he could now.

Chapter Four

By the following evening, Freya breathed a sigh of relief that her working day had been relatively drama free compared to the previous one. Her encounters with Travis had been more than enough to set her mind racing like a Formula One car and dominate her thoughts late into the night.

She and Mimi were able to catch up with admin and ensure they had enough staff in place for the changeovers. When they'd first started Cottage Angels, most people had arrived and left on Saturdays, but there was a growing trend for year-round short breaks which meant cleaners were required for almost every day of the week.

Good ones were like gold dust, so Freya had interviewed two more and taken them on, ready for the busy festive period. Their team of freelancers was growing, to go along with their PA, Hamish, and their valuable list of local tradespeople who were ready to respond to any urgent jobs at a moment's notice.

Hamish was on emergency call that evening, just in case of disaster, so Freya locked up the office and headed round to her mum's before anticipating a quiet night in front of her log burner at her own cottage down by the lake. As she drove to her mother's through the heart of the village, the Christmas lights, as yet unlit, swung in the wind. They were due to be switched on at the weekend as part of the Christmas Fair.

She couldn't wait; it was a gloomy time of year when dark fell by mid-afternoon and the lights would cheer everyone up and herald the start of Christmas and a flood of visitors. She didn't mind the bustle and long hours that came with the holiday season; keeping busy kept her mind off more gloomy thoughts, about past losses and regrets.

She wondered if her mother had heard that Travis was back yet. News travelled at warp speed in the small community. She'd know soon enough: she was already parking outside her mum's bungalow in a cul-de-sac near the rugby club.

Her mum opened the door, very red in the face with flour in her normally perfect blow-dry.

'Quick. Come in, love. Can you shut the door behind you? I've got to get these mince pies out of the oven before they burn. Oh, and mind the boxes in the hall! I've had another delivery!'

Negotiating an array of packages and cartons, Freya made it into the kitchen where her mother was extracting several trays from the oven and cursing. The room felt roasting after the crisp night air, though the aromas of baking were wonderful.

Cooling racks and plates littered every surface. 'Blimey, Mum. Are you setting up in business? There must be a hundred pies here.'

'Don't I know it,' her mother said, closing the oven door with a deep sigh. 'I foolishly agreed to help with the WI stall at the Christmas Fair. We're doing mince pies and mulled wine, and a raffle. We need four hundred in total. These are going in the freezer.'

Freya reached out to the nearest rack. 'They won't miss one will, they?'

Her mother rolled her eyes. 'I suppose not.' She smiled. 'I'll put the kettle on.'

'No, I'll do that. Looks like you need the rest.'

A short time later, the two of them were sitting in the lounge with coffee. Freya tucked in to her pie but her mum declared herself 'sick of the sight and smell of them' and had opted for a glass of Baileys instead.

She plonked her feet on a stool. 'Thank God, those are out of the way. I will never agree to help again. I never was a domestic goddess.'

'Frankly, I'm amazed you made any at all, but they are really good, Mum.'

'Hmm. I watched a ton of online videos first but I was on the verge of ordering the lot from the village bakery. I'd probably have been drummed out of the WI if I had.'

Freya laughed and wasn't surprised her mother had used video tutorials. She had an Instagram account called @Glamoversixty with tens of thousands of followers. 'They're great. What are all the boxes?'

'I'm not sure because I haven't opened them all yet. I'm expecting some makeup and a fancy facial steamer and some hair straighteners. Some of it could be Christmas stuff but most are for the spring. I can't possibly use or review all of it so I'm going to donate some of it to the tombola at the fair.'

'Are the slippers new?' she said, admiring her mum's sheepskin mules.

Her mother waggled her feet. 'Yes, they're from a Lakes company. Lovely, aren't they? Kate Winslet was seen in a very similar pair in a gossip mag last month.'

'Very nice. Will you review them?'

'Already made a reel about them. I wore them to my Pilates class. They're not just for lounging by the fireside, you know. Shall we open some boxes? You can film me, if you don't mind. I'd better get this flour out of my hair first.'

For the next half hour, Freya filmed her mum 'unboxing' some of the haul of free stuff sent to her by companies hoping to have their products featured on her Instagram. Most of it was unsolicited, some of it useful and beautiful – some of it bizarre, like the nose hair clippers that emerged from an oversized carton.

'I'll see if Neil fancies a go with those,' her mum said. 'Now, this looks interesting . . .' she said, removing a black oblong box from inside its cardboard outer. 'What's in here?'

'Chocolates? A silk dressing gown?' Freya mouthed silently, aware she was still filming.

Her mother put the box on the coffee table, beamed at the camera and rubbed her hands together dramatically. 'Oooo! This package looks intriguing. I'm really quite excited. Could it be the new ceramic hair straighteners I'm hoping to try out? Let's see . . . oh, there's lovely gold tissue paper around them . . . I can't wait . . .' Her mum pulled the item from the tissue and her jaw dropped.

'Oh my God, Mum! That's not—' Freya cut herself off, realising her shriek of horror was on film.

'I think it might be,' her mother said, holding what appeared to be a gold-plated sex toy by one of its 'ears'. 'Well I shan't be donating that to the WI tombola!' she declared, her face scarlet. 'Quick, delete that video. What do they think I'll be doing with it? Filming myself and broadcasting it to the world?'

After the initial shock of opening the sex toy, Freya and her mum dissolved into giggles. Sandra buried it beneath its layers of tissue and marked the box with a silver pen: **NOT for tombola!!!**

Freya had to admit there was not a dull moment with her mother these days. None of her friends had mums who were 'social media influencers' and even Roxanne had declared it as 'cool'. It certainly had given her mum a new lease of life since she'd sold the boutique she used to own in the village.

In addition to the freebies, she was often invited to product launches and influencer events while the revenue from her Instagram activities was a welcome addition to her Pilates teaching. Freya was quietly proud of her and very grateful that her mum had helped her set up and curate the Cottage Angels Instagram feed, even if Travis had made a slightly sarcastic remark about the towel art. She felt irritated with him again, and at herself for finding his blue eyes mesmerising for even a nanosecond.

'Right,' she said, mentally sweeping Travis to one side. 'Shall I tell you the latest drama about Roxanne and the flowers?'

For a while they chatted about the wedding, and the upcoming rehearsal. The groom, Ravi, was a doctor, as were the best man and numerous guests, so a Thursday was the only day they'd all been able to take as holiday together.

'Must have saved them a fortune at the Langdale Manor, not choosing a Saturday,' Freya's mum pointed out.

'Quite a lot. Roxanne's parents were thrilled when they chose midweek,' Freya said, amused at her mum's shrewdness.

She realised that fifteen minutes had gone by and her mum still hadn't alluded to Travis. She guessed she was safe – for now – and moved onto the topic of Christmas Day, one that she and her mum had always looked forward to and spent together, even if they were invited to friends'. Without her dad around, the day was special and symbolic of the bond between mum and daughter.

'I was wondering if you wanted to get something different for Christmas dinner? One of the hamper suppliers said he can get me some lovely duck breasts.'

'Christmas dinner?' her mother echoed as if she'd never heard of such a thing.

'Yes,' Freya said, wondering if her mum had been listening. 'I thought we could make a special day of it. Just the two of us – or three if Neil wants to come. I wasn't sure if he'd be spending it with his own family.'

'That's a lovely thought, Freya, and it would have been great but I'm afraid I'm going to be away at Christmas too.' Her mother tittered, causing Freya's alarm bells to ring. 'In fact, I'm going to be at sea too.'

'At *sea*?' Now it was Freya's turn to echo her mum's words.

'Yes, Neil has asked me to go on a cruise with him to the Caribbean and the States. His sister is a travel agent and she's done us a fantastic deal and it's visiting so many places that are on my bucket list . . . Miami, Grand Cayman and Mexico . . . then we fly to the West Coast for a tour of LA, the California desert, and the Grand Canyon. It might be my only chance and I can get loads of photos for my Instagram.'

'It . . . certainly sounds incredible.' Freya was still taking in the news her mother was jetting – and sailing – off with Neil for Christmas. Her mother sounded wildly excited and

Freya didn't blame her with that list of exotic and glamorous destinations.

'I thought you'd be OK with it? You've lots of friends you'll want to spend time with and it is just this once . . .' Her mum's face fell.

Freya opened her mouth to reassure her but her mum was in full flight.

'I mean if you feel *completely* at a loss, I could always see if there's a single cabin available so you could join us,' she went on.

'No!' Freya blurted out more loudly than she'd thought, horrified at the prospect of playing gooseberry to her mother and Neil. 'Thanks for the offer, but you go and enjoy yourselves. I'll be *fine*.'

Sandra's shoulders sank in relief. 'Oh, that's a relief. I expect Mimi will have you. I can ask her mum for you if you like,' she suggested, as if she was planning a play date for Freya.

'No! Mum, please don't do that. If Mimi invites me that's fine, but she has her own brood to look after. You know there's masses of them.'

'Well, I don't want you to be on your own. I know Roxanne will be on her honeymoon so you can't go round to her place. I'm afraid it means I'll miss the wedding too.'

It was too late to worry about any of that, Freya thought, slightly more hurt than she would dream of letting on. However, her mother had been alone for a long time and had been much been happier since Neil had come onto the scene. 'I just didn't realise it was that – so serious – between you and Neil.'

Neil was an inoffensive man, though rather prone to wanting to report people for parking outside his house and other minor infringements of village 'regulations'. He was a kind man, had his own house and a friendly if slobbery Labrador called Benson.

A knowing smile touched her mother's lips. 'I know what you're thinking but don't worry. Neil could never replace your dad but he's very thoughtful, he's good company and we enjoy the same things. His foxtrot is wonderful too – I've learned so much from him. I think it's time for me to show some commitment, don't you think?'

'"Show some commitment"?' Freya was struck mute.

'Sorry, darling, that sounded tactless and I didn't mean it to. I wasn't referring to you and – well, anyone at all. I meant me.'

'I know what you meant,' Freya managed.

'Phew. Thank goodness for that. You see, now Neil's asked me to go with him, it feels like crunch time. This holiday will give us the opportunity to spend so much more time together.' She sighed wistfully. 'And it will be so lovely to enjoy some sunshine at this gloomy time of year. There'll be lots of dancing too. It's one of my biggest regrets: that I didn't dance more with your father, though he was a New Romantic to be honest, more into Duran Duran and Orange Juice than ballroom. Did I tell you about the time I went backstage with Tony Hadley?'

'You did, Mum.' *Many times*, thought Freya, forestalling yet another re-run of the night her mother had been invited into the Spandau Ballet dressing room – fortunately for nothing more than a glass of fizzy cider and an autograph. 'It all sounds wonderful. You go and have a fabulous time.' Freya didn't dare ask if they'd booked a double cabin . . . She shuddered. Of course, they would have.

'I hope so and . . .' Her mother wavered, a wary expression spreading over her face. 'Your dad's been gone a long time now. I'm sure he wouldn't have wanted me to mope about, being miserable, would he?'

'It's been thirty years,' Freya said softly. Most of her life . . .

Freya harboured a terrible secret: part of her was relieved that she didn't remember her father, because it had saved her from the personal pain of loss and grief. Yet she did remember the sympathy – the pity – that had followed her around when she was a little older.

She remembered distant relatives, old schoolfriends and work colleagues of her mother – even the hairdresser and local newsagent – smiling at her, sometimes pressing free sweets and pound coins on her if she were a beggar. They would talk over her head to her mum, their voices hushed and reverent. They meant well: Freya was glad they were kind to her mother but even at five, she knew what pity sounded like. At that age, everyone had had a dad. She didn't want to be special.

How must her mother have felt, bearing her own loss and knowing her daughter would never know her father? Was it selfish of Freya to be secretly, silently relieved?

As for now, Freya had her whole life ahead of her, if the fates allowed, and many Christmases to spend how she wanted to. Would it be so awful for her mother to dance the night away on a sunshine cruise?

She smiled broadly. 'You go and have a lovely time. I'll be fine.'

'Thank you, love. I knew you'd understand. Now, I'd like your opinion on some bikinis I've ordered. I had to get them online at this time of year but you know . . .'

Her mother had been friends with Neil, who she'd met at her ballroom dance class, for the past few months, but Freya must have missed what was under her nose: that friendship had grown into affection – and maybe more.

Would it be so awful to spend Christmas on her own, lying on the sofa eating her own weight in chocs, drinking Baileys and watching Netflix shows that her mother would never enjoy?

'Now, look, what do you think of these bikinis?. You don't think I'm too old for them, do you?' her mother said, cutting into her thoughts and holding up two flowery bottoms and tops.

'No, you have a great figure. You're fully entitled to rock a bikini.'

'I shan't appear in them on my feed, though. Not without a cover-up. Remember when Penny and Graham decided to do that naked shot in the hot tub?'

'Oh, God, how could I forget,' Freya declared, remembering the photo of two of her mum's influencer friends who'd been given a freebie by a spa company.

'I could have told them those bubbles wouldn't cover all their bits. You could tell they were starkers! I'm surprised they weren't banned! It broke the internet!' Sandra said with a giggle.

Freya thought it might break her phone screen if she had to witness such a scene featuring Neil and her mother.

Sandra delved into a box and unearthed more resort wear. 'I've ordered some matching sarongs and a kaftan too – and the company sent me this free nighty. To be honest,' her mum said, wrinkling her nose, 'the nighty isn't really me. Do you want to come up and take a look?'

'Yes. Sounds exciting . . .'

A while later, having admired a succession of items of

flowery, floaty items of 'cruisewear', and having actually rather liked the 'nighty' – a silk slip from a designer brand – Freya declined another coffee.

'Thanks, but I'd better have an early night. I'm on call tomorrow so it's a long day, then there's a traders' association breakfast meeting the morning after. It's to finalise all the details for the Christmas Fair because Cottage Angels are sponsoring both events.' There was Roxanne's wedding rehearsal too, Freya might have added.

Her mother looked suitably impressed. 'You've done very well for yourself,' she said, inducing a glow of pride in Freya. 'After all that hard work, you wouldn't throw it all away, would you?'

The glow vanished and the hairs on Freya's arms stood on end. 'What do you mean?'

'The business. Your life here. You wouldn't want to – give it all up or go away?'

Freya replaced her coat over the sofa back. 'Give up the business? Why would I do that? Where's this come from?'

'Nowhere. It's only me, thinking silly thoughts. I know you'd never make a mistake again . . .'

'A mistake *again*?' She folded her arms, braced for a confrontation. 'Mum, what are you talking about?'

'Well, I – can't help noticing that he's back.'

'He?'

'Yes. Travis Marshall. He's bought the gallery in the centre of town and I heard he was renting one of your properties. It looks like he's come back for good.'

'I have no idea of his long-term plans but yes, he has bought the gallery and he has taken a place on a long-term let, but what's that got to do with me?'

'I know you were sweet on him. You were cut up when you decided to end it but it was the right decision. You were far too young and you'd both have regretted tying yourselves down so young, I'm sure of it.'

No, Mum – you persuaded me to end it. 'Sweet' on him? What a limp, beige way of describing the feelings she'd had for Travis. Cut up? That was accurate.

She'd felt as if a piece of her heart – and her soul – had been ripped from her body when she'd told Travis she'd had to end their relationship.

'It was a very long time ago, though . . .' her mother said, perhaps picking up on Freya's stunned silence, though not the thoughts passing through her mind like leaden clouds over the lake.

'A *very* long time ago,' Freya echoed, picking up her coat and pecking her mum on the cheek. 'Now, I really have to go, Mum. Like I said, I've an early start. I've no idea what Travis Marshall's plans are and frankly, I couldn't care less.'

Chapter Five

'Shouldn't we have cut a ribbon?' Hamza said, shivering on the pavement beside Travis in the chilly morning.

It was one of the smaller units in town, amid a row of former cottages just off the main street. Its location was its biggest attraction: central enough to attract plenty of passing trade, but slightly off the busy road.

'Maybe I'll do that on launch day,' Travis replied, his heart beating a little faster as he turned the key. It was a little stiff but who cared. He had his own gallery, something he'd dreamed of for years but never thought would happen.

The key turned and he pushed at the door, but it refused to budge. 'Probably stuck in the damp. It has been shut up for a couple of months . . .'

'Need a hand?' Hamza said, a split second before Travis shouldered the door hard and let out a scream.

'Bloody hell!' Hamza loomed in the doorway. 'Are you OK?'

Travis gazed up at his friend from the tiles, having crashed through when the door had flown back on its hinges. He dusted himself off. 'Yep. Just about. I'll have to sort out that door though. Can't have the customers falling into the shop.' He squinted. Very little daylight penetrated the grimy windows on this dark winter morning.

'I think the light switches must be in the back,' he said, his voice echoing in the empty space. 'Reminds me of entering those caves in Cambodia,' Travis said, switching on his phone torch and wincing at the racket as Hamza shoved the door to behind him.

'As long as a million bats don't suddenly fly out, we'll be OK,' Hamza said.

'You never know . . . It smells pretty bad.' He wrinkled his nose and shivered. After months of standing empty, the space smelled strongly of damp and felt chillier than the street outside. 'Hopefully the heating controls are in the back too. The details said there's a small staff room behind the framing area with a boiler and services. Ouch!'

He stumbled and shone his torch over an empty wooden crate. 'Be careful, mate,' he warned. 'There's a lot of rubbish on the floor.'

By torchlight, they picked their way through the discarded boxes and old newspaper to the framing area which was separated from the main gallery by a low wall.

Travis shone the beam over the framing machine. That at least looked reasonably modern though covered in dust. He located the switches and the gallery was flooded with bright light.

'Ah.' Hamza exhaled.

'Kinda wished I'd left it in the dark,' Travis muttered.

The walls, long stripped of artwork, were bare and yellowing. The paint was chipped and peeling, the stone and plaster showing through in patches. The strip light trays were thick with flies.

Hamza held out his hands. 'You could say it's a blank canvas.'

'That's being generous. Damn. I hadn't seen inside until this morning. How are we going to get it into shape in six days?'

'With a lot of hard work,' Hamza murmured. When even his usual positive attitude seemed to have vanished, Travis knew things must be grim. 'I'm guessing it's not what you expected.'

'You guess right. The agent's photos showed the place when it was open. Must have been taken years ago.' He sighed. 'It's my fault. I should have asked Bree to come in and take a look at it properly. It's not her fault. She hadn't been inside for years, only peered through the window while it was still an art gallery.'

Hamza pointed to the narrow staircase in the corner. 'What's upstairs?'

'Stock room, allegedly. I was hoping to turn it into a space for running post-processing workshops for clients, though God knows what's lurking up there. I hope I haven't bitten off more than I can chew.'

Hamza grinned. 'I guess a journey of a thousand miles has to start with a first step.'

'Thanks. Very reassuring.' He heaved a sigh. 'I guess we'd better clear out the rubbish but first, I'll call in a local electrician to check the wiring. We don't want the place going up in flames. We're not going to be able to find a plasterer in time, but I'll have to fill the walls and give it a lick of paint. I think I'm going to be here late.'

'Why don't we make a list and I'll head off to the builders' merchants for some supplies?' Hamza offered.

'Good idea. There's one in Windermere. We need filler, paint, brushes, sugar soap, cleaning stuff generally. Take my pick-up and my credit card.'

'On it.'

'Hamza,' Travis said. 'Thanks. I know you said you'd come to help me but I never expected this mess. Feel free to bail out now if you need to.'

He grinned. 'You're welcome. What else would I be doing other than worrying about my love life? Anyway, we love a challenge. At least there are no poisonous snakes or deadly spiders.'

'I dunno. There's some dodgy-looking stuff in those light fittings. I . . . um . . . also think there's a dead rat by the back door.'

'None of it is as scary as dealing with relationships, though, is it?' Hamza said rather sadly. 'See ya,' he said, leaving Travis doing star jumps on the stone floor to try and warm up.

By the time Hamza returned, Travis was hot, sweaty and stripped to his T-shirt. He'd tackled the rubbish like a demon, determined to clear the lot if it killed him. He'd flung it into the trade skips behind the shop and disposed of 'Roland'. He'd established the boiler was working, kind of, and nipped out to buy a kettle and mugs from the hardware shop down the street.

The afternoon was spent cleaning down the walls and doing a bit of DIY filling, in preparation for painting them white. It was dark by four but Travis knew their work was only just starting. Hamza handed him a mug as he put down his mobile with a groan of frustration.

'Can't get an electrician for over a week. They're all busy on existing customers' jobs or booked up to help with the Christmas Fair. I did wonder . . .'

'Keep trying tomorrow,' Hamza said.

'I will. The painting's a priority now. This is going to be like one of those TV DIY challenges.'

'Without the massive team of designers and experts offering their services for free?'

'Yup. I guess it's just us.'

'Just you from tomorrow night. Don't forget I have to set off after dinner. I'm sorry I must leave you in the lurch . . .' Hamza said.

'No, you're not. It's a fantastic job that no one in their right mind would turn down. We've already got loads done,' he said, hating to have made his friend feel guilty. 'And just like the TV shows, I know we'll be ready to open on the day!'

If he didn't sleep, if he worked all the hours and if he could persuade Bree and Seb to lend a hand, Travis thought. It would be a very late night for both of them and he had to get up at the crack of dawn to attend the traders' association Christmas Fair breakfast meeting.

He was too busy to spare the time, really, but he also knew he'd be crazy to miss it. It would be a great chance to network with the other village businesses, find out how he could make the most of his launch day – if he made it – and besides, Freya was sure to be there.

Chapter Six

Travis made a beeline for Freya as she was hovering by the breakfast buffet in the community hall.

'Morning!' he chirped, an annoyingly cocky grin splashed across his face.

'Mmm.' Cough. 'M-morning,' she spluttered after hastily swallowing a piece of croissant.

He grabbed a mug of coffee from the table next to her. 'This is yours, I presume? It looks like your shade of lipstick.'

She raised her eyebrows. 'I'm amazed you noticed.'

'I'm a photographer. It's my job to notice detail.'

With a roll of her eyes, Freya sipped her Americano, though she too had noticed details . . . The untamed curls and stubble hinted that he'd just fallen out of bed.

She affected a bored tone. 'I didn't expect to see you here.'

'Sorry to disappoint you, but I got a last-minute invite because I'm launching the gallery at the Christmas Fair.' He grimaced. 'That's the plan, though judging by the state of the gallery premises, I might not be ready until Christmas. I almost didn't make it this morning. Me and Hamza were up late trying to sort the place out.'

So that accounted for the 'just rolled out of bed' look, Freya concluded. 'Are the premises that bad?' she asked, abandoning the pretence at boredom. She really was interested to know about the gallery, and it seemed a much safer topic than the colour of her lips.

'It's been empty for months and it needs a lot of work.' He sighed then said briskly, 'That's my problem. I thought it was a good idea to come along to do some networking and find out as much as I can about the fair. Actually, it was Jos Beresford who suggested I come along.'

'*Jos* invited you?' Freya slid a glance at the suited, upright blond man chatting with some of the fair organisers on the other side of the room. She'd rather hoped he might be too busy doing conveyancing and wills to bother with the breakfast meeting. With Jos and Travis together, the place was becoming rather crowded with her old flames, not, thank God, that either was fully aware of the other's connection to her.

'Kind of. He called in while Hamza and me were setting up the place yesterday. You know his office is only three doors down . . . he claimed he was there to see if I'd like to join the traders' association as a full member but I think he was just being nosy.'

'He might have been genuine. He is deputy chair,' she replied haughtily.

Travis smirked. 'Of course. Excuse me for being cynical.'

'Why change the habit of a lifetime?' she flashed back, then regretted her sharpness. 'Um – how's Squirrel Cabin? Nothing you need, is there? The owners sent us an email saying we're your emergency contact while you're staying.'

'Nothing to complain of, unless you can do something about turning the tawny owls down. They're keeping me and Hamza awake at night with their courting.'

'Want me to come up and have a word with the local wildlife?' she said sarcastically.

'Not really. I love it, actually. We had three roe deer and a red squirrel in the garden the night we moved in.'

'I wouldn't have thought they were exotic enough for you.'

'Once a photographer, always a photographer. Wildlife doesn't have to be exotic to be interesting. I'd forgotten how fascinating it can be observing the creatures on your own doorstep.' He delivered the comment with a glint in his eyes that implied he'd been observing *her* – or was she imagining it? He rubbed his hands together. 'I'll grab a coffee and one of these pastries. I'm starving.'

Freya finished the croissant while Travis devoured a cinnamon bun and a pain au chocolat in quick succession. She was in the middle of refilling her coffee mug when Brian, the head of the traders' association, called everyone to order.

An adult version of musical chairs commenced, catching both her and Travis off-guard and resulting in them squeezing onto the two end chairs in the front row.

From his seat on the dais next to Brian, Jos Beresford gave Freya a curt nod, which she returned with a brief smile – and which he duly ignored.

She sighed inwardly. She could hardly expect to be his favourite person but, after eighteen months, she might have thought he'd have thawed a little towards her and started to forgive.

The meeting started, with final instructions for the

Christmas Fair intoned at length by Brian, followed by lots of questions and some grumbling from a few of the traders.

Next to her, Travis took a quick glance at his watch.

'Pitches must all be the same size. I'll be going round with my tape measure to double check. Mrs Bickerstaff from the flower shop was very upset by an unwelcome intrusion into her area last year.'

Freya made the mistake of a side glance at Travis. He was sitting bolt upright in his chair, staring at Brian, with eyes wide in astonishment and mouth agog.

She knew that look: it heralded mischief.

'And before I forget,' Brian went on. 'Dave from the cobblers has asked me to remind you all that his back passage must be kept clear at all times. Someone saw fit to store their generator in it last year and none of us want to see a repeat of that, do we?'

Brian eyed everyone sternly. Freya sensed Travis shift in his seat and stiffen his posture, as if he was trying to suppress the urge to erupt. She didn't dare catch his eye or even glance in his direction or risk bursting into giggles. It was like being back in their biology class during the human reproduction module.

'Now, onto the subject of stall erection and dismantling . . .' Brian intoned. 'Stalls must – and I repeat *must* – be erected by Friday evening at seven p.m. and dismantled by nine a.m. sharp on Sunday morning so the roads can be reopened.'

Muffled snorts broke out across the room. On the podium, Jos was stony-faced beside Brian.

With his arms folded tightly and his thighs taut with tension, Travis was like a coiled spring. She knew he was about to explode and if he did, she didn't think she could restrain herself either.

'So, are there any questions before I close the meeting?' Brian asked with a glare at the room.

Travis raised his hand, his face composed into a picture of innocence. Freya gripped the edges of her chair, fighting down the tidal wave of mirth building in her chest.

'Thank you, Brian,' Travis said. 'I'd like to ask something, as a new business owner. What would be the consequences if my erection isn't down by the specified time?'

Jos folded his arms tighter, his firm jaw tight with disapproval.

Brian glared at Travis. 'If it isn't down by nine, lad,' he declared, 'you can expect a visit from me.'

The room erupted, and along with it, Freya. Tears streamed from her eyes and her stomach hurt.

Poor Brian looked bemused and furious, and Jos rose imperiously to his feet.

'OK. OK. That's enough! You all know what to do on Friday and personally, I want to thank Brian for his hard work in making the Christmas Fair happen. It's down to him and the committee that we have this event at all! This is a critical period for the town's traders and I hope you *all* realise that – new and old.'

He glared at Freya and Travis, just like a head teacher spotting two particularly disruptive pupils, which set Freya off again. She slapped her palm over her mouth, feeling guilty but unable to stop her giggles.

There were murmurings of assent, shouts of 'Thank you, Brian' and muted applause before the meeting broke up.

Freya sprang out of her seat and hissed in Travis's ear.

'How could you do that? I thought I might explode.'

'You *did* explode,' he said with a wicked gleam. 'I just couldn't resist. It's all so deadly serious.'

'It is serious! Oh, poor Brian. He does such a lot of work for the traders, I feel terrible.'

'I know.' Travis gave a dramatic sigh. 'But he would keep going on about back passages and erections. I couldn't help myself.'

'If you came here to make friends and influence people, you've got a funny way of doing it. You really are *very* wicked . . .' Freya said, dabbing at her damp cheeks with a tissue.

'Not as wicked as I'd like to be,' he murmured.

Before Freya had time to digest or respond to his comment, she spotted Brian making a beeline for them.

'Sorry, have to go to the ladies'. Redo my face,' she gabbled and escaped. Her mascara must be smeared all over her eyes. Bloody Travis, he'd only been back two days and they were sniggering like schoolkids, sharing in-jokes, and ganging up against the rest of the stuffy old world. She shook herself. They weren't kids now and it had been wrong to laugh at Brian. Should she apologise or would that make it worse?

She walked out of the ladies' to find Jos waiting in the foyer of the community hall.

'Freya!'

He bore down on her, glaring at her from ice-blue eyes. His 'classically handsome' (according to her mother) face wore a thunderous expression.

'You two should grow up,' he snapped. 'This isn't the back row of the classroom.'

Freya's hackles rose. 'It was a *joke*, Jos.'

'At Brian's expense.'

'Yes, well I'm sorry. It wasn't me who said it and Brian was rather asking for trouble.'

'You encouraged him.'

'Who? Travis? Or Brian?'

'Travis! Just like at school.'

She bridled. 'Now look here. Travis has only been back a few days. I haven't spoken to him for years and I am not his keeper. He can say what he likes. Half the room was in hysterics.'

Jos snorted in derision. 'The juvenile half. You didn't need to join in but I guess it's what I should have expected. You never did take anything seriously, did you?'

Freya's reply momentarily stuck in her throat. 'What's that supposed to mean?' she murmured.

'Life's a game to you, isn't it? A lark and a laugh? And now he's back, Jack the Lad, I expect you'll be thick as thieves again.'

Jos glared down at her, handsome, upright and stiff, like an angry marble sculpture come to life and brimming with reproach.

Freya drew herself up too, but she was still a foot below him. 'That's hardly fair, Jos and as you well know, my life hasn't been "a lark". As for Travis, he's nothing to do with me and even if he was, frankly it's none of your business.'

Jos's eyes blazed then he slumped. 'I apologise for the "lark" comment. It was unworthy of me but you know, Freya . . . I find it hard to stand by and see you led astray. I do still care.'

'Thanks for your concern but I'm not a Herdwick sheep. I am an independent businesswoman who was on her way back from the ladies' when you hijacked me. If you could step aside, I'd really like to go back to work.'

He nodded and Freya sallied past him, not looking back but feeling his reproachful gaze burning into her back. She didn't know where Travis had got to and she certainly wasn't going to give Jos the satisfaction of trotting after him.

After fixing her face, Freya walked out of the community centre to find Travis leaning against the wall, scrolling through his phone. She would have to be more careful in case people started seeing them 'ganging up' or God forbid, as a couple, which they very much weren't.

Travis hurried to meet her. 'Hi. I waited for you. Wanted to see if you were OK?'

'Why wouldn't I be?'

'I saw Jos haranguing you. He didn't look too friendly. I do hope it wasn't anything to do with me.'

'Actually, it had everything to do with you,' Freya said sharply.

He grimaced. 'Shit.'

'He didn't take kindly to us – you – winding up Brian.'

'I don't know how Jos could sit there and not laugh himself.'

'Probably the poker face he's developed when he's in court,' Freya said.

Travis sniffed. 'Probably due to the poker up his arse, more like.'

'He's OK,' she said, feeling sorry for Jos and determined to play devil's advocate. Jos was so obviously still hurt after they'd split up. 'He's a good guy and he can't help being so intense. Solicitors have to be serious. It goes with the job.'

'Well, he'd no business hassling you for something I did. I have apologised to Brian, by the way, and said I'd join the traders' association as I was so impressed by how well run it is.'

'You are incorrigible!'

'Hopefully,' he flung back. 'Though I agree, I don't want to be making enemies as soon as I'm back, now do I?' He became serious. 'Should I have a word with Jos? Take the blame?'

'Absolutely not,' she burst out, then lowered her voice. 'I can fight my own battles. Jos is a – well, he's not easy to handle. He'll simmer down though it's unlikely he'll ever forgive you for taking the piss out of the association.'

'Hmm. He always was an intense kind of guy. I expect he's settled down with a glamorous wife and a brood of perfect kids now.'

She ignored the ripple of unease in her stomach. 'He's not married but I've no idea about his current love life. We don't really speak unless it's to do with business.'

Travis nodded. 'Hmm. Well, I should get back to the gallery . . . Hamza will be wondering where I've got to and there's a mountain of stuff to do to get ready for the launch.'

'I need to get to work too. Mimi's holding the fort on her own.'

Yet he couldn't seem to actually leave and neither could she. For a moment, he seemed as if he was about to say more – to ask her something. He shoved his hands deep in his jeans' pockets, his signature sign of nerves.

'See you around, then?' he said gruffly.

Freya lifted her chin. 'I can hardly fail to, can I?'

He nodded and she watched him saunter off up the street, the winter sunlight shining around his tousled curls like a halo on a fallen angel.

Chapter Seven

Once out of sight of Freya, Travis trudged back to the gallery. His jaunty mood was largely an act as the scale of his task was thrown into focus again. Most of the other shops were let and looked smart and thriving, whether they were familiar fixtures or fresh enterprises.

The traditional butchers was still bustling, now cheek by jowl with a trendy cocktail bar. There was a walking boot shop that had been there since he was a boy, next to a vape shop which certainly hadn't. The contrast of old and new matched his own feelings about being back in Bannerdale: at once a part of the scenery yet also the new kid in town. He couldn't decide which role he felt least uncomfortable with.

As the sun finally rose over the fells, the place was waking up and winter sunlight bathed the snow-topped ridges and peaks to the northern side of the village. He itched to be up there, taking pictures of the sunrise turning the snow and bracken russet red – perhaps spotting a red squirrel or a roe deer. No. He didn't dare take any more photos until he had the gallery stocked for Saturday's fair.

Jokes apart, the breakfast meeting had been a sobering reminder that he was now a businessperson with responsibilities, rents and staff to pay like any other trader, including Freya herself. Perhaps that's why he'd been making light of the whole event: trying to cover his own apprehension about his new venture under a sarcastic veneer.

Wow. What was he saying? He sounded exactly like Jos Beresford who'd lived in Bannerdale, but hadn't been at their school. His parents had sent him to a private school and while Travis had played on the village football team with him, they'd never really got on.

The scene from the meeting flooded back to him: Jos looming over Freya. He'd certainly got it in for her too, for some reason. Travis had almost stepped in but then realised she didn't need a knight charging in . . . Maybe Jos fancied her. Who could blame him?

Sitting next to her had been an exquisite form of torment: pleasurable and frustrating – but mostly frustrating. He half-wished he hadn't wound Brian up but it was worth it to make Freya giggle like a teenager.

For a short while, he'd been transported back to the unalloyed silliness of youth, and thoroughly enjoyed it – but now he was weighed down by reality.

He reached the gallery, hoping Hamza had been OK without him.

The smell of fresh paint hit him as soon as he opened the door.

He'd have to hope it subsided before Saturday morning but at least the place did look fresher. It was still damp despite the heating being on and he still hadn't managed to get hold of an electrician.

'Hello! We've had a delivery while you were out,' Hamza called from the rear of the shop where the framing and printing equipment had been dusted down and checked over. Mercifully, it was working.

Hamza was busy unpacking frames from the boxes, which now covered much of the floor. Some contained mounts and frames that he'd brought in, while others were ready printed pictures that he'd had to outsource because he hadn't had time to get his own printer up and running. They needed stock and lots of it ready for the opening.

He experienced a mild ripple of panic. They opened in a few days' time and the shelves and walls were currently empty.

'How was the meeting?'

Travis thought back to Freya, rocking with mirth beside him and then hinting she'd rather avoid his presence completely. 'As you'd expect,' he said, 'dull as dishwater.'

'Really?' Hamza raised an eyebrow.

'Yeah.' Travis sighed, 'It also reminded me of why I left Bannerdale in the first place. Small town pettiness – but also comfortingly trivial. If you know what I mean.'

'I think I do . . .' Hamza said, though the puzzled frown said otherwise.

Travis wasn't going to mention Freya and was relieved when a man in a hi-vis jacket poked his head round the door. 'Hi, mate. Got your sign here.'

Travis thanked the driver and manhandled the large plastic-wrapped package through the door.

The sign was bigger than he'd expected so he and Hamza laid it on the floor and cut the tape open, unwrapping the bubble wrap and uncovering the lettering.

Peak Perspectives.
Gallery and photography tours
by Travis Marshall FRPS

'Wow . . .' Hamza let out a breath.

Travis couldn't speak as he rose from his knees to stand beside his friend. Normally he wasn't the slightest bit impressed by qualifications and 'guff' but he had to swallow a lump in his throat.

This was real and writ large in front of his eyes: he had his own business, his own premises – and his name on the front of it.

That FRPS – Fellow of the Royal Photographic Society – had been very hard won. They didn't hand out the Distinction lightly and it had required the submission of a portfolio of his very best work. He'd acquired the fellowship for his landscape work, but he could have submitted a natural history portfolio too.

He could only have dreamed of it when he was a boy first picking up a second-hand camera on an online auction site. His heart swelled with pride and emotion. He'd come a long, long way.

'Penny for them?' Hamza stood at his shoulder.

'I was just thinking . . .' Travis felt embarrassed about voicing his feelings. 'This. I'm probably being stupid but it feels . . . surreal. Not something, someone like me could have ever achieved . . . *should* have achieved.'

Hamza patted his back. 'It's real, buddy. Celebrate it. Believe in it. You should be proud.' With a broad smile, he swept his arm around the room. 'Now all we need to do is actually put some of your work on the walls otherwise no one will be able to buy it!'

'True,' Travis said. 'Shall we get the sign up first to show we mean business?'

'I'll bring the stepladder and tool kit from the back. Then we need to get cracking, it's going to be a very long day – make that days.'

Mid-afternoon, Bree came by with Travis's nephew, Dylan, who'd started at the village nursery school the previous September, and his niece, Rosie, in a buggy. Another bonus of being back in Bannerdale was that he got to spend time with his family. Bree was also going to work at the gallery on Saturdays and one day a week while Travis led photography tours. Her husband would be looking after the kids.

Bree held onto Dylan tightly and didn't venture beyond the rear staff area at Travis's warning.

'Much as I'd love to let you inside, there's so much glass and stuff round, it's not safe,' he said, taking Dylan's hand so Bree could peer into the main gallery. Rosie was safely strapped in her buggy and more interested in her toy giraffe.

She wrinkled her nose in dismay. 'It does look a bit of a tip.'

He wasn't the least bit offended by his sister's plain speaking; he was used to her by now and very grateful for all she'd done for him and Seb. 'Thanks, hopefully it'll look a lot different by Saturday. Are you sure it won't be too much?' he said, spotting her eyes widen at the mess in the gallery.

Bree shook her head. 'No. I'll be climbing the walls with these two all day every day and having a job will make me feel a bit more like a proper adult again. The money will be nice too.'

'Sorry I can't pay you more.'

'So am I.' She laughed. 'It's OK, you're already paying me more than I'd get in any other retail job and the hours suit me.' A mischievous smile crept onto her face. 'Anything to keep you here for a while. Besides you look as if you could do with the help!'

'Ha ha. Thanks Bree.'

'You're welcome,' she said then squealed as Dylan broke free of Travis and darted forward, shouting 'Camerrarrrras!'

'Come here!' Bree shouted.

Fortunately, Hamza scooped him up and returned him to his mother.

'He's a budding photographer,' Hamza said with a wry smile.

Bree squeaked in horror. 'He can see Travis's stuff on that table. He's been watching some kids' programme about wildlife filming.'

'Good to start young,' Hamza said.

Travis crouched down to Dylan's level. 'If you want to take some pictures, buddy, I'll show you very soon but maybe with a camera you can actually hold.'

'Thank you, Unca Tardis.'

Travis burst out laughing at the mangling of his name.

'He doesn't know what a Tardis is,' Bree said. 'Come on, trouble.'

Dylan allowed his mother to take his hand and she kept hold of it while expertly manoeuvring the buggy towards the shop door with one hand. Travis opened it wide and helped her down the low step. 'See you on Saturday. Dylan's looking forward to seeing the lights being switched on.'

'And Santa!' he cried. 'In his boat.'

'Santa. Of course. He's arriving on one of the steamers at

the boat pier,' she explained to a baffled Hamza. 'Then he gets a lift to the village in an open-top car.'

She smiled at Dylan before fixing Travis with the kind of glare reserved for when he'd been in trouble at school – again. 'I'll be here at eight-thirty on Saturday so you'd better get your act together by then. You might be the big hotshot photographer but you do need something to sell.'

'I'll make sure he does,' Hamza said, going back inside the shop.

Travis saw her off at the door. 'I got your message about looking in on Seb,' he said. 'I see what you mean.'

'Thanks.' She sighed. 'I wanted to talk to you about him but not in front of your friend. I told you Seb needs some support.'

'I'm going to take him to the pub, see if I can spark his interest in playing again. Do you know why he stopped?'

'No, but he's gone downhill since he did. Thanks for helping.'

'I'll do my best.'

Travis locked the door behind her and went into the back to put the camera away in its case.

'Bree's kids are cute,' Hamza said, piling up frames and mounts.

'True. They're also a handful.'

'She seems to cope.'

'She runs a tight ship. Her husband's a decent bloke and she deserves one after our upbringing. It's good to see the two of them happy.'

Hamza paused. 'You ever think of having kids?'

Travis held his camera. 'No . . . maybe once but now. I'm thirty-two. I'm single. I've seen what can go wrong.'

'I think it's a bit too soon to make that decision, mate,' Hamza said.

'Maybe . . . How about you?' Travis asked.

'Yeah, I'd like some. My folks would like me to have some.'

'With Caz?'

Hamza shrugged. 'That's just it. I don't know and I'm not sure she does. We had words while you were out at the meeting. You know that mock wedding you had to take part in? It chimed with me when you said it was all set up to fulfil the adults' fantasies. I get that. That's how I feel: that a wedding . . . might all be a huge theatrical event, all a performance for our families.'

'Hmm.' Travis laid down the camera and folded his arms. 'You need to have a serious talk. I mean it. You probably shouldn't even be here. You should be with Caz, deciding what you two really want.'

Hamza sighed. 'Maybe. Maybe I thought that working round the clock to renovate this place would be easier.' He smiled wryly. 'And I'm off to Scotland tomorrow morning so I can't see her until Christmas.'

Travis shook his head. 'I can't solve that for you, buddy. Look, if you want to take a break and have a proper chat, we can do. Or if you need to call her back, I'll give you some privacy.'

'Nah. I appreciate the offer but can we just work?' Hamza grinned and swept a hand around the shop, taking in the chaos. 'We sure need to. For now, I just wanna hide away and get some space.'

'OK.'

Travis had felt exactly the same after he'd split up with

Freya, except he'd been a teenager and his escape had been to run away to the city and throw every ounce of energy into honing his photography skills.

He should thank Freya for that. Once he knew there was nothing to keep him in Bannerdale, he'd single-mindedly pursued his dream. If they'd stayed together, married, he wasn't sure he'd ever have had the life he did now.

He'd worked part-time in a camera shop to help fund his studies and spent every spare hour in the outdoors with the uni photography club. It was hard to get a foot in the door and he'd had to carry on working for the camera shop, and take on any assignment going to supplement his income. He'd lost count of the number of engaged couples and pets he'd photographed, and the mind-numbing PR jobs he'd done for the local council and businesses.

Eventually, though, his wildlife and landscape shots had begun to gain him respect and a following. He'd built up his contacts and had started taking his own clients out on tours.

The breakthrough had really come when he'd won a prestigious prize for young photographers, which had attracted the attention of the media, leading to commissions – and to a growing list of customers for his tours.

It had meant spending most of his time travelling, either around the UK or abroad, and he hardly saw his studio flat in London. He'd rarely been able to get home to Bannerdale to visit his family and he'd hardly seen his father above a couple of times since he'd left school.

His lifestyle had never been conducive to relationships and the ones he'd had had been flings. His whole life had been consumed by his job – and Freya had most definitely been better off without him.

He shook himself. Now was not the time to dwell on the past.

He had his own gallery, and even if it needed a ton of work, it was finally coming together.

If he could fix the damp problem, make the place safe and get something on the walls to sell, he might even make it for the opening on Saturday morning.

Chapter Eight

Roxanne was lurking at the side of the church, having a cheeky vape when Freya arrived for the wedding rehearsal.

Bannerdale church was illuminated for the Christmas season, and lights glowed behind the stained-glass windows. Signs were hung on the fence inviting people to the various services to be held over the festive period. It was warm and welcoming, and felt a complete contrast to the day she'd run away from the altar all those years ago.

'Psst!' Roxanne beckoned her from a cloud of vapour. 'Don't tell anyone. Ravi thinks I've given up completely.'

'Your secret's safe with me.'

'We'll have to go inside shortly but I said I needed some air. Ravi's probably guessed what I'm up to.' She dropped the vape inside her handbag. 'I also wanted to talk to you before we go inside. Is this the first time since . . . you know . . .'

'No. I've been back for carol services and Mimi's kids' christenings. Haven't been for a wedding yet. You know we never got as far as the rehearsal with Jos . . .' She smiled wryly. 'That's one thing to be grateful for, I suppose.'

'I do know it was a big ask, and as for the first time,' Roxanne grinned, 'I will always *always* be sorry for sticking my tongue out at you at that ridiculous mock wedding. I'm sure it didn't help. You looked terrified.'

Freya laughed and felt her tense body relaxing. 'I've forgiven you and you pulling a face wasn't the problem. It was the pressure, the expectation.'

'All those people in the church waiting. Even I was freaked out by that. My mum and dad had been going on and on about it for weeks, they'd flown my granny and grandad over from St Lucia to see me, you know!'

'I never knew that!'

'Well, it was a good excuse to get them over but I was worried I might make a fool of myself. Granny asked why I wasn't the bride . . .'

Freya squeaked in horror. 'I'd no idea. I wish you had been. You might have stuck it out, not bolted and made yourself the laughing stock.'

'It must have been horrible for you.'

'Everyone was relying on me, my mum, the teachers, all the kids but it wasn't only that. It was Dad . . .'

'Your dad?' Roxanne frowned.

'Mum kept going on about how proud he'd have been and that he'd be looking down on me. I don't believe that now, of course, but back then, the idea creeped me out.' She tried to laugh at herself. 'That sounds ridiculous now.'

Roxanne's face crumpled into sympathy. 'Oh hun, I'm so sorry. Even though you can't remember him, having him snatched away when you were tiny must have had some effect. I bet that stupid bloody wedding triggered you in some way. It could still be affecting you now.'

Freya decided to laugh off the comment with a shrug. 'Possibly. Who knows and who'd ever have thought we'd turn out to be best friends after how we were at primary school?'

'Life has a way of throwing curve balls at you, that's for sure, but meeting you is a good one. I'm so glad Mum and Dad let me go to the village schools. I'd have hated going to one miles away in a posh uniform or even worse, a boarding school!'

Freya was pleased too. Roxanne's parents had made a fortune with a party supplies website before moving to a big house on the edge of Bannerdale when Roxanne was a baby, but they still sent her to the local primary and high schools. They'd eventually become good mates after playing on the school netball team together.

'We might never have been friends if they had sent you away.' Freya linked her arm through Roxanne's. 'Come on, everyone's waiting for us. They might think we've bunked off and gone to Raffaello's early.'

'Don't give me ideas. This "wedding rehearsal dinner" thing is all a bit too American for me, but it was Ravi's mum's idea and they've travelled quite a way so the least we can do is feed them.'

They went into the church, where Ravi and both sets of parents were already chatting to the vicar. The best man, an Italian-born colleague of Ravi's, was on duty at the hospital where they both worked so they'd have to manage without him.

Perennially cheerful, the vicar led them through the 'processional order', making sure everyone knew where to stand and when to sit down – and who to exit the church with. Roxanne's cousin was doing a reading but she worked for the local radio and was on air and didn't need to practise anyway. The whole thing was over in half an hour, and they exited the church into the chilly evening.

Roxanne and the two families drove off to the restaurant but Freya had walked from the office and after a brief chat with the vicar about the forthcoming carol concert, she set off on foot. It was raining heavily so she put up her umbrella and started off down the path but stopped.

Under the lych gate, she glimpsed Seb Marshall engaged in a heated conversation with a man in a full-length hooded coat, the kind that wild swimmers wore but had become fashionable as outdoor wear. Raised voices reached her but the drumming of rain on her brolly meant she couldn't hear what was being said.

Seb had been several years below them at school. She remembered him as a talented musician but cheeky and gobby towards the older pupils – and some of the teachers. Nowadays, he worked at the mini-market though he used to do a few gigs in the local area too.

When she popped in for last-minute groceries and sandwiches, he was always polite enough to her but she wasn't sure he had any idea that she'd been engaged to Travis. She didn't know what Travis had told the rest of the family about him proposing – and her breaking it off – if anything. His older sister, Bree, still lived nearby and had a couple of young children. Freya knew her to nod to but that was about it.

A shout reached her. She wanted to be on her way to the rehearsal dinner but the pair were blocking the lych gate. Freya hung back, reluctant to get too close but also unwilling to leave Seb with this man who was pointing his finger at him.

With a shout of anger, the hooded guy stormed off, leaving Seb alone. He seemed paralysed and briefly rubbed his hand over his eyes, as if wiping away tears.

Freya hurried down the path to join him under the gateway. 'Seb? Are you OK?'

He whipped round, face twisted in rage. He also looked terribly young and when he realised who she was, his anger softened to sullenness.

'Me? Yeah, I'm absolutely fine and dandy.'

'Are you sure?' she asked gently.

'Why wouldn't I be?' he snapped.

'I don't know. I saw you with that guy and he seemed to be hassling you.'

'Hassling me?' Seb scoffed. 'Thanks for your concern, but I can handle him.'

'OK. OK.' Still unconvinced, Freya noticed Seb's soaking work uniform.

He exhaled and managed a very brief smile. 'Look, thanks for asking about me but I'm fine. See ya.'

With shoulders hunched, he trudged up the street towards the centre of the village. Freya walked briskly towards the restaurant, feeling that Travis's concerns about his brother were probably justified. Should she mention what she'd seen, though? It would only worry Travis more and cause more trouble between the brothers – and what business was it of hers?

She was still mulling it over when she walked into Raffaello's where the fizz and banter were already flowing between the two wedding clans.

Chapter Nine

'Mr Marshall! Are you in there? It's the police.'

Travis knew he was in the middle of a nightmare but he couldn't do a damn thing about it. The silence suffocated him and the darkness was syrupy thick. He felt he could almost reach out and touch it, if only his arms would work. He was paralysed and yet he had a desperate urge to move, to escape because someone was hammering on the door of his room, trying to get inside to get him.

'Hamza!'

His shout penetrated the darkness and he opened his eyes to more darkness – this time, real, not nightmarish oblivion. He also realised that he was alone. Hamza wouldn't answer because his friend had left after dinner the previous evening, driving off into the night, still asking if Travis would be OK and beating himself up about having to leave for the assignment.

So who the hell was that hammering on the door of the cabin?

'Travis Marshall! Are you in there? It's the police!'

Shivering in his boxers, still dazed with sleep, Travis

swin hod on the light and went to the door. His night vision was now non-existent and when he peered through the glass, he was barely able to make out the figure under the porch.

As his eyes adjusted, he realised that his nightmare was real in one sense: there was an officer in uniform outside. His stomach lurched. His first thought was it was something to do with his father . . . something terrible – but why would the cops track him down, not Bree or their mother?

He unlocked the door on a blast of freezing air, dreading what was to come.

'Travis?'

Rain dripped off the officer's hat, and he was blinking through round spectacles, but he also looked familiar.

'Kelvin?' Travis murmured.

'Yes, it's me. Didn't think you'd recognise me.' The officer grinned.

'I'd never forget you,' Travis said, recalling a geeky lad who was obsessed with fantasy novels and had been secretary of the camera club – the only school group that Travis had ever taken the slightest interest in.

'You've done well for yourself. Always knew you would. Shedloads of talent; your pictures were always miles better than anyone else's.'

This was all very flattering but Travis was more astonished that Kelvin seemed to have forgotten why he'd banged on the cabin door and dragged him out of bed. 'Thanks – erm, can I ask what you want?'

Kelvin's smile evaporated. 'Oh, yes, sorry. I was a bit star struck there. Very unprofessional. I'm afraid there's been a bit of an accident . . .'

'A *bit* of an accident?' Travis's heart rate soared again.

'Nothing *too* serious. It's your brother, Seb. He was knocked off his bike.'

'Seb? Jesus!' Travis's hand flew to his mouth.

'Don't worry! He's OK. He's bruised and twisted his ankle . . . A few cuts and grazes too. He was shaken up but he says he's feeling OK now.' Kelvin flashed him another reassuring grin, but Travis was more alarmed than ever.

'Why the hell was he on his bike in the middle of the night?'

Kelvin frowned. 'It's not the middle of the night. It's half-past seven now.' He held up his watch as if Travis was stupid. 'The accident happened around five o'clock when Seb was on his way to the early shift at the mini-market.'

'Oh God . . . yes. I understand now. But he hasn't called me . . .'

'He tried but there was no answer and he didn't want to worry your sister. I was the one called to the scene and as I know him, I said I'd come round and tell you.'

Travis swore. 'Sorry. Arghh. I forgot to charge my phone last night. So you're *sure* he's going to be OK?'

'Fortunately, it wasn't as bad as it looked initially. He was lying on the pavement and there was a lot of blood but don't worry!' Kelvin added hastily, probably seeing Travis's face blanch. 'The cuts are superficial and he's going to be fine. He's messaged me from the urgent care in Kendal half an hour ago. I think they'll let him come home later. He – er – says he needs a lift.'

Travis rolled his eyes in his head, feeling marginally relieved. 'A lift? Yeah, that sounds like Seb. Thanks for coming over. I appreciate it.'

'You're welcome. He's a good lad, Seb, if he can stay out of any more trouble.'

'He will,' Travis said. 'I'd better get dressed and head over to the hospital. Thanks again, Kelvin.'

Travis plugged in his phone and it started beeping with messages from Seb. He'd gone back to the gallery to do some more work after Hamza had left, fallen into bed about one a.m. and forgotten to charge his mobile.

He sent a quick reply to say he was on his way, before dragging on some clothes and driving off through the grey dawn. It was a painfully slow journey, the rush-hour traffic travelling like snails in the slush and his wipers making little impact on the thick sleet. Most of the hotels had Christmas lights up but Travis had never felt less festive.

His relief that Seb was OK-ish was tempered by the contemplation of what might have happened. What's more, Kelvin's appearance at the door had brought back bitter memories of another raw December morning that haunted him to this day.

It had been years ago, when he was in the sixth form and hadn't yet plucked up the courage to ask Freya out – the morning that school was breaking up for the holidays. Except it hadn't been Christmas for his family.

The police had chosen that morning to raid the house, searching for his dad.

His mum had been on a night shift, cleaning at a local hotel, and Bree had already moved in with Gav, which left only Travis in the house with Seb. He'd never forget the confusion, the fear, the chaos: his father, protesting, swearing his innocence, cursing the police officers, as he was led away in handcuffs . . . Seb hiding behind Travis's back . . .

85

Travis soothing him and saying 'It's all right. It'll be OK . . .'

His father shouting: 'You bastards! Breaking in here while my kids were asleep!'

A female officer – barely older than him – had walked back up the path and asked: 'Do you need someone to come and look after you? I don't think we should leave a bunch of kids alone.'

'I'm not a bloody kid. I'm eighteen!' Travis had lied, terrified that he and Seb might be taken into care. 'And anyway, Mum'll be back any minute.'

'If you're sure.'

'I'm sure,' he'd snarled, shaking but acting the big man. 'You've done enough damage. You've taken my dad, now get out of our house.'

She'd been trying to do the right thing but Travis had been too traumatised, too angry and way too young for nuance. His aggression had been born of bravado but he was also angry when he looked around and saw the mess: smashed crockery, a broken chair, chaos, as his father had fought off the officers and failed. His father's fault – and the cops' for terrifying the household, coming in heavy when they must have known the young family would be in their beds.

He'd hated them in that moment, even though he knew they were doing their jobs – but did they have to do it so aggressively? They'd gone, and Travis had spent the next half an hour calming Seb down and watching a twelve-year-old boy sob openly.

Their mother had come back to find Seb munching toast while Travis gave him some coins so he could get chips for lunch. She'd ranted and raved and stormed off to the police station, leaving the boys to go to school.

By then word had got round that their father had been taken away. Fingers pointed, sniggers followed him and the drama of the morning had become exaggerated to several vans of armed officers turning up, to helicopters and dogs searching for their father.

The last day of school: the only two kids who didn't want to finish early for the holidays, who didn't want to go home for Christmas. Some fecking Christmas . . .

'Thank God for that!' Travis shouted, finally turning into the hospital car park.

His phone had been beeping with texts – presumably from Seb – on the way to the hospital but it was only when he arrived at the hospital that he could reply again. A short time later, he found the emergency care department.

Seb was sitting outside in the waiting area, flicking through his phone.

'Bloody hell, how did this happen?' he said. His brother glanced up at him, though he was barely recognisable as the cheeky, good-looking lad Travis loved and despaired of. He had some spectacular bruises, a puffy eye and steri-strips across a badly grazed cheek. 'You look like you did fifteen rounds with Tyson Fury.'

'Driver clipped the bike and I wobbled and came off in the ice. I slid along the path and grazed my face and arms . . . but that's not the worst of it. You should see my bum.'

Travis grimaced. 'No thanks. You said nothing's broken?'

'Luckily not. I lost some skin off my arse and legs. They did a scan on my head but my brain's OK.'

'Was there a brain to find?' Travis said, perching on a nearby chair.

'Ha ha. You are so funny.' Seb laughed sarcastically then winced.

Despite the jokes, Travis could tell his brother had been unnerved and in truth, he was pretty shaken himself. It could have been so much worse.

'Have you told Bree yet?'

He scoffed. 'God, no. She doesn't know. The driver dialled 999. Kelvin turned up at the same time as the ambulance and said he'd let you know as soon as he could. He's OK for a cop.'

'Yeah . . . I had a hell of a shock when he banged on my door before dawn.'

'I bet. It's happened before though . . .' Seb said, referring to their father. 'Can you imagine if he'd gone round to Bree's with the kids in bed? We know how that feels.'

'Yes. Probably best you called me. Are you allowed to go home?'

'I think so. I'll check with the nurses. I know one of them.' He let out a low whistle. 'She comes into the shop sometimes. Always makes my day. Trouble is she was the one who cleared the grit out of my cuts and she's now seen more of me than I have. Not sure I can look her in the eye the next time she wants a loaf and a bottle of milk.'

'Oh, I'm sure you'll manage somehow,' Travis said. 'Let's find out if you're free to leave and I'll take you home.'

An hour later, Seb was limping out to the car with Travis supporting him. Travis shivered and not because of the chilly morning air. He was horrified at the thought of his kid brother lying in the road, injured – and hardly dared dwell on the possibility of losing him.

After helping Seb up the stairs to the flat, he made mugs of tea and toast.

'Thanks. I'm bloody starving.'

'You're welcome.' Travis watched him devour four rounds and polished off a couple himself. It had been one hell of a morning and he still had to go into the gallery and start work. 'I think we do need to tell Bree,' he ventured.

'No! She'll go mad.'

'Why?' Travis was puzzled at the panic in Seb's voice, while also thinking that his sister had been there for Travis.

'Because I don't want you making a fuss about me – or her. She'll probably go mad and think I was pissed. The pair of you have got to stop nannying me. I don't need it and I definitely don't want it.'

'Tough. She's going to think you've been in a bar brawl when she sees the state of you and as for "nannying you", I promised Bree I'd help.'

'I knew it! That's why you came back, isn't it?' He groaned in despair then winced. 'Ow.'

'Well, I should have been there for you.'

'Bro, you haven't "been there" for me since school and I've survived. Why would I drag you back here to Bannerdale now?'

The statement stung like iodine in a cut – because it was so true. 'OK,' he said, deflated. 'She's worried about you.'

Seb snorted. 'You mean she's worried I'll turn into Dad?'

'No. I . . . and there's no reason why you should. Or any of us should.'

'Really? There was a time Bree thought *you* would.'

'What?' Travis exclaimed.

'After you took off to Manchester to be a big shot. She

89

didn't think you'd make it. Neither did Mum. They thought you'd just bugger around. I believed in you though,' Seb said. 'I was young and naïve I suppose – but I was also right.'

Travis was floored by Seb's brutal honesty. 'Bree's never said anything like that to me. She always encouraged me.'

'Lucky you. She's always having a go at me.' He adopted a wheedling high-pitched tone. '"Oh, be careful who you trust, Seb, I don't like some of those guys you hang around with. Are you drinking too much? Don't lose that steady job, you won't get another one, you don't want to end up like Dad."'

Some of it did sound so uncannily like their sister that Travis *almost* wanted to laugh, but he wasn't in the mood to be amused. 'You don't have to end up like Dad. He made his own choices. Being a useless father and a criminal isn't genetic.'

Seb snorted. 'You said it. Can you hammer it home with Bree too?'

'She cares about you. You can't deny we've not had the best start. It's harder for people like us – it's tough without someone looking out for you.'

'Then why did you leave? You didn't stay to look out for me when you could see a better life in the big wide world?'

It was another statement that went straight to the target and stuck like a barb. 'That's true. I *did* leave – but you could do the same.'

Seb sniffed. 'How?'

'Pick up your guitar. Get better. Fail. Keep going. Hold down a job while you get some gigs again. Look for a path that makes you smile not despair. Give it your best shot.'

Travis could picture his sister throwing up her hands in horror at the suggestion. He was supposed to be watching over his brother, not encouraging him to leave and go into a precarious trade where temptation – in the form of drink, drugs and hangers-on – would be all around. However, he also knew the danger of feeling you only had a lifetime of grind and barely getting by ahead of you.

Seb listened intently and Travis thought he was finally getting through.

'Wow,' he said when Travis stopped speaking. 'Bro? Will you do something for me?'

'If I can . . .'

'Stop sounding like you swallowed a self-help manual. I prefer you screaming down my ear than turning into a self-important prick. Now, if you really want to look after your poor invalid brother, you can make me another mug of tea.'

That cut the conversation dead. Travis knew there was little more he could do – for now. He could only hope some of his words had got through and he liked to practise what he preached. He hadn't given up trying to pursue his own dream – he certainly wasn't going to give up on Seb.

Chapter Ten

'And you're sure you'll be OK without me? I'll be back just after New Year! I've left you a couple of small presents but I wanted to bring you something really nice back from my travels.'

'Mum, you don't have to worry,' Freya said as her mother caught her in a final *final* hug on the doorstep of her house. She'd spent the previous evening helping her mum pack, a challenge considering the amount of 'resort wear' that Sandra had accumulated. Freya had put on her a brave face but her mum had several times if she'd be OK.

'Sandra!' Neil called from the garden gate. 'The taxi's waiting. The driver can't hang around any longer or we'll miss our flight. You know what the traffic is like on the M6!'

'All right. I'm coming!' Sandra rolled her eyes good-humouredly at Freya and lowered her voice. 'We've got loads of time. Neil ordered the taxi far too early.'

'More time to relax before your flight to Miami,' Freya said. 'And I'll be absolutely *fine*.'

'Great. And thanks for taking in all the parcels for me. See you when I get back, darling. Oh, and help yourself to anything you like the look of in the wardrobes. It's so lucky we're the same size, and I'll never have a chance to wear it all! I think those leather trousers would look fab on you!'

'Thanks, Mum . . .' Freya said, not sure the mustard-yellow trousers would go down well while greeting disgruntled guests at the office. Even so, she was pretty pleased with the slip nighty she'd snaffled from her mum's stash.

With a last air kiss, her mother finally hurried towards the taxi, her new travel handbag lopped over her shoulder. With its numerous organiser pockets, matching documents clutch and reusable PVC sachet for liquids, no savvy traveller should venture forth without it. Freya smiled; she knew the spiel off by heart, having filmed her mum demonstrating it in a video that had attracted many thousand views and hundreds of comments.

Neil opened the door for her, and a hand waved out of the window. 'Byeeeee . . .'

The taxi drove off and the cul-de-sac was quiet again.

After popping back inside for her own bags, Freya locked her mother's door and set off through the grey dawn to work.

'OK. I'll see what I can do, Mrs Kingsley-Wolfe. I'm so sorry you haven't found the mattress to your liking but as you're leaving tomorrow, it's too late to rectify the situation. I'll certainly give your feed—'

Freya winced as the irate guest cut her off mid-phrase.

'As I was about to *say*,' she said, jumping on a nanosecond's pause in the tirade. 'I'll certainly pass on your feedback to the owners, but there are two other double bedrooms in the property. Were none of those suitable?'

Just in time, she held the phone away from her ear to avoid a perforated eardrum. On the other side of the office, Mimi winced at Mrs K-W's shrill outrage. Every word was clearly audible even without the speaker on.

Freya gripped the phone and kept her tone as neutral as she could. 'It's unfortunate that you didn't like the décor in the other rooms, but at this stage of your holiday and in view of the alternative sleeping options, I'm afraid we can't really ask the property owner to refund the rental back. Or any part of it.'

Freya braced herself as the phone vibrated with fury. Listening in on the whole exchange, Mimi mouthed a swear word. Eventually there was a brief silence, presumably as Mrs K-W paused to draw in oxygen before she passed out.

'If you want to take it further, Mrs Kingsley-Wolfe, that's your prerogative. However I'd rather you didn't use that kind of language to me or my staff. Now, if there's nothing further you wish to draw to our attention, I think it's time we ended this discussion.'

Having no intention of allowing Mrs K-W to make further comment, Freya put the phone down and let out a small scream.

Mimi came over to her desk. 'Deep breaths,' she said. 'Though Mrs K-W and her husband would drive a saint to murder. I think it's time we started fighting back.'

'Agreed!' Freya said, feeling a little bruised by the encounter, even though she was used to difficult conversations. 'She's tried to get her money back on three separate properties over the past year and a half – and that's just the ones we look after. I think it's time we flagged her up to the booking agents and owners and slapped a ban on her renting any more holiday homes. She and her husband are scammers.'

'They are – and it says a lot that they've never actually tried to sue. I'll put the kettle on. Take a break. You need it.'

Mimi wasn't wrong. It had been a long day checking that festive hampers would be delivered to all of the properties they looked after, on the correct changeover days before the Christmas holidays. Owners relied on Cottage Angels to make sure guests were kept happy – and rebooking their properties.

However, it was relentless work and would only grow more demanding as the cottages started to fill up for the festive season – which nowadays had become earlier as people booked pre-Christmas breaks, lured by the snow and events like the Christmas Fair.

She'd also been on emergency call three evenings running, each of which had resulted in callouts to a heating system that had failed, a sweet elderly couple who couldn't turn off the smoke alarm and a man complaining that he couldn't get Babe Station X on his telly. She'd arranged a hearing engineer, reset the alarm and explained – by phone in case he got the wrong idea – to the man that not every channel he was used to at home was available in a remote Lakeland village.

Luckily, Mimi was on duty that evening and Freya was planning on going home and curling up with a Christmas novel by her favourite author, hopefully banishing Travis from her brain. Unfortunately, that thought brought him right back to the forefront of her mind.

She wondered how he'd be spending the evening – with Hamza probably, in the pub or cosied up by the log burner with a takeout, endlessly obsessing over photos.

She must have had her eyes closed because Mimi's voice startled her. 'It's past five, I'll lock up. You go home and relax.'

'I plan on doing just that,' Freya said

She switched off her computer and was putting her laptop away in its bag when Mimi's mobile rang.

Freya tried not to listen in but the topic of the call was obvious – as was the disappointment in her colleague's voice and face.

'No. Argh. I'd have loved to. Oh, I'm so sorry but I'm on call tonight.'

There was more conversation before she ended the call with 'Give my love to Robbie. Tell him I'm sorry and wish him all the luck in the world. I'll watch the video. You too.'

Mimi switched off her phone and Freya was horrified to see tears glistening in her eyes.

'Is everything OK?' Freya asked. 'Is it the kids?'

'Nothing bad,' Mimi said, pasting on a smile. 'Good, in fact. That was Cal,' she explained referring to her husband. 'It's Robbie's Christmas play tonight – they're *doing The Snowman* and he was meant to be just a woodland creature but the boy playing the lead role has broken his wrist and Robbie's the understudy.'

'Wow. So he's playing . . .'

'The Boy yes. He's worked so hard on learning the part but never thought he'd get the chance. He'll be so excited and nervous. Cal phoned to see if I can go but it's fine. I've said I can't do it. I can't risk the phone going off in the middle and dashing off. Well, I suppose I could . . . but I'd be on edge all night and we have seats in the front row – I don't want to rush out in the middle and Robbie seeing me leaving. It might put him off.'

'You won't have to rush off anywhere,' Freya declared. 'Because I'll take the emergency cover. You can't miss this.'

96

'You've done it three nights in a row!'

'And? It won't kill me. Nothing might go wrong – but if you're on call and at the play, it most certainly will because that's sod's law. I didn't have any plans, anyway.'

Mimi threw her arms around Freya. 'You are the best partner. I'll make it up to you, I promise.'

'You already have, covering for me while I have the day off for Roxanne's wedding. You just have a fantastic time and take lots of photos for me. I'll lock up.'

'OK, I'll go straight to the school from here. Thank you so much. I owe you!'

'Off you go.'

After gathering her bags, Mimi flew out of the office, phone clamped to her ear as she gave the good news to her husband.

Freya lingered, half wondering whether to stay in the office and do some admin. They were on duty twenty-four-seven technically but most people seemed to call by ten p.m. if they could. Only in the direst emergencies – fire or flood or burglary – had she ever been hauled out of bed.

One thing was for sure. She now couldn't go home and relax with a glass of wine.

She hung around an hour longer, half-heartedly tackling some paperwork before her rumbling stomach nudged her into locking up. She would call for a takeaway from the village to have at home. She deserved a treat . . . She felt guilty. She mustn't put on any weight before Roxanne's wedding or she wouldn't fit into that slinky bridesmaid's dress. She'd walk to the office the rest of the week to work it off.

Although it was raining, she left her car at the office car park and walked the short distance to the Thai takeaway. Its lights glowed invitingly – but so did the windows of the gallery however, which were blazing with light even though it was seven p.m.

The bright new sign made her smile. Peak Perspectives. Nice name.

Peak Perspectives.
Gallery and photography tours
by Travis Marshall FRPS

As she read the words, an unexpected lump of emotion formed in her throat. It felt very much like pride, which surprised and startled her.

The smart and professional sign, however, didn't match the scene through the window. There was what could only be described as chaos inside, with boxes, frames and canvases seeming to fill the small space.

She peered through the window just in time to see Travis hurl a cardboard box across the room as if he was trying to kill it.

Chapter Eleven

Not wanting to be caught spying on him, she hung back a little as he marched over to pick up the box which had knocked a picture off the wall. She heard a shout but couldn't make out the words but guessed they were curses.

He swung around suddenly and the next thing she knew he was at the door, unlocking it. It was too late to run away now.

'Good evening,' she said cheerfully. 'Are you having fun?'

'No,' he snapped. 'As you can probably tell!' He let out a groan. 'Sorry, but I've had a bit of a mare over the past couple of days. Um. Do you want to come in? It's pouring down.'

She was about to make her excuses when she saw the desperation in his eyes. He clearly needed someone to vent to and she didn't have the heart to walk away.

'I could sure do with a break,' he added. 'And you're getting wet.'

'OK.' She stepped inside, gingerly to avoid breaking anything lying on the floor. The smell of fresh paint hit her and an underlying smell of damp. The strip light was flickering.

She took off the hood of her waterproof, hoping she wasn't dripping on anything important. 'You've been busy,' she said.

'You're telling me. You should have seen the place when we first opened the door. We spent the first day and a half filling walls and painting.'

'It looks fresh and bright now,' she said, determined to focus on the positives while wondering how he would be ready for Saturday morning. 'But I'm guessing you're having a few issues?'

'Just a bit. I need someone to check the electrics before we open but all the sparkies are too busy to do a little job for a newcomer – which I can hardly blame them for. The place smells and I need to get some stock on the walls.'

She sniffed. 'The paint whiff will go when you can get some air flowing through.'

He wrinkled his nose. 'The damp won't. I've got a couple of buckets in the loo at the back. I think we have a leak.'

'Hmm. It's a problem with these old stone and slate buildings. It should improve but it might be caused by a leaky gutter. Have you thought about calling a roofer in and hiring a dehumidifier?'

'I tried the roofers. They're busy, like the electricians, and Hamza said the builders' merchants didn't have any dehumidifiers left.'

'Well . . .' she began. 'We do. A lot of the cottages can be damp so our maintenance team keep a couple in stock. I could lend you one.'

His eyes lit up as if she'd given him a million quid. 'Could you? I'll pay the rental of course.'

'Don't worry about that,' she said. 'Um. If you like, I could call in a favour and ask the roofer to come round tomorrow? The electricians are super busy but I might be able to persuade one to squeeze in an extra job.'

Travis threw up his hands in relief. For a second, Freya thought he might also throw his arms around her in a hug. Instead, he said. 'You'd do that for me?'

'I'd do it for anyone in the village who needed help,' she said carefully.

'Yeah. Of course,' he muttered, backing away and pushing his hands through his hair. 'I'd be incredibly grateful.'

'There's no need.'

'I'd have to pay you, though.'

'We can come to some arrangement but the important thing is that you're safe and legal to open.'

'Yes. Thanks. This is a weight off my mind. All I need to worry about now is sorting out the stock.'

Freya nodded, irrationally pleased by Travis's gratitude. 'You'll have Hamza to help you, though?'

'Well. No. He was only ever staying a few days. He's started an assignment in Scotland to film eagles and otters, and some rare geese.

'Rare geese . . .' Freya repeated.

'Yes. Right up his street. He's great with birds. He was all set to refuse but I knew he couldn't turn down a prestigious job like this. His footage will end up on prime-time TV.'

'He mustn't miss that,' Freya said. 'What about Seb? Could he lend a hand?'

Travis laughed. 'He might have been able to but he's laid up after coming off his bike the other night. I had to pick him up from hospital.'

'Oh my God. Is he OK?'

'He'll mend but I was worried. It could have been much worse. I can't ask Bree to help because she's enough on her plate with the kids and she's working for me on Saturday. She's a star.' His brief but warm smile was like a ray of sunshine lifting the gloom. He clearly loved his sister, and Seb too, even if it was a thorny relationship.

'You say Seb came off his bike. It was an accident?'

Travis frowned. 'Yes, apparently. A driver clipped him and he fell onto the pavement. I think the driver might be prosecuted but it wasn't a hit and run. The guy was distraught according to Seb.'

'That's a relief,' Freya said.

'Is it?' Travis gave her a hard stare. 'Yes, I guess so . . .'

'I'm sorry,' Freya said. 'I must sound callous. I only meant it was a relief that Seb wasn't knocked off on purpose.'

'Why would anyone do that?' Travis asked sharply, instantly on the alert.

'They wouldn't. I'm sure,' Freya said, regretting her hasty words. On the other hand, she felt Travis deserved to know about his brother's altercation with the hooded guy.

'I saw him a couple of nights ago as I was leaving Roxanne's wedding rehearsal. He was talking – arguing – with a man under the church lych gate.'

'What man?' Travis said then let out a groan of frustration. 'Was it Fenno?'

'Who?'

'Luke Fennel. He used to hang around with Seb. Get him into trouble most of the time!'

'Oh, I remember him. I guess it could have been because it was dark and raining. He was wearing one of those full-length jackets – you know, like a dryrobe?'

'A drytube?' Travis swore under his breath. 'That sounds like Fenno. And Seb didn't give you a clue?'

'No. I spoke to him after the guy had gone and asked if he was OK. He politely told me to mind my own business.'

Travis exhaled sharply. 'I'm sorry. That's typical of him at the moment.'

'It's fine. He's young and proud and I wouldn't even have interfered except he seemed a bit upset by this guy. I hope I did the right thing? I'm sure he won't appreciate me telling you so can you be discreet if you mention it to him? To be honest, he'll know I told you if you do. Nobody else was around.'

'I'll be tactful. I can be if I have to, you know.' His ironic smile disarmed Freya. 'Thanks for looking out for Seb and telling me. Sorry you caught me at a bad moment,' he said, looking shamefaced.

'We all have those kinds of days. I spent this morning trying to deal with a woman who tried to scam all of her holiday rental back again. Actually, I wasn't meant to be coming past at this time. I'm on call unexpectedly because Mimi's gone to a school play and I was off to the Thai for a takeaway.' Impulse overtook her. 'Have you eaten? Do you want me to get you some food while I'm at it?'

The smile grew wider. 'That sounds the best idea I've heard all day.'

'OK. I'll go for the food but I don't want to interrupt you as you're – um – so busy. I was going to take mine home.'

'No. Don't do that!' There was desperation in his voice again. 'Please. I could do with a break – if you're here, I'll take a proper one while I eat dinner.'

'OK. I'm on call though so if I have dash off to sort out someone's blocked loo, you'll know why.'

'You don't have to do that, surely?'

'No. But I'd have to spend ages placating the guests and find an emergency plumber.' She crossed her fingers. 'Hopefully I'll finish my pad Thai before anything like that happens.'

'Pad Thai?' He gave a sigh of pleasure. 'With prawns or chicken?'

She laughed, feeling a tingle of nervous excitement. 'Both if you like.'

'I like very much. I'm starving.'

She called in her order and twenty minutes later was back with the pad Thai and a couple of bottles of Singha beer.

Travis had cleared a space on the framing table and found two stools from the tiny kitchenette at the rear.

He opened one of the bottles. 'Beer?'

'Not while I'm on call. I'll have to drive home too. They're for you, I thought you needed them. I'll have water. I shouldn't have had the Thai really. '

'Why's that?' he said, tipping the bottle to his own mouth.

She laughed. 'I want to make sure I can fit into my bridesmaid's dress for Roxanne's wedding.'

He lowered the bottle and raised an eyebrow 'You're a *bridesmaid*?'

'Yes,' she said, bristling inwardly at the surprise in his tone. The words: 'I don't run out of every wedding I'm involved in' were on the tip of her tongue.

'Well, you look great to me,' he said. 'You'd look great dressed in anything.'

She'd walked right into that one. She hoped he didn't think she was fishing for compliments even though his comment had pleased her far more than it ought to have done. She took the lid off her takeout and inhaled deeply. 'This smells too good to waste and it's a bit late for going on a diet now anyway,' she said, making light of her comment. 'The wedding's in a week.'

'Really?' His fork hovered over the noodles. 'December is an . . . unusual time – for a wedding.'

'It was one of the only times Ravi – the groom – and his best man and ushers could all get time off together. They work in a hospital,' Freya said. 'Ravi's a consultant.'

'Ah.' With no more comment, Travis dug into his meal.

While they ate, he gave her an update on the gallery. 'We really are making progress, though it doesn't look like it. The reason there's such a mess is that I spent most of today mounting and framing stock ready to start hanging on the walls tomorrow. I'd just had an email when you saw me, saying the canvases I ordered might be running late and as you know, time isn't on my side.'

'No . . . I've sent an email to the maintenance team so hopefully they'll make you a priority tomorrow.'

'That is such a weight off my mind.' He hesitated, looked around at the chaos and grimaced. 'Without Hamza, it looks like I'm going to be camped here for the night anyway.'

Freya followed his gaze. Even with the 'progress' he'd made, she had to agree. 'It's a big job and it's Friday tomorrow.'

When they'd finished eating, Travis cleared the empty cartons into the bin.

Freya checked her phone but there was only a missed call from her mother. That could wait. It was half-past eight and yet she no longer felt tired.

Travis came back, a second beer in his hand.

'I was wondering . . . if you fancied taking a look at some of my stuff before I start hanging it. I'd be . . . um . . . grateful.'

'Me?' she said, amazed. 'I don't know anything about photography.'

'I'd appreciate the opinion of a . . . potential customer, not that I expect you to buy anything!' he qualified. 'Only Hamza and me, we're both too close to our jobs to truly understand what people might want to buy.'

The prospect of helping Travis rather than going home to an empty cottage was far too tempting. 'If you really think my opinion is worth anything, then I'll do my best,' she said, ignoring a million reasons why it wasn't a good idea to be alone with him for the evening.

'I've always valued your opinion,' he said, flashing her a smile that set her pulse into overdrive.

'It's almost midnight!'

Freya hadn't noticed the time flying by and Travis hadn't mentioned it. She'd certainly never meant to stay so late, never meant to stay at all, but looking around her, she was glad she'd helped. As a result of their joint efforts, the walls were a tribute to the place they both lived in: a place Freya did appreciate but, perhaps, had begun to take for granted.

Now she saw it afresh through the eyes of Travis: a place of great beauty, drama, danger and awe-inspiring magnificence.

Most of the prints were of the hills and lakes in her own backyard but there was also a corner devoted to Travis's travels in other corners of the UK and the world.

She felt she could almost reach out and touch the grizzly bears fishing for salmon in a Canadian river and gasped at the colours of the Northern Lights in Lapland.

'These are magnificent,' Freya said, hardly able to tear her eyes away from images that sucked her right into the heart of the wild places.

She shivered. 'I can almost feel that bear's breath on my neck.'

Travis laughed. 'I've smelled a grizzly's breath and believe me, you don't want to get that close.'

She swung round to him. 'You're joking?'

'OK, maybe not quite that close. Luckily, the trackers we were with managed to scare him away before we became his supper.'

'That's too close for comfort for me,' Freya said.

'It was . . . an experience I wouldn't want to repeat. Now, if you don't fancy making friends with a grizzly, wait til you see *this*.'

Buzzing with what Freya could only describe as boyish excitement, he went to the back of the shop where a huge picture obscured by thick polythene was propped up against the wall.

'Thanks to you helping me, the decks are now clear enough to hang this on that wall. I was going to wait until tomorrow but as you're here . . . would you like to give me a hand?'

She was infected by his enthusiasm. 'I'd love to.'

'It's pretty heavy,' he warned. 'It's a six-by-four canvas on a wooden frame.'

She rolled her eyes. 'I think I can handle it.'

Even so, her arms felt the strain as she lifted one end of the canvas off the floor. Keeping it upright, they carried it from the framing area into the gallery space. Breathing a little more heavily, she was secretly glad to rest it against the shelves.

Travis fetched a craft knife and slit open the plastic wrapping.

'I haven't seen it yet, so I hope it's turned out OK.'

He removed the plastic and stood back.

'Wow. It's *huge!*' Freya burst out, then instantly regretted the innuendo.

'It certainly is . . .

Travis's grin was equally massive, staring at the canvas print with pride shining in his eyes.

Freya was relieved he made no further comment on her slip of the tongue, instead focused on the picture.

It was glorious in its simplicity. A masterpiece of understatement. You wanted to keep staring at it.

It showed a white-out, a blizzard on a bare mountain plateau with no living thing until . . . Freya allowed herself to be drawn further into the photo. Against the swirling snow, amid the storm of sleet and billowing drifts were two amber eyes – and as she looked deeper, she could make out the nose, the ears and the outline of the mountain hare, peering at the camera with wary eyes, perfectly adapted to his snowy environment.

'I wanted to make a statement,' he said. 'It's not too big, is it?'

She rejected a dozen different answers for a simple, 'No. A statement is good.'

'Where is this?'

'Cairngorms. Unfortunately there aren't any left in the Lake District now. I decided to take a risk. There are lots of Lakeland scenes. I'll be running tours up to Scotland to photograph them.'

He suddenly seemed unsure.

They hung the canvas and stepped back to admire their handiwork.

'It looks amazing.'

He stepped close to her, his eyes full of passion – for his work, and – was it still possible – for *her*? 'You should come up there with me some time. I'll show you the hares, pine martens, red deer, sea eagles. It's an experience you'll never forget.'

This Travis was the enthusiastic boy – young man – she'd known and . . . *had* she loved him?

'I'm sure I wouldn't,' she said, physically closer to him than she'd been for many long years . . . nearer to kissing him, and more, than those heady teenage days. A moment would all it would take, a heartbeat to capture his mouth with hers, to be wrapped in his arms, to tear off each other's clothes and trash the gallery, lay on the framing table, prints and glass smashing on the tiles.

He was so close, that she could feel the heat from his body, and her need for him in every cell.

He leaned forward and his lips met hers, so soft and warm and delicious. If he hadn't been holding the canvas, they *would* have been ripping off each other's clothes – she was transported back to the past, to the days when nothing mattered but seeing him again, holding him, planning their future and to hell with the whole world.

This was not the past. Her mother had certainly done everything in her power to convince her she'd be 'far better off waiting until she was more mature'. Travis's reaction to her breaking off the engagement – taking off – had seemed to back up her comments that he was 'wild, impulsive and selfish'.

'I'd better get my coat!

Her voice came out as squeak as she sprang away from

him, horrified that her fantasies had been a whisker away from becoming reality. 'It's really late and – oh no – I should have been monitoring my phone A guest might have called.'

'Oh,' Travis said, sounding deflated. 'I'll get it for you.' He went off to the kitchen, and handed it over, looking crestfallen.

'Thank you.' She dug her mobile out of the bag and exhaled in relief. 'No calls, thank goodness.'

'That's something . . .' Travis murmured, sounding dejected as he shoved his hands in his jeans' pockets.

While he seemed disappointed their 'moment' had been cut off, Freya injected a forced cheeriness into her own voice, determined to return their relationship to the purely professional. 'If you can give me some leaflets, I'll add them to the visitor guidebooks in the properties we look after.'

'Thanks. It's good of you to do that for me,' he said in a stilted way that was most unlike him.

'Of course. It's the least I'd do for a fellow businessperson. We look out for each other here in Bannerdale.'

'A fellow businessperson . . .' He stared at her with a deep frown. 'Is that what we are?'

'Yes.' She affected a puzzled look, though she felt shaky inside under his scrutiny. 'Is that so bad?'

'No . . . there are worse things we could be, I suppose,' he said and opened the door for her. 'Goodnight, Freya. As fellow *businesspeople*, I'm sure our paths will cross again.'

The door closed quietly behind her before she'd got three paces up the street.

Chapter Twelve

Despite being knackered after his epic day at the gallery, Travis was still awake at one a.m., reliving that kiss – and rueing the sudden ending to it. If they'd carried on, then anything could have happened – and he wished it had.

Or did he?

He groaned and thumped his pillow. It was the thought of anything happening that was keeping him awake. He'd only been back in Bannerdale for a week and the two of them already seemed on the verge of having a massive falling out.

Underneath the veneer of 'maturity,' they clearly hadn't grown up at all.

After a fitful night, the six a.m. alarm went off so he rolled out of bed and into the shower. It was still dark and he shivered in the chilly air of the cabin. He'd pick up some breakfast from the sandwich shop . . . treat Seb too as he was dropping by to 'help' on his day off. Hopefully, he might be able to get to the bottom of why Fenno had been hassling his brother again.

Travis was hanging a picture of Derwentwater when Seb

hobbled into the gallery not long after Travis had got there himself. Apart from the limp and a bruise on his face, he looked more like his old self. You healed fast when you were young, Travis thought ruefully.

'I'm feeling better. Phoned my manager and I'm back at work next week. They're putting me on the afternoon shift on the tills until I'm more mobile.'

'That's good.'

He looked round. 'So, here I am ready to help. Fenno went past yesterday afternoon and said it looked like shit but actually, it looks OK to me.'

Fenno . . . The name instantly made Travis's hackles rise. 'Thanks for the vote of confidence,' he replied, unwilling to let on that Freya had helped him. 'I didn't know you were still seeing Fenno . . .'

'Sometimes,' Seb said and flashed a defiant glare at Travis. 'And before you say anything, he's one of the good guys now. He's got an apprenticeship with a boat repair place on the lake.'

'I didn't say anything!'

Seb narrowed his eyes. 'I could tell what you were thinking.'

'I wish I had that gift,' Travis said tartly, at a loss how Seb could think that Fenno was a good guy after the altercation they'd had outside the church. It was further proof of how far his brother was under the man's influence. 'Are you sure you're fit enough to help me out?' Travis said.

Seb scoffed. 'Of course. I'm not an old guy like you,'

'You cheeky sod. I'm only thirty-two.'

'Exactly. Ancient. And anyway, now Hamza's buggered off to film these golden eagles, you'll be on your own.'

Travis frowned. 'Who told you Hamza's gone to film eagles – and by the way it's sea eagles. I didn't mention that.'

'Freya Bolton told me. I saw her outside the doc's this morning. She was on her way to her office and she asked me how I was.' He grinned. 'She seemed worried an old guy like you couldn't manage on your own.'

Travis put the hammer on the counter with a thud. 'She did not say that!'

Seb smirked in delight at having wound his brother up. 'Well, not exactly that but she obviously is looking out for you. She cares.' He said it in a simpering voice. 'Just like when you were lovesick teenagers.'

Travis wondered whether now was the time to introduce the topic of dryrobe guy but the situation was still fragile and he thought it best to save that subject until they'd bonded a bit more.

'She's arranged for the builder and electrician to come, that's it.'

'Sure, she did . . .' Seb smirked.

Ignoring the comment, Travis handed a craft knife to Seb. 'Can you manage to open some boxes? You can sit down to do it.'

'Oh, I don't know if I can be trusted with such a complex task but I can give it a go.'

'I'd be so grateful . . .' Travis simpered.

Seb scored a line down the parcel tape. He pulled out a series of A4 prints wrapped in cellophane and nodded appreciatively.

'You know, Trav. Some of this stuff isn't total crap.' He glanced up at the mountain hare and whistled. 'This isn't one of yours, is it?'

'No, it's by one of my numerous assistants. Of course, it's one of mine!'

Seb hobbled closer. 'It's not bad.'

'Thanks. If you talk less and work more, you can get them sorted into those baskets so the customers can buy them tomorrow.'

The two of them set to work, opening the rest of the stock and arranging it in boxes, with the larger stuff on wooden racks. The smaller canvases finally arrived against the odds, and Travis was able to hang some of those.

As he worked, Seb's words about Freya caring resonated with him. She'd always been a caring person. OK, she'd run out of the church like Usain Bolt at the mock wedding, but Travis hadn't really blamed her – eventually. For a while, he'd had to bear the brunt of the other kids asking him if she'd run off because he'd smelled skanky, or he'd tried to kiss her (they could see full well he hadn't!) or because she was scared of him because of his dad.

For a while – about three months – he hadn't forgiven her but eventually, he'd convinced himself he was over it. There was enough to worry about at home, because his father was 'away' again and his mum had toddler Seb to care for and was trying to work two jobs. Travis had to help with looking after him while trying to help out around the house.

He slid a glance at Seb who was intent on sorting prints into some kind of theme. All the times he'd changed his nappy and wiped his snotty little nose . . . stuck up for him at school . . . Seb had no idea.

They worked hard until mid-afternoon when a female voice with a Cumbrian accent called a greeting from the open rear door and in walked a petite young woman with black hair caught up in a scrunchie. She was wearing work boots, trousers with a hundred pockets and a plaid shirt three sizes too large.

'Can I help you?' Travis said. 'We're not open until tomorrow.'

She laughed. 'I hope not with that leak over the back door. I'm the roofer.'

He peered at her, remembering her pretty face from school but unable to square it with the roofers' overalls. 'Araya? It can't be.'

'Yeah. It's me.' She grinned.

Travis smiled. Her parents owned the Thai restaurant whose food he'd eaten the previous evening.

'You weren't expecting some hulking great bloke with his bum hanging out of his trousers, were you?'

'Um. No. I wasn't sure who to expect.'

'Well, you've got me. Me and my brother set up our own roofing company.' She grinned. 'I never minded heights. Remember that abseiling trip at school?'

'You did it twice while the rest of us kids were cowering at the bottom.'

She grinned. 'Yup.'

'Coffee?'

'Go on, then but I'll have it outside while I look at this back roof.'

Travis made the coffee and watched while Araya nipped up the ladder and inspected the roof. He wasn't surprised the old place had issues because most of the stone and slate buildings in the village dated back to Victorian times – some even older. It gave them heaps of character – and sadly, meant they needed loads of maintenance.

Back on terra firma, Araya pointed out the issue to him, while Seb spectated from the doorway pretending to sip a cup of tea.

'There's nothing terminal for *now*,' she said, mug in hand. 'See those broken slates above the rear entrance? They're what's caused your leak. I've actually got some similar slates in the van from a job I've been doing for Freya so I can sort it now if you like.'

Travis heaved a sigh of relief. 'Thanks for coming so quickly. I'm really grateful.'

'Don't thank me. Thank Freya. Once the roof is sealed again, you can start to dry the place out properly. Freya said she'll send the dehumidifier along as soon as.'

'She's a real hero,' Seb said with a wistful sigh.

Travis glared at him. 'Shouldn't you be unloading boxes?'

'I was just having a bit of fresh air while I take a break. Nice work, Araya.'

'Thanks. I'd employ you as labourer if you didn't have the dodgy leg. I heard you came off your bike.'

'From who?'

'Constable Kelvin.' She chuckled. 'He's one of Mum and Dad's best customers. News travels fast in Bannerdale. Hope your leg's better soon.'

Seb slunk back inside while Araya set to work, so Travis left her to it and went back inside to find his brother Seb bursting with glee.

'Some bloke with a dehumidifier just arrived. Says Freya made him stop doing another job to rush over here. See, I told you she's willing to bend over backwards to help you.'

'Great because I need all the help I can get if I'm to open tomorrow in time for the fair,' Travis said. 'Now, do you think

116

you can manage to unpack those boxes or are you going to spend the rest of the day drooling over the roofer?'

Seb mimed a fishing reel action. 'Gotcha!'

Travis rolled his eyes. 'There's a Stanley knife next to you, though you could use your razor-sharp wit, I suppose.'

As sunset approached, Travis noticed that Seb was tiring.

'You should go home and rest that leg,' Travis said. 'Thanks for your help.'

'Like I said, an old guy needs a hand.'

Travis rolled his eyes.

'It's looking better,' Seb declared with undisguised pride.

'Yeah, I'm beginning to think I might make it in time for the launch.' There hadn't seemed a good time to mention the dryrobe man with Seb flagging.

Despite being tired, Seb left mid-afternoon with a smile on his face, leaving Travis in a more positive mood. Today had been a good day in so many ways; the gallery was looking almost there; if he stayed late that evening he should be ready to open in time – thanks to Seb and Freya.

He felt he was making progress with his brother – as for Freya, well, that was still a mystery to him. She always had been a mystery, he'd always felt on shifting sands, never convinced of her true feelings for him. Right from that stupid mock wedding to their real but short-lived engagement, he could never predict whether she'd run out on him. Even when she had agreed to marry him, even if she changed her mind for an evening, it had been with a guarded reluctance as if she was terrified of what she'd agreed to – terrified of making the commitment to him, or anyone.

He was pretty certain about one thing: she still fancied him. With a sigh of manly pride at that thought, he decided to clear up the dust before going home to crash out. The previous tenant had left an old hoover in the storeroom so Travis lugged it into the gallery and shoved the yellowing plug into the socket.

He wasn't sure which happened first, the flash, the bang – or him flying across the room and landing on his arse.

Chapter Thirteen

'Travis!'

Thank God the door was unlocked. It banged back against the wall as Freya dashed into the gallery where Travis was now trying to stand up with all the grace and skill of a newborn giraffe.

'Whoa, slowly!' Kneeling on the floor next to him, she levered him upright with a hand under his elbow.

'I'm OK,' he said hoarsely. 'Just a b-bit sh-shocked. Ha!'

'That's because you've been electrocuted!'

'No shit, Sherlock.' He tried to grin but his jaw felt tingly.

'It's not funny!' She glared at him. 'You could have been killed.' She pulled out her phone. 'I'm calling an ambulance.'

Travis tried to grab her phone. 'You'll do no such thing. I'm f-fine.'

She held the mobile out of his reach. 'All right, *but* you should get a check-up at the local hospital. I saw the flash and you flying backwards. Are you *sure* you feel OK? Let me look at your hands.'

He held them out and they were now rock steady.

'No burns. You didn't get knocked out?'

'No. It all happened so fast.' Still holding onto his hands, she searched his face, checking his eyes were focusing.

'There is one thing though,' he said, grimacing in pain.

Her stomach turned over. 'What?'

'I can pick up Radio One.'

She dropped his hands and folded her arms. 'It's not funny! What the hell were you doing?'

'Plugging in the vacuum cleaner.' He flipped a thumb at the blackened hose lying on the floor. The nearby socket was tinged with soot.

She suppressed a shudder. 'Hasn't the electrician been yet?'

'I think you can guess the answer to that.'

Shaking her head, she pushed a button on her phone and held it to her ear, causing Travis to protest loudly. 'Look, I'm *fine*.'

'Chill. I'm not calling the medics. I'm phoning the electrician to see where he is. Now, sit down on that chair and do *not* touch anything else.'

'I don't remember you being this bossy,' he muttered before dutifully sitting on the chair.

Keeping a close eye on him, Freya made her call and relayed the upshot of the conversation to Travis.

'He's had to go to an emergency job and then he was stuck in a jam in Windermere, but he's ten minutes away. *Stay there,*' she ordered when he attempted to rise.

'I wouldn't dare move a muscle,' he said solemnly, gripping the edge of the chair.

'Hmm.' She aimed a laser stare at him. 'You probably *are* OK.'

'Thanks. Actually, I mean it. If I *had* been seriously injured, it would have been fortunate you happened to be passing by the gallery.'

'I wasn't passing by. I came to collect those leaflets you promised me.'

'Ah. I'll sort them out now,' he said, and went into the framing area. 'If I have your permission to move out of my seat?'

She had to admit, he wasn't looking so pale as he had been, but it could have been so much worse. She shivered, and swiftly put that horrible prospect to the back of her mind.

'I suppose so,' she said as sternly as she could.

It was only now she was sure he was fine that her heart finally stopped racing and she could and take in her surroundings property.

Now the floor was clear of boxes and bubble wrap, she could walk around the room, hardly recognising it even from the previous evening. Framed prints and canvases covered the walks, expertly mounted on wooden battens and gallery wire. Wooden racks had been placed at the lower level and filled with cellophane-wrapped mounted prints in different sizes. There were also half a dozen easels set up, that she guessed were waiting to be filled with key pieces.

And, there on the end wall, the mountain hare peered out from its snowy wilderness, watching everyone with a wary eye.

Travis returned with a box of leaflets and put them on a counter.

Freya swung to face him. 'Apart from almost killing yourself, you've done an amazing job. I'm impressed.'

He smiled. 'Pleased to hear it. It's been a lot of work.'

'I can see that. It looks great, Travis,' she said, swelling with pride on his behalf and thinking that the bad boy of Bannerdale, the 'waste of space' as his father had once called him, had come a long way.

'I already owe you. The roofer came – she was a surprise.'

Freya laughed. 'Thought she might be.'

'She fixed the roof and the place is drying out thanks to you. Seb's been here most of the day, but I couldn't have done it without your help too.'

'I *was* only here a few hours.'

'It's still a work in progress but I'm almost there,' he said. 'At least the place is watertight,' he said. 'Araya fixed a couple of slates and your maintenance man dropped the dehumidifier in.' He moved closer, his eyes full of a genuinely warm appreciation that made her glow all over. 'I really can't thank you enough.'

'You're welcome,' she said, aware of what had happened the previous evening when they'd got too close. A van pulled up outside the gallery and she hurried towards the door. 'Oh look, Danny's here. Let's hope he doesn't close you down for being a death trap.'

A couple of hours later, Danny the electrician had replaced the faulty circuit boards and checked that the rest of the electrics were safe. A few of the spotlights had failed so he replaced those with some he had on the van.

While he worked, Freya helped Travis hang and display the final boxes of stock, until every wall was a love song to the mountains and lakes in all its moods and seasons, from daffodils nodding by Ullswater, to tarns covered in rosy waterlilies, from russet fells perfectly reflected in the lakes to snow-topped peak of Helvellyn.

'I – I have to ask. When did you take all these if you've been away so long?'

'Some are from the early days. Others from visits home while I was at college and when I could pop back.'

'I never knew you'd been back so often.'

'Not that often and only for a night or two. I've spent the past ten years flitting around the UK and abroad doing tours and commissions. I'd come to take pictures until dark, sometimes at night too. I didn't come to socialise.' He walked up to a canvas of an iconic view from the hillside down on Buttermere, his back to her, gazing at it. 'I came for the landscape.'

Was she hurt by the comment? Though why should she be? What he said was so matter of fact, she couldn't be. She really believed that it was true – or did she only want to believe it was true? There had been nothing for Travis in Bannerdale except the scenery and his brother and sister, of course.

She'd never tried to get in touch with him after he'd left.

Her mother had been very relieved.

The electrician walked in from the staffroom, carrying a bag of tools. 'Everything's safe now. I'll give you a quote for the extra lighting rails you want installing and the computer sockets upstairs but for now, let's just say you shouldn't have any more unexpected shocks.' He grinned. 'Apart from the power bill, of course.'

Freya laughed alongside Travis who shook Danny's hand. 'Thanks, mate, I really appreciate it.'

'Thank you, Danny,' Freya added, giving him a peck on the cheek.

'Anything for you,' he said, adding, 'Good luck with the opening, mate.'

They were left alone. The light of the shop windows showed

wispy snowflakes falling softly. It was past seven and Freya's stomach rumbled. She'd grabbed a sandwich at her desk hours ago.

Travis heaved a sigh of relief. 'Thanks for rescuing me,' he said with a grin. 'Again. Will you let me buy you dinner as a thank you?'

Looking into those beguiling eyes was a mistake.

'I shouldn't . . .'

He frowned. 'Why not?'

'Because – it isn't safe?' The moment she'd let the words slip out, she regretted them. She wasn't sure how she could explain her feelings to herself, let alone articulate them to the man she'd rejected. She'd been thinking about Roxanne's comments at the rehearsal, about her being affected by the loss of her dad even though she couldn't remember. To her, it seemed normal that loved ones were snatched away.

He laughed. 'Why, are you worried about being electrocuted?'

That wasn't what she meant and he must have known it, but he chose to ignore the comment. 'OK, but we're not bringing takeaway back here again,' she said, determined not to be alone with him for the evening.

'I wasn't thinking of a takeout. Let's get out of here. I'm starving and desperate for a pint. I think we're allowed to celebrate and what's the point in celebrating an achievement – or anything – on your own?'

She took his point and his enthusiasm was infectious. It would be petty and anti-social to refuse. Her stomach growled again.

'I am hungry,' she said. 'OK, yes. Thanks,' she added with a quick smile. 'Where shall we go? You're the new kid in town. You choose.'

'No, you suggest somewhere. I'll pay.'

Most of the stalls had already been erected ready for the morning, although the workers had gone home now. On a busy Friday evening with visitors flocking to the Christmas Fair, it wouldn't be easy finding a restaurant with a free table.

However, Freya recommended a new Indian restaurant where she knew the owner and he insisted on clearing a space in the window. Freya hadn't the heart to refuse and she and Travis squeezed around the bistro table.

The food, however, was excellent.

He scooped up his lamb rogan josh with a chunk of naan. 'This is delicious.'

'It is . . .' she said, feeling as if she was dining in a goldfish bowl.

He topped up her glass with red wine.

'I shouldn't.'

'I thought we were celebrating.'

'You are. You're the one who's achieved the impossible and transformed the gallery from a wreck to a business in under a week.'

'Only with a lot of help from my friends and you pulling a lot of strings.'

She raised her glass. 'I haven't done much. Here's to you. Bree must be proud of you.'

'She's pleased I'm back at all.' He lowered his glass and seemed to contemplate the wine for a moment. 'Yeah. I just wish . . .' He sighed. 'I wish Mum could see it.'

'Why not contact her, then? Invite her to come down to see it?'

'I saw her a few months ago when I was on a job up north.

She lives near Durham with her partner so we met in a local pub. I hadn't decided to buy this place yet.' He paused.

Freya listened, but said nothing, as if speaking now would burst a fragile bubble.

'She's made a totally different life for herself. She's a supervisor in a care home and her partner's working away which seems to suit her. The moment Seb was off her hands, she left Bannerdale as fast as she *could*. She was very young when she married my dad and I think she decided to go off and have the life she'd always wanted – free from responsibility – before it was too late. I can hardly blame her.'

'What about your dad?'

'Mum says he's living in Glasgow in some kind of halfway house since his last stint in jail but I'm not bothered about him. He checked out of our lives years ago.'

'I'm sorry. I don't think I ever realised how rough things were for you,' Freya said, remembering how Travis had always put on a tough front where his dad was concerned. She guessed he'd wanted to escape from that side of his life when he was with her and she'd probably wanted to avoid heavy conversations too. Now, she would have been ready to listen and offer consolation and advice: the way that people in a mature relationship did. You took someone for better and for worse . . .

'Mum did her best, considering she was left on her own with three young kids on and off for years. She fed us and kept a roof over our heads until Seb left to go to college. Bree was already living with a bloke then and he ended up sharing with a bunch of local lads.' He hesitated. 'They were troublemakers to be honest and he went along with them. Ended up being cautioned by the police a few times and in the magistrate's court for criminal damage and shoplifting. You live here. He must have a reputation.'

'That must have been while I was working away from Bannerdale in hospitality for years,' she said truthfully. 'I certainly haven't heard anything about him lately. He always seems pretty friendly when I pop into the mini-market.'

'It was lucky those guys moved away and he got a job. Jobs plural, he lost a few but he's managed to hold down the supermarket job for the past six months. He's lucky to have that with his record but the manager is a mate of Bree's and she put in a good word for him.'

'How old is he now?'

'He still acts like a teenager. When I went round to his flat the other night I was surprised I didn't find enough wildlife to make a documentary.'

Freya winced. 'Ouch. Sounds like he could do with our services.'

'I wouldn't let you within fifty feet of the place,' Travis declared. 'I'm ashamed of it to be honest.'

'He's young, he's single, cleaning won't be high on his agenda.' She smiled. 'To be honest, it's not high on most people's agendas. You should see the people who turn up in Porsches to a huge holiday place and leave it looking like a herd of rhinos have been living there. They don't even empty the bins or the fridges, yet they're barking down the phone if there aren't enough pods for the coffee maker or the wi-fi drops out for a nanosecond.'

He smiled. 'I can't imagine what you have to deal with.'

'We're used to it. I can handle nightmare guests but occasionally it's with a smile on my face and a metaphorical dagger in my hand.'

'You always stood up for yourself. I admired it.'

'What? The great Travis Marshall? Scary Travis who everyone was half in awe of, half terrified of.'

'Trust me, it was all bravado. I was hiding the fact I felt inferior – Dad in jail, Mum sending me to school in dirty clothes. I had to develop a very thick shell.'

Her heart softened further and she realised that they were talking about issues they'd never discussed before. They were, finally, now it was too late, opening up to each other. 'Look at you now though. At the top of your game in a job most people can only dream of.'

He laughed dismissively as if he suddenly regretted revealing so much. 'Yeah. I suppose I'd better ask for the bill.'

After he'd tapped the machine and the waiter went for their coats, Travis said, 'I'll walk you home.'

'No need. I've walked home alone before, you know.' She didn't want him so near her cottage at that time of night.

'Travis. About last night.'

'I'm guessing you wish that had never happened?'

She tried to laugh it off. 'Do I need to answer that?'

'By the look on your face, no. You came to help me and we ended up – doing that. If you're worried about me inviting myself into your place, it won't happen again.'

It won't happen again: he sounded very determined, so why did her heart sink a little? Did she secretly hope there might be another kiss, another chance? Did that mean she still had feelings?

Before she could formulate a coherent reply, Travis spoke again, so softly, it was barely audible.

'Unless you want it to, of course . . .'

Sparks shot through her and heat rose through her body

to her cheeks. Involuntarily, she raised her fingers to feel the warmth blooming there, blooming everywhere like spring after a long and endless winter.

'Hellooooo!!!'

A loud rap on the window made her jump and a gurning face appeared.

'Oh, God. It's Seb.'

'Not now,' Travis mouthed and was out of his chair in a second.

'Wait . . .' Freya said but he was out of the door. She took their coats from the waiter and followed him outside.

Seb was with two guys she vaguely recognised, who were hanging back, grinning.

'Hi, Seb. I thought you were going home for an early night.'

'I could say the same for you.' Seb smirked at Freya. 'Evening, Freya. Didn't take my brother long.'

'It's a thank-you dinner.'

'I bet it is.'

One of the guys, stinking of beer, slapped Seb on the back. 'We'll leave you to it, mate. Big Brother is watching you now.'

Seb staggered and was only prevented from toppling to the pavement by Travis flinging an arm around his shoulders.

His 'friends' burst out laughing and walked off. 'See ya then.'

Seb sniggered. 'Thanks, Trav.'

'Don't thank me,' Travis growled, shooting an anguished look at Freya. 'I can't leave him. He's pissed.'

'I am not!' Seb shot back. 'I can't afford to get pissed these days.'

'You're having a pretty good try.'

He laughed, then hung onto Travis, slurring. 'Maybe I do need a hand.'

'If you want to come up to his flat with me, I'll walk you home after,' Travis said, desperation in his voice.

'I don't need walking home. It's ten minutes away,' Freya said. 'Besides, Seb needs you. Do you need a hand?'

'No, we'll be OK,' Travis said,

'I do,' Seb said. 'Sorry for spoiling your evening, Frey-ar.'

'You haven't,' Freya said quickly. 'Travis, I'll be fine. I'll see you in the morning at the fair.'

'Oh God, is it tomorrow?' Seb muttered.

'Shut up and try to stay upright until I can get you in the flat,' Travis said, shooting a desperate look over his shoulder at Freya.

She watched him help his brother limp down the street towards the alley where his flat was and then heard a plaintive cry from Seb, bent double on the pavement. 'I think I'm gonna throw up.'

Chapter Fourteen

So, this was it: launch day and the Christmas Fair. It was still an hour to sunrise when Travis arrived at the gallery after a late night looking after Seb.

Travis had stayed until he was certain his brother had stopped being sick and made him drink some water and take some paracetamol, before he'd finally walked home to Squirrel Cabin.

At this early hour, he'd expected to be the only one around but the streets were already busy with traders unloading everything from bottles of gin and jars of chutneys to wooden toys and Christmas puddings. Some were already decorating their stalls with tinsel and fairy lights and he caught the scent of spices on the air from down the street where Araya and her parents were setting up an outdoor kitchen outside their shop.

Brian was presiding over it all, bundled up in a sheepskin coat and tweed cap, and ticking off items from a clipboard. Still feeling guilty for taking the piss at the breakfast meeting, Travis called a cheery good morning to him before unlocking the door on his empire.

He lingered by the light switch, half expecting to go flying across the space but this time when he flicked the lights, there was no drama – unless you counted the rush of excitement that came when he saw the gallery bedecked with his life's work.

Was the moisture in his eyes down to disbelief or the chill of a winter morning?

Was all this really *his*?

He'd had exhibitions of his work in galleries before but never so many pictures on display in such a compact space – never, of course, in his own gallery.

'You southern softy,' he muttered, embarrassed at his indulgence in self-congratulations, before marching to the staff area to switch on the heating – couldn't have his first customers freezing their bits off.

This was absolutely not the moment to rest on his laurels; today was just the start of establishing himself in Bannerdale, of building a customer base and a reputation. He had bills to pay, and more importantly staff. Bree would be along in a little while, ready to serve customers and make sure their orders for prints were processed correctly and sent off before Christmas. In the New Year, when the shop was quieter, she was going to learn to use the framing equipment so Travis could take on more courses and trips.

Bree would be looking after the card machine and taking payments. He smiled to himself; funny but he was more scared of that than of the fiendishly complex cameras and lenses he owned. He'd brought two to the shop as he knew they'd be a huge talking point with customers.

Freya had done him another good turn in putting his leaflets about the gallery and tours in every holiday home they looked after. That was advertising he'd have had to pay for. There would always be passing trade, holidaymakers who came into the gallery and booked a workshop on impulse, but his website was the vital place where people could find out about him and book direct.

He spent the next two hours tidying everything up, polishing frames and glass until it gleamed, and adding pricelists to the cards.

Travis popped his head around the door, delighted to see the sun shining over the fells. Generators hummed, and the streets were now buzzing with traders serving early-bird customers. The speakers were playing time-honoured festive favourites, reminding Travis of Seb; there had been no point broaching the subject of his brother's music – or lack of it – the previous evening, and he was far too busy today.

'Morning!' The greeting was accompanied by a sharp rap on the door.

Travis opened the door to Jos Beresford. Square-jawed, taciturn and wearing a trapper hat, he looked like he could have stepped off the set of a Hollywood movie set in the Rockies.

'Come in,' Travis said, with a smile, determined to build bridges with his fellow traders.

'Thanks.' Jos stepped in and exhaled in surprise. 'You made it, then? Some of us didn't think you'd be ready in time,' Jos said, peering around Travis into the rear of the gallery. 'But I can see you proved us wrong.'

'By the skin of my teeth,' said Travis, maintaining the smile with more difficulty. 'Do you want a quick tour?'

'I shouldn't. I'm meant to be supervising the whole event but I want to support a fellow trader, so I can spare a few minutes.'

I wasn't begging you, thought Travis but bit back his sarcasm. 'Come in, then. Mind the step.'

Jos stepped further into the gallery, making appreciative noises. 'You've done a good job,' he said. 'Hope that doesn't sound patronising?'

'Not at all, mate. I welcome any feedback,' Travis said.

'Well, I have to say, you've transformed it. My office did the conveyancing on the place and I heard it was in a right state when the previous owner left.'

'Your office?' Travis exclaimed. 'I used Caterfields – not Beresfords. Not deliberately,' Travis added hastily.

Jos smirked. 'We *own* Caterfields. Took them over a couple of years ago but let them keep their name because it's well known in Bannerdale. We now have two practices here plus the Beresfords in Windermere and another practice we're buying in Kendal.'

'Wow. Sounds like you're on your way to an empire.'

'Hardly.' Jos smiled. 'But you have to start somewhere, don't you?'

That was rich, Travis thought. Jos's father had put him through law school and made him a partner straight out of university. Travis had had to start from scratch, with nothing and a father who'd told him he'd never be anything. Travis checked himself, aware that he had a chip on his shoulder and it wasn't Jos's fault that he'd been born into a well-to-do family. He mustn't take it out on the guy.

'The real hard work begins now, though, eh?' Jos said, lingering in front of the snow hare canvas, as if mesmerised.

'The real work?' Travis echoed.

'Building up a business. Sticking at it. Staying around long enough to make it work.' Jos swung round. 'You've achieved a lot – it can't have been easy on your own.'

'Well, I had some help . . .'

'Ah. From Freya?'

'Freya . . .' Travis hadn't even mentioned her. How did Jos know she'd been at the gallery two nights running?

'Your brother told me she'd been working here late,' Jos said smoothly. 'I bumped into him in the pub the other evening.'

Seb . . . Travis let out an inner groan but could hardly blame his brother for stating plain facts to Jos. 'Freya put me in touch with some of the local tradespeople. And er – she helped me clear up one evening.'

Jos smirked. 'Yes, I saw you were thick as thieves at the meeting.'

'Hardly!'

'I guess you had a lot of catching up to do.'

'Not much . . .' Travis muttered.

Jos turned back to the mountain hare. 'This is a remarkable picture. It feels as if its eyes are watching you everywhere you go.' He swung round to Travis again. 'Has Freya told you we were planning to get married?'

Chapter Fifteen

Travis had barely a second to recover. Instinctively, he knew that he mustn't act surprised or shocked – or even interested, because that's what this man wanted. He wanted to provoke a reaction and he'd deliberately tried to distract Travis by mentioning the hare photo.

'No . . . she didn't,' he said, trying to affect a mildly interested – but only out of politeness – tone. Inside, his guts had tightened and his mind was in turmoil. Bloody Jos had him in his sights like an eagle spotting the hare and preparing to swoop.

Jos raised his eyebrows. 'Funny. I thought she would have.'

Travis shrugged. 'Why would she? I haven't had any contact with her since I went to college.'

'Really? I thought you might at least have emailed each other or something.'

'No.' Travis hesitated but couldn't help himself. 'When was this?' he said as casually as he could. 'You and Freya getting married?'

'Oh, a little while ago,' Jos said. 'Last summer.'

'Last *summer*?' he exclaimed. That was recent history in Travis's book.

'Yes. Eighteen months ago. It was scheduled for June the twenty-first.'

'And it's all . . . over now?' Travis said.

'I think that's pretty obvious,' Jos replied stonily.

'Well, I'm sorry you split up, mate.'

'Don't be sorry, I'm glad it's over and as for us "splitting up," that sounds like it was a joint decision and it wasn't. Freya broke off our engagement two weeks before the wedding.'

'Two weeks?' Travis's exclamation echoed around the shop but it was too late to pretend he wasn't interested now. The genie was out of the bottle.

'Yes, obviously everything was booked. Cars, flowers, the church and the venue, of course. We'd chosen the Lakeside Hotel.' Jos smirked. 'Only the best.'

'The Lakeside?' Travis echoed 'And Freya called it off?'

'Yes. Rather late in the day, I think you'd agree. The wedding insurance wouldn't pay out, of course, not for the bride getting cold feet. To be fair, Freya did offer to use her life savings to pay for it but I refused. I'm not that petty and of course, I was in a better position to take the hit than Freya and her mother,' he added, 'with the new branches and all.'

'Wow . . .' Travis muttered, though he didn't care if Jos had branches on Mars and Uranus; it was the fact Freya had called off their wedding that had left him dumbstruck.

There was a silence during which Jos was staring at him, unnerving him.

'You haven't asked me why,' Jos said.

'No, I, um . . . didn't think it was any of my business.' What else could Travis say, though he had his own theory why Freya and Jos should not have married. Personally, he thought the man was arrogant and self-important, but Travis was also self-aware enough to realise that his own prejudices against Jos might – had – affected his view.

'I can tell you're pretending you're not interested,' Jos said coolly. 'Though I suspect you are.' He was clearly in the mood to offload, and perhaps had been in that mood since the day Freya had told him the wedding was off.

'I don't need to hear more—'

Jos cut him off. 'She never really gave me a reason,' he said, curling his lip. 'Just some guff about not being able to offer the commitment a lifelong relationship deserved.' He scoffed. 'Told me I'd be grateful to her one day. Well, I must admit that made it worse – for a little while, but she was right . . .' He sniffed. 'Who wants to be saddled with a partner who isn't prepared to give you the love and respect you deserve?'

Though stunned, Travis didn't like his tone. 'She must have had a good reason,' he said, gruffly, determined not to criticise Freya in any way.

'Yeah. Well, like I said, she's done me a favour. And anyway . . .' Jos declared. 'You know how it feels, eh? She left you at the altar.'

'We were eight,' Travis said coldly. 'It wasn't a real wedding.'

'Sign of things to come, though, eh?'

Jos laughed but Travis stayed stony-faced. He didn't think the analogy was funny or fair at all, and he was furious at Jos's nastiness towards Freya.

'I'm sorry you feel so bitter,' he said.

'Bitter?' Jos snorted in derision. 'You're joking, aren't you? I'm relieved. Far better to take the hit of the cancelled wedding than end up with a messy divorce a few years down the line with kids involved.' He rolled his eyes. 'I probably saved myself money in the long run.'

Never had Travis seen a man with less self-awareness than Jos Beresford. Far from being over Freya, the man radiated resentment and hostility. Unease ripped through him: she'd felt enough for Jos to agree to marry him, just as she had for him. Yet he considered himself poles apart from Jos Beresford. That disturbed him.

'I just thought I'd warn you,' Jos said, with a sneer. 'You know, I don't think Freya is capable of truly loving anyone.'

The words flew like an arrow into Travis's heart. Even so, he wasn't going to let Jos get the slightest hint that his words had hit home and wounded.

'I don't need warning about Freya or anyone, thanks,' he snapped. 'And thanks for calling to wish me well,' he added, his words laden with sarcasm, 'but I have to get on.'

Travis moved forward, corralling Jos by the door. 'You're right, I should go. I probably shouldn't have wasted my time even telling you. Freya has taken up enough of my time for a lifetime. Good luck today. I expect I'll see you later at the lights switch-on.'

To Travis's relief, he caught a glimpse of a tweed cap appear in the doorway of the gallery. 'I think Brian's looking for you!' he declared, waving madly at the bemused Brian. 'Yeah. Bloody hell, it's almost time to open.'

With that, Jos was gone, leaving Travis reeling in the gallery, thoughts spilling over into a whirlpool of regrets and questions. Should he ask her why she'd split up with Jos? Get her side of the story?

Wasn't that between her and Jos alone, even if Jos had tried to make it his business?

Couples broke off engagements all the time. Some people broke them off twice.

Jos was everything Travis wasn't – or hadn't been. Well to do, good family, good school, committed to staying in Bannerdale – committed to Freya. OK, he was a pompous prat, but she must have felt enough to get engaged to the man and take things all the way to the wire.

Even so, Jos's cruel words clanged in his mind like church bells ringing out of control.

I don't think Freya is capable of truly loving anyone.

That was bullshit, wasn't it? The opinion of a bitter ex who was trying to wound a rival any way he could.

Damn. He was as obsessed with Freya as Jos still was.

Snatching up a box of leaflets, he marched outside, trying to paste a smile on his face in case customers were around. Although it was frosty, the sun was bright and people were already milling around the stalls. His nose twitched as the aroma of cinnamon lattes and freshly baked gingerbread wafted past – the fair was well and truly open and he'd never get a second chance to make a first impression.

While arranging the leaflets on a small table outside the gallery, Freya walked up the street towards him, smiling.

'Just thought I'd bring you this.' She held up a bottle bag. With her cheeks pink from the cold, and bright eyes, she looked more gorgeous than ever but Travis couldn't stop thinking about Jos. How well did he actually know her if she'd been engaged to someone like Jos: stuffy, pompous and obsessed with money – the opposite to the way Travis thought about himself?

'I didn't expect anything,' he said, trying to cover his disturbing thoughts. 'But thank you. Come in.'

'Only for a moment, I'm on the way to our stall.'

Inside, she handed over a card and a bottle of fizz. 'Congratulations.' Unlike the electrician, however, there was no warm hug or kiss on the cheek.

'Thanks,' he said, forcing a smile to his face. 'I, um . . . appreciate it.'

'No problem. I suggest you have it later rather than now though.'

'I will . . . it's, um, kind of you.'

'*Kind?*' Her brow wrinkled in puzzlement at his formal words. 'It's the least I can do, for a fellow trader.' Her eyes shone and hinted that perhaps she wished they were much more than that.

He didn't know how to react and he was angry at Jos and angry at himself for letting the man make him question everything he thought he knew about Freya and sour his thinking about her. It was stupid of him to be influenced but he couldn't simply ignore what he'd heard or the way it made him feel.

'Oh, you have customers.' She turned to see a middle-aged couple peering through the door, deciding whether to venture inside.

He swore softly then put on his cheery customer face. 'Do I? So soon? Bree's not even here.'

'Then you'd better go on the charm offensive.'

Freya marched over and opened the door. 'Morning,' she said as the woman clutched a leaflet.

'Is he open?' the man asked.

'Oh yes,' Freya said. 'Why don't you be his first customers?'

'First *ever*?' the woman said, delightedly.

'Yes.'

'In that case, we must come in. We absolutely love his pictures. He's so talented . . .'

As they gushed, Travis could only glimpse Freya's back as she hurried out of his doorway, the pompom on her hat bobbing. He was as poleaxed by her as he'd ever been in his youth, touched by her kindness yet nonplussed by Jos's disclosures.

Moments after he'd sold his first prints to the couple, Bree arrived, and in no time, the gallery began to fill up with curious locals, tourists and photo nerds. Travis had no choice but to set aside the explosive revelations.

'I am *totally* knackered,' Bree declared, flopping down in the chair in the kitchenette at lunchtime. 'Why did I let myself be talked into this?'

Travis sipped from his water bottle, parched and hoarse after a madcap morning of chatting and smiling until his jaw ached. He'd spent the morning talking cameras, signing up people for courses and selling gift vouchers for new ones in the New Year. He'd only been outside once, dashing to fetch Cumberland hot dogs from the nearest food stand.

'*Have yourself a merry little Christmas . . .*'

'I love this one!' Bree declared as the Ralph Blane classic started up again from the speakers. She took the hot dog from Travis and licked the ketchup from the end. 'Bliss. Lunch I haven't had to make. Thanks.'

'Least I could do.' He leaned against the counter, tucking into his own hot dog. 'It won't be like this every weekend, I promise. It's just the novelty of me being here and the Christmas rush. You'll probably be bored sick once January comes.'

'I don't think so. There'll be framing and the admin to do.'

'Having second thoughts?' he said.

She laughed. 'No. Even though I'm knackered, I'm enjoying it. It's so lovely not to have to talk about nappy rash and kids' TV – and actually, I like enthusing about where I live. People love your work, Trav. I'm quite enjoying basking in your limelight of a celebrity photographer.'

Travis rolled his eyes, embarrassed. 'I'm not a celebrity, I'm not even well known.'

'You could have fooled me. At least a dozen people have said they adore your work and have seen it in wildlife and photography magazines.'

'There's always some diehards. I've seen three people who've been on my courses before. They all signed up for more. I even got a booking for the Iceland tour.'

'I gave out a ton of leaflets and we've sold quite a bit of stock.'

Ping

The shop bell rang.

Bree was halfway down her hot dog and chewed furiously.

'Don't rush,' Travis ordered. 'Finish your lunch. I'll go. I recognise the woman. She's been on some of my other courses.'

Travis showed the lady in, resigning himself to a cold hot dog. While she signed up to his Landscapes of the Lakes trip, Bree came back out to serve an elderly man wanting to buy a large canvas of his favourite scene as a Christmas present for his wife.

'I asked her to marry me up there,' he said wistfully, while Bree arranged for the print to be sent to his home.

'That's romantic,' Bree said.

'Not really. She turned me down.' The old guy grinned. 'I asked her again a few months later while we were queuing for some chips and she accepted. This will make her laugh. She can't claim I didn't try to be romantic the first time.'

The afternoon went by in a flash. Every time Travis tried to grab a moment to go outside, in the hope of seeing Freya, he was pinned down in the gallery.

The sun had sunk and dusk was falling, and the torrent of customers slowed to a trickle. Bree wandered over to the kitchen to make a coffee and came back with two mugs and a raised eyebrow. 'I see Freya dropped by before I came.'

'Yes, she brought a good luck card.'

'And the bottle of fizz with the tag marked "Best wishes, F"?'

'Maybe.' He waited a few seconds before his next comment, knowing it could lead to more questions from his sister that he wasn't prepared to answer.

'You might have told me she'd been engaged to Jos Beresford.'

Bree paused, the stack of cards in her hands. 'Why would you even want to know?'

Travis looked at her. 'Touché.'

'You showed no interest in her whatsoever when you left. You never asked about her or looked her up on your rare visits so I assumed you'd moved on long ago.'

'I *have* moved on.'

'Then why would you care that she'd been engaged to Jos?' Bree scrutinised him. 'Did *she* tell you?'

'No, he did. He said she broke it off two weeks before the wedding.'

'That's true . . . but I've never spoken to Freya about it, or any of her mates. I'm older than her so we were hardly likely to be friends at school, and nowadays I don't have anything

144

to do with her other than to say "hello" if we happen to bump into each other in the shops or out walking.'

Travis wondered if there was a slight edge to Bree's tone. 'OK. It's fine. Forget I asked. It doesn't matter, anyway.'

Bree had abandoned the card stacking and fixed him with the kind of steely gaze that used to spell trouble when he was younger.

'I saw how hurt you were when you and Freya split up and I know that was what made you take off.'

'It wasn't only her,' Travis said curtly. 'It was a long time ago.'

'Exactly. You were kids and I don't hold anything against Freya now. She seems a nice enough person and she's done well for herself.' Bree gave him the laser eye. 'I take it that you *are* still interested in her now, though?'

'No. As a matter of fact, I'm not. We probably wouldn't have crossed each other's paths if she hadn't been at the cabin when I arrived, or at the traders' meeting.'

'Or pulled the electrician and roofer off other jobs to help you?'

He tried to laugh. 'She didn't as far as I'm aware. How do you know that?'

'Araya told me.'

'Jesus, this place . . .' he muttered. Bree was hitting very close to home and she didn't even know Freya had spent two nights helping him.

'It's a small town. You did grow up here so you know what it's like,' Bree said. 'As long as you're OK with the situation. I don't want you to get hurt again.'

'I don't intend to,' he muttered, which wasn't the same as 'I won't'.

A loudspeaker blared out and Travis seized the opportunity to end the conversation. 'Come on, let's close for a few minutes so we can see the switch-on. Customers will all be watching it too.'

'Yes, I'd love to, maybe I can find Gav and the kids. They must be somewhere.'

After locking up, he followed Bree into the street, though it was difficult to make their way to the market square where hundreds of locals and tourists were crowded in front of the stage area. Under clear skies, the late afternoon had turned bitingly cold and everyone was bundled up in padded coats and woolly gloves which lent a very festive atmosphere. Some folk were gathered around a glowing brazier roasting hot chestnuts or clutching steaming cups of mulled wine.

Small children shrieked with excitement from a traditional carousel. Was that Dylan waving from one of the toy cars? He wasn't sure but had a misty memory of riding in one himself, turning the wheel like a racing driver . . . He must have been barely older than Dylan was now.

With the carousel organ blending with the carols, Travis was transported back in time. The lights might be eco-friendly LEDs but that was about the only change from his youth. He remembered wandering through town with his arm around Freya's back, excited because he'd saved up enough to buy her a ring from the catalogue store.

That evening, in her room, while her mother was out, he'd proposed and the next day she'd given him the ring back – he'd been so stunned by her change of heart, that he'd refused to take it.

'There they are!' Bree said, waving in excitement as she spotted Gav and the children. 'Looks like they've been to the doughnut stall – and I told him not to let them have too much sugary stuff!'

Travis hid a smile and followed his sister to join the rest of the family. Rosie looked impossibly cute in a reindeer hat. Bree took her and planted a kiss on her rosy cheeks.

Dylan held up a half-eaten doughnut in his sugary fingers. 'Don't want any more, Unca Tardis,' he said.

Gav laughed. 'Uncle Travis might not want it.'

'Oh, I do,' he said. 'Haven't had these for years.'

Dylan giggled as Travis popped the rest of the doughnut in his mouth and made exaggerated sighs of ecstasy while he chewed it, much to Dylan's delight.

'Mmm. Delicious,' he said when he'd swallowed it.

Dylan was laughing hysterically and Rosie squealing with excitement at a balloon vendor when there were crackles from the stage microphone. The piped music ceased and faces turned towards the stage, a hush of expectation descending on the crowd.

Wearing a Santa hat and a suit, Jos was holding the microphone and in earnest conversation with Brian and a woman Travis didn't recognise.

'Jos looks as jolly as constipated bulldog,' Bree whispered in Travis's ear. 'I don't think festivity suits him.'

He smiled but was struck by an uncomfortable thought. At least Jos had made his life in Bannerdale, while Travis had been absent. No matter how much he disliked the man, Jos had been there for Freya while Travis had got as far away as possible.

He moved forward a little and caught sight of her with Mimi, standing at the side of the stage, in a cream bobble hat, looking gorgeous. Should he be relieved or glad that she and Jos had never made it up the aisle? Would he have been just as wrong for her as Jos? Had it been Jos's stolidness – his predictability – that had appealed to Freya?

'Hello, everyone,' Jos intoned. 'This is finally the moment when Bannerdale lights up. I'd like to invite Councillor Gabril to push the button.'

The councillor stepped up, and Jos started a countdown that everyone joined in with.

Ten, nine, eight . . . three, two, one!

Applause and cheering rang out as light and colour lit up the streets and the tree flicked into life. Bulbs were strung across the main street, and the lampposts were decorated with illuminated Santas, stars and holly leaves. Dylan was beside himself and asking if it was Christmas Day yet. Bree was pointing out the Christmas tree to Rosie who was reaching up as if she could catch the star at the top.

Freya was only a few metres away and Travis caught her eye. She smiled. His stomach did a flip. He was in serious trouble if she had the power to melt him with a look.

She threaded her way towards him. After a brief conversation about how the day had gone in the gallery, she issued an invitation.

'There's a load of us meeting up at the Tap Room around eight-thirty. It gives time to clear away some of the stalls before the erectors move in, or should I say the de-erectors.' She giggled. 'Oh God, I sound like Brian again. Must be the mulled wine I had from the WI stall.'

Travis laughed then hesitated. 'I was going to go home and have an early night.'

Her face fell and he felt bad. 'Well, we'll be in there if you change your mind. When I've helped Mimi and Hamish clear our stall, I'm off home for a long hot bath and a bite to eat before I go out again. Actually, Mimi's waving to me now. I'd better go. See you later – maybe.'

After locking the gallery, Travis went back to the cabin for a shower before heading again for the twinkling lights of the village, trying to put Jos's vindictive comments into perspective. He shouldn't be influenced by the tainted opinions of a bitter ex . . . Even so, coming home had been so much more complicated than he'd ever dreamed. So much more disturbing and emotional – he'd kidded himself that it was Seb who needed the support, it was him.

Chapter Sixteen

Freya spotted Travis before he saw her. Pint in hand, he was scanning the large but crowded space as if searching for familiar faces.

She was guessing he'd never been in the Tap Room before as it was a recent conversion of an old craft brewery and former mill. It had been opened out to the roof trusses with metal joists, with part of the water wheel mechanism retained at the end of the bar. A former yard and storage warehouse area to one side had its own entrance and served as a function room for parties, gigs and events.

She lifted a hand and was rewarded with a fleeting smile as he made his way over to a table that included Araya, Roxanne, Ravi and various businesspeople from the village. She'd had the bath she'd mentioned but it hadn't been as relaxing as she'd made out, because she'd been wondering about Travis's distant mood earlier in the day and at the lights switch-on.

He joined the table and everyone started chatting about the day, asking him how the launch had gone, and about his work. Freya saw him visibly relax and come to life when talking about his photography. She relaxed too, deciding that he'd simply been on edge and exhausted after the launch week and his issues with his brother.

It was a while before she had a chance for a quiet word about Seb.

'How's Seb? Have you found out any more about the man hassling him by the church?'

'No. there hasn't been a good moment to ask him so far. The situation's . . . delicate, shall we say, and I don't want to ruin any progress I might have made. Not that I'm sure I have made much progress,' Travis said gloomily. 'The really scary part is that he's not playing his music. Until a few months ago, Bree said he used to love doing gigs at the local pubs with some of his, shall we say, more supportive mates who used to look out for him. She bumped into Carly Raffaello the other night. She told Bree Seb had been invited to do a session a few times but he's turned them down flat.'

Freya winced. 'That doesn't sound good. You think if he would start playing again, it would help him regain his confidence?'

'It's worth a try.'

'Hmm.' She paused for a moment but then voiced an idea that had been forming for a few days. 'What about that?' She pointed to a poster on the wall behind him.

He twisted round to check out the poster advertising an open mic night at the Tap Room the following week.

'In theory, that's a great idea but there's no way he'd agree to it. He'd sus that straight away. I must admit I have asked him to come out for a drink sometime so here is as good a place as any but if he's seen the posters, he'd still be suspicious.'

'I thought of that. The event is in the back room where they have the gigs and functions. If you use the bar entrance and pretend you'd no idea it was on, he might not go ballistic – he might even stay and listen at least?'

Mulling it over, Travis hummed. 'I'd like to try it but still can't see him being fooled.'

'OK, hear this. Roxanne's asked me to meet up at Raffaello's for a pre-wedding counsel of war?'

'Counsel of *what*?'

'War.' Freya shrugged. 'That's what she calls it. It's meant to be a quiet drink where she can have a good bitch about all her pre-wedding moans and I can listen and agree with her. I guess I could ask her to meet here instead?'

'That's . . . nice,' he said without much enthusiasm. 'But how does that help me get Seb here?'

Freya was slightly regretting her subterfuge, but it was too late to back out. 'I thought that maybe . . . you could mention that you heard we were coming to the Tap Room and you just felt like turning up by coincidence?'

He frowned. 'Right . . . you mean, I should pretend like I'm interested in you or something and want him to be my wingman so it doesn't look weird when I walk in and you're there with Roxanne?'

She cringed, having dug a hole of her own making. 'Yeah. If it's not too much of a stretch to *act* as if you are interested in me,' she said haughtily. 'Seb might fall for it, as he spotted us the other night outside the restaurant.'

'I suppose,' Travis said with a sigh. 'It's *vaguely* plausible.'

Was he winding her up? His lack of enthusiasm was galling after she'd come up with the idea. 'Look, I'm only suggesting this to help you out! You said you were worried about him and wanted him to start playing again and I've offered a solution. It's not compulsory,' she added sniffily.

'No, No, it's a good idea. I *think*.'

'It's the only idea I have,' she said, snatching up her bag as if to leave the table.

'That's one more idea than me.'

'I'll ask Roxanne to switch venues and if you turn up, you turn up. It's up to you.' She affected a large yawn. 'It's late and I'm sure we're both done for after the past few days. I'm going home.'

'Wait, Freya. Thanks for the suggestion. I'll, er, hint to Seb that I want him to come with me on Tuesday. But if he *does* agree, you'll have to act all surprised to see me and maybe annoyed and aloof?'

Freya shrugged on her coat. 'I can promise you *that* part will definitely be easy.'

After mulling over a variety of reasons for switching the pre-wedding drinks to the Tap Room, Freya decided on the simplest: honesty. Roxanne was happy to oblige and seemed quite excited at the prospect of taking part in a 'sting' on Seb.

One they'd positioned themselves where they had a clear view of the door to the bar, Freya placed a cocktail on the table in front of Roxanne.

'Seb must never get to hear of the plan. He'll kill Travis if he finds out we've been cooking up a scheme and I don't think I'd be his favourite person either. That's *if* Travis can even get him in here without him noticing the open mic sign by the function room door.'

'I feel like we're in *Line of Duty* on an undercover operation . . .'

Roxanne sounded gleeful but Freya's laughter was mostly nerves. Tonight could go horribly wrong for so many reasons. So far, there was no sign of Travis, though he'd been primed to turn up about fifteen minutes after Roxanne and her, if possible.

Her phone pinged and she scrolled through the screen and snorted. 'It's Mum. I get alerts when she posts. They're onboard ship now. Prepare yourself.'

Roxanne took the phone and her perfectly waxed brows shot up her forehead. 'Oh my God, is that Neil in the budgie smugglers?'

'I'm afraid so. I think they were a freebie and she hates to waste anything.'

'Ew. I can't unsee that but your mum looks amazing in that crochet beach cover-up. Do you know where she got it from? Don't tell her but I wouldn't mind one for my honeymoon.'

'I think she might have mentioned the brand in her hashtags,' Freya said, trying not to focus on Neil's turquoise trunks. As a builder, he kept himself in reasonable shape for a man of his age, but Daniel Craig he wasn't. Freya allowed herself the thought that the only man who *might* look good in them was Travis.

'Can you forward the post to me so I can check out the tags?' Roxanne said.

'Sure.' Freya did as requested then closed the app.

'Trunks aside, they do look happy,' Roxanne said.

'I know. It's lovely for Mum because she wasn't sure how they'd manage sharing a small cabin on their first big holiday together.' Freya had never seen her mum look so excited as in the past few posts from her cruise. Neil seemed very happy in their WhatsApp calls too but then, they were on holiday.

'Talking of romance . . .' Roxanne said with a mischievous

154

glint in her eye. 'You and Travis. He's meant to be pretending that he's interested in you – though he's not really – to persuade Seb to come in here with him because you might be here on the off-chance, rather than any other of ten drinking venues in the village?'

'Not on the *off-chance*,' Freya corrected. 'Travis has told Seb that he heard me mention we were coming here for a pre-wedding drink. So, it's not a coincidence.'

Roxanne rolled her eyes. 'What a tangled web you weave and I can't for the life of me think how the two of you are going to convince anyone that you're the slightest bit interested in each other.' She punctuated this less-than-innocent statement with a slurp of her cocktail.

Freya decided it was best not to rise to the bait and started a conversation about the wedding flowers: an issue she knew had caused more 'wedmin' and angst than almost any other aspect of the nuptials.

As expected, Roxanne immediately threw up her hands and launched into the latest update.

'Well, the florist *finally* managed to track down some flowers that are native to St Lucia, though Ravi found out how much they were going to cost and said he thought that Flowergate was getting out of hand, and then we had a big row but he got bleeped by the hospital and by the time he'd got back, he was too knackered to care, so we *are* having the flowers and my dad is so happy and they will look amazing so everything is fine.'

When Roxanne paused for breath, Freya commented, 'Well, it'll be lovely to have a nod to your dad's family.' Mr Jameson had been born in St Lucia before his parents had emigrated to the UK when he was a baby, and Roxanne had become fixated on the flowers as a way of 'bringing both families together in symbolic yet meaningful way'.

'Yes. So that's done and we've almost finished the table plan. You'll be on the top table, of course, next to Nico. I can't wait for you two to meet each other.'

'What about Nico's partner?' Freya said, her antennae twitching. 'Won't they want to sit together?'

'Oh, they've split up,' Roxanne said airily. 'Didn't I tell you? She went off with one of the directors of her advertising firm. Nico was heartbroken to start with, though Ravi thinks he's better off without her. He's single again – like you – so that's made the top table planning and walking out of church so much simpler. I always think it's a bit weird when a best man and chief bridesmaid have to link arms and walk down the aisle, when they're married to other people. At least you'll look like you could be a *real* couple.'

Freya had no answer to this but fortunately, it was the exact moment when Travis and Seb made their entrance into the bar.

Roxanne dug Freya in the ribs. 'Uh huh! It's them!' she said in a stage whisper. 'Should we act as if we don't want them to notice us – or we do?' Roxanne said with a smirk.

'Try to act normally,' Freya said, having no idea how to do that.

Travis was visibly on edge, checking his watch, smiling too much – only someone who knew him as well as she would guess. Surely Seb would have detected Travis was twitchy too? For now he seemed OK, chatting to one of the waiting staff while Travis bought the drinks.

She told herself to chill: the plan was going better than she'd hoped – so far.

A few minutes later, the two men made their way through the packed pub towards their table.

'Fancy seeing you here!' Roxanne declared with a level of enthusiasm that made Freya cringe.

Seb smirked. 'Yeah. Fancy that . . .'

'It's heaving in here. Why don't you sit down?' Roxanne patted the bench seat next to her. 'There's plenty of room if Freya squeezes up. Seb can sit opposite.'

'Thanks,' Travis said, sliding onto the seat next to Freya. 'You OK for drinks?'

'Fine,' she murmured.

Seb grinned. 'It's busy in here for midweek.'

Freya felt Travis stiffen with tension. It was clear Seb hadn't cottoned on to the event yet, though goodness knew how. This thought didn't fill her with joy; it might have been better if he had realised it was open mic night yet still agreed to go.

Freya started up a conversation about the Christmas Fair, and how well it had gone, and a mercifully brief conversation about Roxanne's wedding followed. She didn't mind what they talked about as long as Seb seemed relaxed. After a while, he excused himself to go to the gents'.

Roxanne exhaled and fanned herself. 'This isn't fun. I think I'm going to have a heart attack.'

'You are?' Travis muttered. 'You should be in my position. Is it normal to be terrified of your little brother?'

'It is if you've lured him here under false pretences,' Freya muttered. 'Oh God, is that a sound check?' She heard a mic announcement from the function room. 'How has he not realised?'

'Maybe he has and doesn't care,' Roxanne murmured.

'And pigs might fly,' Travis said. 'Uh huh. He's coming back . . .'

Seb returned, still smiling and seemingly unaware of the deception. He settled back in the seat and started scrolling through his phone.

'Hey, man! Long time, no see!'

Freya saw Travis's face blanch as a rail-thin man in leather trousers slapped Seb on the back.

He turned and grinned. 'Hello, Nate.'

'It's good to see you,' Nate said. 'Are you here for the open mic thing?'

Seb frowned. 'What open mic thing?'

Nate flipped a thumb towards the function room. 'It's in there. Anyone can turn up. Starts in an hour, you just need to put your name down.'

'I didn't know it was happening. I'm here for a quiet pint with my brother and his friends . . .' He turned to Travis and gave him a beaming smile. Freya had a horrible feeling that Travis was in very hot water. 'Aren't we, bro?'

'Oh, OK, but if you fancy it another time . . . At least come in and listen,' Nate said. 'We miss you, man. We'd love you to start playing again. Are you sure you won't join us tonight just for one number?'

'Sorry, I haven't got my guitar,' Seb muttered.

'OK, but any time, you know where to find me,' Nate said.

Nate walked off and Seb stood up. 'I'm sorry, ladies, but I'm going to have to leave you. I need to have a word with my brother. I'll see you outside, Travis.' He marched off towards the door.

'Oh dear, that went well,' Roxanne murmured before slurping up her cocktail.

'Shit.' Travis rubbed his hand over his mouth in despair.

Freya let out a groan. 'Sorry. I wish I'd never suggested it!'

'No, it's me who should be sorry for even thinking it would work.' He hooked his jacket off his chair. 'I must go. If I don't open the gallery in the morning, you'll know there's been a murder and I'm the victim.'

Chapter Seventeen

Seb rounded on Travis the moment they were outside the bar. 'Why did you bring me here? I knew there was something up, you were as twitchy as hell, but I thought it was because of Freya. Now, I'm guessing it nothing to do with her, did it?'

'I only thought you might like to join in.'

'Join in?' Seb scoffed. 'Man, you can't just turn up and play in front of people like it's karaoke night. I don't have my guitar if you hadn't noticed.'

'You could sign up now and go and get it from the flat?'

'You are joking?' Seb said, then shook his head. 'No, it's worse. You're *serious*. I haven't rehearsed. I haven't even sung or played for weeks. These events are for artists to showcase their latest work, not make an arse of themselves.'

Travis held up his hands in surrender. 'OK. OK. Simmer down. I just thought it was a safe space. That it would be a way in again . . .'

'To what? To be the laughing stock? There's no safe space when you perform. You go out on a limb; you take the risk and the only way you can even contemplate that is if you spend every waking minute preparing.'

'I'm sorry, I thought you could just rock up and play. Like in the old days. With the band . . .' Travis stopped speaking, aware of how limp that sounded.

'The old days are gone.' Seb stormed off, leaving Travis standing in the street, swearing at himself. His worst expectations of the night had been realised and now he'd lost any trust he'd built up with Seb, if he'd ever done that.

He'd also worried and embarrassed Freya in front of Roxanne. It wasn't her fault at all, it was his for agreeing to such a scheme. Great.

He thought about going straight back into the bar and leaving his brother, but changed his mind. He wasn't going to give up yet. He had questions to ask and since the genie was now out of the bottle, this was as good a time as any.

A chink of light glimmered beneath the flat door, so at least Seb hadn't gone to one of the other pubs as Travis had feared.

Bracing himself for a broadside, he rapped on the door. 'Seb?' There was no answer.

'Please let me in. I swear I'm not here to lecture you.'

After an agonising few seconds, the door was pulled open. 'That would be a first but you'd better come in before the neighbours complain about your whining.' With a stony glare, Seb held the door back so Travis could enter.

Travis prepared to grovel as he'd never done before. 'I'm sorry. I shouldn't have done that to you. It was crass, and stupid. I ought to have asked you.'

'I still wouldn't have played.'

'OK.'

He didn't know what to say next in case it ignited another row but he couldn't simply stand silently with Seb glaring at him, squaring up to each other like boxers in the ring.

'If you don't want to talk about it, I can go away again,' he said as neutrally as he could. 'But I do care, and if someone's been hassling you . . .'

'Hassling me?'

'Yeah. Freya happened to mention she'd seen a guy arguing with you outside the church.'

Seb curled a lip. 'She told you, then? I knew she would.'

'She's worried about you.'

'So you're both interfering now? A regular social work team. Great.'

'You keep Freya out of this!' Travis snapped then forced himself to calm down. 'Is there anything I need to know? Anything I can do to help or get this guy off your back.'

Seb glowered at him. 'Only if you want to cause more trouble between me and my mates. It was Fenno, and he was a bit lairy because he'd been to a mate's party. I told him to grow up and he didn't like it but that was it. We've made up now.' Seb made a kissy kissy sound. 'OK with you?'

'Fenno . . .' Travis shook his head slowly. 'I might have known.'

'Then, hurrah! Aren't you clever?'

'There's no need to be sarcastic. I'm not clever, I just care about you and I want you to be happy.'

'As if it was that easy,' Seb snapped, then went on angrily, 'I know you think you're being helpful. Really though, what do you know? You do what you *love* for a living. What do you actually know about wasting your life in a job you don't want to do and that will go on forever?'

'Then do something different,' Travis threw back. 'Screw wasting your life. Try and make it with your music.'

Seb scoffed. 'You live in Cloud Cuckoo land. I'll never make it like you have, so stop thinking I can!'

Despair filled Travis, followed by the chill of deep sadness. 'You won't make it with that attitude. You're your own worst enemy!'

He'd meant to jolt Seb out of his inertia, but he immediately wished he could claw back every word.

'I think you should leave and don't try and manage me again or we really will fall out.' Seb opened the front door and Travis walked out, hearing the door slam behind him.

Chapter Eighteen

'Are you ready?'
'Shouldn't I be asking you that?' Freya said to Roxanne as they shivered in the vestry of Bannerdale church.

Roxanne shimmered like an ice princess in her white sequinned dress and fur-trimmed cloak. They'd been left alone briefly while Roxanne's dad had nipped to the loo for a 'last-minute pee' and the vicar was touching up her lipstick in the cloakroom mirror.

Freya resisted the urge to rub at her lower arms to get the blood flowing again. It was a perfect day for a winter wedding, with snow still lying in the churchyard and frost sparkling like a million diamonds. However, the elbow-length sleeves of a faux-fur bolero over a satin slip dress weren't up to the chill of a Lakeland day when frost still lay on the grass in the afternoon.

'You must be freezing,' Roxanne said. 'I *knew* I should have brought hot toddies.'

'Later!' Freya said, disguising the chattering of her teeth with laughter. 'Or we might not make it into the church.'

Roxanne didn't laugh. 'I can see the goosebumps. I *knew* I should have chosen long sleeves but the short ones look so much better and I promise you'll be warm at the reception. That blush pink really suits you. I'm so envious of you with that willowy figure.'

Freya felt embarrassed. 'Thanks, but you're the bride and you look completely *amazing*.'

'Thank you . . . but . . .' Roxanne touched Freya's bare wrist. 'Are *you* ready?' Roxanne asked. 'I'm so grateful you agreed to be bridesmaid. I know it was a big ask . . . It's bound to stir up old feelings.' She didn't say Jos's name out loud but Freya knew who her friend was alluding to.

If Roxanne was jittery, she didn't show it, unlike Freya who was a glutinous mass of nerves. How pathetic was that? The bridesmaid was supposed to be the cool, calm and collected one.

'Of course. I'm fine.'

Roxanne gave her the gentlest of hugs.

'It is an honour and a privilege to be your bridesmaid and this is your day. Yours and Ravi's. Let's do this.'

Roxanne's dad emerged from the loo. 'Eee. That's better!'

'Glad to hear it, Dad, but you might like to do up your fly before we walk down the aisle.'

Freya suppressed a giggle as he glanced down in horror at his trousers.

'Always a good idea,' said the vicar with a smile. 'Now, shall we do this?'

Roxanne's father took his daughter's arm. 'You look beautiful, love.'

The tender endearment cut through Freya like a knife. They could almost have been echoes of the words her mum might have used on her wedding day that never was. The one that was meant to be perfect and she'd bailed out of, almost at the last minute. No wonder Jos was hurt. He wasn't a bad man, just not the man she could have made a lifetime commitment to.

The organ volume rose with the triumphant notes of the 'Wedding March' and they were off, Freya a few feet behind the bride, gliding up the aisle of Bannerdale church.

Her smile fixed in place, she focused on Roxanne: it was her day, her moment. Freya was solemn yet joyful, telling herself she was invisible compared to her friend – a dull pinprick of light in the glare of the sun.

She knew a few of the people in the church; the odd one or two or might have been potential guests at her own big day. She was rather relieved that her mother was probably lying on a steamer chair on the deck of a cruise ship, as she'd be unable to resist making some pointed comment about Jos.

Ravi gazed at Roxanne with total devotion and her friend was equally smitten, neither of them apparently with a moment's doubt about committing to each other for the rest of their lives – in theory, at least. How wonderful to have that certainty, thought Freya, taking the bouquet for safekeeping. How terrifying . . .

'Dearly beloved . . .'

They were off: ten minutes away – maybe less – from a lifetime's commitment. So simple and yet so impossible to comprehend.

It was over. On Nico's arm, Freya followed the bride and groom out into the churchyard, the guests spilling out behind them. They huddled together in groups for warmth, like the penguins in one of Travis's photos.

'Woah!'

Nico steadied Freya as her heel slipped on the icy flagstones outside the church. 'OK?' he asked.

'Yes, just about. Thanks.'

'Mind out, Julie, you don't want to go arse over tit,' Roxanne's dad muttered behind them.

'Paul, please don't use language like that in church!'

'We're not *in* church now, my dearest, and it's bloody lethal out here. Why haven't they put some salt down. Why did we have to have a wedding when it's minus five? We can't keep people out here for long. Your mother will have hypothermia!'

'Shh.'

Freya had to laugh, it was either that or succumb to the sub-zero conditions along with Roxanne's granny. She tried not to shiver, as the photographer arranged her and the best man with the bride and groom for the first group shot.

He had to shout to be heard over a group of kids having a snowball fight with some lingering overnight snow they'd scraped off the tombstones.

'Ouch!' Freya cried as a bullet-hard ball of ice hit her on the side of the arm.

'Will you please stop that, Damien!' his mother cried as the culprit danced in front of the bridal party, pulling faces at the camera.

'Just the main bridal party in this shot,' the photographer cried in despair.

Damien's mum yanked his arm. 'Behave or you'll go home this minute!' she ordered.

'Good! I'm bored! And my tie is hurting my neck.'

'Sorry,' she mouthed, dragging the boy away.

'Can we please start now?' the photographer wailed. 'I'm

on a very tight schedule and as you've noticed, it's a bit chilly.'

Freya stood next Nico, willing the whole thing to be over as quickly as possible and hoping her teeth didn't chatter too loudly.

The photographer raised the camera, shouted 'Big smiles!' took a step back and vanished.

Chapter Nineteen

'Oh my God! He's fallen over the wall!' Roxanne's scream reverberated off the tombstones.

Ravi and Nico, however, were already on their way to the church gate.

'It's four feet down to that car park!' Roxanne screeched. 'He might be dead! Help! Is there a doctor in the house?'

From the throng of guests at least ten people dashed forward, abandoning handbags and top hats on the ground.

'I don't think he'll be short of medical attention,' Freya said, watching the guests swarming towards the photographer. 'You stay here with your dad while I take a look.'

'Be careful. I don't want you slipping down there too!'

Freya teetered her way to the edge of the churchyard where the photographer was lying in a space marked 'Reserved: Wedding Cars' surrounded by medics in heels and morning suits issuing orders to each other. He'd obviously lost his footing and toppled backwards over the retaining wall.

The non-medical guests gathered around Freya, pointing at the scene below.

'Oh, the poor man!'

'He's not dead. He's sitting up.'

'Quick, Darren! Get this on TikTok!'

With a whole crash team of consultants and nursing staff, the photographer was soon being covered in jackets and assessed by Ravi, Nico and their mates.

'I'm OK,' the photographer insisted.

'Don't move,' Ravi ordered. 'You might have a head or spinal injury.'

'I didn't hit my head but my ankle hurts like hell. More importantly, I've broken my best camera. It's worth eight grand!'

'That's what insurance is for; you need to go to hospital.'

'No, I'm OK. My camera . . .' he wailed.

'Sorry, an ambulance is already on its way,' Nico cut in. He turned to Ravi. 'Look, mate. You go to Roxanne. I'll take charge here until the paramedics arrive.'

The photographer tried to sit up again. 'I'm fine. Bloody hell, I've got the complete cast of *Casualty* looking after me, already!'

'We're real doctors,' Ravi said stonily then declared: 'I'm not leaving you.'

Standing beside Freya, Roxanne burst into tears.

Freya put her arm around her. 'It'll be OK,' she soothed, leading her friend back to the church. 'Let's be grateful he's OK and we had so many experts on the spot. I'm sure someone else can look after the guy now.'

Inside, the vicar took charge of Roxanne and asked the guests not to go outside. Word came through that the ambulance had arrived and the photographer had been persuaded to go to hospital.

'*Obviously* I'm worried about the photographer,' Roxanne whispered to Freya. 'But we've only just started the photos and he was booked to stay until the end of the reception.'

'There will be lots of other people taking pictures,' Freya soothed.

'On their phones, and I bet most are of the photographer falling over! We won't have a proper record of the day. Oh, this was meant to be perfect.' Roxanne fanned at her teary eyes. 'The best day of my life and it's all turning into a disaster.'

'Not quite,' Freya said, handing Roxanne a clean tissue. 'At least you did turn up for the ceremony.'

'True,' Roxanne said, with a gentle hug for Freya. 'Are you OK?'

'I'm fine,' Freya said, although she could no longer feel her toes. 'And as for the photos . . . I do have an idea . . .'

The moment she'd given voice to the thought that had entered her mind, she regretted speaking.

'What?' Roxanne's eyes lit up hopefully.

'I could try Travis. He used to do weddings when he was younger.' Freya avoided adding that Travis had mentioned he'd loathed taking wedding photos and had only done it to earn a bit of money when he was starting out.

Roxanne lowered her tissue. 'Do you think he would?'

'I don't know. He might, though he does have the gallery to run.'

Roxanne hugged her again. 'You are the best bridesmaid ever.'

'He might not be able to!' Freya warned.

'If anyone can persuade him, it's you.'

'I wouldn't bet on it after the cock-up with Seb . . .' she muttered to herself, leaving Roxanne huddled in the vestry under an old surplice with her mum fussing over her like a mother hen.

Freya poked her head through the door of the bridal car and slapped on a winning smile for the chauffeur. 'Any chance of a lift to town?'

It was only a short walk but in a long dress and heels, she wasn't sure she'd make it without adding to the casualty list. 'If you could drop me outside the new photo gallery and wait for me, please?'

A few minutes later, she was hitching up her dress to climb out of the Rolls and tottering up to the shop.

She could see Travis and Bree inside by the desk, talking to two customers. He looked busy, probably making a sale – and what would Bree think of her interrupting them?

If anyone can persuade him, it's you.

Roxanne had far too much confidence in her. Maybe she was the last person Travis would want to drop everything for to spend a day doing a job he loathed. She'd heard nothing from him since the open mic debacle.

Travis was at the door in a moment, staring at the Rolls on the double yellows outside his shop.

'Freya? What are you doing here? You're supposed to be at the wedding?'

'Don't worry, I haven't chickened out this time. Ravi and Roxy are married but the photographer fell over the church wall and has had to go to hospital for a check-up. His camera's ruined.'

'The poor bloke!' Travis's face was a picture of horror. 'I bet that kit was worth a fortune.'

'His *kit?*' Freya echoed.

Bree and the two customers were staring at her too.

172

'You'd better come into the back,' he said. 'Bree, would you mind looking after these customers, please? Sorry,' he added, ushering Freya into the back.

'Are *you* OK?' he asked.

'Yes. People keep asking me but yes. I came to . . . well . . . to ask a favour. A huge favour and it's a bit of a cheek. A *massive* cheek, actually, but anyway, there are people snapping away with phones and cameras but they're all *amateurs* and Roxanne wanted something special and I said I – I would ask—'

She faltered as Travis stared at her in naked astonishment. 'Look, forget I asked. It was a stupid idea because you're busy and you said you'd hated doing weddings and you have customers – I'll go.'

'Freya!' Her rested his hand on wrist briefly. 'Take a breath.'

She found her chest so tight with cold and rushing that it was difficult to gain enough oxygen to speak again.

'Are you saying you want me to take some wedding pictures right *now*?' Travis said while Freya steadied her breathing.

She nodded. 'I'd be so grateful. Roxanne would too. Everyone would.'

'No need for gratitude. I'll speak to Bree and get my camera – and here.' He pulled his coat from the peg and thrust it into her arms. 'Put this on before you freeze to death.'

Chapter Twenty

Outside Bannerdale Church, Travis unloaded his gear from the rear of his car. While he collected his equipment Freya had gone on ahead in the Rolls to let Roxanne and the wedding party know he was on his way.

Adrenaline pumped through him. He hadn't done a wedding for over ten years, and only then because a close friend had asked, and he'd needed the cash to fund a foreign tour. He didn't have the right kit and lenses, he was horribly rusty with photographing people – and the expectations on him would be sky-high.

Yet how could he possibly have refused Freya? It was fortunate that Bree had called in and was able to look after the shop for him. Otherwise, he'd have had to close, which he could ill afford to this near to Christmas.

When she'd turned up at the gallery, her cheeks pink with cold, looking stunning in that dress – he'd almost dropped the picture glass he'd been holding. His throat had turned dry and he'd been thrust back to the night he'd proposed to her and they'd decided to run away.

She'd been beautiful then and she still was now, swamped by his mountain jacket, waving frantically from the church door with the rest of the wedding party.

He came to his senses. Freya needed him – but she didn't need *him*. She'd only come flying into the shop because she wanted his professional skills.

With his camera and tripod, he joined them by the front door. The bridge, groom, best man and Roxanne's parents looked at him as if he was their saviour. His stomach fluttered with a rare dose of nerves. This wasn't his field of expertise and very different from his day job. So many times he'd gone out looking for an animal and failed to see it. That was nature and there was usually another chance. Not today: this was – hopefully – once in a lifetime and he dare not disappoint.

'Thank God you're here, lad!' Mr Jameson said, shaking his hand furiously. Travis remembered the man from school when he'd come in to help with rugby practice. He'd actually encouraged Travis to join a club but he'd been too interested in heading for the hills at the weekends.

'Lucky I wasn't out on the fells leading a course,' he said, trying to manage expectations and remind the party of his real job. He smiled, realising they needed him to take charge and be confident. 'In view of the time and the temperature, we'll just take a few pictures out here in the churchyard and the bulk at the reception,' he said. 'The Langdale Manor has beautiful grounds from what I can remember.'

'It's the best hotel in the Lakes,' Roxanne's mother declared then rubbed her hands together nervously. 'Are you sure you know what you're doing?'

'Mum!' Roxanne cried. 'Travis is famous.'

'Oh, I'm sorry. I thought he only did squirrels?'

Travis saw Freya cringe but he grinned, highly amused. 'I'll do my best given the short notice, Mrs Jameson. Shall we grab a few group shots so we can all get out of this freezing weather and over to the hotel?'

Drawing on all his old skills from his past, Travis marshalled the immediate wedding party and a few close relatives and friends together. It wasn't like lying in wait for a pine marten or a grizzly bear; in many ways it was much less predictable . . .

Calling people to order, getting them all to smile and look at the camera when they were nervous, hated being the centre of attention, were cold, hungry and probably a bit bored, was never easy.

It didn't help that his camera kept being drawn to Freya, focusing on tiny details that made him want to linger forever. The colour of her dress was perfect for her; he wasn't sure how to describe it except it matched the rosy hue of her cheeks. Even the nape of her neck was a work of art, a few wispy tendrils of hair tickling the bare skin. He'd never wanted her as much as he did now – which was inconvenient when they were in the middle of a hundred wedding guests.

He dragged his attention back to the family shots. He'd abandoned a group shot of everyone since some of the older and youngest guests had already been taken to the hotel to keep warm.

He managed a couple of pictures of Roxanne and Ravi together in the churchyard before suggesting – firmly – that it was time for everyone to head for the hotel as the bride was turning blue.

So, he thought as he drove to the hotel, the first part of the job was over. Now, all he had to do was spend an hour

176

shooting a few photos in the grounds and function room, then leave them to it.

Driving through the stone pillars at the entrance to the Langdale Manor took his breath away momentarily. The building was even grander and more exclusive than his memories of it. His mum had briefly had a job as a chamber maid there and taken him with her one day and it had seemed like a medieval castle. This was no surprise, as the place had been built for a Victorian industrialist, with towers and a crenelated roof resembling a fairy tale palace. The grounds stretched down in terraces to the lakeshore, with a range of high fells opposite reflected in the still waters.

Most of the guests were inside, doubtless quaffing mulled wine by the log fires, but the bride and groom – with Freya – were waiting by the main entrance. Freya was swaddled in his coat and a pair of monogrammed hotel wellies, and some genius from the hotel seemed to have supplied Roxanne and Ravi with full-length puffer coats.

'We absolutely *must* have some pictures of the two of us by the boat house if it's OK?' Roxanne asked. 'It's so beautiful with the lake behind it and the fells topped with snow. It was going to be one of our hero shots for the album.'

Travis could hardly say no and in truth, he was also entranced by the location. It would be no hardship to take some photos there.

'Why not?' he said.

'Freya, would you come with us to hold my bouquet?' Roxanne asked sweetly.

'Of course,' Freya said, taking the flowers and catching Travis's eye. 'Thank you,' she mouthed.

He felt he'd been conferred a favour by a beautiful but

177

haughty princess. His pulse skittered. Hadn't their relationship always been like that?

'Here's the transport,' Ravi said as a golf buggy glided towards them.

They all squeezed in, Travis sitting in the back seat next to Freya, trying not to get any of his gear on her dress.

'I am grateful,' she murmured as they were driven past statues and terraced lawns to the lakeshore, where a stone boat house stood at the water's edge, a mini castle in its own right.

'It's no problem . . .' Travis said.

Roxanne was helped out of the buggy by Ravi, her face rapt. 'That's the honeymoon suite on top of the boat house,' she said, breathily. 'We're spending the night there before we fly off on honeymoon tomorrow.'

Travis tried not to think of spending the night there with Freya.

'Sounds great,' he said gruffly, avoiding her eye. 'Now, guys, I think if you both stand *here*, we'll have all the drama of the fells behind you.'

Freya stood by, holding the bouquet when required and the cloak for a few minutes while Roxanne posed in her sleeveless dress as if it was the middle of the summer. Travis had already noticed the light softening and the sun slipping lower towards the fell tops. In this 'golden hour' the light hit Freya perfectly, giving her skin and hair a soft glow.

'Could we just have a teeny few on the jetty?' Roxanne wheedled.

Ravi intervened. 'Roxy. I expect Travis wants to get back to work.'

'To *work*? Oh – oh, I thought he was staying for the

reception. There's the first dance too – and the party. Our real – I mean the first – photographer was booked for a full day.' Roxanne smiled sweetly at Travis. 'We will pay you the full fee, and a bonus, of course.'

'It's not that,' Travis began to protest.

Freya jumped in. 'I only asked Travis to come and take a few pictures at the church in an emergency,' she said. 'I didn't ask him to stay all day.'

'Oh. Oh . . .' Roxanne's face crumpled. 'I understand. I just – I kind of thought that as he was here already with all his equipment, he might . . .'

'I . . . could stay for a short time,' he said. 'Maybe do some poses with the cake? That sort of thing?'

Roxanne's face lit up. 'Would you?'

'I'll have to phone Bree. She's looking after the gallery,' he said, imagining his sister's reaction when she heard she'd be left alone.

He kicked himself for even offering but how could he turn Roxanne down?

'Are you sure?' Freya said, coming closer.

Sure? He wasn't sure about anything, other than she looked amazing and was setting off fireworks inside him every time he looked at her, or heard her voice . . .

'Yes,' he lied. 'I'll call Bree now and tell her to close early if she can't cope.'

'But this is your busy time. You've just opened and it's almost Christmas.'

'It's half-past two now. We close at four-thirty. I'll offer Bree the fee Roxanne is paying me.'

Freya nodded though there was doubt in her eyes. 'If you *really* don't mind.'

'It's your friend's special day,' he said with a smile. 'How could I mind?'

While the three of them went into the hotel, Travis called Bree, expecting the hairdryer treatment down the phone.

'It's been manic,' she said, which caused Travis to feel a fresh pang of guilt. 'But I've managed. In fact, I've rather enjoyed it. Bet I've sold a lot more than you would have.'

'I don't doubt it,' Travis said, amused and secretly proud of his sister's competitive spirit. 'You're doing a stellar job and I've got something that might alleviate the pain of you being thrown in at the deep end.'

Sure enough the offer of a substantial fee, more than he could possibly pay her for her shift, was enough to console her considerably.

'I can't take all your fee, though!' she said. 'I'll share it.'

'We'll see,' said Travis. 'I haven't shown them the pictures yet. They might change their minds about the cash when they see them.'

'Don't be daft,' Bree scoffed. 'You'll do a much better job than that bloke they'd booked originally. Have you heard how he is by the way?'

'Just cuts and bruises apparently, though he's still there having a scan to double check. Thank you, Bree, I do appreciate it. Lock up for me, please, will you? I've a feeling this might go on a bit.'

Chapter Twenty-One

Freya's place on the top table gave her a bird's eye view of Travis, taking photos of the speeches, the couple posed by cake and candid shots of the guests. However, they were both far too busy with their duties to speak to each other.

She was seated next to Nico, whose speech about Ravi's adventures as a medical student brought the house down, though Roxanne and her mother were almost hiding behind their menu cards at several points, wondering what he was going to say next.

He'd pitched it exactly right and left everyone with a toast to the happy couple. Mr Jameson left everyone dabbing their eyes with his heartfelt speech to his daughter and her new husband. It was sincere and gently humorous, and not too rehearsed.

Freya would have been made of stone not to imagine her own father standing up and wishing her a 'lifetime of happiness', though she had no recollection of his face and had never heard his voice apart from a video of him telling a joke at a family party.

A realisation socked her in the gut: could his passing be one of the reasons she couldn't imagine a stable future for herself? Even if she didn't consciously recall him, she must have some memories of him: like treasure on the bottom of the sea, lying too deep to reach or even see, yet there all the same.

'Here. Have this.'

She felt a whisper against her ear and Nico's fingers brush hers under the table. He'd pushed the rose-pink handkerchief from his morning jacket into her hand.

She reached up to her cheek and found it damp with tears.

'It's all very emotional. I'm almost in bits myself.'

His cheeky smile told her otherwise. He thought she was crying at Mr Jameson's speech, little did he know it was for a loss she'd never really mourned in the first place, and perhaps for the loss of what might have been: relationships, children . . .

She smiled. 'It is. Thanks.'

It had been dark for several hours by the time the meal and the speeches were over. Freya got up, longing to seek out Travis to thank him but Roxanne wanted to speak to her.

'Travis is a total star. I know I shouldn't have kept him here but I did want the photos and also – I wondered if *you* wanted him to stay here longer?'

'Roxy! That's outrageous.'

'Sorry, it was wrong of me. Have you been OK?'

'Yes, until you told me that.'

'Come on, you know the bride is always on matchmaking opportunity. You now have Nico and Travis to choose from.'

Before Freya could protest, Roxanne hugged her. 'I've had such a wonderful day. I just want everyone to be as happy as I feel with Ravi.'

Freya couldn't be cross with her friend for long and especially not on her wedding day. 'I am happy. I've had a fantastic time and I still am, and more important, I have loved being a part of your special day. Ravi is a brilliant guy and I can see how much you love each other. That's all I could ever ask for.'

'Oh, don't set me off!' Roxanne cried. 'I've already had to retouch my makeup three times.'

'It's true. Today has been . . . even better than I expected.'

'And Travis being here isn't a small part of that? He's been amazing.' Roxanne turned her head to indicate Travis. He was, finally, taking a break, sipping a pint of Coke by the bar, and looking, Freya admitted, a little frazzled but absolutely gorgeous. Her heart skipped several beats. The way he'd stepped in was chivalrous. 'I'm not sure he'd have done it for anyone else but you.'

Freya snorted. 'He would.'

'Hmm . . .'

Ravi arrived, slipping his arms around his wife's waist. 'Roxy, the band are ready to set up. They're double checking what you want them to play for our first dance?'

'I remember the days of arguments about it and hope I said something easy as I've had rather a lot of champagne.'

'It'll come as a surprise, then,' and he led her away.

They were the picture of newlywed bliss, Freya thought, fuelled by a lot of champagne. Finally, the relentless tide of romance and high emotions – not to mention the fact she'd been up since five a.m. – had worn her down. There'd been so many points at which she'd told herself: *this could have been me*. So many times, she'd asked herself: *what if?* What if . . . what?

Once again, she chased away the fruitless thoughts and made her way over to the bar. She took her wine and turned round to find Travis standing beside a pillar, almost hidden by a large potted palm – with his lens trained on *her*.

Noticing her a fraction too late, he lowered the camera hastily. Freya held his gaze, daring him to look away and after a few moments' hesitation, he walked over to join her.

Although she was sure he had been taking pictures of her specifically, it seemed arrogant to ask.

'How's it going?' They both said the same phrase at once and both laughed out loud.

'You go . . .' Travis started, overlapped by Freya with, 'You speak first . . .'

The next second consisted of them both with mouths clamped shut until Freya broke the deadlock: 'How are you? Have you had chance for a break?'

'Not much but I don't need one. The time's flown by.'

She wasn't sure she believed him. 'Have you eaten?'

'The staff offered me some food but I was too busy to eat. I've lain on mountains and in bird hides for hours on end. I'm used to harsh environments.' He grinned.

'Is this one?'

'It could have been, but to be honest, it hasn't been as challenging as I expected.'

Freya frowned, not quite sure of his meaning. 'In what way?'

'Everyone's behaved, by and large, and been willing to have their photo taken.' He smiled. 'Once the fizz was flowing, most of the guests unwound and I got some pretty good candid shots. I'd much rather take those than the formal poses.'

'More like capturing wildlife?' Freya said, enjoying the twinkle in his eye that reminded her of the old Travis.

'Much more. That's all we are really, isn't it? Wild animals with a veneer of civility. Although I've done weddings where there's been some pretty vicious behaviour.'

'What?' Freya said. 'Actual fights?'

'Fist fights. Cat fights. Verbal venom. If you've ever seen hares boxing or two stags locking horns, you're prepared for a wedding and before you ask, I did keep shooting at times, just in case evidence was required.'

Freya sipped her wine and giggled. 'Thank goodness that's not happened today.'

Travis leaned in towards her. '*Yet.*'

'I know I've said it before but thank you for agreeing to this. It's meant the world to Roxy – and I can't wait to see the pictures.' She had a vision of his camera again, trained on her from behind the pillar. What else had he captured? 'Um. Any chance of me taking a sneaky look now?'

'Sorry. Nice try but no can do. The bride gets first view.'

'Of course,' she said hastily, embarrassed for asking. 'It's Roxy's day. You deserve a break. There's a buffet in a little while. You have to eat or you'll keel over.'

'I'll have to take a rain check on that. I'll stay for the first dance then I think my job is done.'

'You've gone beyond the call of duty.'

They had to stop talking.

'Ladies and gentlemen. The bride and groom will now take to the floor for their first dance as Mr and Mrs Sahota!'

A huge round of applause and cheering, punctuated by enthusiastic whistles. Guests flocked to the dance floor.

'I have to get this,' Travis said, picking up his camera and moving to the edge of the dance floor.

Freya made her way to the front, cheering them on as they started to dance. Roxanne laughed. They hadn't rehearsed anything: no *Strictly* moves, flash mobs or YouTube viral videos – just a newlywed couple shuffling around the floor, slightly self-conscious, a little bit drunk and deliriously happy.

They didn't notice the phones held up to record the moment or Travis snapping away from a discreet distance.

Travis returned to Freya after a couple of minutes, leaving the bride and groom to finish their dance to raucous applause.

The singer took to the mic. 'Three cheers for Mr and Mrs Sahota!'

'Doesn't Roxy look amazing?' Freya said.

'Yes. Nice dress.'

'Is that all you can say?'

He smiled. 'I'm more used to looking at filters than dresses. She looks lovely.' His smile faded and his eyes dared her to look away. 'But not as lovely as you.'

If he'd smiled or had a glint in his eye, she would have laughed at him, but she couldn't. She knew him too well and that he meant every word.

'I don't think you can say that on a bride's wedding day,' she said as lightly as she could.

He shrugged. 'I just did. Roxanne looks stunning but you're the most beautiful woman in the room.'

'Travis . . . no, stop it . . .'

'Why?'

'Because . . .' She might feel something for him? It might not end there?

She was left speechless, any words drowned out by the raucous applause and the shouts of the lead singer. 'Now, ladies and gentlemen, may we invite you all to take to the floor so we can get this party started!'

A faster tempo track began and Mr and Mrs Jameson and the Sahotas were on the floor, throwing shapes.

'I must get pics of the parents dancing or Roxy and Ravi will never forgive me,' Travis said, leaving Freya stranded and stunned by the edge of the floor.

He *mustn't* say stuff like that at a wedding, or any day: words that made her body zing with desire and turned the key on feelings that had been locked away so long.

Travis was a blur somewhere behind the guests gyrating on the dance floor, all ages of them – hiding away behind the camera somewhere.

A hand touched her arm, making it tingle. She spun round, ready to beg him not to touch her.

'Nico!'

That handsome face was smiling down at her, jacket and tie discarded, eyes gleaming with amusement.

'I believe it's traditional for the best man to dance with the chief bridesmaid after the bride and groom?' he said.

'Is it? I haven't heard that before.'

'Maybe I just made it up.' He held out his hand. 'You can, of course, refuse.'

'If it's tradition, then I can't.' She smiled back. 'Thank you.'

The tempo slowed and his hands settled on her waist, lightly and expertly, pulling her a little closer but not too close. They turned round, covering the floor, slowly turning round and round. Over his shoulder, she searched every corner of the room for Travis yet there was no sign of him.

Roxanne caught her eye and beamed delightedly. Freya smiled back.

'I think we've been set up,' Nico said.

'It wouldn't surprise me.'

She was in the arms of this handsome, single, Italian surgeon. She imagined her mother watching, in paroxysms of ecstasy.

The dance ended, but Nico kept his hands on her waist.

'Can I get you a drink?' he said.

Roxanne was watching them from the bar like a hawk observing a rabbit along with Mrs Jameson, an auntie and a cousin. If the group had had binoculars, Freya was sure they'd trained them on her and Nico, hoping the two of them would pair up – and mate – right in front of them.

'Freya?' Nico's eyes were filled with concern.

'Thank you, but . . . not now. I, um, need to go to the bathroom to do my makeup.'

She left him, almost tripping over her dress in her haste to reach the double doors that led out of the ballroom. She could only imagine Roxanne and co.'s disappointment in watching one of the pair fly away from the other.

In the foyer, Ravi was saying goodbye to several relations.

'Ravi!' Freya flashed a smile at the relatives and cut in. 'Sorry to bother you but have you seen Travis?'

'He's gone home,' Ravi said. 'I think he's knackered after working all day and he said he had a tour to lead first thing.'

Freya's heart sank into her wedding shoes. 'Oh. I see.'

'It wasn't that long ago. Couple of minutes? Do you need him?

'No, I only wanted to say thanks.'

'I did that for you. He's a top bloke, stepping in like that.'

'He is. Thanks.'

Leaving Ravi being hugged his family, Freya trudged back towards the ballroom, crushed with disappointment, desperate to know more. Travis couldn't leave, not after saying . . . what he'd said. His words had come out of the blue, with the force of a hammer.

She turned around and hurried to the door. She wanted to run but that would have attracted attention and she'd probably trip over her bloody heels . . . oh, sod it!

She took them off, hitched up her dress in her free hand and jogged towards the hotel entrance and into the stone porch.

The cold snatched her breath away and it was snowing. The car park was white over, and frost sparkled on the box trees standing sentinel at the entrance. She couldn't go out in her bare feet – but wasn't that Travis's car parked by the far hedge, with the boot open? Was that shadowy figure him?

Abandoning her heels, she grabbed a pair of wellies from the rack in the porch and pulled one on, hopping around and almost toppling over in her haste. They were five sizes too large for her and she strode into the darkness like Jack the Giant Killer in his seven-league boots, except she was slithering and squashing through the snow.

Travis closed the boot with a slam and climbed into the car.

'Wait! Argh!'

Freya stumbled, swore but by a miracle, stayed upright.

His car engine started.

'Hang on!'

His reversing lights glowed white in the darkness.

She took three giant strides. The car inched backwards in the snow.

'No!' She banged on the roof. 'Wait!'

The engine stopped dead and the door flew open.

Travis jumped out and his eyes widened in shock. 'Freya? Are you OK? What's the matter?'

'Y-you are,' she said, gulping in the air. 'You can't leave. You have to stay with me.'

Chapter Twenty-Two

'I *have* to stay?' Travis stared at her.
'Yes.'

'You're freezing and wet. Your dress . . .'

'Am I?'

His voice reawakened her senses. Cold, wet satin fabric clung to her legs and she realised she was trembling.

He shrugged off his coat and draped it around her shoulders, transferring the warmth of his body to her chilled flesh. 'That's the second one I've loaned you today,' he said, 'I don't have another one. Come on, let's get you inside.'

His arm settled around her shoulders and he guided her towards the doors.

Freya noticed the six-inch tear in her hem and winced. 'I'll have to change. I hope Roxanne doesn't see me like this.' She stopped suddenly. 'And you *can't* be seen with me either.'

He frowned. 'Why not?'

'Because . . . Look,' she added desperately. 'Travis, just do as I say. Let me go inside and then follow me in. Is there another way into the hotel you could use?'

'What? Like through the kitchens?' he shot back. 'I'm not sure they'd approve of me marching in while they're doing dinner.'

'I'm being serious!'

'OK, then, seriously, there are several staff entrances from the grounds. I used them with Roxy and Ravi earlier, but why all the secrecy?'

'I'll tell you in my room, but please, *don't* go.'

'Freya,' he said solemnly. 'I can promise you I'm not going anywhere.'

The promise in his smile sparked an internal glow that heated her faster than any fire. 'See you in a minute,' she said, already on her way.

He caught her arm, gently. 'Wait. I don't have your room number.'

'It's twenty-three,' she said. 'In the tower wing.'

Without a glance back, she left him, returning to the hotel, ditching the wellies and collecting her shoes – praying that no one noticed her rushing through the door to the guest wings in a wet dress and borrowed jacket.

She closed the door, shed his coat and glimpsed the flushed-cheeked woman in the mirror. Her hair was damp, her crystal comb sparkling with melting snow. As for her torn dress – she'd have to have it repaired . . .

'The bed!'

Her four-poster had been turned down and rose petals scattered on the sheets, lamplight softly glowing and a warm honeyed scent perfuming in the air. Every nerve ending caught alight and he wasn't even in the room yet. She wanted him and it had to be now. However crazy it was, however wrong it would seem in the morning, she needed him.

The knock at the door was so soft.

She almost jumped out of her skin. No going back.

Opening it a sliver, she spied Travis, his tousled hair as damp as her own, as jittery as she felt. Was it lust or nerves or a heady cocktail of both?

'Room service, madam?' The roguish glint in his eyes almost made her self-combust.

'No one saw you?' she said, locking the door behind him.

'Housekeeping, a couple of teenagers snogging in the corridor.' He glanced at the room, his gaze lingering on the four-poster bed where his jacket lay. She hadn't left it there on purpose – had she?

'Why did you leave without saying goodbye?' she asked.

His gaze settled on hers. 'I saw you with Nico. You were dancing.'

'Nico?' she echoed.

'Yeah. The tall, dark, loaded Italian surgeon, unless you hadn't noticed.'

'Is he loaded?' she exclaimed in amazement. 'He didn't tell me.'

'I'm sure he'd have got round to it,' he said spikily. 'He mentioned his Ferrari and Tuscan villa twice while I was taking the photos earlier.'

Freya could torment him – and herself – no longer. 'Actually, I did know,' she said, closing on him. 'I was winding you up.'

He shook his head in disbelief, exhaled and closed the space between them. 'Freya,' he murmured, reaching up to caress her cheek with the back of his fingers. 'After a day of looking at you in that dress, I don't think it's possible for me to be wound up anymore.'

He pulled her gently into his arms, the soft-rough wool of

his sweater brushing her cleavage, sending splinters of desire shooting through her. His mouth swooped on hers, suffusing her chilled body with heat. Freya sought him too, exploring his mouth, pressing more tightly against him, wanting his skin on her skin, and him deep inside her.

She tugged his shirt out of his jeans, slipped her hands under the brushed cotton, flattened them against his smooth flesh, feeling his muscles tauten under her fingertips. He drew down the zip and the satin slithered down her body to the floor, leaving her in her bra and knickers: mere lacy scraps of satin that matched the dress.

'Wow,' Travis said on a breath, his eyes like saucers. 'Just *wow*.'

'I don't usually wear . . . this sort of thing . . .'

'I promise I'm not judging.' His voice was hoarse, tinged with urgency.

In moments, her very expensive bra was lying on the floor, followed by her knickers and Travis's jeans. They sank into the duvet, naked, Travis kissing his way down her neck, between her breasts and telling her he wanted her so much he might pass out.

Freya opened her eyes and turned her head to one side. It was still dark but there was enough light from under the door to reveal that she wasn't alone for the first time in over eighteen months.

Travis lay face down, one arm flung across the pillow.

With a contented sigh, he shifted in his sleep and the duvet slipped off the bed, exposing his muscular behind. Freya was unable to take her eyes off it, fascinated and impressed and wondering how she'd done the very thing she'd vowed never to do under any circumstances.

She'd been a bit tipsy when she'd run out into the snow after him but not so that she didn't know exactly what she was doing when she'd begged him to come back inside. She'd done all the running, she'd issued the orders and was in control. The night's events – all of them – flooded back and made her squirm with lust all over again.

They'd both had the presence of mind to be sensible for at least ten seconds, judging by the empty foil packets on the bedside table.

Sensible . . . She'd been sensible far too often and for too long, so she could allow herself her moment of madness, surely?

Who could be sensible when faced with the sight of a naked Travis, his body made strong and muscular by years of hiking up mountains carrying heavy camera gear?

She allowed herself a little while longer to wonder at his gorgeous bottom before he suddenly turned, yanking the duvet off her with a startled expression as if he had no idea how he'd ended up in her bed.

'Morning,' she said, looking down on him.

'Er . . .' He pushed his hair out of his eyes. 'Yeah.' Then: 'Oh my God! I'm supposed to be leading a tour.'

He leaped out of bed, got tangled in the duvet and slipped, stubbing his toe on the chair.

'Argh. I should be halfway up a mountain. Argh. It's my first tour, I've got six people waiting at the shop . . .' He glanced at his wrist and found it bare. 'Oh God, what time is it?'

Freya fished it from her side of the bed. 'Quarter to eight.'

'Oh.' His shoulders dropped and he exhaled. 'I'm meeting them at nine. There's still time to make it.'

'I suggest you get dressed first. You'd definitely cause a stir if you turned up like that.'

He clamped his mouth shut as if he'd only then realised he was naked. Freya wanted to giggle before he stared at her and realised that she was naked too.

'Oh. I – wow.' He shook his head in wonder, the right kind of wonder. 'Maybe I should forget the tour.'

He climbed back onto the bed.

'Don't you need time to prepare?' she said half-heartedly as he lay down beside her.

'No. I've got all my gear in the car and trust me,' he added, with a cheeky grin, 'I know what I'm doing by now.'

Afterwards, while Travis dashed into the shower, yelping and cursing because he couldn't wait for the water to heat up, Freya lay under the sheet, hoping the tempest of emotions rolling over her would pass like a summer storm.

A whirlwind had hit the room over the past ten hours. Items of clothing were abandoned on the desk, on the floor. Were those her knickers on the tea tray?

It had happened, she'd slept with Travis and it had been momentous and wonderful and she wanted to do it again and again. She was an addict, succumbing to her first fix after years of abstinence that she'd thought would last forever.

Towelling down, he thundered back into the bedroom. 'Where's my clothes? I won't have time to go home and change now. I'll have to go commando.'

That kind of talk *really* wasn't helping her.

Uttering a stream of creative curses, Travis hopped around, pulling on his jeans, unearthing his T-shirt from the tangle of bedclothes.

'I'm starving. OK if I have these?' He started stuffing the complimentary biscuits, fruit and bottled water into his jacket pockets.

She sat up. 'You can have anything you like but Travis, we *have* to talk about what's happened here.'

He cast a look around the room. 'Looks like World War Three happened to me.'

'I mean what happened between *us*.'

He grinned. 'That was pretty explosive too.'

The physical intimacy had been mind-blowing but she was also scared of where it might lead: to him getting hurt, to them both getting hurt and messing up their lives again. Life had been so much simpler before Travis had walked back into it – and so much duller and safer . . .

She swung her legs out of bed. 'It was, she said. 'But it absolutely can't happen again . . .'

His grin faded instantly. 'Please don't say that. Not after last night. And I have to go.' He crossed the room to the door but she was after him.

'You haven't let me finish, it can't happen again *unless* . . .

'Unless what?' He grasped the door handle.

'Unless you agree to my conditions. *Strict* conditions – but I need time to explain. I don't want you rushing off and not listening.'

'I'll do anything.' His gaze raked her body. 'Anything you say to keep on doing what we just did.' His lips met hers, in a deep and tender kiss that ended way too soon. 'Now, I have to go. I'll see you later. Just tell me where and when.'

Chapter Twenty-Three

'Hi, come in. Excuse the mess. I'm editing some of the pictures I took on the tour today.'

Travis opened the door to Squirrel Cabin for Freya that evening. She'd called in after work and the moment she stepped inside she was enveloped in its warmth, her nostrils inhaling the soft scent of wood smoke from the glowing burner.

The cabin was almost unrecognisable from the day she'd prepared it for his arrival. Every surface was littered with camera bags, lenses, filters and low-tech stuff like maps and ring binders. Next to a steaming mug of coffee, two MacBooks were open side by side on the dining table, showing a photograph of a snowy mountain ridge.

On the surface, it looked cosy and welcoming and safe but Freya had butterflies in her stomach. She'd suggested meeting at his place as a compromise. His territory, her ultimatum: that seemed fair, but now she had the feeling she'd walked into the lair of a messy, albeit friendly, grizzly bear.

'You made it then?'

'By the skin of my teeth.'

'Sorry,' he said, following her gaze around the room. 'I probably should have let the cleaners work their magic, but I'm not used to being waited on and how can they possibly clean this place up with my junk everywhere?'

'It's fine. I'm glad to see you made yourself at home.' More than that, he'd imbued every corner, nook and cranny with his very essence.

'Coffee?' he said. 'I just made a pot.'

'Thanks.'

The few seconds he took to pour her out some coffee and find the milk were the only time she had to gather herself. She'd rehearsed what she was going to say over and over, keeping it light yet firm. Roxanne's wedding had churned up a heap of memories and insecurities, with Jos, with Travis and even going back to her childhood.

He swept a couple of files off a chair before handing the mug to her.

'Thanks.' She nodded at the MacBook whose photo had faded to a screensaver of a waterfall she recognised as Aira Force at Ullswater.

'How did the tour go?' she said, aware she was only delaying the crunch moment.

He smiled. 'Good. Very good considering the rush I was in.' His cheeky grin made the blood rush to her cheeks when she recalled the way they'd said goodbye earlier. 'Three of the group signed up for my Tarns tour in the spring and one booked for the Iceland trip this summer. We got some good shots and they all seemed pretty enthusiastic.' He rolled his eyes. 'Apart from the man who said he could have been a professional if he hadn't devoted his life to commercial insurance broking.'

She wrinkled her nose. 'One of those?'

''Fraid so. Turned up in a big Bentley SUV, with brand new hiking boots and a camera he'd no clue how to use. I get them sometimes: all the gear, no idea.'

She laughed, amused at his world-weariness.

He perched on the sofa. 'But you didn't come here to talk about photography, did you?'

Her stomach fluttered. 'No.' He'd opened the door for her, now she had to walk through it, quickly and confidently. 'Does anyone know about last night? You didn't tell Bree we were together?'

A deep frown. 'I saw her for a few minutes when the tour group met. She'd no clue I hadn't been home.'

'Oh . . . only I thought someone might have seen you when you left. Your car was there.'

'I sneaked out the back door the same way I sneaked in. Everyone was sleeping off their hangovers and if anyone asks, I'll say I had too much to drink and called a cab to take me home.' He folded his arms. 'Why is it so important that no one knows we're together?'

'Because we're *not* together. Not in public. I don't want the gossip and the . . . expectation. Not from our families, or friends or anyone.' She couldn't stand the pressure on herself – the pressure to admit she felt more for him than lust.

'OK. I can understand that. I don't mind being discreet.' He seemed to relax and smile. 'I think it could be pretty sexy conducting an illicit affair. In fact, now would be the idea opportunity to practise. I presume no one knows *you* came here . . .'

Damn, he didn't seem to be taking her warnings seriously. Freya tried again. 'They don't, and I feel the same about you: the practising, I mean.'

'Wow.' He raised his eyebrows.

'You're surprised I'm so upfront? That a woman would be.'

He laughed. 'Not surprised – delighted.' The laughter melted into a smouldering look of desire. 'I'd love to go to bed with you again. Right now.'

'Then let's just do it. As often as we want.' With her resistance dissolving by the second, Freya steeled herself. 'But here's my second condition.'

'Right . . .'

'As well as being discreet, we must *not* get serious. It's fun times, the pub, dinner and lots of sex – but absolutely no commitment. I'm rubbish at it. My track record proves it. With you – and—' She almost added with Jos but stopped in time. 'It would all go wrong.' And if she never allowed herself to love again, she couldn't suffer the pain of losing him.

'Right . . .' Travis said in a tone that let her know he felt the situation was anything but right. 'I respect you being upfront but shouldn't we sit down and talk this through more before we jump into bed?' He groaned. 'I can't actually believe I just said that but I'm thinking of you – of us. Both of us.'

Freya drew herself up, more determined than ever. 'This is the talk. The *only* talk. Let's get it right, there isn't going to be some big epiphany, some lightbulb moment. You want sex, I want sex. I do . . . really like you, Travis. Life's never boring with you, but as for staying together, til death us do part, in sickness and health – I have the worst track record when it comes to commitment; you live an exciting life and although you have the gallery, I don't think Bannerdale will be big enough for you somehow.'

He looked at the floor. 'Not *big* enough for me?'

'It wasn't before,' she said.

'So this arrangement is to protect you – or me?'

'Both.'

'You were the one who broke it off,' he said so gently, she couldn't be angry.

'Yes, I did and like I said, commitment's not for me. Not at the moment. You must know I'm right.'

'Maybe. Maybe you are.' He laughed but his laughter held a chill that sent shivers through her. 'Maybe this should be the template for relationships. No strings, no promises.'

She hadn't realised her hands were shaking, this was more emotional than she'd expected. She'd thought she could breeze in, offer him no-strings sex and he'd keep things light. Yet her heart ached as she spoke and her honesty sounded more brutal than refreshing.

'I'm not suggesting it would suit everyone. Just that it's the right thing for us, right now. If you're not comfortable with that, I'll understand.'

'Oh, I'm very comfortable with having lots of sex with you.'

'Without expecting anything else?' she said, needing to know unequivocally.

'With no expectations. You made it perfectly clear you didn't want anything when we were young. More importantly, you've made it perfectly clear now that you're not looking for long-term with me or . . .' He faltered. 'Or anyone for now.'

'I think we're mature enough to keep this as friends with benefits,' he said, adding lightly, 'I have as much intention of making this into some big romance as you do.'

She heaved a huge sigh. Even as the weight was lifted from her mind, the weight of relief at telling him, replaced by a different kind of weight that came from – where? She didn't know how to name it.

She forced a smile to her face. 'OK. Whew. That's out of the way – I was worried you might want to end it all before it had even started.'

'After last night?' His eyes sparked with desire again. 'I'm not crazy.'

'I worked that out. So, do you think we should forget the coffee and continue the arrangement? Unless of course,' she said, sweeping her hand at the laptops, 'you're too busy?'

He was on his feet, taking her hand in moments. 'Oh, I think I can find the time.'

Chapter Twenty-Four

The following evening, Freya lay back on the pillow in cottage with a sigh of pleasure. 'Whew, that was . . . pretty mind-blowing.'

'For a moment, I thought you were going to give me marks out of ten.'

'What do you mean?' She propped herself up on one elbow, staring down at Travis, who'd called round after the gallery had closed. Travis smiled. 'You looked so intense, so angry when you er . . . were in the throes—'

She squealed in horror. 'You were not watching me when I was . . . how could you!'

'I couldn't help it and besides I love making you feel like that: making you lose control. Even if,' he said, a cheeky grin creeping onto his lips, 'you did look as if you'd been plugged into the electricity.'

'You horrible man!' Freya said, her cheeks firing up. 'Well, at least I made you take off that bloody smart watch.'

Travis scowled. 'I've no idea why.'

'Because I read an article about men with smart watches

using them to monitor their heart rate during sex, and logging how many times they do it in the health app.'

Breaking into laughter, he pulled her on top of him. 'I swear to you that the last thing I was doing while we were having sex was monitoring my heart rate. It would probably have exploded the watch anyway.'

'You think?' Freya rested on her elbows, pinning him down. Her toes raked his calves.

'Definitely. Though I might put it back on so I can tell when I'll be ready to go again.'

'No! I'm on duty. What if a guest needs me while I'm in bed with you?' Freya struggled to her feet, but Travis pulled her back down.

'I need you,' he said before swooping down on her lips for a kiss.

Later, they cracked open beers and sat in front of the fire, digging into noodles with chopsticks. Wrapped in a fluffy robe, Freya had her feet in his lap. The TV was on mute and a holiday ad flickered on the screen showing silver-haired couples dining on the deck of a ship.

'Mum's probably lying on a private island with Neil . . .' she said.

'Do you mind?' Travis scooped up his noodles.

'Not now. I was a bit taken aback when she first told me they were off on the cruise together. I hadn't realised things were that serious with him, but now, I think she deserves to be happy and as things have turned out, it suits me to be home alone for Christmas.'

He smiled. 'I'm glad you're home alone . . . I like the tree.'

'You do?' Freya looked at her tree, a modest-sized silver tinsel affair standing proudly in the corner of the room. 'Mum gave it to me. She bought a new artificial one and thought I might like it. I treated myself to new decorations. Most of our properties have been dressed for Christmas since the first of the month by professionals, or we use the owners own decs. It's what guests expect unless they've come here specifically to get away from it all.'

He laughed. 'Bree made me "add some seasonal touches" to the gallery. She said I'd look a real Grinch otherwise.'

'You don't like Christmas?'

'We never made a big thing of it. Couldn't afford to. Mum did her best but Dad was usually away or in the pub. There was one year . . .'

'Yes?'

'One year when it snowed like hell and the village was cut off all over the holiday. I must have been about eleven.'

She sat up. 'I remember that!'

'We came down to find three sledges under the tree. I'm not sure Bree was impressed because she was fourteen by then, but Seb was *so* excited. Mum was quietly fuming, asking Dad where they'd come from. He told her not to ask but we didn't care. We couldn't wait to try them out so Dad took us up to the field above Bannerdale Park. We had the best time ever.' His eyes lit up with pleasure at the memory of it. 'I don't remember him being at home again. It was our last Christmas together . . . He left and never came back. I think the sledges were a guilty gift to salve his conscience.'

'I'm sorry, Travis.'

'No need for the tiny violin. You and your mum have been on your own for years.'

'Not often. We usually got invited to one or other of my grans.'

'I remember your granny. She gave me and Seb packets of Haribo once. I think she felt sorry for us.'

'She passed away a few years ago. She was a force of nature. We went to Neil's last year and Mimi's the year before – and we went to Tenerife once. To be honest, Mum was always glad to come home and I just wanted to get the Big Day over with and go out with my mates over the holidays.'

'I've been abroad most times, or on my own – I declined a lot of invitations. I don't want to be the bloke they ask out of pity.'

'They wouldn't have done that, but I do know what you mean.'

He ran his hand up her thigh. 'We do need to talk about Christmas Day. Bree's invited me and Seb for lunch.'

'Oh?' Freya said. 'That's nice.'

'It would be difficult for me to say no and anyway it's been a long time since we were together.'

'Why would you say no?'

'Well, I thought we might spend Christmas together and I know Bree would be OK with it, but unless we go public – to her and Seb, which is kind of the same thing – it could be awkward to explain why you're there.'

'There's no need. I'll be fine,' Freya said blithely, thinking that somehow, spending Christmas Day together with or without his family, felt like a step on from 'no strings attached'.

'We can spend the evening together though. I can get away.'

'I don't want to spoil your day. It's important you and the family have time together.'

'Bree's looking forward to it. Seb needs it . . .' He sighed.

'He was so pissed off about the open mic night. I'm not sure he's forgiven me yet.'

'He'll simmer down,' Freya said, realising how much family meant to him. If she'd thought she could have Travis to herself – she was wrong. Was she naïve to think she could compartmentalise their relationship? Was it even realistic to keep it under wraps? Then again, it was no one's business but their own. Why did couples become public property?

'Maybe.' Travis stuck the empty noodle carton on the table and balanced the chopsticks inside. 'It was a terrible idea to think he wouldn't mind. He'd specifically asked me to stop managing him.'

'He will come round, if you can prove to him you aren't.'

'Naw. It would never work.'

'It'll never work unless you try.'

He shook his head. 'I should probably stick to minding my own business. Jeez, I've got enough of it. I've a tour in the week. One of your guests as it happens.'

'Really? The leaflets helped?'

'They did. There's a group of friends staying at Garside Lodge. They saw the leaflet, went on my website and phoned Bree while I was at the wedding. I said I'd do a trip for them midweek. They wanted to make a day of it so Bree suggested arranging picnics from the posh deli in the village. I'm picking up hampers with hot chocolate and mulled wine to have after the shoot. It's added value to the trip. More than worth my while. People are looking for "experiences" now, something unique and a special treat.'

'I'm impressed. Well done Bree.'

'She's full of good ideas. I just wish Seb was that easy to please.'

'Hmm.' Freya's eye was drawn to Travis's camera bag in the corner of the sitting room. He hadn't wanted to leave it in his car in the public car park near her cottage.

'Have you thought,' she said, treading carefully, 'about taking Seb on a shoot?'

'What? With these four clients? I don't think that's a good idea?'

'No. Though they might like it.' Freya laughed. 'I was thinking of just the two of you. Brothers. Take him out on a shoot. I don't mean a commercial one, I mean for pleasure. Share your passion for what you do.'

'My passion?' Travis didn't smile as she expected. He rubbed his finger along the blade of her foot, lost in thought – almost sadness on his face. Despair even. He must be so worried about his brother.

She touched his arm. 'He'll find his way. Your coming back here is probably unsettling for more than me.'

His head lifted. 'Let's not compete on that one.' He ran his chopstick down her sole.

'Hey! No!'

'Ticklish?'

'Yes, and now I have chow mein sauce on my foot.'

'I could lick it off,' he said, then pulled a face. 'Yuk.'

She smiled. 'That's what you said when the vicar told us to hold hands.'

'I had my reputation to maintain,' he said, 'And let's face it, your palms were very sweaty.'

'I was terrified. I thought I was going to throw up.'

'Good job you ran out of the church then.'

'You are impossible.'

'I do try.'

She caught sight of at the clock. She could ask him to stay over. She wanted to.

'Is that my cue to leave?' he said.

Freya hesitated then muttered. 'You . . . don't have to . . .'

He raised his eyebrows. 'Oh, but what if the *neighbours* saw us?'

She was stung by his sarcasm yet also felt slightly foolish. 'Travis . . . I was only trying to stick to our arrangement.'

'And staying over at each other's places isn't part of it? How's that going to work?'

'It isn't. I realise that. It isn't practical – and not much fun, so that's why I'm inviting you to stay.'

'Hmm.' He affected great interest in her ankle, half circling it with his fingers and thumb, before replying. 'That's very tempting but I have to be on the road by five. There's snow forecast and I want to be ready to capture the sunrise over the Solway and I've left my long lens at the cabin. Not to mention, I have a little job to do involving a wedding.'

'Are you blowing me off for a lens?'

'I'm afraid so,' he said, lifting her feet from his lap gently. 'This is what happens when you get involved with a photographer.'

She got up. 'When will we see the wedding photos?'

'I promised to have them ready for when Roxy and Ravi are back from honeymoon after Christmas.'

She nodded. 'I won't ask for a preview. That's their prerogative.'

'I wouldn't have shown you,' he said sternly.

She lifted her arms around his neck and kissed him. 'Not even if I tried very hard to persuade you?'

'No. Although . . . I'm not sure how long I could hold out under severe pressure.'

She laughed and handed him his coat. 'Then I'd better not put you to the test.'

He sighed. 'I'm not sure whether to be disappointed or relieved. I'll see you tomorrow. Dinner at Squirrel Cabin?'

'I'm on phone duty at the office but I can finish at ten. Enjoy the fells. Think of me delivering Christmas hampers to thirty properties. See you tomorrow night.'

'I can't wait.'

She sighed, savouring the past few days of delicious sex and Travis's company. This arrangement was going even better than she'd expected.

Chapter Twenty-Five

Squirrel Cabin was as inviting as a fridge when Travis walked in after leaving Freya's cottage. He turned on the lamps, drew the curtains and lit the wood burner, thinking of how he could still have been in bed with her.

His excuse was a genuine one: he did have a dawn shoot and he did need time to prepare his equipment. However, if he had stayed, there was a good chance he'd never have made it out of her cottage in the morning.

It had been better to walk away while he could.

Too late for that, mate.

That inner voice telling him he should never have agreed to the no-strings sex pact *at all* was a bloody nuisance. Dismissing it, he started laying out his equipment for the shoot and reminded himself how lucky he was to be back in his favourite location in the whole world.

It was one of his reasons for returning: to be within touching distance of familiar spots on days like this. Many professionals would kill to have such locations on their doorstep: the landscape would be some compensation for spending a lonely night with only the owls for company.

He didn't want to dwell on what he was missing, so he turned his thoughts to her idea about Seb. It was hard enough dragging himself out of bed at four a.m., let alone luring his brother from his pit to go up the fells in the snow.

Travis reminded himself of Freya's words: *It'll never work unless you try,* when he followed Seb into his favourite lakeside cafe on the Sunday morning. He'd found out that his brother had the Monday off and hoped he'd have nothing planned. Now, all he had to do was persuade him to get up at six a.m. and set off into the icy dawn.

'Why am I suspicious that you asked me here?' Seb said, spearing a Cumberland sausage on his fork. 'I'm a big believer that there's no such thing as a free breakfast.'

'In this case, there is,' Travis said, shaking ketchup on his own fry up. 'This is a peace offering. I was wrong to trick you into going to the open mic night and I wish I hadn't been so arsey about you and Dad.'

'My God!' Seb gasped, mid-way to popping the sausage in his mouth. 'My brother admits he's wrong! Let me record this so I know it really happened.'

Travis laughed. 'No need. I was out of order. He bit into a piece of bacon, and then sighed appreciatively. 'I've missed this place so much. There's nowhere does a brekkie like here, and nowhere with a view like this. I wish I'd brought my camera . . .'

An hour later, to Travis's amazement, the plan had worked – and Freya had, once again, been proved right.

* * *

'Remind me again, why the hell I agreed to this?' Seb grumbled from deep within the bundle of layers Travis had provided.

Smiling to himself, Travis drove through the darkness towards the spot he'd chosen on the fellside above the lake. 'Bro, this is going to be one of the best experiences of your life.'

Seb raised a sceptical eyebrow. 'Of my *life*?'

'Today will be worth it, I promise,' Travis said, switching the focus onto the shoot. It needed to be fun, to try and engage his brother's attention. He needed to concentrate and not be thinking ahead to dinner that evening, and what might be for dessert, if he and Freya even made it that far.

'Are you sure this isn't some scam of yours and you're taking me to audition for some bloody TV talent show?'

'You're not that good.'

'You cheeky sod! I'm better than a lot of the chancers on those shows!' Seb declared, giving Travis fresh hope. Did he detect a hint of professional pride in his brother's tone? There must be some sense that he'd been a good musician once – and still was.

Eventually, the car warmed up and Seb deigned to take off his trapper hat. It was still pitch black so Travis handed out a head torch.

Seb put his hat back on and strapped on the torch, swearing ripely. 'It has to be minus five up here.'

'Minus six according to the car,' Travis said, unloading gear from the back seat. 'Don't worry, we'll soon be warm.' He handed Seb a camera backpack.

'Whoa! It weighs a ton!'

'Don't drop it! There's ten grand's worth of kit in there!'

'Ten grand? Fecking hell!'

With a grin, Travis patted Seb's arm reassuringly. 'Chill. You've got my old gear. I wouldn't dream of letting you near the new stuff.'

'Thanks for the vote of confidence.' Seb slipped the foam straps over his shoulder and winced. 'You're crazy, Travis. Have I ever told you?'

'Shut up and follow me and be careful. If you fall off the path and I lose my gear, I'll never forgive you.'

The path up to the tarn wasn't that steep, and not at all exposed: Travis would never have put his brother in danger but it was slippery underfoot.

'Warm enough, now?' he said.

Seb pulled a face. 'I'm sweating.'

'That's why I don't put too many layers on before I set off. You soon get toasty carrying all the stuff. I keep an extra layer in my bag to put on when I'm hanging around.'

'Now you tell me.'

It was hard work, tramping over rough ground by torchlight, and they were both breathing hard by the time they reached the tarn itself, their breath forming clouds in the chilly air.

'Wait here a sec.' The sky was changing from velvet black to indigo in the east. He pointed to a small flat area that gave a great view of the lake.

'This is the blue hour. Right. Let's find a good spot and get ready.'

Seb finally stopped grumbling and started to take an interest in the camera settings and technicalities. Travis had known it was impossible for him not to give it his whole attention but had been worried he might be bored. However, he seemed to take mastering the technicalities to be a challenge. Travis couldn't care less what pictures Seb took.

Soon, Travis himself became lost in the moment, capturing the light changing minute by minute – sometimes second by second.

'Look!' he whispered, pointing out a small herd of fallow deer who had wandered out of the woods to graze on the lower slopes of the fells. 'Now the sun's rising, this is the golden hour, the perfect time to get pictures of wildlife and landscapes.'

Shutters whirred and clicked as he and Seb fired off hundreds of pictures of the deer, the sunrise and the lake.

An hour had passed by and Seb was flagging so Travis deployed the hot coffee and bacon butties he'd made the night before. They were cold but two ravenous young brothers weren't going to mind about that.

'Thanks.' Seb munched away, seemingly lost in thought.

Travis didn't blame him. Although it was bitterly cold, he wouldn't have wished to be anywhere else in the world at that moment, except in Freya's bed. Standing by Seb's side, watching the sun rise over the lake with snow lying on the fell tops, and the light burnishing the bracken with flame – all reflected in the mirrored surface – was awesome.

He didn't care if he'd got anything worth using in the gallery; he just wanted to share the moment with Seb and try to build a relationship he'd neglected so woefully over the past decade. A pang of guilt seized him. It had felt so right to leave everything behind after Freya had hurt him, but he'd ended up abandoning his whole family to lick his wounds.

He was as guilty of running away as she was from him, and from Jos Beresford.

He had to find out why she'd called off their wedding so suddenly but what business was it of his? She'd insisted – begged – for no emotional attachment so why would he pry? What difference could it possibly make if he knew the reasons? Perhaps she'd left Jos for the very reason she didn't want to get involved with him. She was terrified of commitment.

Seb broke into his thoughts. 'Haven't been up here for years,' he said. 'The last time was with Carl Hazelmere. We climbed the fell, came up here for a sneaky smoke of something.'

'Carl?' Travis recalled the stocky boy with ginger curls, at one time inseparable from Seb. The guitarist in Seb's band and worth ten of some of the guys Bree said Seb had been hanging around with. 'Is he still living in Bannerdale?'

'You're joking. He did a music tech degree at uni. Said I could stay with him any time.'

'And have you?'

'He asked me a couple of times. I went once but I never went back. I felt out of place. His mates were . . .'

'Snotty with you?' Travis said, bristling on his brother's behalf.

Seb snorted. 'I think I could have handled it better if they *had* been stuck-up gits. No. They were all very polite, trying to include me in everything: the pub, a meal, a gig. Carl was super eager to make sure I was having a good time, but . . . it wasn't their fault. It was me. I was the miserable bugger. "You seem a bit aloof," he said to me.' Seb wrinkled his nose. '"Aloof". I'd never heard him use a word like that before. If he'd called me bolshy or salty, I'd have laughed.'

Travis almost smiled. He could picture the exchange, the whole weekend. He knew how it felt to be patronised, however unintentionally. 'Carl wouldn't have meant anything. He was a good lad, like his family. I remember his mum was a dinner lady at school and his dad worked on the lake ferry.'

'He's changed. I've seen his Facebook posts. He joined some classical group.'

'I didn't know he could play the piano?'

'He could play just about anything. Him and his "group" make TikTok videos now. They wear tuxedos and do covers . . .'

Travis burst out laughing. 'I can't see Carl in a tux.'

'He looks a right tit,' Seb sneered. 'They get loads of views though. You wouldn't believe it.'

'I would. It's the same with photographers. You can make a living just off YouTube tutorials. I've done a few myself so don't knock it. You should try TikTok. Look at all these music influencers.'

'I don't want to be "famous". I just want to . . .' He suddenly checked himself and clammed up.

'Just want to be what?' Travis said.

Seb shrugged then shook his head. 'Don't try to cure me, bro. I thought today was about *you*, not me.'

'It's about both of us,' Travis said briskly, getting to his feet. 'I think we've got enough shots of the lake. Do you want to try and find some more wildlife?'

Travis led Seb towards the woods they'd passed on the way up. 'If we're in luck we might see a red squirrel,' he said, directing Seb towards a small clearing in the woods. 'There's a feeder up there and we might catch them scampering in the trees or even on the ground but we'll have to be patient.'

'I'm up for it,' Seb said, lifting his lens to show readiness, much to Travis's amusement.

'We can hide behind that bush. See if we get lucky.'

'I wouldn't bet on it, with me along,' said Seb archly.

'Come on, let's put the tarp down and get into position and from now on, be very quiet.'

'Told you . . .' Seb murmured half an hour later. 'I'm a jinx.'

'Shh . . .'

'It's freezing and I'm numb with cold,' Seb whispered, rolling over to face Travis. 'Let's call it a—' He stopped abruptly, his eyes on stalks. 'Oh. My. God,' he mouthed, raising his lens slowly. 'There's one behind you.'

Hardly daring to breathe, Travis rolled over to face the same way as Seb. There, nibbling on a hazelnut under a tree, was a red squirrel. It had chosen to sit in a pocket of snow and looked impossibly cute.

'My hands are shaking,' Seb whispered.

'Take a breath . . .'

Despite all his experience, Travis still felt the spike of adrenaline when a wild creature came in view of his lens. It might only be a red squirrel, but the excitement of seeing a beautiful – and increasingly rare – animal always gave him a buzz. He was past the stage of shaky hands but he was anxious for Seb. He wanted his brother to get a shot of the squirrel more than he wanted to capture it.

Eventually, the squirrel scampered off up a tree.

'Wow.'

'Let's take a look at what we got. You first.'

Seb scrolled through the images on his camera screen. Some were out of focus, others had cut half of the animal off. He groaned in disappointment.

'Man, I was shaking like a leaf. For a freaking *squirrel*.'

'Keep scrolling.' Travis prayed silently that at least one frame would be in focus.

After the first few shots, the images gradually sharpened as Seb had relaxed a bit and got his eye in. Several had the creature looking straight at him, and with a nut in its paws. Then—

'Bingo,' Travis declared.

There in perfect clarity, was the squirrel staring right at the camera, its deep red coat a vibrant contrast with the snow. The image was so sharp, you could see every hair in its distinctive tufted ears and the tiny claws on its paws as it held the nut.

'Well done, bro. This is a great shot.'

'I got lucky,' Seb replied, zooming in and out of the image as if he couldn't believe it was actually on his camera.

Travis laughed. 'Believe me, there'd be no wildlife photography if someone didn't get lucky once in a while.'

'So, I'll soon have it on the cover of *Countryside* calendar?' Seb said jokily.

'Better than that. I'll make it into a card for the gallery.'

Seb lowered the camera and pointed at Travis. 'You are so funny.'

'What's funny?'

'You almost had me there.'

Travis was saddened and angry. Their upbringing – their father's behaviour – must have affected Seb too, and now his confidence was at such a low ebb that he couldn't believe any praise. 'I'm not having you on, bro. I mean it. That photo is gold. I'll sell lots of them to people who come in and don't want to buy a big print – or can't afford to – they'll buy that card. Maybe two or three. One for them, one for a friend, they'll take it home, and get a cheap frame and keep it and think they've nabbed a piece of artwork. They'll order it online too.'

220

'In that case I should ask for royalties.'

'I'll give you a cut.'

Seb snorted. 'Now, I know you're joking!'

'Well, you'll have to see if I am when you get your fifty pence.'

'Fifty pence!'

'Probably more than that. I'll definitely give you a share of what I sell on prints from my website but there's no point putting it on a big stock photo site. The market is saturated. Professionals have to make most of their money from leading tours and retail sales now.'

'You *are* serious.'

'Yeah. I wish I'd taken it – and the number of times I say that is rarer than unicorn droppings.'

Travis meant every word. In one way, Seb had been fortunate today but Travis couldn't be happier. They stayed another half an hour but the squirrel didn't return and the light was fading. Travis could have stayed all night but Seb's patience was worn out. There was no more luck and there might never be for him. Luck really was preparation meeting opportunity.

Despite his heavy camera equipment, he felt as if his mental load had been lightened a little. He hadn't seen Seb so at ease with himself since his arrival in Bannerdale. With Seb still buzzing from the day, they walked down to the car and he drove home.

'Fancy a brew?' Travis said as he neared the turn-off for the track to the cabin.

'I would do but I think you might be happier on your own.' He gestured to a car with a Cottage Angels sign, turning into the track that led to the cabin. 'That's Freya's car, isn't it?'

'Maybe,' Travis replied as casually as his could, while his

pulse had quickened. 'She must have come to um, change the sheets.'

Seb raised an eyebrow but said no more. 'I need to get home, have a quick kip and a shower ready for my late shift. Today wasn't as boring as I thought it might be,' he said with a twinkle in his eye. 'And I'm expecting to be able to pack in work when those photo royalties start rolling in.'

Travis rolled his eyes. 'I'm glad you enjoyed it but take my advice: don't give up the day job yet.'

A minute later, Travis hurried from his car into the cabin, wondering why Freya *was* there. He hadn't arranged to meet her. Nonetheless, excitement rippled through him at the prospect of seeing her again. The lights were on in the sitting room and bedroom.

'Hi there! It's me!' Abandoning his gear on the floor, he strode into the bedroom.

Freya was tugging a pillowcase from a pillow, a canvas linen bag on the floor next to her.

'There's no need to do that,' he exclaimed, dashing forward to help. 'I can make my own bed and wash the sheets. I don't want you to wait on me.'

Freya laid down the pillow, with the case half on. Her cheeks were pink after coming in from the cold, and she'd never looked lovelier. She smiled. 'They need to take these to the professional laundry anyway. The housekeeping team are busy with Christmas prep so I thought I'd do it while I was here.'

He knuckled his forehead. 'I hadn't realised it was change-over day.'

'It's fine. You looked like you've been doing far more interesting things than stripping beds. Seb seemed happy.'

'Yes . . . that was a great idea you had. I took him up into

222

the high woods on Kirkstone Fell. He got a great shot of a red in the snow. He's buzzing.'

'That's great. I'm pleased.'

He pulled her into his arms. 'Don't change the bed.'

She laughed softly. 'It needs doing . . .'

'Sure, but not by you and definitely not now.'

Chapter Twenty-Six

When Freya arrived back at the cabin after work that evening, Travis was standing by the fridge, hands on hips.

'Hello!' she called, walking in. He turned guiltily. 'What's the matter?' she said.

'I was going to cook but I'm afraid dinner's going to have to be a couple of ready meals from a petrol station shop.' He laid the two cartons on the countertop. 'They only had turkey meals left in the chiller cabinet . . .'

Freya was amused by his sheepish expression. 'That's fine. It'll be my first Christmas dinner of the year.'

'Phew. I grabbed them on the way home from the gallery. I went into do some processing and time flew by. It's been non-stop since I took Seb on the shoot.'

She shed her coat. 'How did it go? We – er – didn't get round to discussing it earlier.'

He drew her into his arms. 'I had other things on my mind.'

'I was supposed to be changing the bed, not testing it out.'

'Did it pass?'

'Oh. I think so though I'm not sure the springs will hold out if we keep using it so, um, energetically.'

Travis laughed. 'I'll get you a drink.'

'Better do, before we end up there again. I want to hear about Seb. I'll admit it was a long shot and I didn't think he'd agree.'

'Nor me but it went far better than I'd hoped. The light was great and Seb managed to grab a fantastic squirrel picture. I was pretty pissed off to be honest.' He smiled. 'Not really. I was stoked for him. I'll probably have it made into cards for the gallery.'

'I'm really pleased. You did well to persuade him to come.'

'I was amazed he agreed. Even more amazed he managed to get out of bed at six a.m. in the dark and freezing cold. He seemed . . . more like his old self by the end of the afternoon. Thanks for the suggestion. Sorry I can't repay you with anything better than a ready meal.'

'You don't owe me anything. Neither of us owe each other anything.'

'No.' A shadow crossed his face but he soon chased it away with a grin. 'You lay the table while I rustle up this gourmet fare.'

Why had she felt the need to subtly – or none too subtly – remind him of the terms of their 'relationship'? Was it because things were getting far too cosy between them? After dinner, Freya curled up on the sofa while Travis showed her some of the pictures from earlier. He'd had a beer but she'd stuck to a zero-alcohol brand so she could drive home. With the wood burner glowing and the wind howling outside, the prospect of heading back to the cottage alone was becoming less appealing by the minute.

'What was that?' Travis exclaimed, as a loud crack came from outside.

Freya winced. 'A branch might have come down. Some of those trees are pretty close.'

'I'd better check,' he said.

'I'll come with you.'

'No, you stay inside.'

While he shrugged on his coat and boots, Freya tugged the curtain aside and tried to peer into the night. Flakes swirled but it was so dark she couldn't see how thick the snow was.

Travis opened the front door and an icy blast made the fire in the wood burner flicker. From the window, she saw his torchlight picking out snow on the car roofs and branches shaking in the wind. The snow was certainly starting to settle, and if she was going to leave, it would have to be soon.

He came back in, snowflakes melting in his hair. 'A big branch has come down behind the house and there's a blizzard out there!' Hastily, he closed the door.

She laughed. 'You've been away from Bannerdale too long if you call this a blizzard, but I agree, if I don't go now, I might not get out of here tonight.'

'And you have to get up for work in the morning?' he said.

'No, as a matter of fact – technically, if Mimi doesn't call in a panic, it's my day off . . .'

'Then, don't go,' he said, taking her in his arms. 'Stay the night with me. What harm can it do?'

Not quite a blizzard . . . The morning brought postcard-blue skies, with a few centimetres of snow lying around the cabin, undisturbed by footprints of any kind. The sun was just rising over the high fells, lending them an Alpine look.

Travis handed her a second coffee after she'd already demolished a plate of toast.

'Pretty spectacular, isn't it?' he said, staring out of the window beside her.

'Stunning.' It couldn't have looked more Christmassy, she thought. 'The guests are going to absolutely love it *if* they can make it to some of the more remote cottages. I'd better be ready to step in if Mimi and Hamish can't cope.'

'I thought it was your day off.'

'It is but if you hadn't noticed, I need to go home and change into clean clothes just in case.'

'That could easily be remedied.'

'Don't you have to open up the gallery?' she asked.

'It doesn't open until ten-thirty. That's plenty of time.' His tone held a hint of sexy promise.

Freya tore herself away from the heat of his gaze to the snowy scene outside. She remembered his childhood reminiscence about the sledges and had an impulse to re-enact it for him, even if at the time, the experience had been bittersweet.

'Actually, I had a different kind of activity on my mind,' she said. 'How do you fancy going sledging?'

'Sledging?' He frowned. 'What, now?'

Despite his bemused reaction, Freya ploughed on. 'Yes. The owners keep a couple of old toboggans in the shed behind the cabin. I thought we could take them to the field below the woods.'

Visions of whizzing down a steep slope, shrieking with excitement and terror, filled her mind.

'I haven't been sledging since . . .' he said, swallowing. Freya held her breath for a second, hoping she hadn't soured the moment.

'Of course,' she ventured. 'If you're too scared . . .'

'Scared?' Travis exclaimed. 'You must be joking!' He clapped his hands together. 'Come on, then, bet I can go faster.'

'Wheeeomigod!'

She was going way too fast. The slope was far too steep. She was never going to stop. 'Helpppp . . .'

The sledge hit a drift and Freya fell off, shrieking with laughter. A second later, Travis was flat on his back alongside her, whooping like a schoolboy. 'That was brilliant! Shall we do it again?'

'You bet!'

They hurried back up the hill, boots sinking in the snow, breathing heavily. The field was so much steeper than she remembered from her childhood yet it was still exhilarating.

'Race you this time?' she said, laughing at the way Travis dwarfed the red plastic sledge.

'One, two, three . . . go!'

She launched herself and then careered downhill, trying to steer the sledge while also trying to go as fast as she could.

To her dismay, Travis appeared beside her, a whisker ahead, making her lose her concentration. The sledge veered off course and flipped her into a drift, and she face-planted into the icy snow.

She levered herself up from the snow, blinking moisture from her eyes. Travis's grinning face appeared above her. He extended his hand. 'Are you OK?'

She let him help her to her feet. 'Yeah, apart from you cheating.'

'I did *not* cheat!' he cried.

'You set off on "three" not on go.'

'No way!'

Her skin stung with the cold but her body was buzzing with endorphins.

Travis took off his glove and brushed snow from her cheek. His eyes were concerned, and his touch was gentle, fingers warm against her chilly skin. 'Are you sure you're OK?'

'Absolutely fine!' she declared, grabbing the toboggan leash. 'Best of five?'

Travis snatched up his own sledge. 'I won't need five!'

In the end, they lost count of the runs and who'd 'won'. Her jeans were soaked, her hands were cold despite the waterproof mitts and her thighs were burning from hauling the sledge up and down the hillock.

After the final run, once they'd pulled themselves out of the snow, Freya pointed out other people trooping up the path to the field, dragging sledges in their wake.

'We're not alone,' she said to Travis.

'I'm surprised we had the place to ourselves this long on a snowy morning.' He checked his watch. 'Talking of which, it's almost ten o clock.'

'Really? I can't believe it.'

'Time flies when you're having fun.' He smiled. 'Sadly, I should go to the gallery or Bree really will kill me. It should be a busy day with so many people arriving for Christmas looking for gifts.'

'You'd better get a move on and I have to go too. I'm soaked,' she said while they walked back to the cabin. 'I need to get home to the cottage and have a hot shower.'

'I'd like to join you.'

'Don't tempt me!' Freya cried. 'Thanks for the sledge idea. I had the best time. And I did beat you.'

'Oh really? I thought we lost count?'

'Maybe . . . see you later at my place?'

'Sure, I've a workshop tomorrow but I can come over tonight.'

'Why don't you stay?' The invitation had tumbled out before she'd had time to think and the surprise in Travis's eyes was unmistakable.

'If you're sure, I'd love to. I'll make sure I have all my kit and a change of clothes so I can make an early start.'

Freya went into the cabin only to collect her handbag, before jumping in the car and gingerly driving down the track into the village. The streets were filling up with families and walkers, cramming into the cafes and browsing the shops, with their windows decorated for the festive season. The backdrop of the snowy fells made it look impossibly Christmassy and she was still pulsing with endorphins after the sledging.

Today had been the happiest she'd been for a long time . . . pure unadulterated joy.

She had to stop for a pedestrian crossing outside the solicitor's where Jos Beresford was talking to a woman she assumed was a client. He saw her and nodded curtly. She remembered the Christmas meal she'd spent at his parents' house, sitting around their table not long after they'd become engaged, and a chill came over her.

In hindsight, that was probably one of the earliest moments when she sensed something wasn't right between her and Jos. Ignoring that niggling feeling had led to so much hurt for him and herself. It was one of the biggest regrets of her life that she hadn't recognised the signs earlier – hadn't known herself much better. She should have learned from the way she allowed herself to be persuaded to break off her engagement with Travis. No wonder she now felt she couldn't let any man get too close, commit to anyone.

Then there was Travis: being continually let down by his father must have left scars deeper than she'd even realised. Was that why he was so angry and upset when she'd broken off their overnight engagement? She'd been too young to fully understand back then.

Was the accusation Jos had flung at her when they'd split up true – that she was 'toxic' as far as relationships were concerned? Or had it only been 'right man, wrong time' – then wrong man, right time?

And now?

Wrong man, wrong time . . . How did you *know*?

What if she did overcome her fears and want more? She'd issued an ultimatum to him that now felt impossible to go back on.

Chapter Twenty-Seven

'What's this?' Travis grimaced as a Michael Buble song played from a Bluetooth speaker by the cash desk. He'd arrived a few minutes late, with damp hair from the sledging.

Bree tapped the phone and said, 'I'm going to play some Christmas music. Haven't you noticed it's happening in a few days' time? You did ask me to do some extra hours so you could focus on getting the last-minute orders out?'

'Yes, thanks. Appreciate it.'

'Gav won't. This was his day off but to be honest, I'm enjoying working here more than I thought and sorting you out. I re-jigged the ordering system by the way. Whoever set it up for you made it overly complicated.'

'Erm. I set it up,' Travis admitted sheepishly.

'Hmm. That figures.' Bree grinned. 'You'll find it a lot simpler to use now and find exactly who's ordered what and the pricing, delivery status and so on. I've just stopped you from sending a canvas of a grizzly bear to a woman who'd ordered a cute bunny.'

'Thanks,' Travis said. 'You're a star. I'm sorry the admin systems were a mess. I had to set everything up in such a hurry. The past few weeks have been crazy; I feel I'm always in a rush.'

Bree narrowed her eyes. 'I can see that. Your hair's wet – raced out of the shower after sleeping late, did we?'

'You know me too well,' said Travis. 'And you're probably right about the Christmas music.'

'Don't be a Grinch. I can't avoid it if I wanted to. I've got a nativity play at Dylan's nursery, Rosie's going to a Christmas party at Baby Gym, I need to get all the fresh food for Christmas dinner and collect the turkey, and the carol concert is coming up. I've been roped into helping with the refreshments while Gav's in charge of the kids.'

'You're a saint.'

'More like a prize mug.' She sighed. 'I keep reminding myself it's for a good cause. The money's split between a kids' charity and the church hall. You *are* going, aren't you. As a local businessperson you should be supporting it. Show your commitment to the community.' She smirked. 'Cottage Angels are sponsoring it.'

'So I heard.' Travis tried to sound casual. 'Actually, I am going. The vicar asked me if I'd take some official photographs.'

'You never said!'

'She mentioned it after Roxanne's wedding and I thought she might have forgotten but she sent me an email about it this morning.'

'That's good. You're turning into a fine, upstanding member of the community.'

Travis grimaced. 'I hope not, though I seem to be turning into the go-to guy for any photography jobs.'

While Bree dealt with a handful of early customers, Travis set to work on printing and folding the squirrel cards. He'd edited the image slightly on his computer but it hadn't needed much and he'd left the inside of the card blank. On the rear, he'd added the Peak Perspectives logo and a credit to Seb Marshall. Finally, he added them to the card display by the door and several more to the box by the cash area.

With only a few days to Christmas, a degree of panic gift buying had set in, and Travis was thankful for it.

Bree was rushed off her feet, dealing with customers while he was almost hoarse from chatting to them about workshops, locations, camera settings, lenses and filters.

While some simply wanted to boast about their own skills, many were fascinated to hear from a professional, who was 'living the dream'. He'd have no need to work at all if he had a tenner every time someone asked him 'how did you get into this?' – usually from middle-aged men looking for a second career. Travis didn't knock their ambition; he knew plenty of 'amateurs' who'd quit their jobs to go full-time, but you had to be good, media savvy and prepared to put in long, long hours.

At lunchtime, Bree handed over a hot paper bag that smelled amazing.

'Wow. What's this?'

'Turkey pasty from the bakery. I got one for myself.'

She tore a chunk off the pasty and blew on it to cool it as she always had. He felt a rush of affection towards her: Bree had always been a constant in his life and Seb's, the lodestone even when her brothers had wandered far away, physically and metaphorically. He was delighted she was loving her work in the gallery, for both their sakes.

'Thanks, Bree,' he said, watching her chew her pasty cautiously. 'For everything.'

She glanced up in surprise. 'What's brought this on?'

He shrugged. 'Nothing in particular . . . I'm just grateful for your help with the gallery and for looking out for Seb.'

'Well, I'm not alone now, am I? You're back to help. He enjoyed that photography trip. Mentioned it twice when he came round the other day.'

'Good. I wasn't sure he'd enjoy it but I'm glad.'

'It was a great idea.'

Replying with a smile, Travis didn't tell her it was Freya's idea.

'Call me sentimental,' Bree went on. 'But I'm really looking forward to having everyone together for Christmas. Last year Seb promised he'd be round for dinner but he ended up in the pub all day with his mates. He rolled in drunk after closing time and woke up the kids. Rosie was colicky and I was absolutely knackered. There wasn't much festive spirit on my part and he ended up storming out and going back to his flat.'

Travis could picture the scene. 'I'm sorry I've not been much help myself.'

'Well, if I'd been offered the chance to swan off on all-expenses-paid trip to see the Northern Lights, I'd have done it too.'

'It wasn't all "swanning off". I did have to work. It was the coldest I've ever been and I was obliged to be nice to people I couldn't escape from for two whole weeks. I also put on half a stone.'

Bree pouted. 'Poor you. My heart bleeds.' Then she rolled her eyes. 'I'm winding you up. I'd have gone nuts if you'd cancelled a trip like that to spend the day in our madhouse.'

'The kids are darlings.' Travis smiled.

'Only because they're not yours and "Unca Tardis" can do no wrong.'

He smiled. 'Dylan must be so excited.'

'He's been hyper since Hallowe'en,' Bree said drily then sighed wistfully. 'All that matters is that you're here now and . . .' She held up crossed fingers. 'Seb has promised to turn up for lunch sober this year. It'll be lovely to have a Christmas with us all together like a proper family.'

'We've always been a "proper family",' Travis replied. 'Whatever that is.'

'I never felt it was for us,' Bree said. 'What with Dad away and then vanished. Poor Mum. Now I'm a parent, I can understand the pressures she was under. I might give her a call.'

Travis nodded. It was great to see Bree happy and he was delighted their working arrangement suited them both so well, but he was uneasy.

He didn't want to leave Freya alone even for half the day, even though she'd said she'd be fine. It didn't feel like a 'proper Christmas' to him without her, even if it was all under wraps.

'I've ordered a whole turkey this year,' Bree went on. 'Well, I told Gav to order it and make sure there was enough for the four of us. I want us to have all the trimmings: party games, everything.'

'Sounds great . . .' Travis murmured, torn in two but knowing he couldn't possibly let his sister down. She'd done so much for him and Seb; she deserved her 'perfect' Christmas.

Yet so did Freya.

Should he ask her to come along? Ask Bree if she minded? Both of those things broke their 'agreement'.

The shop bell dinged. 'Here we go,' she said, the pasty halfway to her mouth.

'You finish your lunch,' Travis ordered, tossing the empty bag in the bin. He really had to ask Freya again how she'd like to spend Christmas Day and hope it was with him.

Throughout the afternoon, customers began to flood in, buying pictures and cards, booking the odd workshop or purchasing vouchers for photography-mad relatives. He sold another squirrel card and someone ordered a bigger print of it.

Seb would be made up.

Bree went home, leaving Travis to lock up.

He was eagerly anticipating his evening with Freya, but he had a call to make first. With the squirrel card secure in his laptop bag, he walked down the alley that led to Seb's flat. He hoped his brother's confidence would be boosted further by seeing the card and hearing that it had gone on sale. Even better, that Travis had sold two that day.

He opened the main door and stepped onto the stairs – then stopped.

He could hear music. At first, he'd thought it was the radio but then he realised it wasn't. It was someone singing live, quietly and accompanied by the soft sounds of a guitar.

He took another step, two and the stairs creaked. The music paused. Travis stopped, one foot on the top step that led to Seb's landing. He was almost too scared to breathe.

The music started again: a guitar intro.

Travis felt as if he was treading on eggshells as he crept up to the landing, listening to the mesmerising sound of the guitar and Seb's voice, soft and lilting. He recognised the ballad . . . an oldie. A real oldie from the dawn of time, but that he hadn't heard for years.

'The first cut is the deepest . . .'

He breathed in sharply then exhaled as softly as he could. That song . . . how it tore at his heartstrings. It reminded him of the good times: the three of them and their mum. She used to play it on CD, the Rod Stewart version – until they were sick of it. She'd sing along and actually, she didn't have a bad voice which must have been where Seb got his vocal talent from.

And yet, it also brought back the dark times. He'd played it himself when Freya and he had split up, seeking comfort in the misery of someone else who understood how painful the loss of your first love was. Looking back, he'd tried to rationalise those feelings and diminish them as teenage angst yet hearing Seb's haunting voice, which held a kind of broken innocence, brought them to life again.

That night he'd said goodbye to Freya and she'd taken a piece of his heart with her – a piece that was still in her possession if only she knew. Maybe she *did* sense it and that's why she was refusing to let him get close.

He knew the words off by heart; and knew that the song was coming to its end.

He turned and crept back down the stairs. Seb didn't need an audience – and not a hostile one – perhaps not ever, but at least he was doing the thing he loved again and that was all that mattered.

Travis told Freya about Seb over pasta carbonara and a bottle of Pinot Grigio at her cottage.

'Thanks, that was slightly better than a microwave turkey dinner,' he said as she lounged on the sofa with her bare feet in his lap.

She chuckled.

'I have good news. I went round to Seb's on my way home and I heard him playing his guitar.'

'Really?' Her eyes lit up with pleasure. 'That sounds a really positive sign.'

'Yeah. I decided not to disturb him in case he stopped. I think your idea might have worked.'

'Maybe,' she said. 'Or perhaps he just decided to start again anyway. I'm not taking any credit for it. Whatever has triggered this, I'm happy for him.'

'Even so, thanks. I'm not sure I'd have thought of – or dared – ask him on the shoot for fear of getting my head bitten off. If he'd said no, it might have ended in a row. I guess,' he said, 'we can both be pig-headed.'

'You don't say . . .'

He massaged her feet, enjoying the feel of the soft flesh. He circled her ankle, thinking how beautiful it was.

She twitched. 'That tickles.'

'But you like it.' He leaned forward and kissed her deeply. 'Shall we have an early night?'

'At seven p.m.?' He just smiled, took her hand and led her upstairs to bed.

The next morning, Travis was in early at the gallery to mount and frame, and pack some orders he'd taken during the week, ready for the courier to collect. The village was already filling up with tourists and shoppers, making last-minute purchases.

During a brief lull, Seb popped his head around the door.

'Sorry to bother you, but can I ask a favour?'

'Sure,' Travis said, pleased to be needed for a change.

Seb shoved his hands in his pockets awkwardly. 'I er, could do with . . . er . . . borrowing a camera? The cheap one will do, I know I can't be trusted with anything decent.'

'None of them are cheap,' Travis said, warily. 'What's this for?'

'Remember the bloke who was at the open mic night? Nate? I, er, happened to mention I'd been taking photos with you and he asked me if I'd mind doing a few shots of his band for their website and socials. Before you ask, he wanted something more professional than mobile phone shots.'

'You're going to take them?'

'Don't sound so surprised. They want outdoor shots and you showed me the basics on the camera so – I said I'd give it a try. I wasn't going to volunteer your services. They couldn't afford you and anyway, they're offering a small fee and I need the money.'

Travis gasped in mock horror, yet he was secretly pleased that Seb was taking an interest.

'I only need the camera for a couple of hours I promise I'll be careful. I'll be back with it before you know.'

'I can loan you one of my Canons and a lens, I suppose.'

'Thanks. You're a star.'

'I am when you want something.' He smiled wryly. 'Before I get the camera, I've got something else to show you. Come into the back.'

Seb followed him into the framing area where Travis lifted a cardboard box onto the table. 'These arrived this morning. I was about to put them on display.'

Seb gawped at the box as if it contained the crown jewels. 'It's not . . . is it?'

'Open it and see,' Travis said.

Seb lifted the cardboard flaps and took out the card featuring his squirrel. He stared at it, at a loss for words.

'You like?' Travis said.

Seb held the card up. 'It's awesome – in fact I can't believe I took this. Are you sure it isn't one of yours?'

'No! I wouldn't do that to you. It's all your own work. I've put them by the till and added some to the card rack. In fact, I've already sold two.'

'Two! Thanks, bro.'

Seb's expression of delight was enough to bring tears to Travis's eyes but he managed to put on a gruff voice to disguise his emotion. 'Now, let's have a look at this camera. I'll run through the basics again and give you some tips on taking PR shots for the band.'

'Be careful . . .' Travis warned, a while later, watching Seb walk out of the shop, whistling. His heart swelled with pride – and relief. Things were definitely looking up, as far as his brother was concerned at least.

Chapter Twenty-Eight

'Mimi! A Christmas miracle has happened.'

Freya called through to the office from the Cottage Angels reception area. A large package had just been deposited at the desk by the couriers.

'The banner's come!' she declared.

Mimi heaved a massive sigh of relief. 'Phew! I was beginning to think it wouldn't arrive in time for the concert. Let's have a look at it, then.'

The two of them managed to open the large canvas banner, checking that there were no faults or typos on it. It was their showcase item of promo for the carol concert, specially commissioned to be hung in front of the stage.

Held on December 23rd, the concert was always a highlight of the Bannerdale festive celebrations and, Freya thought, heralded the moment when you really felt as if Christmas had arrived. She'd always enjoyed going along, first as a child with her mum and friends and even in her teenage years, though she'd affected a blasé attitude to it, claiming she only went along for her mother's sake.

Even when she'd been away at uni, she'd made a point of always being home and going to the concert with her mother. In fact, this might be the first time Sandra Bolton had missed it.

Freya didn't have time off until the office closed on Christmas Eve afternoon and she could finally meet up with Travis at her place and they could both relax.

She got home from the office late and flopped onto the sofa with a hot chocolate when a WhatsApp call came through from her mother. Bronzed, and with a glamorous updo, she was wearing a sleeveless cocktail dress and chandelier earrings.

'Hello! Hope you can hear me, there are so many people on deck, only I thought I'd call before the fireworks went off!'

Freya turned her phone volume up so she could hear her mother better.

'You're very glam,' Freya said, thinking how happy her mum looked.

'Oh, yes, we've just been to the captain's gala dinner and we were invited onto his table. The food was amazing and now we're all outside waiting for the firework spectacular over Cozumel.'

'I saw the photos of you snorkelling on Instagram. It looks amazing and warmer than here.'

'It's glorious. The sea temperature was like a warm bath and you should see the coral . . . We're having a wonderful time.' Her enthusiasm tailed off. 'But I keep worrying about you. Neil and I both do. You're not on your own on Christmas Day, are you? Because Auntie Hazel emailed me the other day and I said we'd left you behind and she said you'd be very welcome at hers.'

Left you behind? Even though her mother and Neil meant well, Freya felt like a puppy that had been abandoned.

'Mum, I am absolutely fine. Work's super busy what with people arriving for Christmas, and Cottage Angels is sponsoring the village carol service so there's loads to do with that and er, the usual Christmassy stuff. I'll be fine.'

'OK but your Auntie Hazel will be thrilled to see you. Uncle Graham has dug out some old videos of you and your cousins when you were all tiny. She says there's a hilarious one of you all splashing each other in the paddling pools and then your cousin decides to water the garden, the little horror . . .'

Great, the option of watching videos of herself, probably naked, and her cousin doing a wee on the roses, in front of a bunch of distant relatives.

'It's very kind of them to ask, but I've plans!' she said, only slightly hysterically. For some of it, Freya thought, with mixed feelings.

'So you're going to Mimi's after all?' Her mum heaved a sigh.

'Um—' Freya was saved from an outright lie by a loud bang.

'Sorry, darling, that was a massive rocket! But you'll have a lovely time at Mimi's . . .' Loud pops and crackles drowned out the rest of her mother's words, then Freya saw her wave her hand and a grinning Neil appear behind her, waving madly.

'Have to go,' her mother trilled. 'Call you from our next port. Your Auntie Hazel will be disappointed but it's a weight off my mind that you won't be alone on Christmas Day.'

Chapter Twenty-Nine

'How'd it go, then?' Travis asked when Seb shuffled into the gallery later, buckling under the weight of the camera bag. It was almost time to close up after a very busy day. 'Are you ready to take on a new career as a music PR?'

His flippancy vanished when he saw Seb's gloomy expression.

'What's up? Didn't the shoot go well?'

'It went well. I got some good shots. Nate and the guys were really happy.'

'That's good . . . isn't it?'

Seb rested the bag on the framing table with extreme care. 'I, er . . . there's no easy way of saying this, bro . . .'

The hairs on the back of Travis's neck stood on end. 'No way of saying what?'

'I downloaded the pictures of the shoot OK, but then there was an accident.'

'What accident? Travis folded his arms. 'Don't tell me you dropped the camera in a beck?' He laughed and pointed a finger at Seb. 'This is a wind-up, yeah?'

'I wish it was. No, someone else dropped it. Not in a beck, though.'

'*Someone else* dropped it? Who?' Travis said sharply.

'I was in the pub with the guys from the band after the shoot and Fenno was there and he asked me about what I'd been doing.' Seb kept his eyes on the floor. 'And I let him hold the camera and it slipped and fell onto the tiles in the bar.'

'Fenno?' Travis groaned. 'That tosser again?'

'He's not a tosser.'

'He's the one who got you into trouble last time. What were you doing with him and his moronic mates? Bet you were pratting about!'

'No, I wasn't! It was an accident like I said.'

'Was Fenno pissed? Were you?'

'No! I was stone-cold sober and I'm gutted! I was dreading telling you this because I knew you'd go ballistic! Look, I'm really really sorry, but can't you claim on the insurance?'

The insurance. Travis was riled by Seb's casual attitude. 'Well, yeah, I guess but it won't cover the lot. There's a big excess.'

Seb covered his mouth with his hand. 'Shit. I'd expected you'd get the lot back.'

'No – but that's not the point! You should never have let him touch it. I asked you to be careful. I was happy to let you take it. I was glad to see you take an interest but you had to show off, didn't you?'

Seb stared at the ground.

Travis threw up his hands and let out a cry of frustration.

'Have you finished?' Seb said quietly.

'Not really. Jesus, Seb. Why do you do this stuff?'

'I don't know, Trav. Maybe because I thought I'd enjoy it. I never set out to break the camera. I never asked Fenno to drop it! If you didn't trust me, why did you even lend me the bloody thing!'

'Because I never expected you to be so cavalier with my stuff. You're hopeless!'

Seb opened his mouth then shut it. His eyes glistened and Travis wanted to kick himself. His brother looked on the verge of tears. 'Bro, I didn't mean that. Honestly. I was just shocked – and a bit pissed off.'

'I worked that out,' Seb said quietly.

'It was an accident. I realise that and the insurance will cover most of it, bar a few hundred. I can take that hit. Cameras get broken all the time.'

'Do they?' Seb lifted his eyes. 'Not by you, though. I bet you take care of your stuff. I'm sorry I didn't.'

Travis reached out to pat his shoulder but Seb flinched away. 'No. You're right. I am hopeless. Everything I touch turns to shit.' He turned for the door. 'Stop trying to turn me into something I'm not: a useful member of society. It'll be easier for both of us.'

Seb pulled the door open as Freya arrived and pushed past her.

'Sorry,' he muttered, but hurried away from the shop.

Travis jogged over, watching his brother skulk off up the street like a wounded animal.

'What's the matter with Seb?' she said.

'I've upset him,' Travis said, filled with despair. 'I need to go after him.'

'Wait.' Freya put her hand on his arm. 'Looks like you need to leave him to cool down. Maybe both of you need to give each other some space.'

He traipsed back into the shop and sat down, his head in

his hands. He told her what had happened, the broken camera on the counter seeming trivial against the damage to the fragile relationship with his brother.

'You can fix this,' she said firmly.

'I admire your optimism but I feel I've kicked him back down just as he was rising. Why didn't I think before I spoke? The moment he mentioned that bunch of idiots was involved, I saw red.'

'Because you were frustrated and you care about him?' she offered.

'He sees me as having come back purely to get on his case. I don't blame him, but you know the worst part? The way I reacted reminded me of my dad. I called Seb "hopeless".' He swore silently, feeling queasy at the remembrance of his words. 'That's last thing he needs to hear. Sometimes I feel that I'm repeating my dad's mistakes where Seb is concerned.'

'I doubt it. From what you've told me, your father didn't care enough about any of you to take an interest in your lives whereas you care too much.'

'Maybe.' He sighed deeply, feeling out of his depth but grateful for her insight. 'Sometimes I think we can't escape from the past; it comes back to haunt us. Why think things could be any different?'

'They *can*.' She put her arms around his waist and saying sternly. 'Go and see him later or first thing tomorrow. Don't let this fester between you.'

Travis opened the curtains of the cabin, to find pink tingeing the sky as the day began. It was forecast to be bitingly cold but clear, with blue skies. He had time to head up to the fells with his camera before he opened the gallery.

It was then he spotted an envelope on the doormat. Recognising the handwriting instantly, he opened it and his stomach clenched.

Dressed in a smart trouser suit, Freya walked into the living room.

'What have I done?' he murmured, pulling banknotes from the envelope, and holding them out to her. 'Seb must have put this through the door late last night.'

She took the money from him, dismay on her face. 'There must be several hundred quid here.'

'Where did he get the money for this?' Travis said, feeling close to tears. 'You know what? I'm beginning to think it's not Seb who's hopeless, it's me.'

Chapter Thirty

On her way into work, Freya called in at the mini-market for birthday muffins for Hamish, yet it was Seb and Travis who were at the forefront of her mind. Seb wasn't her responsibility or part of her family and yet she'd started to feel that way.

On leaving the shop, she found Seb lurking down the side by the trade bins, a cigarette in his hand, staring into space. It was bitter cold and he was only wearing his uniform.

She hesitated before approaching him and then took the plunge. 'Hiya. I didn't think you smoked.'

He shrugged. 'I gave up but . . . I scrounged this from a mate. I can't afford it anyway.'

She had to choose her words very carefully. 'Seb, tell me to mind my own business but when I, um, popped into the gallery earlier this morning, Travis mentioned you'd given him some money.'

'*He* told you that?' He gave her a hard stare. She knew he didn't believe a word of her attempts to pretend she'd casually dropped by first thing.

'I think he was, um . . . a bit bothered by something he'd said to you . . . over a broken camera.' Freya realised she'd dug a massive hole for herself and Seb wasn't buying any of it.

'So, let me get this right,' he said carefully. 'Trav told you we'd had a massive row and that I'd pushed an envelope through the door. Because he'd share that with anyone who "dropped by"?'

She squirmed. She couldn't keep lying to Seb, not if she wanted to gain his trust.

'I caught him at a bad moment and he's worried about you,' she said, answering his question without actually answering it.

'Sure he is.' Seb took a long drag of his cigarette.

'You know he didn't mean what he said . . . Look this is probably way out of order, but I think he's worried that you . . . might have made life difficult for yourself by giving him that money.'

'You mean he's worried I nicked something or borrowed it from one of my moronic mates?'

'He didn't say that,' Freya said calmly. 'And he didn't ask me to come here. It's me being nosy and um . . . concerned. As a friend,' she added.

Seb shook his head, a bitter smile briefly passing over his lips. He threw the unfinished cigarette onto the ground and ground it into the mud with his boot.

'I sold my guitars.'

Freya inhaled sharply. 'Oh God.'

He shrugged. 'It was either that or default on my rent.'

'Oh, Seb. I'm sorry you felt you had to do that. You shouldn't have.' She knew Travis would be devastated. 'Where are they?'

'Music shop in Windermere.'

251

'You need them back.'

'I can't. I need to pay Travis for the insurance excess. I know it won't cover the whole lot, but I won't take money from him. It was my decision to sell them.'

'He'd be gutted if he knew.'

'Do *not* tell him!' Seb's eyes were wild. 'Don't. I wanted to do this. I want to sort out my own mess for a change.'

'I won't let on but you have to get those instruments back.'

He laughed. 'How?'

'I'll . . . I'll loan you the money.'

'Loan?' He shook his head. 'Freya, even if I could bear to take your hard-earned cash, it would take me ages to pay you back.'

'I have savings. I can afford it,' she said. 'I'll wait while you pay me back as and when. Call it an investment.'

He snorted. 'In what?' He eyed her suspiciously. 'Why would you help me? Why do you care so much?'

'I don't like seeing you torture yourself.'

His searching gaze reminded her of his brother. 'Or you don't like Travis torturing himself? Why do I think this is about helping him, not me?' He stared at her. 'You're shagging each other again, aren't you?'

'That's none of your business!'

'I'll take that as a yes.'

'Please don't – I . . . I am sorry I interfered but the offer still stands. There's nothing serious between me and Travis.'

His eyebrows shot up. 'Friends with benefits, is it?'

Freya pressed her lips together.

His eyes bored into her, seeing everything. 'OK. It's none of my business but you should know that Travis is a sensitive soul,' Seb sneered. 'He plays the hard man but he's a bloody romantic at heart. I know you two went out when I was young and that you split up. I was only thirteen but I heard Mum moaning about it, Bree too.'

Moaning about her, Freya guessed. 'That was years ago. And like I said, there's nothing heavy going on now.'

'OK.' He held up his hands. 'Look, I do appreciate you trying to help – both of us – but why is it so important to you that I get my guitars back.'

'I shouldn't tell you this but Travis heard you playing the other night.'

'What?'

'He went round to the flat and heard you, but he walked out because he didn't want to disturb you.'

'Man, he really does tell you everything.' Seb kept his eyes on the ground, almost as if he was ashamed of being caught playing again.

'Not everything but he was so pleased to hear you again, that I guess he couldn't help himself. It just came out when we were together. I'm sorry you're upset he shared it with me.'

'Upset?' Seb exhaled. 'I'm not upset. I . . .' He frowned. 'I'm amazed that it meant that much to him. In a way it scares me that he's so keen to "save" me. I'm not sure I can live up to his expectations. I'm never going to be a big shot like him. I'll always be average at best.'

'If by average, you mean normal, regular and like the rest of us mere mortals, then join the club,' Freya said, fearing she was treading on eggshells but determined to say her piece. 'We all have our demons and bad experiences we can't shake off, anxieties, a ton of baggage.'

He looked at her thoughtfully. 'You mean you and my brother?'

'Yeah. I guess. We've got to deal with them but don't try and beat yourself up on top of surviving day to day.'

There was a pause during which Freya was on tenterhooks then Seb let out a huge sigh. 'I won't lie. It gutted me to sell my instruments and I'd love to have them back but even if I accepted your frankly crazy offer, I can't repay you. Not for months.'

'I understand that but maybe there's another way of you repaying the debt, if you really want to.'

His puzzled frown changed to a smile of realisation. 'Ah, you want me to work for *you*? Cleaning toilets and making beds?' He grinned. 'That I can understand and y'know, it's not the stupidest idea I've ever heard.'

Freya smiled, her plan hatching along with her fear that Seb might not agree to her terms. It was too late to back down now, though. 'Come into the office straight after your shift and I'll tell you more.'

Chapter Thirty-One

Butterflies took flight in Freya's stomach as she helped Mimi unload their banner from the car outside the village hall.

'Careful,' Mimi warned. 'It's icy and this thing is heavy.'

It felt as if half the village was there, checking lighting and sound systems, setting out chairs and busying themselves in the kitchen area ready for the concert that evening. The vicar was the compere for the evening and was in deep discussion with two women who were acting as 'stage managers'. The sound of excited kids singing and laughing came from the room behind the stage that had been designated as a warm-up area.

With its tinsel-covered walls and tree adorned with handmade decorations, the hall had a homely feel that she'd always found rather comforting. This afternoon, the usual odour of floor polish had been eclipsed by the scent of mince pies and mulled wine from the kitchen area.

She and Mimi fastened the banner to the rear of the stage. Several members of the traders' association were helping to set up including the electrician, Brian and Jos Beresford.

They'd almost finished when Jos came over. 'Do you need a hand?'

'We're OK, thanks.'

He stood back and admired the banner – at least she thought he was admiring it. 'It looks impressive,' he said.

Freya smiled.

'You don't think I mean it?'

She glanced up in surprise then laughed. 'Of course I do. Thanks.'

'Good because I only have your best interests at heart. I always did – I still do.'

Freya was lost for a reply. She didn't want to say anything that might start an awkward conversation, or to hurt or encourage him.

'Ah, Freya. Glad I caught you!' Brian interrupted, brandishing a clipboard. It was one time when Freya was grateful for his officiousness. 'I'd like to check that your banner is securely fixed. It could cause a nasty injury if it fell off the stage during the performance. There are children around.'

'It's *very* securely fixed, thank you, Brian,' Freya said with a sweet smile but steel in her voice. 'So there's no need to worry.'

Jos patted Brian on the shoulder. 'Brian, I'm sure it will be fine. Freya and Mimi know what they're doing and this isn't an official traders' association event so we don't need to be concerned about insurance issues – in the very unlikely event of an incident, I'm sure Freya and Mimi have their public liability insurance sorted out.'

'We certainly do,' Freya soothed.

Brian puffed up. 'Well, better to be safe than sorry, but as I'm not required, I've plenty of other jobs to be getting on with.'

'It's very kind of you to give so much time to the event,' Freya said, feeling guilty and slightly miffed at being 'saved' from Brian by Jos. There was something slightly paternalistic about him that she'd only noticed since they'd split up. He was a decent man, but she could never have been wholly herself with him.

The thought filled her with a mix of relief, sadness – and shame that she hadn't recognised how unsuited they were before she'd let things go so far. Being unsure of her feelings had caused them both a lot of pain and she wouldn't let that happen again, with Travis or any man.

After Brian had scuttled off, Jos lingered. 'Is Travis coming? I know he's been asked to take the photographs, but you never know if he'll actually turn up.'

'Of course he's coming,' Freya said. 'He wouldn't let you down.'

Jos raised his eyebrows. 'You seem very certain of that.'

'If he commits to do something, then he'll do it,' she said firmly.

'I'm glad some people do,' he muttered.

She bridled. 'That's hardly fair.'

'I know and I'm sorry. I shouldn't have said it, but I can't stop caring about you.' His eyes held desperation that filled her with dismay.

'I'm sorry too, but you have to try. We both have to go on with our lives and now's definitely not the time to talk about this.' She waved frantically at Mimi. 'Mimi! Can you help me collect the children's goody bags?'

He nodded and she walked outside to the car, feeling his resentful eyes burning into her back. She was already on edge about the event and by defending Travis, she'd probably confirmed Jos's obvious suspicions that the two of them were closer than friends. When she returned with the goody bags, she heaved a sigh of relief to see him halfway up a stepladder on the stage.

Freya and Mimi had spent ages filling the bags with colouring books, felt tips and Christmas chocolates, ready to hand out to the younger children at the end of the concert. Freya took the bags into the kitchen and finally, she and Mimi drove back to the office.

'Right, I'll be back after we've had tea,' Mimi said, flicking the remote on her Focus.

'I'm popping home to get changed too,' Freya replied, though she felt too edgy for much food.

Mimi gave her a searching look. 'Are you OK? You seemed a bit . . . twitchy at the hall. I noticed Jos talking to you. He hasn't been a pain, has he?'

'No. No . . . he was just being Jos.' Freya smiled. 'I am a bit twitchy because I want things to go well tonight. We are the main sponsors and it feels like a big deal.'

Mimi patted her arm. 'Why is it a big deal? We've done our bit and provided the cash and prizes. All we need to do is sit back and enjoy the concert. See you soon.'

With an air kiss, Mimi left, leaving Freya alone in the car park. She checked her phone for a message she'd been hoping to receive for the past hour. There was nothing so she jumped in her car and drove home, wishing she really could just sit back and relax.

Early birds were already arriving at the hall by the time Freya returned, freshly showered and in an emerald velvet jumpsuit she'd bought specially for the occasion.

She went into the canteen area with a hamper for the interval raffle and left it on the table by the goody bags. On her way back into the hall, Travis met her.

'I love the antlers,' he said, tweaking the top of her reindeer headband.

'You made me jump!'

He pinged her antlers again. 'You look gorgeous.'

'Thanks. I feel a bit nervous.'

'I can't think why.'

'Maybe because Cottage Angels haven't been main sponsors before. I want to make a good impression. Is, um, Bree coming tonight?'

'She's on her way. She always loved the concert. It wasn't Mum's thing but she hauled us along a couple of times. Said she'd never do it again though after Seb raided the goody bags for chocolate and was sick during "Good King Wenceslas". He was banned by Mum after that, much to his delight.'

Freya laughed. 'It doesn't sound like his thing, I must admit.'

'Nah. According to Bree, he's gone to Lancaster to visit some mates apparently.'

'Are you still worried about him?'

'Yes. I always worry and that's not right. I'm not his father but since I've come back, I'm in danger of trying to take on that role. The business with the camera was a disaster.'

'Has he said any more about it?'

'No. I've called him to try and smooth things over and he seems OK, but he won't have the money back and I still don't know where he got it from.' He sighed. 'I can't worry about him tonight. I have enough to do.'

She nodded. 'It must feel strange to be playing a key role after all this time.'

'Strictly behind the camera. The idea of being the centre of attention makes me break out in a cold sweat. No one notices the photographer.'

'You attracted enough attention at school,' Freya said.

'It was all bravado. It was a front. You knew that. Later, it suited me to be invisible.' He held up the camera. 'If I've got to be around people, at least I can hide behind my lens. I can make them the focus of attention, not me. It suits me to be invisible.'

With the way he looked tonight, rugged, handsome and in his element, Freya thought otherwise. She'd spotted a lot of the villagers taking a very great interest at him, though she certainly wasn't going to tell him that.

Chapter Thirty-Two

Travis carried on snapping away, noticing a lot from behind the lens, some of which he wasn't meant to see. He was sure the vicar hadn't meant him to take pictures of the choir master reading *Fifty Shades* behind his song book or Brian trying on a turkey hat for size when he thought no one was looking.

He was probably meant to stick to safe, posed shots of people grinning at the camera, but then again, the vicar *had* told him to 'capture the spirit of the occasion' so he felt justified.

Of course, the photos might not all make it to the official website. That included dozens of Freya shining like a precious jewel in a jumpsuit that looked sensational on her.

The volume of chatter rose once the hall was almost full so he moved to the back of the room, where he could capture some shots of the singers without disturbing them.

Freya found her way into the viewfinder again, chatting to two bearded guys in the front row who Travis recognised as proprietors of the village hardware store. Freya was smiling a *lot*, though her body language was stiff. He could tell she was on edge, almost as if she was part of a performance herself. Was it simply because this was a big night for her business, and it rightly meant a lot to her? Or was it because Jos Beresford kept gawping at her every five minutes?

Travis laughed at himself. Who was he to criticise Jos when he couldn't take his eyes off her either? He was the lucky man sharing her bed, yet somehow he didn't feel lucky.

The lights dimmed and he lowered the lens.

A spotlight lit the stage and the vicar, resplendent in a purple glittery trouser suit and dog collar, sashayed onto the stage. The shutter whirred and he became aware of Freya next to him, smelling of frangipani, her velvet sleeve brushing his arm.

'Hello,' she whispered but his reply was lost in thunderous applause as the curtains parted and the village choir let rip with 'Deck the Halls.'

Travis was so busy capturing the atmosphere as soloists and groups performed a medley of carols and Christmas hits that the time flew by and the interval came. It was thirsty work so he slipped into the kitchen to collect a soft drink.

Stalwarts of the traders' association were dishing out refreshments, although Brian was knocking back more mulled wine than he was handing out.

Freya kept sliding him looks that made him long to sweep her up in his arms and carry her home to Squirrel Cottage. He managed to make his way through the hungry hordes to her and whispered in her ear.

'If we were on our own, I'd drag you off to bed. You look incredible.'

Her cheeks flushed. 'You can't say things like that to me when people watching.'

'I don't care. I want to unzip that jumpsuit right now.' His pulse beat faster at the image in his mind.

With a fixed smile, Freya nodded a hello at someone across the room before returning her gaze to Travis. 'That might cause a stir,' she murmured.

Ladies and gentlemen, please can you return to your seats for the second part of our Christmas concert which starts in three minutes!'

At the sound of the vicar's voice, the kitchen began to empty, and Travis returned to his post at the rear of the hall.

As with all second halves, the audience were in the mood to party, largely thanks to the mulled wine. The church choir sang 'The Holly and the Ivy', which was followed by a band doing a version of Elvis's 'Blue Christmas'. It was an eclectic mix that made Travis smile.

The vicar spoke into the mic, a grin on her face. 'Now, we have a special highlight that I am so excited about.'

Intrigued and inebriated 'oh's rippled around the audience.

'I wonder what this is,' Freya whispered.

'For one night only, I ask you to give a huge round of applause to our new supergroup, Brian and the Snails – with their unique version of a Bruce Springsteen classic!'

The curtains parted to a huge collective gasp followed by squeals of delight, revealing a sight that Travis never imagined in his wildest dreams.

Brian sat at a keyboard in an electric-blue zoot suit, accompanied by a white-haired guy on drums and a seventy-plus man in ripped jeans on lead vocals.

'Did you know about this?' he hissed in Freya's ear.

She held up her hands, her eyes wide in astonishment. 'Do I look as if I did?'

People were cheering as Brian and his fellow musicians launched into 'Santa Claus is Coming to Town'. Everyone started singing along and even Jos was clapping in a suitably dignified way.

Travis moved into the aisle to get some photos, still hardly able to believe his eyes at the sight of Brian on his feet, thumping the keys like a rock star.

The song ended and the audience were on their feet, screaming for more but the curtains had closed, hiding Brian and the Snails from view.

'What the hell was in that mulled wine?' Travis declared.

'I think it's probably Ribena with a drop of brandy,' Freya said.

'A *drop?*'

The vicar stepped into the light again, waiting for the noise to die down and people to settle in their seats.

'Thank you, thank you everyone and a huge thanks to Brian and his Snails for bringing the house down. Now, the bad news is that our concert is almost at an end.'

The vicar acknowledged the good-natured boos of disappointment from the audience. 'I said, "almost," because for our finale, we have another very special treat for you.'

'What's this? Jos comes on dressed as Mariah Carey?' Travis murmured to Freya.

'I'd like to see that,' Freya muttered.

Suddenly, the stage was plunged into darkness. A hush descended on the audience and Travis raised his camera.

A few moments later, a single spotlight shone on a stool and mic in the centre of the stage. Into the pool of light walked a familiar figure carrying a guitar.

'*Seb?*'

'Shh!' A woman glared at Travis from the back row but he hadn't been able to stop himself from blurting his brother's name out loud.

'*Silent night, holy night, all is calm . . .*'

There were more gasps, of surprise and delight, but this time, the audience were silent – rapt as Seb gently coaxed the opening notes of the carol from his guitar. His lilting yet earthy voice was like the touch of a hand, soothing the audience. The arrangement was beautiful too and Travis guessed it was one of Seb's own.

Tears pricked the back of his eyes. How could this be? How had Seb been persuaded to step up on stage in front of half the village after so long?

The song ended and the audience burst into warm applause. Travis was almost too shocked to join in. Freya, in contrast, was clapping enthusiastically.

'Thanks, guys,' Seb said, a little shyly. 'Now, I think you'll also know this one.

'*O, little town of Bethlehem, how still we see thee lie . . .*'

They did, and there were 'oh's and 'ah's as Seb played and sing the well-loved favourite.

At the end, the audience erupted again but Seb called for a hush.

'You've been a fantastic audience. Finally, this one is for someone special in the audience. It's an oldie but a goody and it reminds me of good times with my family. Most of all, it's for you, Travis and you, Bree.'

'*Have yourself a merry little Christmas . . .*'

Travis rubbed his eyes with his hand but the tears kept coming. He had to get out of the room but he had to stay and hear the end. His hands shook too much to take any photos but everyone around him was holding up phones. He looked for Bree to see her reaction but could only see the back of her head.

Finally, the song ended and the audience erupted into applause.

Travis joined in, whooping and whistling.

Freya was on her feet cheering, along with the rest of the audience.

He leaned close to her ear. 'Did you know anything about this?'

Shrugging, she applauded and whooped even louder.

Wreathed in delighted smiles, the vicar strode onto the stage, raising her hands to calm people down. 'Thank you, thank you for that. Seb is a very talented young man as is every single person who took part in our carol concert tonight. I want to thank them all for giving up their time and entertaining us all. Thanks to all the front of house team, backstage crew and tonight couldn't have happened without the . . .'

She went on to thank a long list of people whose names became a blur to Travis, who still had a lump in his throat at the appearance of his brother on stage.

He was desperate to find him and congratulate him but there was one last surprise from the vicar.

'So, before we go, let's end this Christmas carol concert with a rousing performance of "We Wish You a Merry Christmas". I want you all to join in and raise the roof!'

Freya was singing enthusiastically alongside him, but Travis had only one aim. He slipped into the aisle and started to take photos to capture the moment. The choir, their song sheets lifted, mouths open. The audience belting out the song at the tops of their voices, smiles and people clapping along. Bree, looking suspiciously like her mascara had run. Most of all: Seb at the heart of it, playing and singing at the heart of a choir of kids and adults.

A pang of guilt seized him as he remembered his harsh words to Seb, even if they had been delivered in anger.

He dismissed the thought. He wouldn't let anything sour this moment: Seb's moment.

The song ended, with another raucous round of cheering and applause and then the lights went on, and the exodus started. Travis had never been sentimental about Christmas but this evening had injected even his cynical heart with a powerful dose of festive spirit.

'I have to find Seb – and Bree,' he said to Freya.

'OK. Tell him I thought he was amazing.' She smiled. 'I need to talk to Mimi and her family.'

Leaving her, he made his way through the lingering members of the audience to find Bree giving Seb a bear hug.

'Whoa, I can't breathe.'

'I don't care. If I want to give you a big hug, I will. I am so proud of you!'

'It's not Wembley, you know,' Seb said. 'Just a couple of easy carols in the village hall.'

'Stop that! You were brilliant.' Finally letting him go, she stood back. 'Wasn't he, Travis?'

'He was pretty good,' Travis said.

Bree batted him om the arm. '*Pretty* good? He was amazing. I cried!'

'I was seriously impressed,' Travis said, refusing to let on that the emotion had also got to him. 'You're a dark horse too. I had no idea you'd be performing.

Seb grinned. 'Well, I hate to be predictable.'

Travis leaned in to hug him and murmured. 'Bro, I'm sorry about the other day . . .'

'Not now,' Seb said. 'Let's save "the talk" for later. If ever.'

'I *do* want to talk,' Travis insisted. 'I want to know what made you play again – here?'

'Ah, Sebastian!' The vicar swooped down on them, sparkling in sequins and smiles. 'It seems to be the moment for hugs, so let me give you a great big one.'

Trapped like a rabbit in the headlights, Seb had no choice but to allow himself to be hugged. Bree exchanged a smirk with Travis. Seb might love performing but he only enjoyed the spotlight on stage; this attention might all prove a bit much after he'd been in the doldrums for so long.

Finally releasing Seb, the vicar chatted for them for a while before flitting off to thank the children's choir leader. Travis caught sight of Freya, now alone after Mimi had left the hall.

Seb had retrieved his guitar from the chair. 'I need to go back to the flat and get some sleep. I'm at work tomorrow and it's Christmas Eve so the place will be crazy from when we first open.'

'Good, well I'll be going too. I bet Gav's climbing the walls because Dylan is completely hyper, asking if Santa will have set off by now and will he see the sign in the garden and what if the sleigh has a breakdown. I can't wait for Christmas morning to finally come. You haven't forgotten about Christmas dinner?' Bree added sternly.

Travis's euphoric mood dipped instantly. His gaze slid to Freya; all might be starting to go well with Seb, but he still hadn't come up with a solution to being in two places at once.

Travis walked with Seb to his flat, chatting about the

concert. The moment they were inside, he handed over the envelope of cash which Seb had shoved through his door.

'Here, have this and before you ask, I was going to give it back before I saw you at the concert. I hope you believe me. This isn't some kind of reward for being a good boy.'

Seb stared at the envelope. 'I believe you, but I can't take your money.'

Travis put it on the table. 'OK but I'm sure not taking it back home with me. Think of it as an investment.'

'An "investment?"' Seb stared at him. 'Why do you call it that?'

'An investment. Buy something for your music.'

Seb seemed about to say something, then nodded. 'If you really want me to, then thanks. I did see a new strap in the Windermere music shop.'

'Good,' said Travis in relief. 'What I want to know is – and I don't care what the answer is – what made you play again?'

'That day we went up the fell. I started thinking. No, not about being a photographer, You've got that sewn up. I don't have the patience for that. I enjoyed the day and it was a buzz to take that squirrel picture but I know it was flukey. It would take years to be as good as you, years of dedication, patience and getting to know the wildlife even if I was interested which I'm not. And most importantly, if I had the talent, which I don't.'

Travis smiled. 'You don't need it.'

'But . . . it made me realise that I already have something I do have the patience for and the love for. Maybe even a tiny bit of talent. Not enough to do it professionally but enough to entertain myself. Some people seem to believe in me too so I guess I owe them.'

'People?' Travis said.

'You, Bree . . . and, um, as I came off stage, Carly Raffaello grabbed me. They still have the weekend music nights at the bar. It's mostly jazz and blues, but they're looking for some younger, more contemporary performers alongside the oldies.'

Travis smiled, knowing oldies meant anyone over thirty-five in Seb's eyes.

'Carly asked me if I want to do a Friday evening session while people are scoffing tapas and necking cocktails. It's a mature crowd, not exactly my scene, but they're going to pay me and you know it might lead to stuff and I'd be earning money . . . I could pay you back at some point.'

'If you insist but I'd keep your cash until you're headlining Glastonbury. It sounds great,' Travis said, filled with relief. 'I'll come and heckle.'

Seb laughed then eyed him shrewdly. 'You and Freya?'

Travis shrugged. 'I dunno. You'll have to ask her if she'll come.'

Seb shook his head and snorted. 'Sure I will.'

'You do that,' Travis said, feeling uncomfortable under his brother's scrutiny. 'I've no idea of her plans for New Year.'

'So, let me get this right,' Seb said slowly and deliberately. 'You're not shagging her and she's not shagging you? What are you two playing at?'

'You cheeky sod. I'm not telling you my business.'

'Ah, so there is *something* to tell.' Seb gave him a piercing look.

Refusing to take the bait, Travis got up. 'I'll see you at Bree's. You will make it, won't you?'

'I won't let her down. I'm working late tomorrow so you needn't worry about me being pissed in the pub with my mates. I'll be tucked up in bed by midnight, hoping Santa comes.' He smiled. 'I'm guessing you'll be doing the same.'

'Something like that but I think Santa might be bypassing the cabin.'

'Why's that?'

'I have no intention of being good.'

Chapter Thirty-Three

'Phew. That's it! It's officially Christmas!'

Freya unwound her scarf and tossed it on to the sofa in her cottage. 'If anyone's oven goes up in smoke or their TV decides to give up the ghost for the King's speech, they'll have to manage.'

'You don't mean that,' Travis said, taking her coat from her shoulders.

'Well, we're now officially closed though we do technically offer emergency cover. Luckily, I won't have to do something about it. I did my duty for the last two years and now Hamish is on call . . . not that there's a chance any of the tradespeople will want to go out during their Christmas dinners. Talking of which, that smells good.'

'It's tagine but wait until you taste it before you get too excited.'

After he'd hung up her coat, he urged her into the kitchen where the table was laid ready for dinner, with glasses beside it. To anyone watching through the window, you'd think they were any other couple, finally relaxing after the hectic run-up to, or maybe preparing for Christmas Day itself.

How different reality was. They wouldn't be spending most of the day together. Freya had already decided she wouldn't be languishing on the sofa watching cheesy movies all day. It was forecast to be crisp and cold so she'd decided to take herself off for a long walk on the fells, with a flask of hot toddy. Maybe, with few people around, she might even glimpse a red squirrel . . .

Last night after the concert, after Seb's unexpected appearance, Travis had been in a pensive mood. She could tell he was feeling emotional and instead of dragging her off to bed as he'd promised, their lovemaking had been slow and tender.

She hadn't told him that she'd persuaded Seb to play at the concert. It was to remain a secret between the two of them.

Travis returned with two large glasses of red wine and a bowl of tortilla chips. 'Thanks.' She popped a chip in her mouth then had a sudden thought. 'Oh! I have a present for you.'

He wagged his finger. 'I thought we agreed. No presents.'

'This isn't a present. It's a leftover. I'd have to chuck it away if I didn't bring it. Hold on a minute.' Getting up again, she went into the hallway and returned with a large wicker hamper.

'Wow. Some leftover.'

She put it on the kitchen counter. 'It was meant for one of the luxury places down by the lake but they cancelled at the last minute so I couldn't let it go to waste.' It contained a ham, local chutneys, pâté, a bottle of fizz, fine wines, luxury chocolates and more.

He examined a jar of posh olives. 'You could feed half of Bannerdale with this.'

'You *could* and so I thought – maybe you could take it to lunch with you at Bree's?'

'Maybe I could . . .' He held the jar in his hand. 'Or maybe you could come with me and give it to Bree yourself?'

Taken aback, Freya gave a nervous laugh. 'I don't think that would go down very well.'

'With Bree – or with you?'

'You're serious, aren't you?' She shook her head. 'It's not fair on Bree and besides, big family lunches aren't for me.'

'What do you mean?'

'Nothing. Ignore me.' She walked out of the kitchen to the sitting room but Travis followed swiftly. He caught her hand and pulled her into his arms. 'No way, you can't come out with a statement like that and not explain yourself.'

'I – it's to do with Jos.' Why had she blurted it out? It wasn't something she wanted to discuss, especially not on Christmas Eve but it was too late now. She sat down on the sofa and Travis sat beside her.

'I want to hear your side of the story.'

She stared at him. 'My side? What do you mean?'

'Jos . . . came into the gallery on the day it opened. He had his arse in his hands and he thought it was a good moment to let me know that you split up before the wedding.'

'On your opening day?' Freya said, horrified. 'What did he say?'

'Not . . . that much other than he still didn't know why you'd dumped him. I – I could see he was bitter and he's still not over you. I'm sorry I even mentioned it.'

'No. Don't be sorry. I wish he'd let go, I mean properly let go. Every time I see him, I feel guilty but I wouldn't change anything – apart from telling him sooner. I should have been honest with him from the moment I first realised I'd been living a lie. It was in the middle of Sunday lunch at his parents' house.'

She picked up the glass and took a large gulp.

Travis let out a whistle. 'You told them it was off over the roast beef?'

'Not actually at the table, though believe me, my appetite had gone.' She thought back to the moment she was watching Jos's family as they handed around the roast potatoes and gravy: a normal family ritual for them. The moment she realised she didn't belong and never would – and that she would have to break Jos's heart and turn herself into a villain.

'I realised I couldn't go through with it. It was two weeks before the big day and his parents had invited us for a pre-wedding lunch with all the family, at their house. You know the one: down by the lake not far from the hotel.'

'The massive Arts and Crafts place? They still live there?'

'Yes. It was meant to be a relaxing "family get-together", with the two of us, his parents, his sister and brother and their families.' She forced herself to return to that perfect June day at the beautiful old house, with its carefully tended gardens in full bloom . . . 'His nephews and nieces running around and playing in the treehouse with their mums and dads.'

'Sounds idyllic,' Travis muttered.

'On the face of it. Jos was chasing them and they were laughing. He was loving it. It was all normal stuff, but I was so on edge, I was almost shaking. At first I told myself it was only pre-wedding nerves. I don't think I'd been to a formal meal with the whole clan before. When you come from a small family, like me and Mum, big tribal gatherings can be totally overwhelming.'

'I don't think Mum ever held a formal lunch party,' Travis said drily.

'No and I don't think you'd want to, if it was anything like the Beresfords'.'

Freya thought back to the glossy-haired sister and sister-in-law, his brother and brother-in-law discussing fine wines, his father advising them both on their 'portfolios' and his mother making her expectations clear. 'They're so perfect, so polished and . . .' She felt disloyal. 'They're not bad people, they're just so comfortable in and with their world, and assume everyone is the same.'

'Even Jos?' Travis asked.

'Even him. I felt that he'd merged with his tribe the moment he stepped through the door of his parents' house. As if – I hope this doesn't sound stupid – he picked up a coat at the door and slipped it on and he was one of the clan again.'

'It doesn't sound stupid . . . and maybe I should admire him because I haven't looked after my clan like I should.'

'That's not true! You're nothing like him.'

'So what happened at this tribal gathering?' Travis put in.

'His mother, Fiona, took me upstairs. She claimed she wanted to get my opinion on her wedding outfit, but we passed Jos's old room on the way.'

'Wow. Don't say he still had his signed posters of David Beckham on the walls?'

'You've been in there?' Freya said.

'No, but he was always boasting about them at football practice. His dad knew someone on the Man U board.'

She had to smile. 'No, it had been redecorated very tastefully. It overlooked the garden and she showed me inside. I'd never been in there before. No reason when we always stayed at his place or my cottage.'

He nodded, rather stiffly, so she went on.

'She was showing me the view over the gardens from his window. The kids were playing out there and she was sighing over them when I noticed Jos in the bedroom doorway. His mother hadn't seen him and I can't forget what she said: "Of course, your little ones will be playing out there one day. In the future, the not-too-distant future, I *hope*. Time has a habit of flying by, Freya and you're the wrong side of thirty so I wouldn't wait too long."'

Travis wrinkled his nose. 'Ouch. Not a woman for subtlety, then.'

'No and Jos didn't say anything either. Not even "Hold on a minute, Mum," or "We haven't decided whether we want kids". Because we hadn't talked about it, either of us, and now I think about it, that was a mistake because I realised we both had different expectations. It's not that I *don't* want any, I just didn't want people making assumptions.'

Travis murmured, 'I understand how that feels.'

'And then, over lunch, his father started talking about private schools. The little ones were all at private nurseries and pre-prep.'

'Jesus.'

'And it turned out they all had their names down at the big schools already. The older ones were going to board . . . and Jos's brother said, half-jokingly: "You two had better get your skates on, there's a five-year waiting list for Bodgem Towers."'

277

Travis's eyes widened. 'Please tell me that's not the *actual* name of this school?'

'No! It's not.' She sighed. 'I can't even remember, I was so . . . so dumbfounded and shocked. I couldn't answer. I just laughed it off, while churning away inside. And Jos just said: "Don't worry, I'll have it all in hand". Not even "*We'll* have it in hand" – he just assumed I'd go along with it, feel the same way, and I thought how selfish of me to feel so angry and cheated when I could have all this privilege.' She stopped. It was too late to feel disloyal to Jos now, she may as well tell Travis everything. 'We had a row about it afterwards and he said as much.'

'Hold on a minute,' Travis said bluntly. 'No matter how upset he was, he was out of order to patronise you like that. I'd have been bloody furious with him.'

'I wasn't furious. I was sad. I was devastated because I knew in that moment, that this was not the path I wanted to take in life. It wasn't my path, but it very much was Jos's. I hadn't realised before – I think I was in denial, so swept up in the whole him and me thing. I thought I could have Jos and that would be it.'

She paused for breath before going on. 'You marry someone, you can't separate them from their family, from the expectations they have. You can't simply siphon off that one person, you have to take everything that comes with them, whether you like it or not, and you shouldn't and I didn't want to. So that evening, when we went back to his flat, I told him it was over.'

Shock flickered across Travis's face, fleeting but impossible to miss. In that moment, she knew he was empathising with Jos, knowing how he'd felt.

'I'm guessing it didn't go well,' he said softly.

'No. He was angry, devastated, humiliated, hurt. I didn't blame him. I would have been. I offered to pay for the wedding and he said: "Don't be ridiculous. You can't possibly afford it."'

'Charming.'

'He was right, of course. I'd sunk most of my savings into expanding Cottage Angels but I didn't want to be in debt to him. I said I'd re-mortgage my cottage or borrow it from Mum and he laughed at me and marched out. I thought he'd get over me.'

'I don't think he has,' Travis said. 'Did he try to change your mind?'

'He was convinced there was someone else even though I tried to explain that I would never fit in with his life. Like I said, they're not bad people, but I realised they would never ever be *my* people. I would never be like them. I didn't want to be.'

'I get that,' he said. 'Trying to be someone you're not – to live a lie – would finish me too, but even though Jos's lot are a tribal gang doesn't mean you won't be welcome at Bree's. You said yourself that my family aren't like his and this would only be one day – one meal, with no expectations,'

'Yes, but Bree won't be expecting me.'

'She won't mind. She'll have plenty of food in and we can take the hamper contribution.' He smiled wickedly. 'That champagne will help.'

Freya didn't think a bottle of fizz would compensate Bree for her brother's ex turning up on her doorstep, uninvited.

'If I do turn up, there will be expectations because she'll *know*.'

'Know what?' Travis said airily. 'That we're shagging each other?'

'Well, yes.'

'So?' He shrugged. 'What's wrong with that? I don't want you spending the day on your own roaming around the fells. What if you fell in a ravine or—'

'I'm not going to fall off a cliff. I'll be fine.'

He narrowed his eyes and spoke more seriously. 'OK, let's try this way. What if *I* don't want to spend the day without you. There's a subtle difference.'

Her reply was snatched away. Him needing her – wanting her to go because he wanted to share the whole day with her – was different to him feeling guilty about leaving her.

'It feels a bit too . . .' *Perilously close to a real relationship* was the thought running through her head, but Travis seemed to have read her mind.

'Screw the contract for one day. Let's do the stuff a real couple would. Everyone has Christmas Day off, after all. Then we can go back to the rampant no-strings sex tomorrow.'

He made her laugh. He always did, so why did she have the feeling they were playing a dangerous game?

Chapter Thirty-Four

The moment Bree opened the front door, Dylan shot out like he'd been fired from a cannon.

'Unca Tardis! Santa's been. Come and see what he's brought.'

Travis swept him up. 'You must have been good, then?' He inhaled. 'You smell like a chocolate factory.'

'Mummy said it was OK to have Rudolph for breakfast today.'

Freya smiled at him as he grinned in Travis's arms. 'Well, it *is* Christmas Day,' she said, thinking that if Dylan could eat chocolate for breakfast, she could pretend to be part of Travis's family. She'd only agreed to come to lunch if Travis called Bree and asked her if it was OK. He'd done as she asked and claimed her reply had been 'the more the merrier' and that she was more than happy to welcome Freya. She didn't push it but she was wondering exactly what reasons he'd given his sister for her coming with him.

Travis lowered Dylan to the ground and the child stared at Freya. 'Are you having dinner with us?'

Freya was about to reply when Bree appeared, wearing an

Elf apron. Her grin for Travis faded slightly when she saw Freya but was soon in place again. 'Freya.'

Travis jumped in: 'We've brought some food with us.'

Freya clutched the hamper, half-wishing she'd never been persuaded into coming. 'Bit last minute, thank you for having me,' she said lightly.

'Mummy?' Dylan said plaintively. 'Is our turkey big enough?'

'It's big enough for everyone, poppet.' Bree took Dylan's hand and addressed herself to Freya and Travis. 'Not even my brothers can eat the monster Gav ordered. He got the wrong weight and I was worried we'd be eating turkey curry for weeks.' She rolled her eyes, but Freya still felt uncomfortable.

'*Bree! Who's that at the door?*' Gav's voice came from inside the hall.

'It's Travis and er, Freya.'

'Freya? What's she doing here?'

'Gav. They're on the doorstep!' Bree shouted, the edge of panic hard to disguise, adding, 'I did tell him. He probably wasn't listening as usual!'

Gav appeared, wearing a Santa hat, gawping at Freya as if she was the fairy on top of the Christmas tree. If only she could have flown away, she thought, she'd have been out of there in a heartbeat. 'Oh,' he said. 'Hello. Sorry, forgot you were coming. It's been a crazy morning.'

Squirming, Freya grinned sheepishly. 'I hope the wine in the hamper will help'.

Freya caught the flicker of surprise – or disapproval – in Bree's eyes before she opened the door wide and said cheerfully: 'I'm sure it will. Come on in. Gav will pour us all a drink.'

Freya had to give Bree and Gav credit; after the initial awkward reception, they made Freya more than welcome, almost too welcome, with Bree chattering away about the children, apologising for the chaos and urging Freya to make herself at home amid the wrapping paper and toys and empty cereal bowls.

The easy-going Gav didn't seem to care, probably relieved that he had extra people there to keep Dylan and Rosie entertained while he poured the champagne and helped in the kitchen.

He handed over two glasses of fizz to Freya and Travis. 'So. You two. You're a thing now, are you?'

Following him in with bowls of nuts, Bree shot him a glare. 'Leave them alone, Gav. They don't want you sounding like a granny.'

'We're friends really . . .' Freya said.

'Friends?' Gav said. 'Is that what they call it now?'

'Gav!'

'Sorry, love. I, er, just thought that you two . . . Bree said you were seeing each other once.'

'At *school*,' Bree said.

'It was in the sixth form,' Travis said gruffly. 'And it was a very long time ago.'

Dylan hurtled up. 'I want to play Twister!'

'Me too,' Travis declared. 'Right now.'

'Can't think of anything I'd rather do,' Freya added, putting down her glass. 'Let's go for it.'

'Gav?' Travis asked.

Gav grimaced as if he'd been offered root canal work. 'Er. I need to help Bree in the kitchen.'

A few minutes later, Dylan was giggling helplessly while Freya was wishing she'd gone to yoga class and Travis was muttering that he 'might pull something crucial'. Dylan was spinning the wheel, issuing orders and lying on his back giggling hysterically as the 'grown-ups' contorted themselves into convoluted shapes.

'Sorry about this,' Travis murmured from somewhere behind Freya. She couldn't see his face, only hear him grunting.

'I thought it wasn't the best idea.' She tried to look between her legs to see him. 'Ow!'

'Red hand!' Dylan screeched.

'It was never this hard when I was a kid!' Travis moaned, stretching for a red spot underneath Freya. 'Is he making this up?'

'Yellow foot!' Dylan barked. 'Do it now!'

'He's going to grow up to be a drill sergeant,' Travis muttered. 'Argh. Oh God, I'm going down!'

Freya rolled away too late to prevent Travis from toppling forward on top of her. She lay on her back with him straddling her. They both burst into uncontrollable giggles as Dylan danced around squealing with delight.

'Well, well, bro, if Twister's this much fun, I might have to play it myself.'

Travis sprang up and Freya scrambled up after him. Dylan ran over and hugged his legs and Seb put his guitar down on the sofa and swept his nephew up into his arms. 'How are you, big man?'

'Santa's been!' he declared.

'Has he, now? Who knew?' Seb replied.

Bree walked in, with Rosie in her arms. 'Hello! Better late than never.'

'I'm not late. The *others* are early. Wasn't expecting this to be a party,' Seb said, drawing a glare from Travis and making Freya cringe afresh.

'Well, it is now and I say the more the merrier,' Bree declared. 'Now, who wants a drink? Gav! Mine's a G&T! A large one.'

The next few hours were spent amid organised chaos, with the kids hyper and the room a sea of wrapping paper. Freya and Travis offered to help out but Bree said she'd prefer it if they entertained the children while she and Gav got on with preparing dinner.

Seb didn't make any more comments on Freya's presence and was kept busy by his nephew and niece who wanted to see his guitar.

'After lunch,' he said. 'I promise.'

It was cosy in Bree's living room, with everyone crammed around the table on an assortment of chairs and stools, plus Rosie in a highchair. After lunch, they flopped out on the sofas. Rosie had a nap, Seb played with Dylan while Travis and Freya helped Bree wash up and clear away.

Darkness had fallen again by the time they'd all eaten and drunk their body weight in chocolate and Baileys. Freya took the rubbish outside to the dustbin, lingering to look up at the stars, and the cottage lights scrambling up the side of the fells. A hush had descended on the village streets.

'*O, little town of Bannerdale . . .*' Travis sang quietly from behind her. '*How still we see thee lie . . .* It looks peaceful.'

She turned and he slipped his arms around her waist. 'For one day, at least. I hope I haven't caused trouble by turning up with you.'

'Told you it would be OK,' he said.

'Bree was a bit shocked. I don't blame her but she's made me very welcome.'

'She's all right, my sister.'

Freya shivered. 'Let's go back in before they think the elves have captured us.'

They walked back to the house and heard music.

They walked in to find Seb sitting in the armchair playing 'Jingle Bells', with Dylan attempting to sing it. Rosie was jigging along from on Bree's lap.

'Anyone would think we were in *The Sound of Music*,' Travis said and everyone burst out laughing.

'I can play "Edelweiss" if you'll dress up in those weird leather shorts,' Seb said, sticking on a cheesy grin and strumming the opening bars of the song.

'I'd like to see that too,' Freya said.

Travis opened his mouth to protest but Dylan took charge. 'Play "Jingle Bells", Seb!'

'OK, big man, but only if you sit and listen *quietly*.'

With a shortage of seats, Travis sat on the carpet at Freya's feet. Dylan squeezed onto the sofa between her and Bree, while Gav flopped down in the armchair.

Seb played and sang along to his folky version of 'Jingle Bells' before switching to 'Rudolph the Red-Nosed Reindeer'.

Dylan listened quietly, snuggling up to Freya.

'Shall we take the tempo down a bit?' Seb winked at Bree and started to play 'Silent Night'. Before he'd got to the end of the first verse, Dylan's eyelids drooped. His lashes fluttered on his cheek and he gently flopped over, with his head resting on Freya's lap. She didn't dare move and she didn't want to.

There was a loud snore from the armchair.

Everyone looked and suppressed giggles. Gav was spark out, catching flies.

'I've never sent an audience to sleep before,' Seb murmured, taking the guitar off.

It was such a contrast with Jos's grand house, and the lunch with siblings jostling for power. This fractured family, who'd spent so many Christmases apart, were finally together. Once again Freya reminded herself that she didn't really belong but with Dylan dozing on her, she felt she might have earned her place for a little while.

Travis caught her eye, looking thoughtful – sad almost – then he smiled.

Gav was still sleeping deeply in his chair, causing Bree to roll her eyes good-naturedly. She got up with a 'shh' finger at everyone. Very carefully, she extricated Dylan from Freya's lap. He snuffled and sighed but stayed asleep, while she carried him out of the room.

Freed of his weight and warmth, Freya felt strangely bereft.

Easing himself off the sofa, Travis murmured. 'I'll just use the bathroom and collect our coats. Give Gav and Bree a chance to chill out.'

Seb got up too and found his guitar case from behind the chair. 'I'm off to the pub. Nice to see you, Freya. Have a good evening, you two. I'm sure you will.'

He was silenced by a glare from Travis who flipped a thumb indicating Seb should join him in the hall. Their voices were low and although Freya couldn't hear the exact words, she could guess that Travis might be asking Seb to be discreet about their 'relationship'.

The front door closed softly and the stairs creaked as Travis made his way upstairs. Freya was left alone, wondering whether she should try to tidy away the glasses or wash up – then thinking that Bree might not want her poking around the kitchen alone, after she'd helped to clear up after lunch. She wondered whether to tidy the children's toys into their baskets but didn't want to wake Gav, now snoring again in his chair. Bree had been so busy, she felt she ought to do something.

As quietly as she could, she picked up a fabric basket and started to gather up Rosie's toys. The fluffy squirrel had rolled by the side of the sofa. She reached for it and heard a voice speaking from the teddy.

'Travis?'

It sounded like Bree, but her words were indistinct.

'What?' The answering voice was unmistakeably Travis.

'I need a word with you.'

Freya picked up the squirrel and spotted the baby monitor with its red flashing light. With a glance behind to check if Gav was still asleep, she kneeled beside it, listening to the conversation being relayed through the speaker.

'Now? You'll wake up Dylan and Freya's waiting for me downstairs.'

'You're not getting away yet. I hope you know what you're doing with her'.

Though horrified at hearing herself discussed in this way, Freya leaned down to hear better.

'You said you were fine with her coming.

'I could hardly say no, could I? You'd have been upset and angry with me, and it would have been plain bloody rude to Freya. That doesn't mean I'm happy with the situation. You were a wreck the last time you . . . involved with her!'

'I was eighteen. I've grown up a bit if you hadn't noticed and you've no idea what "the situation" is.' Travis's voice was cold. Freya felt she was witnessing her own car crash.

'Something's going on, that's for sure and it's not "just good friends" either! I hope you know what you're doing, Freya

288

hardly has the greatest track record where relationships are concerned.'

The words were clearer now as Bree's voice rose in volume. Freya clutched the squirrel tighter, straining to hear Travis's reply.

'If you mean Jos Beresford, I heard what happened and I don't care. Besides, we're keeping things casual. It made sense to hook up for Christmas.'

'"Hook up"? You call bringing your ex here for a family Christmas dinner, "hooking up" and "casual".'

'I'm not discussing this with you!' Travis cried and a second later, there was a low wail.

'Shit. Now look what you've done!'

'Me? You're the one who wanted to give me a lecture about my love life.'

'A love life? Is it love? Are you going to let her hurt you all over again? Then take off to lick your wounds!'

Freya stomach churned. The monitor crackled and she put her head closer to it. Gav let out a loud snore.

'You can rest assured, sister dearest, that I'm in no danger whatsoever of being hurt. We're not in love. Not even close, so you can stop worrying.'

Bree's reply was lost amid the wails of a crying baby.

For the next few seconds, Freya was a crouching statue on the carpet, toy in hand, trying to process what she'd heard. At the thud of heavy footsteps from above, she sprang up and whirled round, wondering if Gav had seen or heard any of it.

He was still lost to the world.

Her paralysis gave way to an urgent desire to leave the right there and then, coat or not. She threw the squirrel on the sofa and hurried into the hall, not caring if Gav woke, but hoping Travis would hear her close the lounge door as hard as she dared.

He was already jogging down the stairs, coats over his arms and a thunderous expression on his face. Behind him, the screams of a tired baby rang through the house, then a plaintive howl of 'Mummeeee!' that was unmistakably Dylan.

He shoved Freya's coat at her. 'Come on, we're going.'

'I should, um, thank Bree,' Freya muttered with zero enthusiasm.

'I'd leave it if I were you,' he snapped, pulling the front door open.

Moments later they were out in the frosty street, marching back to Freya's cottage. The cold hit her lungs and her chest tightened but it was the chill between them that froze her far more. Travis didn't know she'd heard . . .

She doesn't have the greatest track record where relationships are concerned.

The words she'd overheard from Bree stung like salt in a wound, because she couldn't deny them – but none hurt as much as Travis saying he wasn't even close to being in love with her.

Chapter Thirty-Five

Freya woke to a cold bed and a note on the pillow.

Gone to take photographs of deer on Hart Fell. Back later. X

Boxing Day. It seemed appropriate, given the conflict of yesterday. There had been a time, for a few hours, when she'd forgotten that she and Travis weren't a 'real' couple. Bree had done her best to make Freya welcome, and she'd loved the family banter over the dinner table and playing with the kids. Rosie and Dylan were adorable . . . then the conversation over the baby monitor had doused any fuzzy festive feeling with icy water.

She couldn't blame Bree for trying to look out for her brother; it's what she'd always done. Travis must have been hurt more deeply than even he'd hinted at, and his reply told her that he'd hardened up since – or had he?

Did he still have deep feelings for her and was only putting on a show of bravado in front of Bree?

It had been a strange and disturbing evening. After they'd got home, Freya had half-heartedly watched a movie and replied to a message from her mum. She'd sent several photos of herself and Neil holding up a Happy Christmas sign and posted more pictures on her Instagram feed. Tagged #thecaptainstable and #AmericanChristmas, they showed her and Neil raising glasses with a bunch of strangers in black tie and cocktail wear.

This morning, Travis was gone.

After a soak in the tub, Freya picked up her phone which had been charging. She hadn't had chance to look at her mum's Insta feed since then, so she opened the app now and scrolled to the latest photo on the account.

What?

No.

Her thumb froze on the screen. She must be dreaming.

Her mother and Neil were wearing cowboy hats and standing outside the Wedding Chapel in Las Vegas, with a grinning Elvis lookalike in the middle of them. They were holding up their hands and the caption read:

JUST MARRIED

Freya blinked and checked out the hashtags. #justmarried #tiedthenot #WeddedBliss #vegaswedding

The phone clattered onto the tiles.

Freya breathed in and out again, trying to process what she'd seen. She'd no idea her mum and Neil were going to Vegas, let alone getting married – and to see it on Instagram without any warning was a hell of a shock.

She picked up her phone to find it still working and buzzing with a WhatsApp call. Her mum and Neil appeared on the screen with neon signs behind them and 'Hound Dog' playing in the background.

'Freya!' her mother shouted above the music. 'Thank goodness we've caught you! you. It's the early hours here but we *had* to get hold of you before you saw it on Instagram. You're not going to believe this but we've got married!'

'Indeed, we have.' Neil slid his arm around her mum's shoulders.

'It was all very last minute but Neil proposed yesterday and while we were in Vegas, we just decided to go for it!'

The seconds ticked by as Freya took in what her mum and Neil were saying.

'Freya?'

She came to her senses and her reply gushed out. 'Oh, oh, that's wonderful news. Congratulations. To both of you.'

'Neil bought me a ring,' her mother said, lifting the pendant from her tanned chest. 'It's slightly too big so I've put it on this chain for now. It's so beautiful though, with a lovely ruby and diamond. I can't wait to show you when I get home.'

She lifted the pendant over her head and held the ring up to the camera. It sparkled in the neon lights. Freya felt her eyes swim. Seeing her mum so happy was wonderful but the news had knocked her for six.

'It's beautiful . . .'

'Thank you, darling. I know this must come as a huge shock but really, when Neil asked me, I thought – why wait? Life's far too short and all that. We can have proper party with you and all our friends and family when we get back.'

'Your mum has made me the happiest man on the planet,' Neil said. 'I hope you'll forgive me?'

'Forgive you?' Freya said, still struggling to take in the news. 'There's nothing to forgive if you've made my mum happy and I know you have.' He really did sound so desperate for her approval, and looked ecstatic, how could she ever not forgive him? 'I can't wait to celebrate with you when you come home. Congratulations to you both.'

After more details about the impromptu ceremony and promises to send her lots more private photos of the wedding, the call ended with kisses and smiles.

Freya lowered her phone, taking a deep breath. Of course she was pleased for her mum and Neil. Of course she was thrilled to see such joy on their faces. Of course she'd never ever want her mother to be lonely.

And yet . . . this was a momentous change in everyone's lives, even though she was a mature adult. Her mum and her – it had been the two of them for so long, they'd been through so much and now Neil was part of their lives.

Another realisation niggled at her: it felt as if everyone was getting their happy ending – or happy beginning. No matter how thrilled she tried to be for her mother, a wall of loneliness hit her. Of course, she wasn't the only person in the world who hadn't settled down with a partner but in this moment, it felt that way.

She went upstairs to her room and pulled out a little folding step so she could reach the furthest corner in the back of the wardrobe. Under a pile of summer tops, was a tin that had once contained mints. She took it out and sat on the bed, staring at it before finally picking it up.

The lid was stiff because it hadn't been open for so long. Inside was a small leather box, still as pristine as the moment she'd been given it.

The ring sparkled in the muted light of a Lakeland winter morning, not as brightly as her mother's, yet still a tiny beacon of hope – or a poignant reminder of love lost.

Travis had loved her once, and she'd loved him. She'd been right to give him up.

Now, she had a second chance if she only she could be brave enough and seize the moment, but the risk was high.

The sun was shining outside. She was like a cat on a hot tin roof, unable to settle. Snatching her coat from the peg, she strode out of the cottage and headed for the hills. her breath misted the air as she powered relentlessly up the same path that Travis had taken before dawn.

Only when her lungs were about to burst and her heart was thumping, did she pause for a rest. To the north, the horseshoe ridge of fells above the village was dusted with snow while Windermere stretched out to the south, sliding towards the low hills where its waters spilled into the river and sea. She paused, watching a fairy-lit ferry decanting passengers at the pier.

When she turned, Travis had emerged from the woodland higher up the fell. He waved and strode along the path from the woods, making straight for her.

If she was going to say anything, why not now, out here in the open? The thought made her stomach clench. Waiting another day, another hour wouldn't make any difference. The time had come.

He was smiling as he approached, oblivious of what she was about to launch at him.

'Hi.'

'How was the photo trip?'

'OK. Good. I got a few pictures of the stags. Sussed out a

new location for a future workshop. The old bothy by the falls at Sweden Bridge.'

'I know it. It's beautiful.'

'Yeah.' He frowned, clearly sensing something was amiss. 'Is everything OK?'

She forced a smile. 'It's fine. More than fine. Mum called me. She and Neil have got married.'

He dumped his camera bag on the ground. 'Married? Bloody hell. Can you do that?'

'You can in Vegas.'

'Did they plan it?'

'Not as far as I know. They've been friends for years. Neil's a widower and Mum worked with his partner before she died a few years ago. I thought they'd stay as friends but then they started seeing each other last spring. I hadn't realised things had gone this far.'

Travis studied her face. 'You like him, though?' he said.

'Yeah, he's nice. Steady, kind . . . he seems to worship Mum. It's just . . .'

'What?'

'Weird. There's always just been Mum and me. There have been other men, on and off, but no one like Neil.'

'That's a long time to be alone,' he murmured.

'Yes, of course and I want her to be happy. No one deserves it more but I never noticed any grand passion.'

'Does there have to be one?'

'I guess I must think that. Otherwise I'd have stuck with Jos, wouldn't I? I didn't love him enough.'

'Are there degrees of love?' Travis asked. 'Levels of it? You can't love someone ninety percent. Not when it comes to a lifetime commitment. It's all or nothing.'

'Or all of your heart for a while. People change, Travis.'

He frowned deeply. 'You mean us?'

'Yes. I tried to tell you this at the time. We were young and Mum needed me. She was terrified that things would go wrong between us.'

'And that I was the wrong man for you?'

'Yes.'

'Did you think that too?'

'We were young. It could have and probably would have gone wrong. It might not have lasted.'

'So much doubt . . . and now?' he demanded.

Now, she wanted to shout: she was as much in love now as she had been all those years ago. She had no excuse now of teenage crush. Should she tell him and risk everything? Then she remembered what she'd overheard at Bree's.

Was he merely putting Bree off the scent or did he mean it?

If she didn't take a chance now, she'd never know the answer – just like her mother and Neil, she had to go for it.

'What if I wanted more?' she said lightly.

'But you don't, do you? That wasn't part of the bargain.'

'No, it wasn't.' She laughed. 'Forget I said it.'

She knew he couldn't forget she said it. Neither of them could. She'd opened the lid of the box, just a little bit but the genie was out and it was an unstoppable force and not a kind one.

'I can't forget you said it, Freya.'

'OK. We agreed that our arrangement should end if something changed between us. Well, I heard you on the baby monitor at Bree's. I heard you say that you weren't in any danger of falling in love with me, and it made me wonder –

ask myself – if you really meant it? Because I'm not sure I can keep the bargain. I want something more.'

This should be the part where he threw his arms around her and declared he felt the same. Instead, he let out a low groan.

'I'm sorry you heard that conversation but,' he added softly, 'you spent so long telling me you don't want more. That you're not cut out for long term. This is such an about turn. They were your terms.'

'It's not an about turn. I've been fooling myself.'

'Are you sure?' His eyes were troubled. 'What exactly is fooling yourself?'

'I get it,' Freya said, her hopes sinking faster by the second. 'Is this some kind of punishment for me leaving you the first time?'

'*Punishment?*' He flinched as if she'd slapped him. 'I . . . could never do that to you. It's not punishment, or revenge. It's self-protection. I don't want to get hurt and you're right. I thought I could do this too. I can't.'

Where were the bells, the fanfares, fireworks exploding – the rush into each other's arms? Where was the rom-com dream ending, credits rolling as they kissed in the rain, against the rising crescendo of a show-stopping anthem?

'There's nothing I can do to prove that it will last again and maybe it won't,' she said, at last. 'I can't guarantee that neither of us will be hurt either.'

'I wouldn't ask you to.' He shoved his hands though his hair. 'I . . . didn't expect this. I've no answer but I do know I couldn't face ending up like Jos, being left on my own after giving everything again. I'm sorry but I just can't do it while I can't trust how you really feel, Freya.'

Jos again – not trusting her again. She'd let people down too often so how could she be surprised Travis wouldn't take the risk? The past was impossible to escape.

'Thank you for being honest,' she said, withering inside. 'Maybe it's best that we spend some time apart . . .' Even as the words left her lips, every cell screamed at him to refuse the offer, say it was the last thing he wanted, tell her he felt the same.

He couldn't even meet her eye. 'Maybe. Yes. That's probably a good idea.'

Chapter Thirty-Six

As expected, the Cottage Angels phone was ringing off the hook when Freya walked into the office on December 27th.

Central heating controllers had failed, loos had leaked, a guest's gerbil had gnawed through a telephone cable (the gerbil hadn't got the message it was a pet-free property) and a professor had called to complain that the wallpaper in his bedroom had given him a migraine and he wanted a full refund.

Freya embraced every call, rolling with punches that were easy to take compared to the emotional blow Travis had delivered. She threw herself in to solving the cock-ups for her guests so that she didn't have to think about the mess in her own life.

The weather had clearly decided the festivities were over too. Strong winds and heavy rain blew in, melting the snow and filling the lake so it overspilled into the fields. The stream that had gurgled benignly through the centre of the village became an angry torrent, swollen by a myriad of tiny becks.

The falls above the village tumbled in a foaming yellow cascade, more than earning their name of 'sour milk'.

When Freya left the office on December 29th, the Christmas lights strung between the lampposts swung angrily in the wind. It was already half-past seven, and she was hoarse from being on the phone all day soothing ruffled feathers and cajoling busy tradespeople out to fix water leaks and dislodged slates.

Peak Perspectives skulked in darkness as she trudged past, reminding her of an empty shell, lifeless without the creative force of its owner.

Freya had never been gladder to slip into the warmth of Raffaello's, where Roxanne had arranged to meet her for a pizza. Tanned and smiling, she was out of her seat to greet Freya the moment she reached the table.

'Hello! I got a bottle of prosecco,' she said, enveloping Freya in a cloud of warmth and exotic perfume. 'Oh, I have missed you.'

'I hope not. You were on your honeymoon!'

'Yes, and it was completely amazing of course but we have been living together for four years and you can't spend all your time in a bed or the hot tub or the couples' hammock.'

'Poor you. It sounds absolutely terrible.' She allowed herself a smile.

'It was awful,' Roxanne said, unable to hide her grin while she poured a glass of fizz for Freya. 'How have *you* been? How was your Christmas? I was a bit worried about you with your mum off on that cruise.'

'Oh – OK.'

'You weren't on your own?' Roxanne demanded anxiously, adding, 'Sorry to sound like your mum.'

'I was fine,' Freya said. 'And actually, I have news about Mum.'

After a calming glug of prosecco, she relayed the call about her mother's wedding.

'Wow. That's a surprise . . . Or is it?'

'Yes and no. The more I think about it, the more I should have seen it coming. I was taken aback at first, but I've had a bit of time to get used to it. They're coming home next week.'

'Let's order and then, would you like to see some of the wedding photos? Don't worry, I've edited them down to a few hundred.'

'A few hundred? I definitely think we better order first,' Freya said brightly, picking up a menu.

The earlier pictures at Roxanne's house and in the church had all been taken by the original photographer. They were OK, with some nice shots of the bridesmaids having their makeup done and pretending to help Roxanne adjust her veil or hold her bouquet. The shots in the church were suitably impressive and brought back happy memories and a lump to her throat.

A picture popped up that was a blur of sky and frosted holly leaves.

'Oh dear! That must have been when the guy fell off the wall. Good job he's OK now,' Roxanne said, swiftly swiping past it. '*Now*, these are the ones that Travis took.'

'Are you pleased?'

'I cried when I saw them. The others are good but these are so . . . real. I mean, he's taken all the usual group shots and managed to make us look as if we weren't shivering with cold, but the ones he took when we weren't aware, are just so special. Look at this one of Ravi and me laughing when we were having a quick swig of whisky from the vicar's emergency hip flask.'

'It's beautiful.'

'My only complaint was that there weren't many of you, other than the group shots. So I asked Travis if he had any more and he said he'd missed off a whole load by mistake and then he sent me through tons. They're amazing. You look so gorgeous.'

'I don't think so!'

'You do. I'm so glad I chose that colour because it sets off your skin and hair and – look at this close-up of you looking out over the lake while you held my bouquet. It's a work of art, as if he could see what you were thinking.'

'I doubt it.' Freya laughed. 'My stomach was rumbling and I was wishing I was inside with some mulled wine and a whole tray of canapes.'

'You weren't?' Roxanne laughed. 'Actually, so were we. Ravi was starving. I love these fun photos. There are some more here of the two of us giggling like schoolkids at the reception – and one of you dancing with Nico.'

'What?'

'You're not looking at him though. You're on another planet.'

It was true. The shot, from the side, showed Freya staring into the distance, her lips pressed together, while Nico leaned so close to her, you couldn't have slotted a credit card between them.

'I worked out you weren't interested.'

'I like him, he's handsome – very – but not for me.'

'Anyone seeing these would think you and Travis were – well, more than exes. No wonder he held these back.'

'If he says it was a mistake, it was, I'm sure.'

Roxanne's frown deepened and she said gently. 'Freya, is there anything you want to tell me? Because, I haven't said anything until now, but I did notice that you vanished before the end of the evening . . . '

Unable to hold back her feelings any longer, Freya held out her glass. 'Top that up and I'll try.'

Roxanne listened, sighed, sympathised and swore in all the right places before subsiding into a brief silence.

'So, there you are. What a mess, eh? I rejected him when he asked me to marry him the first time.'

'For very good reasons.' Roxanne pointed out. 'I knew there was something going on at the reception!'

'Sorry, I didn't plan on doing a disappearing act so early but it just happened. As for rejecting Travis first time round, I'm no longer sure it was for good reasons and it's too late to change now. He comes back to Bannerdale and we get together and I issue an ultimatum of no emotional involvement.'

'Which was never going to end well, honey . . .'

'No . . . I thought it was the best way of dealing with things.'

Roxanne raised her eyebrows.

'And so, I fell as much in love with him as ever and tried and failed to fight it so did what I thought was the brave thing and told him how I felt.'

'It was the brave thing.'

'But it ended in disaster. He doesn't trust me anymore. I can't say I blame him.'

'And that's it? How did it end?'

'He left after Boxing Day afternoon and I haven't seen him or heard from him since.'

'You haven't tried to contact him?'

'No. I thought he needed time . . . now I'm too scared.'

'You're just going to give up, just like that? Proving his point that you're not really that committed? Proving that hey, you've accepted it – life goes on. Are you hoping he'll come begging at your door? Crawling on his knees to apologise and propose again?'

'No, of course not! Shit.' In gesticulating, Freya knocked her glass and prosecco spilled onto her jeans. The group at the next table stared at her.

Calmly, Roxanne handed over a serviette. 'Here, mop it up with this.'

'Thanks.' She dabbed at her jeans, still jabbering about Travis. 'I don't expect him to turn up with armfuls of flowers and champagne. He's too wary of me for that.'

'Then somehow you'll have to *show* him that he can trust you. He's an intense and deep-feeling guy, who's had to suppress his emotions for years in front of his awful father and while he had to take care of his family. Being teased at school must have been horrible and it's no wonder he's developed a thick shell. Underneath, he has and always will be crazy about you. He just needs to be confident you feel the same way.'

Freya threw up her hands in despair. 'I don't know how to make him do that.'

'Start by not taking no for an answer. Start by telling him you need another chance to explain how you feel. He's had time to think – he might be in a more receptive mood now.'

'Hmm . . .'

'Why not go round tonight?'

'Because it's late. I'm with you.'

Roxanne rolled her eyes. 'In the flesh, maybe, but not in spirit. I want the whole Freya with me and you won't be truly present until you sort things out with Travis – or at least, try your utmost to. I don't know if he'll open the door and drag you inside but you can at least give it a go. Take him by surprise . . .

'I suppose I could . . .'

'Great. Come on, let's wolf down these pizzas – you look like you're flaking out – and then I'll walk with you to the cabin and you can do the rest.'

'Faint heart never won fair Travis.'

'What?'

'Who dares wins.' She thrust a menu under Freya's nose. 'Here's the food. Eat and then you can go and risk it all.'

'Damn. That's a blow.'

Roxanne's shoulders slumped in disappointment when Squirrel Cabin came in sight. It had been a wet and windy walk from Raffaello's and a huge let-down when they'd finally found Squirrel Cabin in total darkness and no sign of Travis's car.

'It's probably a sign that I shouldn't be here.'

'No, it's a sign he's gone to the pub. Hmm. You'll have to try again first thing. Ambush him at dawn.'

Freya drove up to the track towards the cabin just before eight in the pre-dawn gloom. She hadn't slept well but was determined to catch Travis before he opened the gallery. She could only hope he hadn't set off early for a shoot but the weather forecast wasn't great so she assumed not.

She wasn't sure about ambushing him before work but only planned to stay long enough to persuade him to meet her later for a proper heart to heart.

That didn't look like it was going to happen. Approaching the parking area, she could see that the cabin was still in darkness . . . but the curtains were still open, as they had been the night before, and there was still no car outside.

Maybe he *had* gone on a shoot.

Or had he had a heavy night at the pub, staggered into bed and was still asleep? Curiosity got the better of her, and she peered through the windows. Daylight was stealing in and she could just about see inside – what she did see shocked her.

'Oh!'

The place was a tip. Clothes were strewn on the floor, and a half-eaten plate of food was on the coffee table next to an almost full glass of beer.

The thing that made her blood chill was the camera equipment and laptop, left on the sofa and chairs with no attempt to hide it.

It looked like the *Mary Celeste*.

Her first thought made her stomach squeeze unpleasantly. What if he'd had an accident and was lying somewhere within the cabin, injured – or worse? The sight of him after the electrical accident still hadn't left her . . . but that was ridiculous. No one, not even Travis, could be electrocuted twice in one month.

However, he *could* – conceivably – have had a different kind of mishap, though God knew what in a tiny one-bedroom cabin. Someone might have broken in and harmed him but violent crime was unheard of in Bannerdale . . . and a burglar would surely have taken his laptop and camera gear . . .

Above all else, his car was gone, which pointed to him having left voluntarily – but why? He hadn't gone on a shoot.

307

Could someone have forced him into his car for another reason? Driving him to the cashpoint for money?

Tearing her eyes from the window, Freya swore loudly. These dramatic imaginings weren't helping. Her rational side told her that would be a perfectly reasonable explanation why Travis had vanished yet left his most precious possessions: like nipping to the garage for some milk and paracetamol.

Maybe she really wasn't meant to try and persuade him how she felt, not yet at least. She strode back to the car, trying to laugh off her fears herself and manage the disappointment of finding him out again after she'd worked herself up all night.

A buzz from her phone made her jump then her heart beat faster, hoping it was Travis. Her spirits immediately sank when the screen revealed Mimi asking her to grab a fresh jar of coffee from the Co-op on her way into the office. Reminded that she had an actual job to do that should take priority over her tortured love life, she drove off to work and tried to knuckle down to the job.

The morning crawled by until she heard an agitated conversation in the reception area between Mimi and a man and woman. A few moments later, Mimi opened the door. 'I'm sure he's OK but of course, you can ask Freya if you think she can possibly help . . . you can leave the pushchair in the office here. I'll keep an eye on Rosie while you talk to Freya,' Mimi said, walking in, followed by Bree and Seb, who was wearing his work uniform.

In that second. Freya had the strangest sensation of the ground falling away from under her.

Seb's agitated face and Bree's anguished expression and them turning up at all at her workplace in the middle of the day could only mean one thing.

'What's happened to him?' she burst out.

Mimi stared at her, totally oblivious to the fact that anything at all had been going on between Freya and Travis. 'I'll go keep an eye on the baby,' she said, closing the office door behind her.

'Nothing – we hope,' Bree said. 'Only we can't raise him. He hasn't turned up at the gallery, he's not answering his mobile and the cabin looks like a bomb hit it.'

'He hasn't even taken his camera.' Seb said. 'Bree called me to say he hadn't come into work so I went up there just now and saw the state of the place. His car's gone so I phoned him and it went straight to voicemail.'

'We're worried,' Bree said, clasping her hands together. 'And we hoped you knew where he was,'

'I – I've no idea. I went up to the cabin myself before work and saw the mess and his camera stuff there and the car gone. I thought he might have popped to the shops and would be back.'

'Have you phoned him?' Bree demanded.

'No, I didn't want to bother him.'

'Have you two had another row?' Bree shot back. 'Have you upset him again? Have you caused him to take off again?'

'Bree . . .' Seb said, clearly embarrassed.

'No, I haven't,' Freya said but realised that wasn't entirely true.

'Things aren't right between you, though, are they? I warned him about getting involved with you again.'

'Bree. This isn't helping!' Seb shouted. 'And it's not our business.'

'It's my business when my brother's taken off without telling anyone again.'

'Look, Travis and I – we were together, but it wasn't serious.'

'It seemed serious to me.'

Freya didn't tell Bree that she'd overheard the baby monitor row. Things were bad enough. Even though she felt shaky and worried – and annoyed with Bree – it was her job to stay calm, especially with Mimi on the other side of the door.

'I don't think he's been home all night,' Seb said. 'I haven't been able to get hold of him since yesterday morning when he replied to a text. I just thought he was busy later but now I think he left sometime yesterday afternoon.'

'But *where*?' Bree wailed.

'I don't know but I swear I want to see Travis safe and home as much as you do,' Freya replied. 'I don't know what I'd do without him.'

Chapter Thirty-Seven

Hamza's jaw dropped when he opened the front door of his flat. 'Man, you look terrible!

'Thanks. You sound exactly like my brother.' A raindrop slid down Travis's chin. 'I had to park two streets away.'

'That's London for you. Come in out of the rain.' Hamza took Travis's wet jacket and hooked it over the banister in his hallway.

'Thanks for letting me stay at short notice. You could have said no . . .'

'Mate, when you send me a message asking "if I'm in" and you're over two hundred miles away, then I know it's important. I'll get us some food. I don't know about you but I'm starving.'

Travis tried to relax, while Hamza made a call to his favourite restaurant.

'I ordered *dejaje demhal* since it's your favourite.'

'My mouth is watering already. Let me pay.'

'No, it's my treat, since I left you in the lurch with the gallery,' Hamza insisted. 'We'll eat first then share our woes.'

'Wocs?' Travis said, dismayed. 'Is this about Caz?'

Hamza gave a resigned shrug. 'Might be. Now, eat.'

Funny, but Travis didn't know how much he needed someone to order him to do the basics: like eat and sleep. Over the past few days, even simple decisions had seemed a struggle. He'd opened the gallery and served a few customers but closed early, feeling exhausted. Freya's bombshell had shattered him. He'd been expecting her at some point to tell him their arrangement was over, not that she wanted it to continue, and wanted more.

He'd been so braced for disappointment, that he hadn't considered the alternative and he had no idea how to react. The scars ran deep when you felt you weren't worthy of love . . . Travis knew that this applied as much to himself as to Seb.

For now, he did as he was told. He ate. Food was nurture, Hamza had once told him, sharing was caring, showing love and respect for friends and strangers.

There was certainly love in the delicious meal, in the tangy salad of aubergine, onion and lemon and flatbreads, and the *dejaje demhal*, with its spicy tomato sauce.

He'd had it several times before when he'd lodged with Hamza's parents. 'This is sensational though not as good as your mum's, of course.'

'Can I record you saying that?' Hamza said.

'By all means. I miss it and you can't get it in Bannerdale. There's a great Thai restaurant though. Seb keeps dropping in. He's spending far too much money in there.'

'Is this because of the roofer you told me about?'

'He likes Araya but I'm not sure how she feels. I hope he won't get his heart broken.'

'Like the two of us?' Hamza said. 'The older, wiser ones?'

'I definitely feel older but not wiser. You tell me about Caz before I unload.'

Having loaded the empty cartons into the bin, they sat on the sofas with bottles of Lucky Saint. Hamza sighed. 'We've agreed to stay just friends. When I got back from the last assignment, she invited me over and we had a talk. To be honest, she started the chat. She told me she was very sorry but she didn't want to marry me – or anyone – right now. She'd been offered a job at a hospital in Perth and she wanted to take it.'

'That's tough. I'm so sorry, mate.'

'Don't be. I *do* love her – as more than a friend but not in the way that you should love someone you're going to spend the rest of your life with. She made it easy for me. She said she suspected I felt the same way as her.

'It was hard, it was upsetting. We both cried, because the death of anything that special is painful, but I sensed she was even more relieved than me. We've kept in touch since, and we can talk freely.'

'What about your families?'

'Dealing with them was harder than breaking off our engagement. My mother was inconsolable. Her mother was angry with both of us but we've stayed firm. They've had to accept it.'

Travis thought of Freya and Jos's parents – the fallout the anger and he felt a pang of pity for Jos.

'I should have been there for you?'

'You couldn't have done anything and I could say the same thing. Now, your turn. I'm guessing Freya is the reason you're here?'

They were on their third non-alcoholic beer by the time

Travis had finished talking and Hamza had listened and empathised and asked questions.

'So I *want* to trust her. She most definitely is the woman I want to spend the rest of my life with. She always has been – I believe that so strongly, it scares me.'

'But you *can't* believe that this time, her feelings are going to last?' Hamza offered.

'Maybe. No, yes. I think so – I'm being a wimp.'

'This is the man talking who'd get within snogging distance of a grizzly to get a great photo?'

'That's not the same, you know it. That's physical courage – actually, that's sheer insanity. Dealing with relationships is much harder and riskier.'

'Remember, this is also the man who took on the care of his family after his father let him down so many times. Who left with nothing to make a life for himself in one of the most competitive professions in the world. Who backed himself and built up his business.'

'You flatter me. Still easier than believing it'll work this time.'

Hamza sipped his beer then smiled. 'Mate, I wish I was in your position. Where the woman I loved more than anything wants to be with me. Caz and I realised we didn't need each other enough to take the risk. You and Freya *do*.'

Travis woke with a crick in his neck and a dry mouth, though not from drinking booze.

He and Hamza had sat up until the small hours, talking – he'd like to say they'd set the world to rights but that wouldn't be accurate. He had, however, unloaded all the ups and downs of his relationship with Freya.

The sound and smell of coffee being made awakened his senses fully and a minute later, Hamza walked into the sitting room.

'Morning buddy. Happy New Year's Eve.'

'Is it? Jeez, I forgot about that. The days have blurred into one since Christmas.'

Travis swung his legs off the couch, gratefully accepting the mug from Hamza. 'Morning.' He sipped and winced. 'God, this could strip bark from the trees if you don't mind me saying.'

'It's Turkish. I thought you needed the caffeine.'

'Hmm.' Travis sipped the syrupy liquid and shuddered. 'It smells better than it tastes.'

'Thanks for your honesty. Get it down you, then come into the kitchen.'

'I'll be bouncing off the walls,' he said, sipping again. His nose twitched. 'What's that great smell?'

'Shakshuka. It's my go-to breakfast lately. My Turkish mate got me into that too.'

Over the shakshuka, Travis asked to borrow Hamza's phone. 'I left mine behind at the cabin,' he said.

'I can't believe that you were out without your mobile!'

'I left in a hurry and I wasn't thinking straight. I'd assumed it was in my coat pocket but obviously not.'

'Does anyone even know you're here?' Hamza asked.

'No.'

He winced. 'Don't you think they *should*?'

'I can't imagine they'd have missed me yet. It's only been eighteen hours since I left home but I guess I ought to send a message. I, er, suppose it might look odd that the gallery's closed, although I hadn't planned to open until tomorrow. I'll have to say you were home and I decided to nip down to see you.'

Hamza laughed out loud. '*Nipped* to London?'

'I've nipped to the other side of the world, so why not?'

Travis pushed his empty bowl away, having wiped it clean with flatbread. 'That shakshuka was bloody amazing.'

'I'm glad you're happy about something at least.' Hamza eyed him sternly. 'Here's my phone. Make some calls and prepare for people to be pissed off. In my opinion, you deserve it!'

After breakfast, Travis drove home and arrived back at the cabin where he had to once again explain himself to Bree, who'd calmed down from boiling point to simmer. As for Freya, he'd simply sent her a text saying he was sorry that he'd worried Bree and Seb to the point where they'd intruded on her working day.

He'd kept the message as short as possible, and as free of emotion as possible. His talk with Hamza hadn't solved his problems. He hadn't expected it too, but once again, his friend had hit the nail on her head: *I realised we didn't need each other enough to take the risk. You and Freya do.*

Could Travis risk his heart again?

By the time he'd got back to the cabin and answered a pile of emails and messages from clients, it was dark again, and he still had to check all was well at the gallery. The streets were already busy with people heading to hotels, bars and restaurants. A few fireworks were already going off in the park by the lake. Travis had never felt less like celebrating and planned to go home to the cabin to lick his wounds.

First he had a more important task: checking on Peak Perspectives which lay in darkness too, as if accusing him of neglect. This was the dream he'd worked for much of his life and he'd abandoned it. Whatever else happened, it was his livelihood now.

He inserted the key in the front door lock and pushed open the door and his heart rate rocketed.

A torch beam wavered at the rear and then there was a crash of glass shattering.

Travis flicked on the lights.

'Dad! What the hell are you doing here?'

Alan Marshall swung round, blinking, surrounded by broken glass.

Boiling with indignation, Travis advanced on him. 'There's no cash in here if that's what you're looking for. I don't keep any camera equipment either.'

'I wasn't looking for cash or your precious cameras!'

He'd once claimed to Travis that he'd been a decent amateur boxer as a teenager but Travis had added it to the list of myths and fantasies his father had perpetuated. He still looked in shape for a man in his late fifties but prison had inevitably taken its toll, and his face was a map of every lie he'd told and scam he'd pulled. His grey hair had been allowed to grow long and was pulled back in a scraggy ponytail.

Travis snorted in disbelief. 'Pull the other one. You must have wanted something.'

'Only to see the gallery. I heard how well you've done and I wanted to take a look.' He took a step towards Travis, his boots crunching on broken glass.

'In the dark? Why didn't you come round while the place was open, like everyone else?'

'I didn't want to cause a scene or embarrass you.'

'So you decided to break in? That's not causing trouble?'

'I didn't break in. The glass is from a tumbler I knocked over on my way in. The back door wasn't even locked.' He smirked. 'Your security is lax, son.'

Travis could have kicked himself. He must have left the rear door unlocked when he'd rushed off to Hamza's. The gallery could have been broken into any time he'd been away. It was a miracle Bree hadn't noticed when she'd gone searching for him but she'd probably assumed it was all secure and not checked the rear door.

'I don't care if you materialised in here like the fecking Ghost of Christmas Past. You weren't invited and you still aren't.' Travis was worried he'd already been to hassle Seb or Bree – or both. Or that he might try it once Travis had sent him packing.

'That's not very hospitable, is it?'

'I'm hospitable to people who are welcome. You aren't and I'd like you to leave.'

He tutted. 'When did you get so bitter? You've everything you want in life, yet you can't spare a crumb of kindness for your old man.'

Travis caught a whiff of booze on his dad's breath.

'Bitter? I'm not bitter. I'm just sad that you pissed your life away. That you left Mum with the three of us and didn't give a shit what happened. That you tried to drag me and Seb down to your level. Well, you won't do that because he's not you, and neither am I. Now, I'd really like you to leave.'

'What will you do if I don't want to?'

'Call the police.'

'The police? You are joking? On your own father?'

Travis pulled out his mobile, hoping his father wouldn't

318

see that his hands were shaking. This confrontation was making him feel sick but he had to make a stand, for his sake and his family's.

'Travis!'

Travis spun round to find Freya in the shop, eyes wide with alarm. She was wearing a shimmering dress under a furry coat.

'I saw the lights on and was worried about—'

His heart sank to his boots. He didn't want her witnessing this kind of scene but it was too late. She came forward. 'Mr Marshall?'

'*Mr* Marshall.' He smirked. 'Now, that's how to speak to a man. Good evening, Freya. My, you've grown a bit.'

'Dad was just about to leave,' Travis said, hating the idea of his father being in the same room as Freya or having the opportunity to upset her.

'Like I said, I came to see if you were OK?'

'Aww, that's nice,' his father sneered. 'Someone cares about you. How lovely. When's the wedding? Second time lucky, is it?'

'What the hell do you mean?'

'I remember her running off from that church. I wasn't inside at the time. I heard you crying in your room that night because some kids were taking the piss out of you at school. Remember?'

'And you came in and laughed at me and told me to man up!' Travis shouted.

Freya laid her hand on his arm. 'Travis, don't let him get to you.'

His father ignored her. 'I also heard about the second time when she dumped you. Proper messed you up, didn't she? Your mum let on, though she wished she hadn't. She tracked

319

me down when Bree was getting married and tried to tell me I should take an interest in the family, you and Seb. She'd heard I was out and hoped I'd turn over a new leaf.' He laughed. 'As if life was that simple.

'Your trouble is that you wear your heart on your sleeve. You need to harden up and stop thinking there's a happy ending out there. You both look at me as if I'm the devil but you'd know life doesn't work out . . .' His voice faltered. 'Not if you'd had the upbringing that I had . . . not if everything you tried turned to shit . . .'

His father was making excuses. Blaming his own childhood for the way he'd treated his family.

'Get out,' Travis said, 'Or I will call the police, and I don't want to do that, Dad. Leave.'

His father took a step forward, as if squaring up to him for a fight, then stumbled. He put his hand on Freya's shoulder. Startled, she overbalanced, almost falling.

'Get off her!' Travis lunged forward and grabbed his father's arm, propelling him towards the door.

'Hey!' his dad protested. 'I didn't mean to push her, I was only steadying myself. I'm not as young as I was.'

Travis let go of him. 'Don't touch her. Leave now, Dad or—'

His father stared him, eyes blazing. 'Or what?

'Stop this, both of you,' Freya ordered.

'Don't worry. I'm going.' He nodded at Freya. 'Happy New Year, love. Good luck to both of you if you're planning on your happy ending, cos you won't get it.'

He marched out of the gallery and slammed the back door.

Travis bolted it behind him and tried to steady his breathing. His father had dredged up his darkest days of his life, the most toxic emotions, the hurt . . .

Crushing all of it down, he strode back into the gallery where Freya was waiting for him. The urge to throw his arms around her was almost overwhelming. 'Are you OK? I'm so sorry!'

'I'm fine, and it wasn't your fault. He didn't mean anything. I think he was unsteady on his feet.'

'He was drunk!' Travis snapped. 'Ignore what he said. He's full of bullshit. Don't let my bloody dad spoil your evening. I'd forgotten it was New Year's Eve.'

She took a breath and regained her composure. 'I was off to the Shoreline. A bunch of us are. Won't you come with me?'

'No, I don't think so. I'd be the spectre at the feast.'

'I'm not leaving you,' she declared.

'You have to go and enjoy yourself. I'll be fine.'

'It doesn't look like it. Come on, you can't stay here on your own or mope in the cabin. I won't take no for an answer.'

He nodded. 'I'll pop in for a drink. Just one. Let's get out of here and this time, I'll make sure I lock the door properly.'

They walked the short distance to the Shoreline Inn, where the firework display had been set up in the beer garden at the edge of the lake. The place was packed with familiar faces including Roxanne, Araya, Mimi and her husband, the local traders, and the vicar. There was no Bree, who he guessed was at home with the kids, or Seb, who'd gone to play a gig at a bar in Windermere.

One drink, he'd vowed, but that turned into several and several trips to the buffet because he hadn't eaten properly since breakfast. He found himself swept up by the atmosphere, talking to people he hadn't seen for years and crowding into the beer garden with Freya, her friends and the other partygoers.

In the summer, the lawns would have been carpeted with people enjoying drinks with the view of the fells on the far side of the lake. Tonight, the velvet darkness of the water was punctuated only by the lights of a few yachts moored in the marina. The moon and stars were hidden under a thick blanket of clouds.

Shadowy figures moved by torchlight on the edge of the shore Around him, chatter and excitement rose like the buzzing of bees, more and more people spilling out of the pub and restaurant onto the terrace.

Travis checked his watch. Only a few seconds to go.

'Ten, nine, eight . . .' Jos shouted.

Every voice joined, in with the countdown.

Seven, six, five . . .

Four, three, two, one!

Cheers rang out and glasses were raised to the sound of rockets fizzing high into the sky then exploding in blinding flashes of white and green. People were hugging and kissing, wishing each other a Happy New Year.

The pops and bangs, explosions went on and on and finally there was one last massive bang that had people shouting in a collective, 'Ah!'

Then the sky over the lake went dark again, just puffs of smoke yet there was still a frenzy of fireworks going off in the grounds of hotels and houses.

'What's that?' Araya pointed towards the village where there was an orange glow.

'Looks like a big bonfire.'

'I don't think so . . . It looks more like a house fire to me,' Freya said. 'In the middle of the village too. Oh God, I hope not.'

Travis's stomach clenched tightly. It couldn't be . . . and yet his skin turned icy cold. The position of the flames, their location in the village . . . He had the strangest feeling.

'Travis?'

He didn't reply, because he was already running out of the garden and into the street. Running until his lungs burst, desperately hoping that he was wrong but knowing he was right. Even if the gallery wasn't alight, the shops and flats nearby had to be. Seb's place could be one of them. Seb would surely still be at the gig? He couldn't take that chance.

Gasping for breath, he ran up the village street and stopped, feeling the heat on his face. The gallery, with all his work inside it, was on fire.

He stopped for a second, smelling the smoke, tasting bitterness on the air. Orange flames licked at the front door, and the Peak Perspectives sign was blistering in the heat but the roof was intact, so maybe the blaze was contained to the front?

He wanted to go inside. He could get around the back of it – maybe save the printing equipment inside. He had to do *something*.

He could run down the alley at the side of the building. and round to the back. It was by the side of the shop if he was quick. If he did it now.

Drinkers from the Red Lion were out in the street, *watching* – spectating while his business burned, some even holding up phones out to film the inferno.

No way would Travis stand by and see his place go up in flames!

Ducking low, he forced himself to brave the heat and reach the alley.

'Hey mate! What you doing?'

'He's nuts!'

Travis was choking on the smoke, but forced himself to press forward, crouching, and spluttering, his nose streaming.

'Leave it, bro!'

Seb was in front of him, trying to push him back.

'Let me go! I need to do something!'

'No!' Freya had now seized his arm, dragging him back while Seb pushed his chest. Their combined force left him powerless and he could hardly see, his eyes stinging.

A crash cut through the air and glass exploded into the street, at the same time as the three of them ducked to the ground. Flames billowed out of the shop front.

A moment later, he found himself on the tarmac, with Freya and Seb next to him.

'Oh God, no.' Travis knelt over Freya. 'Are you OK?'

'Yeah . . . yes . . .' she murmured.

'Me too,' Seb said and allowed himself to be helped up by Travis. 'Let's get the fuck away from the place before we're all killed.'

Glass crunched under Travis's feet as he limped away from the gallery with Freya and Seb. Freya was holding his arm so hard it hurt. 'The fire brigade are coming,' she said, as sirens wailed above the crack of the flames.

'I've lost everything.'

'Bro, you haven't – it's only *stuff* – paper and card.'

'It's my work!'

'That can be replaced,' Freya said.

'And you can't.' Seb hugged him. 'I don't know what I'd do if I lost you, bro.'

Before his eyes, everything he'd worked for his whole life

was burning to ashes. Tears streamed down his face and he let them flow, let everyone think it was the smoke but it was grief: for the loss of the gallery, for the loss of Freya all those years before and his loss of belief in their future.

Chapter Thirty-Eight

Freya shuddered as she contemplated the blackened walls of the gallery. She'd joined Travis the next day after the fire officer had finished his investigations and the insurance had been to inspect the damage. A surveyor and electrician had declared the structure safe and finally allowed them into the building.

Once the flames were out, it became clear that the fire had been localised to the front of the shop. Mercifully, the rear structure was virtually untouched, although there was soot everywhere and the acrid stench of burning filled the air. With the front window and door boarded up, the gallery was a pitiful sight, made worse by torchlight.

Travis seemed numb with shock, and she didn't blame him. Seeing him about to run into a burning building had been one of the most terrifying moments of her life. Luckily, she and Seb had got there in time, or he might have been right in front of the window when it exploded.

She shivered again, as the moment flooded back. 'I hate to state the obvious but it could have been even worse.'

'I know. The watch manager told me it was lucky they got a call to report it so quickly and got here fast or it might have all gone up.' Travis turned to her. 'And it's lucky you stopped me from doing the stupidest thing in the history of the world.'

'It must have been hellish to see the place in flames. Don't beat yourself up for wanting to stop it.'

'Well, I'm only alive thanks to you and Seb.'

'I wouldn't go that far.'

'I would,' he said softly, then looked around him with a deep sigh. 'But you're right. The place *is* salvageable. The surveyor says the structure is sound so we can start the clear-up but I have tours planned at the weekend and a workshop in the upstairs room. I've nowhere to put them.'

He ventured deeper into the damaged section of gallery. Following him, Freya's boots crunched on broken glass.

He picked up the charred canvas of the mountain hare and stared at it, shaking his head.

'You can print another one,' she said.

'I guess,' he said, his voice breaking. Carefully, he propped the hare against the wall even though Freya knew it was unsavable. 'I never thought Dad would resort to this.'

'You don't know he did yet.'

'Don't I?' he said, turning to her. 'You saw how unstable he was last night, how raw. He was angry, but there was more than that. He was frightened and panicking. It's as if he finally saw the damage he'd done, not only to us, but to himself.' He frowned. 'He reminded me of a wounded animal that's been cornered.'

'Do the police know where he is?'

'No – because they're not looking for him.'

'You haven't told them about the row?' she said.

'No. I did think about it but, he's still my dad. I know I threatened to call the police but I – I still wouldn't have done it. I won't do it now.' He gazed at her. 'I can't hate him enough to do that. I can't hate him at all.'

She nodded. 'I do understand. He's family.'

Travis heaved a sigh. 'There's nothing more we can do today. Thanks for coming. I'll start the clear up tomorrow, but I have to find somewhere else for the workshop later this week.'

He really did seem to be carrying the weight of the world on his broad shoulders. 'I can help with the workshops,' she said, taking that part of his burden, at least. 'You can use our office space for now. I've already squared it with Mimi.'

'Thank you.' He lifted eyes full of gratitude to her. 'I . . . don't know what to say.'

'Don't say anything. I'm not looking for thanks. You need time to take it in and you need to get your business back up and running.' Her phone buzzed and she pulled it out of her pocket.

Travis must have noticed her reading the message. 'Please don't tell me you're going to help do that. You've done more than enough. I can see you're busy,' he said.

'I'm not going to help,' she said, shoving her phone back in her pocket. 'Not on my own anyway. I think you should come outside.' She ushered him out of the rear door and into the lane behind. 'The cavalry's here.'

A dozen people were gathered outside, including the florist, baker, Bree, Seb, Mimi, Roxanne, Araya, Brian – and Jos. They were all equipped with brooms and buckets while Brian wheeled an industrial vacuum forward. At the front stood

Roxanne, rocking a Land Girl vibe in oversized overalls and a bandana.

Travis clapped his hands on his head in disbelief. 'What's this?' he declared. 'Ghostbusters?'

Everyone apart from Jos laughed.

'Something like that,' Freya said. 'Everyone wanted to help you but wasn't sure how; so, I got in touch with Brian. He organised the generator to rig up some lights, and there's a skip arriving any moment.

'If you have any trouble with your insurer, refer them to me,' Jos said grumpily.

Still nonplussed, Travis murmured. 'I can't thank you enough.'

Brian stepped forward with a broom in hand. 'Come on then, lad. We haven't got all day. First though, I want everyone in PPE before they enter the building.'

They worked until lunchtime when Travis insisted on fetching sausage rolls and coffee for his clear-up crew. The skip was half full of rubbish, the glazer was scheduled for the next day and the walls had been cleaned so they were in a better state for the plasterer to come later that week. The gallery would be out of action for a while but at least Travis looked less broken.

Gradually, the working party dispersed, leaving just a handful.

'Thank you, Brian,' Travis said, earnestly shaking Brian's hand.

'You're welcome, lad. We all stick together here. I'm sure there's a raft of health and safety issues we've broken but I'll let it slide this one time.'

'Appreciate it,' Travis said solemnly.

Freya took a call while Travis thanked Roxanne and Mimi. When she ended the conversation, they were alone together.

'Travis. That was the fire investigator. I know him.'

'Now why doesn't that surprise me?'

'He used to do all the fire safety checks on our properties. This isn't official and he needs to file a proper report, but he thinks a firework started the fire, possibly pushed through the letterbox. There's no sign of accelerant inside the shop.'

'So, it wasn't Dad?'

'If it's any consolation, the investigator thinks it was probably kids. There were a few incidents locally though none as bad as this. I guess they might be on CCTV, but the police will have to look into that.' She briefly touched his arm in reassurance but withdrew her hand quickly, remembering . . . 'I need a bath. You look as knackered as I feel. I think we should call it a day until tomorrow.'

'You'll be back at work tomorrow,' Travis said.

'I could spare a few hours first thing.'

'You've done so much for me already.'

'Only what a friend would do.'

'A friend?' He smiled fleetingly and sadly. 'I've been doing a lot of thinking while I was away.'

Freya's phone rang out. She should ignore it, but then she saw the name on the screen.

'It's Mum,' she said. 'She's back home.'

'Answer it,' Travis said.

Freya did as she was told and a moment later found Travis outside in the lane. 'She's desperate to see me. She's so excited to show me her ring and tell me about the wedding. I can't put her off.'

'You mustn't. Go and see her. Maybe I'll see you later?'

'I'll call you,' Freya said, leaving him standing alone outside amid a pile of rubbish, but more hopeful than she'd been for days.

'Oh my God, I can't believe all this stuff really all arrived while I've been away!'

Freya found her mother, tanned and smiling, amid a sea of boxes in her living room.

'I moved the stuff in here out of sight.'

'It'll take me a week to open and film this lot.'

'Just as long as I don't have to film it in case of any more "surprises",' Freya muttered.

'Oh, don't worry, I'll rope Neil in to do that. He wanted to wait for you but I told him to collect the dog from kennels. He's coming round later for a celebration, with his son and daughter. I thought we could have a little celebration here, just the families. Is that OK?'

Freya abandoned all hope of seeing Travis that evening. 'That sounds lovely,' she said, sounding as cheerful as she could. 'First, shall we sit down and have a brew? I'm dying for a proper cuppa.'

Minutes later, they were sitting in the cosy kitchen, with two steaming mugs in front of them. Her mum sipped and sighed appreciatively before putting down the drink. 'That's better. Thanks for the tea and thank you, my darling, for being so excited and happy for me. You're not annoyed that we got married on impulse?'

'Mum, how could I be annoyed? I was surprised, it came as a shock, but I'm not annoyed.'

She grasped Freya's hand, her eyes glinting with tears. 'I

know we've been specially close with your father leaving us when you were so young. I've often wondered if we were too close – too dependent on each other. I fear I might have held you back.'

'You haven't. It was my decision to stay around. If I hadn't. I might never have started Cottage Angels. I love being my own boss and I love the Lakes – and I love you.' Freya could hardly squeeze out the words past the lump in her own throat.

'Now stop it because you'll have me in floods and I've done that enough. When Neil proposed, I wept buckets and when he hasn't been alone, I've had a little cry for your dad too. I hope he'd approve.'

'I'm sure he would. Neil is a lovely man.'

'Mmm. He is,' her mother said but the wry 'Mmm' set Freya's antennae twitching.

'Is everything OK? Are you absolutely sure about this – you and Neil?'

Her mum smiled and shook her head. 'As sure as anyone can be. I was smiling because of you not me. Neil is a lovely man, but I'm fully aware that he's not exciting. That's he's a safe choice. Perhaps, in your eyes, a little bit . . . dull?'

Freya was horrified. 'Oh, Mum, I didn't say that!'

'But you think it and you'd be right. He is safe, kind and steady and yes – sometimes a bit conventional, but I love his company, and I'm looking forward to making a new life with him.' She took Freya's hand and stroked it, soothingly like she had when she was a little girl. 'The thing is that a man like Neil would never be right for *you*. You always wanted something exciting and unpredictable. I realise now that Jos wasn't the man for you even though I didn't understand at the time.'

Freya nodded, unable to respond for a moment. Her mum's insight had stunned her, and she was amazed Sandra she'd found the courage to admit it.

'I wish . . .' Freya began. 'I wish I'd acknowledged it sooner and been more honest with myself and Jos.'

'Don't waste any more time on regrets. He'll get over it.'

Freya recalled Jos's desperate face at the carol concert. 'I hope so, because he hasn't quite yet. I caused that.'

'Well, perhaps it's continually seeing you here in his own backyard – single, available – that gives him false hope. Maybe if you were with someone else, he'd move on.'

'I can't find someone else just for Jos's sake,' Freya said firmly. 'I can't be his therapy.'

'No . . . then he'll have to find someone else himself or learn to live on his own, as I have for so long. As you have,' her mum said firmly. She gave Freya a searching look. 'But this isn't about Jos, is it? It's about Travis Marshall. I heard about the gallery fire. You were there.'

Freya gasped. 'Gossip reaches every corner of the world!'

'I had messages from the WI gang. You were a bit of a hero on the night, so I gather. You organised a clean-up party too.'

Freya shook her head. 'Everyone was at the pub. We all ran to the gallery and it was Seb who pulled Travis back too. And lots of locals wanted to help the clear up. I only gathered them together, got them organised.'

'Out of the kindness of your heart?' her mother said with a sceptical eyebrow.

Freya shrugged. 'Something like that.'

She sighed. 'I'm sorry, love. I've been selfish and wanted to keep you too close when I should have encouraged you to spread your wings and find someone exciting . . . someone that I don't approve of. Someone like Travis.' Her mum leaned over for a hug that made Freya want to cry and laugh at the same time. 'If you want to get back with him, you don't need my permission.'

'You're right,' she said, embracing her mum tightly, feeling closer to her than she ever had in her life, but in a different way: as if a closed door had been flung open between them and they were facing each other as equals, as woman to woman, not mother to daughter. 'I don't need your permission. I never have. I made my own decision to break off our engagement when I was young and I'll make my own decisions now.

Throat clogged with emotion, she smiled at her mother. 'I love you and you can rest assured, in the nicest possible way, Mum, what you think or say won't stop me from doing what I want now or in the future.'

Chapter Thirty-Nine

Travis had groaned with frustration when Freya messaged to say she had to stay at home for a family celebration. However, he had no choice but to be patient until she could come round that evening after work.

He wouldn't be alone in the meantime. Seb was on the later shift at work and turned up at first light to help him carry on with the clear-up.

When they stopped for a brew, Seb answered a phone call and came back inside the shop, grinning from ear to ear.

'What's this?' Travis said. 'Good news?'

'You could say that.'

'Hot date with a roofer?

Seb laughed. 'Almost as good. I'm quitting my job.'

Travis sucked in a breath. 'And that's *good* news?'

'Yes, because I'm starting a new one in a week's time. That was the music shop in Windermere. They've offered me the deputy manager's job!'

Travis broke into a grin to match Seb's. 'That's great news. I'm really pleased for you. How long have you been planning this?'

'The owner was at the carol concert and he's a regular at the mini-market too. So you see, my customer service skills haven't gone unnoticed after all.'

Travis laughed, seeing his brother blossom under his very eyes.

'I can also fit some gigs in around the job. Much as I was grateful for the mini-market job, I think I'll be better at selling guitars than baked beans.'

'I'm made up that things are working out for you.'

'Yeah. They are.' He shoved his phone in pocket of his overalls and looked serious. 'I've also got another confession to make.'

'Another one?' Travis braced himself.

'Remember the guy who was hassling me outside the church that night when Freya saw us?'

Once again, the hairs on the back of Travis's neck prickled. 'Fenno? Don't say he's been causing more trouble!'

'Calm down. I told you he wasn't a bad bloke, apart from dropping your camera which *was* an accident.'

Reining in his impulse to overreact, Travis said, 'OK, so what has he been doing?'

'He's done nothing. He never did. It wasn't him outside the church. It was Dad.'

'Dad?' Travis said, feeling his heart squeeze with shock. 'Dad was hassling you?'

'Yeah, and it wasn't the first time. He turned up at the flat about six months ago.'

'Does – does Bree know about this?'

Seb scoffed. 'You're joking! She'd have gone ape shit. As would you, if I'd admitted it was Dad who's been causing trouble.'

Travis agreed, but was still reeling that Seb had shouldered the burden of the visit alone. 'What did he want?'

'What do you think?' Seb rubbed his fingers together. 'Money.'

Travis closed his eyes. Their father was predictable in one respect.

'Of course, he didn't say why he was here at first. He brought a pack of beer and got all matey. "How are you, son? Nice little flat, you've got, boy."' Seb gave a depressingly accurate impression of their father's tone when he was trying to be 'nice', invariably when he'd wanted something or felt guilty for letting the family down again.

Finally, Seb sat down too. 'I had to give him credit. He kept up the patter, said he'd been out of jail for a year and was in "gainful employment", whatever that means in his eyes. I was almost beginning to believe it really was a social call. We were on the second beer before he asked for a loan.'

Travis could imagine how Seb had been given the glimmer of hope that their father might have changed, then had that hope destroyed. He'd been there himself, many times.

'You haven't got any money to lend him,' he said quietly. 'He must have realised that.'

'I think he worked it out pretty fast when he saw the flat and found out I was working in the mini-market. He had a different tactic: he told me to ask Bree – and you.'

'He is unbelievable.' Travis gazed skywards, astonished at his father's audacity – but why should he be so surprised?

'I said I didn't know where you were and I'd rather poke out my eyeballs than ask Bree.'

'And?' Travis said, thinking Seb had some balls to defy their father.

'He was pissed off, of course. He called me a loser, a failure. He—' The break in Seb's voice showed his struggled to rein in the emotions he'd been through at the time. 'He saw the guitar and asked me why I kept it when I'd never be good for anything more than stacking tins of beans on shelves.'

'That's more than he's ever done! You virtually managed that minimarket and Freya's told me you're really great with people.'

'I'll admit I wasn't in the best frame of mind and after he showed up. I felt like I'd been kicked when I was down.'

When Seb opened his mouth to protest, Travis held up his hands. 'I'm sorry you couldn't even tell me he'd called on you. More than that, I'm gutted I called you "hopeless." I've wished the words back every day. No wonder you were so upset.'

Seb stepped forward. 'C'mere. Let's have a manly hug before I change my mind.' He embraced Travis and slapped him on the back, before stepping back, a little sheepishly. 'I'm over it and now all we have to do is get *your* life sorted.'

Travis covered his delight at being hugged, with a grin. 'No need to worry about me,' he said airily. 'I'm fine. The gallery will be ready to reopen by the end of the week, thanks to everyone lending a hand.'

Seb rolled his eyes. 'I didn't mean this place. That's easy to fix. I meant we have to get *you* sorted, Trav. You and your love life.'

'What love life?'

'Exactly. What's going on with you and Freya? You're at war with her, then you're shagging her and she's round for Christmas dinner and then you're both stalking around the village like the sky fell in.'

'It's complicated.' Travis thought about the previous day,

the rush of emotion he'd felt when Freya had bust a gut to help him. How he'd felt when she'd dragged him back from the fire . . . None of those feelings were mere gratitude.

'Not from where I'm standing. I know there's history between you but bro, I'm gonna tell you something she didn't want you to know. It was Freya who encouraged me – or you could say, *blackmailed* me into playing at the concert.'

'*Blackmailed?*' Travis gasped in astonishment. 'How?'

'I sold my guitars to pay you for the camera.'

'Sold them? Oh Jesus. No! You shouldn't have done that.'

'Don't stress. I got them back because Freya loaned me the money to buy them back from the music shop. I thought she wanted me to work for her in return but she made me play at the gig instead. To be honest I didn't want to, but my arm was twisted. She said it would mean a lot to you and the best way I could make it up to you for trashing the camera.'

Still feeling sickened that Seb had sold his precious instruments, Travis was trying to take in the subterfuge that had been taking place under his nose – and what the people he loved had done for his sake. 'And you *agreed?*'

'Yeah, because she was right and I like her and in the end, I couldn't resist the chance to perform. She knew that. As you know, she can be very persuasive when she wants to be.'

Heart swelling with emotion, Travis couldn't deny it.

'Thing is, she didn't do it for my benefit. Not completely anyway. She did it for *you* so I guess that means that she cares for you, bro. And I tell you this. If you had run into that fire, I've a feeling she'd have run right after you.

'So, may I respectfully suggest, dear brother, that you stop pissing about and find her and tell her how you feel about her before I drag you round to her house myself.'

Travis raised his eyebrows, secretly impressed. 'Wow, is this you're managing me? You're bossy. Where did you get it from?'

Seb shrugged. 'No idea. I've done what I can. If you want to piss your life away because you're too scared to take a chance, then do it. It's your funeral. Talking of which, I'll have shoot off soon. I've got a sound check at Raffaello's ready for the gig tonight.'

'I'll be there,' Travis said, still in shock.

'OK but you'd better be there with Freya, or I'll never speak to you again.'

Travis carried on working, waiting and hoping for a message from Freya until dusk fell. It was snowing, coating the rubbish in the skip with a thin film of snowflakes. He slung some empty paint tins on top and decided: he would go round to the Cottage Angels office himself – and damn what anyone thought. He had to talk to Freya now.

First, however, he had to lock up, not that anyone would bother wrecking the place again, he thought bitterly. He walked inside and started, as a grey-haired figure detached itself from the shadows of the gallery space.

'Hello, son.'

'Dad!'

His father flipped a thumb at the cleared space, now a shell again. 'It's not looking bad considering.'

'Considering what?' Travis said, braced for sneering.

'Considering the last time I saw it.'

'When it was fine. It'll look like that again,' Travis said, determined not to take any crap.

'You mistake me. The last time I saw this place, it was going up in flames.'

340

'What?' Travis exclaimed. Freya had been wrong, his father *must* have torched it, no matter what the CCTV showed. 'You were here? You hate me that much?'

'*Hate?*' His father screwed up his face in disgust. 'I've never hated you. Any of you. I've only hated myself for being a failure. I'm sorry not to live up to your expectations but I didn't torch the place. It was me who called the fire brigade.'

'What?'

'I'd been in the pub and came out for a smoke and the flames were flaring up in the window. I don't know who shoved the fireworks through your door but it wasn't me. I called 999 straight away. You can check if you want, because I gave my name.'

'I didn't know . . .'

'Why would you?' He held Travis's astonished gaze. 'You didn't think I'd do something like this?'

'No. No . . .' Travis protested.

'Come on. You did.'

'I wondered after we'd had that dust-up but I . . . know it was an accident. The investigator told me it was kids messing about but you did break in the first time.'

'I know. I shouldn't have but I'd had a few too many and while that's no excuse, I wanted to see what you'd made of the place, I wanted to see inside my son's mind, I suppose.'

'To be fair, you've never really been interested before, Dad,' Travis said sadly.

'Touché.' He nodded at Travis. 'We've had our differences but I'd never destroy what you've made here. I really did come back to see this place and yes, I was short of funds when I saw Seb. I should never have spoken to him like that. The truth is that I'm envious.'

'*Envious?*' Travis echoed in disbelief.

'Envious of what you've done, envious of your talent and the way you stuck at it and made a success of yourself. Seb and Bree too.'

Travis scoffed. 'Funny way of showing it.'

'Yeah. You're right. And don't worry, I'm not going to hang around like the spectre at the feast. When I saw the place in flames for a moment I thought – you might be in there. Then I saw you haring up the street and I thought about stopping you myself and I would have, I swear, if Seb and Freya hadn't beaten me to it.'

'You were *watching*?' Travis exclaimed.

'Until I knew you weren't going to do anything stupid and then I left cos I couldn't do anything to help. I've never been much use, I've certainly never been a role model but I wanted to see you this last time to say I'm pleased for you and Seb and Bree – and if you're going to get together with Freya, her too. What do I know about relationships?' He laughed. 'What do I know about "commitment" and "love"?' He bracketed the words with a sneer. 'Bugger all, but you're not *me*. You never have been and you never will. I came to try and make some kind of peace but can see I'm wasting my time.'

He turned on his heel but Travis called out. 'Wait, Dad. Stay. Talk to me. To Seb and Bree.'

His father smiled sadly. 'No, son. I've said enough. You can pass the message on. I'm sorry and I'm proud of you all but you're better off without me. I swear, I did try to be a normal dad. I tried to support you and make a decent life, or decent as I saw it. I'm not clever, not educated, I'm not one of these pen-pushers who can spend all day in an office . . . and I was never going to get rich by sweeping floors and mending roads. So I did it the only way I knew how and I failed.'

'I can't answer that,' Travis said, weary of hearing the same excuses though realising that this was probably the longest – certainly the most profound – conversation he'd ever had with his father.

'It's too late for answers but I want you to know that I have got a job.'

Travis snorted, unable to hide his incredulity.

'Don't look so amazed.'

'I'm not. OK, I *am*.'

'I appreciate the honesty,' he said wryly. 'And for your information, it's work in a fish market in Scotland – thanks to some ex-offenders' charity my probation officer put me onto. There's a room in a hostel too and I'm going to give it a go and try to live up the "ex" part for a change.'

He added a grin but Travis felt like crying, and didn't know why. 'Then, I wish you all the best. Truly.'

'I know you do, and I appreciate it. Now, shall we shake on it and I'll be on my way?'

Too choked to say much, he grasped his father's hand, realising it was the first physical contact he'd had with him for decades. 'Bye, Dad.'

'Bye, son. Go well.'

That single brief moment of connection was gone, vanishing as fast as water over the falls. Travis clenched his fingers tightly, willing himself not to give way to the fresh loss he felt as his father walked out of the gallery and into the softly falling snow.

Chapter Forty

'Travis!'

Freya literally bumped into Travis walking out of the rear door of the gallery.

He steadied her with hands that were cold as ice. 'Sorry, are you hurt?'

'No, I'm fine.' She recoiled at the sight of his face, which was drained of colour. 'Are you OK? Only I thought I saw your dad a few minutes ago, walking past the office. Has he been here?'

'Yes, he has.'

'Don't say he's caused more trouble?'

'No. No – he wanted to talk. To make some kind of peace with me, and all of us. Do you know what it's like, seeing someone you love being put in handcuffs and led away? Because I did love him once. He was my dad. He still is.'

'I understand. Even though I never knew my father, I feel his presence. Not in a spiritual way but in my mother, her memories, her expectations, the way she tried to be both a mum and a dad to me, to be my whole family. We both have these huge gaps in our lives. Perhaps that drew us to each other. It must have been harder for you. My father will always be a tragic hero, never getting old, always a memory seen through a golden haze by my mother, a mythical figure to me.'

'Whereas mine is tarnished and broken. You know, the first time he was put away, Mum didn't tell me the truth. He just wasn't there one day, as if he'd vanished and Mum told us he was working away on an oil rig. Then I heard the whispers, people pointing at me. Kids who'd been told to keep away from me by their parents in case they were infected with some kind of virus. We were a bad family. No wonder your mum didn't want you chained to me.'

'She was younger then, on her own, she had to protect me even if what she advised was . . . maybe not the right thing for me,' Freya said.

'I felt as if people expected me to fail. They wanted me to fail, to turn out like him so they could say "I told you so".'

'I never did,' Freya said, picking up his chilled hand and holding it.

He smiled at her, with a warmth she hadn't seen for a long time and which filled her with hope. Colour returned to his face as well as his hands.

'What are you smiling at?' he said.

'You. There's a blob of paint on the end of your nose.'

'It's only emulsion. I can wipe it off.'

'I can do it,' she said. 'Wait here. It's an order.'

She wetted a piece of paper towel in the kitchen. 'Keep still.'

Gently, she rubbed the end of his nose. 'You smell of paint,' she murmured.

'Funny that, when I've been painting.'

'Shh.' She rubbed his nose harder until the paint was gone. 'There.'

She dropped her hand.

'You didn't come here to wipe my nose, did you?' he asked, taking the paper towel from her.

Her pulse skittered. 'No, I came to talk to you – about the night of the fire, actually as well as . . . everything else.' She screwed up her courage. 'When we pulled you back, Seb said what I feel: you could never be replaced.'

Her heart raced. She might crash and burn but at least she had tried to fly. He didn't speak, simply looked at her, the crumpled tissue in his hand.

She carried on, taking her risk: the last one she would take with Travis Marshall; the final chance for them both.

'I don't know what I'd do if I lost you. If that's not love, I don't know what it is. I also know . . .' She took a deep breath. 'I've never told anyone this and I hadn't really acknowledged it myself until that night. I think I've grown up secretly terrified that the people I love most will leave me without warning.'

She choked back a sob.

'Freya . . .' He held her hand gently.

'I pushed you away because I didn't have the faith that it would work between us, that you would stay. Jos offered stability and predictability and I thought I wanted that but I also should have known that I would never feel the way about him that I did about you, the way I've always felt about you and the way I do now. The punishment is that I can never prove that.'

He dropped her hand, leaving her bereft again. He couldn't look at her, almost as if he was too overwhelmed. Even after baring her deepest fears, hope was slipping away . . .

He lifted his eyes to her. 'You don't need to prove anything. I understand how it feels to be abandoned by a father, in a different way. I don't know what I'd do without you either. I never have. I ran away, I kept away because coming back would have meant seeing you again and feeling everything again.'

'You *did* come back,' she said, the hopeful spark flaring into life again.

'Bree asked me. Seb needed me but . . . now I know I just needed an excuse. I wanted to come back and thought I could handle you being here, living in the same place. I was wrong. I knew from the first moment I walked into the cabin and you were there. I knew I was lost. I've tried to fight it. I don't want to be hurt again. Who does?'

He held her, gazing intensely into her eyes.

Her heart beat faster. 'How can I guarantee that either of us will never hurt the other again? There's something I need to show you. It's not here. It's at my place. Would you come with me?'

He nodded. 'I don't need an excuse to get out of this place and anyway, our work here is almost done.'

The January sun was sliding towards the horizon as they walked to Freya's cottage, past the greengrocer taking in her produce and the baker turning the closed sign on his door. Lights were switching off in some shops and clicking on in the Thai takeaway, ready for the evening's service. Bannerdale was both shutting down and waking up, life going on around them in its cycle. They were silent, trudging out of the centre and along the lane to her cottage.

Freya let Travis into the cottage. 'Wait here?' she said.

She wasn't long before she returned and handed over her secret treasure.

'What's this?'

'Not mints,' Freya said quietly. 'Open it.'

He took off the lid and his eyes widened when he saw the tiny box inside. 'Is this . . .?' he murmured.

'Yes.'

He flipped the lid and the ring sparkled in the lamplight. 'You kept it . . .'

'Of course. You refused to take it back but I would never have parted with it because I loved you. I still do.'

He covered his mouth with his hand, while the other held the box.

With her heart leaping from her chest, Freya took the ring from it and held it out. 'Look, I'm not going to get down on one knee, but I am going to take the biggest risk of my life – this one last time, one more try.'

His eyes were fixed on her, there was no hiding place.

'Travis Marshall,' she declared. 'Day after day, year after year, I have tried to tell myself that I'd get over you. Tried to convince myself that "grown-up" love shouldn't feel the same as first love. That somehow, "real" love should be steadier, calmer, without the crazy rollercoaster highs and lows. That it must be easier.'

Travis burst out laughing. '*Easier*? If only. It isn't. It hurts as much – and more because we're already scarred and our wounds are so easily ripped open.'

'We don't have to get married. We can make that a condition of being together.'

He took the ring and put it back in the box. 'I can't imagine forever without you, but I can't promise not to propose.' He handed her the box and closed his hand around hers as she took it. 'So I'd like to keep my options open. Those are my terms.'

Feeling a little shaky, she put the box back on the table. She was soaring high, higher than she'd ever been. 'So it's a "yes"?'

'It's a "yes" to whatever you want and a yes to commitment and trust and hope . . . How about if forever started now? This minute and the next?' He reached for her and she melted into his arms. 'And personally, I know exactly what I'd like to do this minute.'

Epilogue

Twenty months later, early autumn

'Hiya, I'm home!'

'Shh. She's asleep,' Freya mouthed the words at Travis rather than said them. Tanned yet looking tired from jet lag, he put his camera bag down on the rug and tiptoed over to Freya who'd been sitting on the sofa for the past half an hour, hoping that he'd be home from his latest trip before their baby daughter went to bed.

The mellow evening sun was shining through the window of the cottage, settling on the baby's head like a halo around a cherub's curls. Elise's hair was fluffy and soft after her bath, and afterwards Freya had dressed her in her sleepsuit and settled down on the sofa to share a picture book with her.

The little girl's eyelashes had soon fluttered against her pink cheeks and her eyes had closed. Now, she was snuffling softly against Freya's chest, smelling deliciously of baby bath foam and milk.

'I'll take her up,' Travis murmured, and the exchange of a precious parcel followed in slow motion. At eleven months old, Elise was no longer the tiny bundle she used to be and made soft moans of protest as Travis gathered her into his arms, though her eyes stayed closed. Wincing at every creak of the stairs, Freya crossed her fingers that her daughter would stay asleep.

If she'd thought she was busy before Baby Elise had arrived, she now knew the full meaning of the word. Elise had been born barely nine months after Travis had moved in with Freya – rather unexpectedly but with a rush of joy that Freya could never have imagined.

Travis was besotted, her mother was ecstatic, and Freya had had to take on an assistant at Cottage Angels so she could work part-time. It was fortunate that both her business and the gallery were thriving. Travis had courses booked months ahead and a healthy stream of customers purchasing prints, especially during the summer months. He had to go abroad for some of the year, leading tours, but Freya still had to pinch herself every time she saw him feeding Elise or taking her to the park and pushing her on the swings.

They were now a family of three: impossible to believe.

Travis's grin was wider than the Cheshire Cat's when he walked back into the room. 'Phew. Made it. She's in the cot, and still fast asleep.'

Freya held up crossed fingers. 'For now.'

He joined her on the sofa, lifting her legs into his lap.

'How was the trip?' she asked, relaxing as he massaged her feet.

'Good, we didn't get eaten by any of the wildlife and two of the people have already booked the Iceland tour.' He gave a wry grin. 'I bought a cuddly polar bear for Elise but I'll wait until morning to give it to her. I've missed you. How have you been?'

'Mum hasn't ripped her hair out while she was babysitting, I managed to get the quality gradings sorted at work and Elise only threw *some* of her spag bol on the walls this evening.'

Travis laughed. 'I'll clean it up.'

Freya smiled. 'It'll wait.' She felt a rush of longing for him. 'Stay here, please. I've missed you too.'

He circled her ankle with his fingers, intent on her skin – or perhaps unwilling to look her in the eye. 'I've been thinking while I've been away,' he began.

She laughed. 'Always dangerous.'

'True . . . but I've been thinking about this particular idea for a while.' He lifted his eyes to hers. 'How would you feel about eloping?'

Goosebumps popped out on her skin, and her stomach flipped, but she knew instantly that they were the excited kind of goosebumps and the thrilling kind of somersaults.

'When you say "eloping," do you mean running away to get married?'

'I do. Why don't we get married and not tell anyone?' His voice held an urgency. 'Just run away and do it, you, me and Elise.'

'I don't think Elise would count as a witness,' Freya said shakily, still processing that Travis was proposing. 'It sounds great but surely we can't just do it? You have to give notice, don't you? Even if there's a space?'

'You only need twenty-nine days' notice, I looked it up. And maybe we'll get lucky and get a cancellation at the register office.'

'Wow. You really have been thinking. Is getting married anything to do with us having Elise?'

'No, it's to do with me wanting to marry *you*.' He grasped her hands in his. 'Because it feels right, right now.' His gaze was intense. 'So, is it a "yes"?'

Freya didn't have to think, she took his face in her hands and kissed him, knowing that nothing had ever felt more right. 'Yes,' she murmured, then louder. 'Yes. Yes. Yes!'

Now, here they were, six weeks later on a wet September morning, driving up in Hamza's van to the jetty that took the launch to the castle on the far side of the lake. Earlier that day they'd been to the register office, with Hamza and one of the office staff as witnesses and Elise as mini bridesmaid.

The drizzle that had fallen while Hamza had taken photos outside the register office hadn't been predicted, Freya mused, but when did any forecast in this rainiest of places turn out as planned?

Life was full of twists and turns and surprises, as their unwitting guests were about to discover.

A wooden launch, its cabin bedecked in bunting, glided towards the jetty on the lake shore. Freya spotted her friends and family gathered on the pier, in waterproofs and under umbrellas. They all thought they were there to belatedly celebrate Elise's first birthday on board one of the traditional wooden ferries that plied the lake. They were right in one way – and so wrong in another.

She tapped Travis on the shoulder. 'Do you think Mum will ever forgive me?'

'I should think she might, by the time of our tenth anniversary,' he replied from the front seat. 'Shall we get this over with?'

Having parked the van, Hamza turned round, smiling. 'I'll fetch the umbrellas and my camera out of the boot.'

'I'll strap Elise into her buggy,' Travis said. 'You stay inside for a moment.'

Playing with a toy beside her, Elise gurgled happily and Freya's butterflies took flight again. She genuinely hoped her mum would forgive her: but then again, her mother had also sprung a surprise.

Travis appeared at the door, looking gorgeous in the first suit he'd ever owned. He didn't seem to care about the rain, more concerned that Elise wouldn't get wet while she was being fastened into her buggy.

Hamza held a golf brolly over Freya as she swung her legs out of the van, trying not to drape her hem in the puddles.

'Well, here you are!'

Peacock-like in turquoise wellies and a purple raincoat, her mother scurried towards them. 'What time do you call this . . .' Her voice tailed off and her eyes widened into saucers.

Behind her Roxanne and Mimi, Bree, Neil and the families were all pointing or had hands over mouths as realisation slowly dawned.

'Why are you in a suit?' she demanded of Travis. 'Why are you wearing a wedding dress . . . oh my God.'

Freya took a deep breath.

'I'll give you three guesses, Mum.'

Her mother let out a shriek. 'No! I can't believe it. You ran off and got married without telling me?'

'Well, you *did* set the precedent,' Freya said, her heart beating faster. 'We decided a few weeks ago and we wanted to do it as quietly as we could, no fuss – like you and Neil

– but now . . . well, we're ready to celebrate with all the people we love most.'

By this stage, everyone had twigged what was happening and rushed up to hug and congratulate them.

Sandra embraced Freya, tears streaming down her face. 'I wish you'd said, I'd have dressed up! Now here I am in my wellies! You look so beautiful, my darling. And you're a dark horse!' she declared to Travis who also gave her a peck on the cheek.

Dylan hurtled up and stomped in a puddle, spraying up water.

Bree dashed forward. 'You'll make Freya's dress all muddy!'

'Uncle Travis likes me to splash in puddles,' Dylan protested. 'He says it makes a good picture!'

'I don't care what Uncle Travis said. I don't want to be drenched before we even get there.'

Rosie kicked up a spray of water. 'I've got new wellies,' she declared.

'I don't mind,' Freya said, laughing. 'I'm sure Elise would do the same if she could get out of the buggy. She's almost walking already.'

Dylan giggled and jumped in a puddle right in front of his mum. 'And now my trousers are all damp and dirty.'

Bree shook her head. 'Gav! Can you please help me get these kids onto this boat in one piece? Dylan! Please leave the ducks alone!'

Even with the rain pattering on her brolly, Freya couldn't stop grinning, swept up on a tide of joy and laughter that no grey sky could dim.

Her mother took charge of the buggy but Travis was scanning the road to the boat jetties anxiously.

'Where's Seb?'

'On his way. Look . . .' Bree pointed to the head of the jetty where a motorbike had stopped.

Carrying his guitar case, Seb climbed off the pillion, followed by its rider who took off her helmet and shook out long dark hair. He'd started dating Araya a few months before and they were planning to move in together.

'Sorry I'm late! The music shop was rammed. Lucky for me that Araya is a speed merchant . . .' He frowned and gawped at Travis. 'Why are you wearing a suit, bro? Where's the funeral?'

Bree batted his arm. 'Seb! You idiot! It's a wedding. These two have sneaked off and got married!'

'Right. OK . . .' With a shrug that implied he'd expected this day forever, Seb pumped Travis's hand up and down then kissed Freya on the cheek. 'You took your time but you got there in the end. Congratulations.'

With a cry of delight, Sandra pointed to the sky. 'Oh, look, there's a peep of blue. They say if there's enough blue to patch a sailor's shirt, the rest of the day will be fine.'

Freya gazed at the glimpse of blue that seemed to be changing by the second – though whether it was expanding or shrinking, she couldn't decide. Most importantly, she didn't really care. It could rain all day long, if it wanted to. She'd never looked for or planned a 'perfect' wedding; she had everything she ever wanted already.

'OK, everyone on board!' Hamza called. He'd been snapping away from the moment Travis and Freya had arrived at the jetty in Hamza's van. Freya had seen him, capturing shots of the children splashing in the water and Elise smiling in her buggy and everyone hugging and kissing and gasping in

357

amazement. She had a feeling they'd be the best wedding photos ever, even if Travis hadn't taken them.

With Hamza's shutter whirring, their guests filed onto the launch: Bree, Gav and the children; Mimi and her family; Seb with his guitar; and Araya in her leathers. Only Neil and Sandra were left on the jetty, looking after Elise in her buggy.

'Not you two. I want some pictures of you together.'

'Whoever knew you could be so bossy?' Travis said, posing with Freya under a huge golf umbrella.

'Ah, and now can we have some of you with Elise?'

Freya's mother heard. 'Neil, can you bring the little one over?'

Neil plucked the wriggling baby from a buggy decorated with white ribbons and handed her to Sandra.

'Oh, she looks like an angel! I've been inundated with lovely clothes for her since I became a granny. Her little wellies are just so cute.'

Freya's heart was too full.

'Dada. Dada. Mumm,' Elise babbled away, plucking at the flowers in Freya's hair.

Travis whispered. 'You are beautiful. You both are and I couldn't love you more.'

'Same . . .'

'OK. That'll do for now. Don't want to keep you out in the rain too long.'

Freya lowered the umbrella. 'Actually, I really do think it's stopped raining.'

Neil stepped forward to retrieve the golf brolly, leaving Freya, Travis and Elise standing under the brightening sky. The sun peeped out shyly, warming her arms and drying out the wooden jetty.

Hamza grabbed some more pictures before finally lowering the camera. 'OK, that'll do for now. Shall we get on board and party?'

Travis laughed. 'I thought you'd never ask.'

A cheer went up when Freya and Travis took their places in the bow and a champagne cork popped.

The launch pulled away, gliding across the lake as glasses were lifted.

'There, I told you!' Sandra cried triumphantly. 'The sun's coming out properly now.'

Travis squeezed Freya's hand and kissed the top of Elise's head as she pointed at the sun shining down as the clouds lifted, slowly but surely, and the green and purple fells rose up to meet the sky.

Acknowledgements

I've loved returning to the Lake District for this book; it's magnificent in all its moods – and weathers! One of the best perks of the job is being able to visit it for legitimate work purposes, which in this book, included visiting some gorgeous photo galleries for inspiration.

My friends, Janice Hume and Phill Ward, who are both talented wildlife photographers, helped me with research for Travis's career. Janice just happens to be an ace bookseller too and is a great champion of my work.

With her sensitive and insightful suggestions, my editor, Rachel Hart, has made a big difference to this story, and I'm always grateful to my eagle-eyed copy editor, Dushi Horti. I'd also like to give a big thank to the whole Avon team, including Helen Huthwaite, Maddie Dunne-Kirby, Gabriella Drinkwater and Ella Young, in particular.

My fabulous agent, Broo Doherty, and I have had an exciting year and long may it continue! Thank you, Broo, for your expertise, advice and friendship.

My life would also be a whole lot less fun without the wise

counsel, cake and laughter I enjoy with my author mates, Liz and Nell aka the Coffee Crew. I'd like to thank the Party People for being a moment away with ideas, commiseration and encouragement.

In Real Life, the Friday Floras are always there for me too, whatever life hurls at us.

Most of all, I want to thank my very special family for their support and love. I love you all, Mum, Dad, John, Charlotte and James.

If you loved *Four Weddings and a Christmas*, then don't miss these festive romances by Phillipa Ashley, set in the magical Lake District . . .

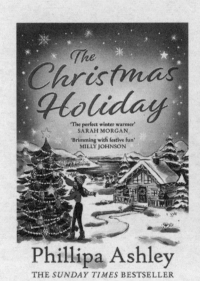

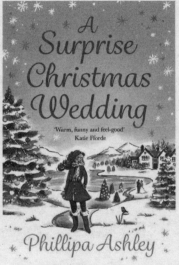

Then explore Phillipa Ashley's glorious Porthmellow series . . .

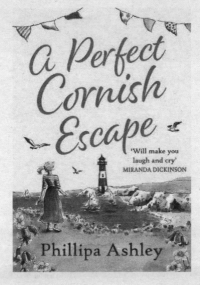

Discover Phillipa Ashley's beautifully escapist Falford series . . .

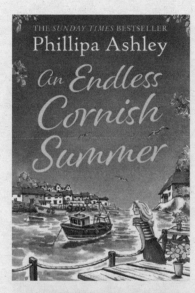

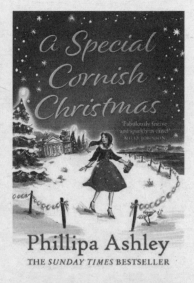

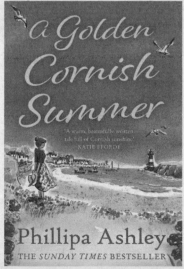

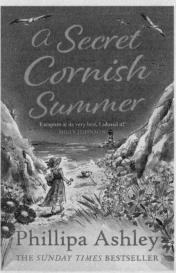

Escape to the Isles of Scilly with this glorious trilogy . . .

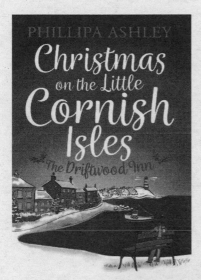

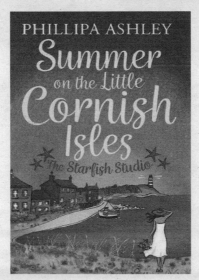

Discover the wonderfully cosy Cornish Café series . . .

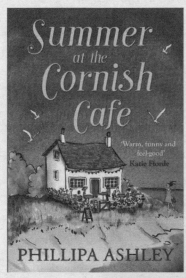

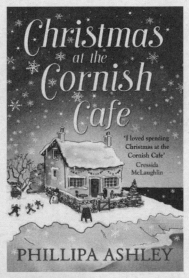

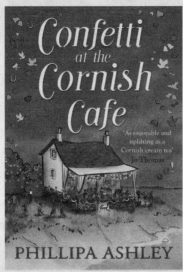